HUNTER'S NEED

SHILOH WALKER

B
BERKLEY SENSATION, NEW YORK

THE BERKLEY PUBLISHING GROUP
Published by the Penguin Group
Penguin Group (USA) Inc.
375 Hudson Street, New York, New York 10014, USA

Penguin Group (Canada), 90 Eglinton Avenue East, Suite 700, Toronto, Ontario M4P 2Y3, Canada
(a division of Pearson Penguin Canada Inc.)
Penguin Books Ltd., 80 Strand, London WC2R 0RL, England
Penguin Group Ireland, 25 St. Stephen's Green, Dublin 2, Ireland (a division of Penguin Books Ltd.)
Penguin Group (Australia), 250 Camberwell Road, Camberwell, Victoria 3124, Australia
(a division of Pearson Australia Group Pty. Ltd.)
Penguin Books India Pvt. Ltd., 11 Community Centre, Panchsheel Park, New Delhi—110 017, India
Penguin Group (NZ), 67 Apollo Drive, Rosedale, North Shore 0632, New Zealand
(a division of Pearson New Zealand Ltd.)
Penguin Books (South Africa) (Pty.) Ltd., 24 Sturdee Avenue, Rosebank, Johannesburg 2196,
South Africa

Penguin Books Ltd., Registered Offices: 80 Strand, London WC2R 0RL, England

HUNTER'S NEED

A Berkley Sensation Book / published by arrangement with the author

PRINTING HISTORY
Berkley Sensation mass-market edition / December 2009

ISBN: 978-0-425-23150-0

BERKLEY® SENSATION
Berkley Sensation Books are published by The Berkley Publishing Group,
a division of Penguin Group (USA) Inc.,
375 Hudson Street, New York, New York 10014.
BERKLEY® SENSATION and the "B" design are trademarks of Penguin Group (USA) Inc.

PRINTED IN THE UNITED STATES OF AMERICA

10 9 8 7 6 5 4 3 2 1

This book is for my editor, Cindy Hwang,
and for every person that emailed me,
asking when Duke would be getting a book.
Hope it's worth the wait.

To Natalie, who is always willing to do a rush job.

And always, for my husband and kids . . . I love you.

CHAPTER 1

STRENGTH.

    Some people have it.

Some people don't.

Analise Morell knew which category she fell into. She wasn't strong. Not at all. While she might wish otherwise, wishing for something didn't make it happen. And reaching for that indefinable something didn't always bring it closer. She'd reached for strength before, and she'd always failed.

Here, she was more acutely aware of just how lacking she was. *Here* being Excelsior, the hallowed home of the Hunters—at least on this side of the world. For four years, she'd trained here, fighting to control her psychic gift, refining her admittedly shoddy shielding ability and working on control. She'd also managed to get her GED and complete the first few years of college courses.

To the mortal world, Excelsior was a private school for gifted and troubled children and teens. Other than her age, Ana supposed she fit into that category well enough.

Psychics weren't exactly the sort of *gifted* the normal person would expect to find here, no more than they'd expect to find fledging witches, shapeshifters or newly made vampires. Excelsior was a whole different world from what mortals would have expected to find.

Not everybody who came to Excelsior would become a Hunter—Ana wouldn't, and she was fine with that. But she'd leave it stronger, smarter and more capable of controlling the gift that had damn near controlled her.

She wouldn't be used again. Not by her gift, and not by somebody else seeking to exploit it.

She may not be strong enough to be one of *them*, but at least she could control herself enough so that she couldn't be used to hurt them, either.

Hurt him.

As though even thinking of him was enough to make him appear, Duke Lawson came striding into the huge gymnasium, walking with a lazy, feline grace. He'd been born Duke Monroe, but like many of the Hunters, he'd left his given name behind with his old life.

There was a faint, almost unconscious smile on his face, one that faded as she stared at him. He came to a halt and she saw his nostrils flare—

His gaze cut to her and she managed to keep from flinching as his dark gray eyes connected with hers. She lifted a hand, waved hesitantly, but he didn't acknowledge her. He just turned away and strode across the rubberized floor. She knew where he was going—the training area on the second level. Right now, there was a class in progress for the advanced students; fighting skills, but not exactly the kind of fighting one would encounter at any legit dojo.

Martial arts were definitely taught, but the advanced students, the ones most likely to be approached about joining the Hunters,weren't just taught basic self-defense. Duke was currently one of the Hunters assigned to help train— she knew, because she did her best to quietly learn everything about him that she could.

As much as she could learn without him realizing it, anyway.

Considering she'd once been party to his kidnapping

and torture, she doubted he'd be too happy knowing that she was obsessed with him. None too happy with knowing that she still dreamed about him, more than four years after the night he'd had the bad luck to meet up with her.

Too fucking twitchy for this, Duke thought as he squared off with a young vampire. Young in vamp years anyway. Shawn Lenning would have celebrated his fiftieth birthday in just a few months if he hadn't been attacked one night. He'd been heading to his car after leaving work. Parked on a side street in a less than respectable area of East St. Louis, he'd heard the sounds of struggle, a woman screaming and he'd gone to help.

But it wasn't just the average rape he'd interrupted. The woman survived, Shawn Lenning was technically listed as missing and presumed dead and his life would never be the same. Duke could sympathize. He knew what it was like to have your entire life changed in the blink of an eye, although at least Duke had been a little prepared. A natural shifter, he'd known pretty much all his life that there was a whole hell of a lot more to the world than mortals thought.

Shawn had simply been human. Courageous and decent, willing to risk his neck for a woman he didn't know, but just a human and he hadn't known a damn thing about natural shifters, vampires, psychics . . .

Pretty blonde psychics with eyes the color of violets and a mouth he could still taste, even four years later.

Life would be easier if he didn't have to know about that particular psychic, Duke suspected. After what she'd done, it wasn't a big surprise that every time he saw her, it hit him on a deep, visceral level.

He still had scars from those days, days that ran together in a pain-filled, delirious blur. Just a few days, but even a few minutes under those circumstances would be too much. She'd used him, figured out what and who he was and toyed with him, making him believe she wanted him and convincing him to leave the club with her.

He'd done just that, but instead of taking him to a motel or some dark, quiet apartment where she lived, she'd taken him to hell. To Cat, a feral vampire with a few mental issues. Something about Ana's gift fucked with his instincts and he'd been blinded to the fact that the house he was following her into was the territory of a feral vamp's.

Blind to everything but Ana, he'd been so caught up in her, in the taste of her mouth, the feel of her body against his, he hadn't realized the danger until it was too late. He'd been shot with silver and in the brief period he'd been unconscious, somebody had chained him up, bound him head to toe with chains of silver and titanium. The silver had drained him, burned him and ate into his flesh, while the titanium was too fucking strong for him to break away.

And that was how he'd spent the next couple of days, until help arrived in the form of Mary Kendall and Duke's old friend Kane. Somebody from his life before. Life before the Hunters. Life before he'd ever met up with a sad-eyed psychic—a life that had been a helluva a lot easier.

He didn't remember much of the days he spent in captivity, beyond Ana. Almost every damn time he swam up out of the black well of pain and weakness brought on by starvation, she'd been there, urging water past his parched throat, giving him just enough to keep him going. A natural shifter, he ate more, drank more than a mortal. A mortal could go a decent amount of time before starvation left them weak. But for a shifter, a couple of days without food was enough to put him in a bad state.

For the thousandth—no, probably the millionth time, he found himself wondering why she'd made the pretense of helping him, of caring if he lived or died under Cat's hand. Found himself wondering why she was here—why she'd come, and why they'd allowed her to stay.

A ham-sized fist caught him on the side of the head and he went flying, coming to a stop only when his body crashed into a reinforced wall. Head spinning, he shoved to his feet and stared across the mat at Shawn. Rubbing his ringing ear, he muttered, "Good one."

Shawn shrugged, a wry smile creasing his dark face. "Not really. You're off."

Off—yeah. He was that. "Maybe." Scanning the students seated at the edge of the mat, he singled out Lindsey Sue Whittaker. Petite, delicate, her head barely reached the middle of Shawn's chest but when the black man saw her rising from the floor, he swore. Lindsey fluttered her lashes at him and blew him a kiss before bending over and stretching out her legs.

Then she straightened and without so much as a blink lunged for him, crossing the distance with a speed no mortal eye could track. Werewolf quick.

As the vampire set about fighting off the werewolf, Duke retreated off the mat and tried to get his head focused and his thoughts off Analise Morell.

"WHO is that?"
Duke glanced up, first at the vampire standing across the pool table, and then toward the door. But even before he saw, he knew. Raking Ana over with a contemptuous gaze, he looked back at the vampire. Dominic—the last name escaped him. Here from Nashville, Tennessee, where he served as a lieutenant for the local master. "Somebody that shouldn't be here."

Dominic snorted. "Well, hell. She's got a lot in common with me, already." He braced his pool stick on the ground and watched as Ana made her way through the people, heading for the small library tucked off to the side of the rec room.

The rec room was crowded, but for a rainy Saturday evening, that was to be expected.

All too aware of the vampire's interest, Duke focused on the pool table. The edgy, twitchy sensation in his gut expanded and he shot a dirty look at the window. He didn't mind water. But he hated getting drenched and if he shifted in that downpour, he'd end up soaked to the bone.

He needed to shift, though. Had to do something to release the edgy, nagging tension that had been building inside him over the past few weeks.

"You know her?"

Duke lined up his shot and took it before straightening and meeting Dominic's gaze. "There's close to five hundred students in this school—you think I know them all?"

Dominic shrugged. "Well, you know her well enough to say she shouldn't be here."

Duke could have bit his tongue off. Yeah. He had said that. "Her name's Ana. She's a psychic, here to get that under control, not because she's Hunter material."

Running his tongue over his teeth, Dominic cocked his head, watched as she disappeared through the doors leading to one of the numerous libraries. "She's cute—blonde. Shit, I love blondes. And I bet she's blonde all over . . . "

She was—a memory he'd tried damn hard to forget came rushing up, the night she'd suckered him in, on the trunk of her car. He'd followed her out there, didn't bother to tell his partner he was heading out, too focused on the woman and the hunger he scented coming from her. Too focused, too impatient to wait, once they'd reached her car, he pulled her against him and kissed her, deaf, dumb and blind to everything but her.

The way her breath caught when he slid his hand under her shirt and cupped her breast.

The way she bit her lip when he slid a hand under her short, snug skirt and pushed it up over her hips before spreading her out on the trunk. In public—where anybody could see—she'd said as much, and he'd whispered, "It's dark. Nobody can see us . . . " Plus, he would have heard anybody coming before they got close, and he just couldn't wait.

Then he made her come, tugging her simple white panties aside and going down on her in the corner of a dark parking lot. Dark, but not so dark his refined vision couldn't make out the pale, smooth perfection of her body and the silvery blonde curls that covered her sex.

His cock stiffened under the tight confines of his jeans at the memory. He swore silently.

Hated it. Hated how a memory could do this to him,

how he could still remember how sweet and soft she'd been—how easily she'd lied to him.

"Ana, you said?"

Jerking his attention back to Dominic, he blinked, then scowled. "What?"

"You said her name was Ana?"

Duke gave the vampire a terse nod.

"She with somebody?"

Duke jerked a shoulder up in a shrug and said, "Beats the hell out of me." Although he knew the answer. No. She was with nobody. She didn't date. She rarely left her room unless it was to be with her brother or hit the library. He shouldn't be surprised to see her here. She wouldn't want to go out in that cold rain to the main library any more than he wanted to go out in it for a run.

A strange smile curled Dominic's lips and he glanced back in the direction of the library, then back at Duke. "You mind if I go talk to her?"

Something inside him screamed, *Yes*. He tried to pretend it was because he liked Dominic, and Ana Morell wasn't a woman to be trusted. He even convinced himself he believed it. He glanced at the table and then back at Dominic. With a nonchalance he didn't feel, he said, "Feel free. We can play later, but I'd watch your back around her."

"The game ain't the reason I'm asking," Dominic drawled, his southern accent a bit more pronounced. Circling around the table, he leaned in close and said in a near-soundless voice, "I bet she isn't with anybody. And I bet it's because anytime a guy thinks about moving in on her, he gets a good look at your face and decides it ain't worth getting his head ripped off."

Duke snorted. "And you think I care who 'moves in on her' for . . . what reason again?"

Dominic laughed. "Hell, maybe *you* don't care. But some part of you does. Body language doesn't lie. Scent doesn't lie."

And that was the bitch of it all, because even if Duke wanted to pretend he didn't want the pretty blonde psychic with the sad, purple eyes and hesitant smile, his body said otherwise. Above the other scents in the room, the scents of life, coffee, food, the lotions a lot of the women loved to rub into their skin, he could smell her. Smell Ana.

He could smell himself, smell the need on him. Knowing how fucking bad he wanted her didn't make it any easier to look at her, though. He looked at her and saw how fucking foolish he'd been, how damn gullible. How pathetic.

Not again. He could want her until hell froze over, but that didn't mean he'd give in.

Across the pool table, he met Dominic's level stare. Then, without saying anything, he hurled his cue stick down and stalked out of the room.

S HE felt his passing like a hot, angry wind, blasting against her shields, snaking through the minute cracks and scalding her.

People were watching her—she felt it as she left the library. She didn't want to, but she couldn't just stay in the library forever, either, which meant she had to go back the way she'd come.

Should have just dealt with the rain and gone to the main library. *Stupid, stupid, stupid.*

Ana stood looking out into the rec room. Clutching the book to her chest, she licked her lips and then glanced from the door where Duke had just disappeared and then back at the pool table where he'd been playing only a few minutes ago.

There was a vampire standing there—she might not have the sense of smell or the eyesight that most of these people had, but she could recognize a vamp easy enough. Instinctive fear curled inside her gut, and she fell back a step before she realized it.

Vampires—she hated them. It had taken her weeks to work up the courage to leave her assigned rooms once the sun had gone down, even longer before she could be near one without fighting the urge to lock herself back in her room and just hide.

Not all of them were evil. Not all of them were like Cat. She knew that.

The one watching her now was a stranger, a man she'd never met and she watched as his gaze left hers to study the room around them, picking up on the censure and distrust and outright hatred.

It was no secret how Ana had landed at Excelsior. Nor was it any secret that most of the students here quietly despised her, resented her presence. Unfortunately, she presented a hazard to them and she had to be trained.

Well, trained or just killed.

The vampire's gaze came back to linger on her face and to her surprise, a slow, sympathetic smile curled his lips. Even through her shields, she sensed his intention before he moved and she jerked her gaze away. She didn't need his sympathy.

Pulling her shoulders back, she started forward, winding through the mass of people, sidestepping those who were lying on the floor, skirting around tables, keeping her distance. She wanted to run. It was a need that left her muscles in knots while her gut clenched and her hands went cold and slick, but she didn't give in.

Running around a bunch of predators that already disliked her seemed a very, very bad idea.

She almost made it through.

Almost.

A familiar voice drawled, "Where you off to, Ana?"

If seeing Duke made her sick with guilt, hearing that voice made her sick with fear. Neal Hollister, a vampire who'd arrived at Excelsior about the same time she had, and he was roughly her age. Like so many vamps, he'd been Changed against his will by a feral vampire, but his sire had an accomplice—a psychic. Neal's distrust of psychics went as deep as Ana's fear of vampires.

He came up quietly, quickly, so quickly she didn't have the time to avoid him as he placed himself in her path. He smiled, flashing his fangs at her, and reached up, toyed with the ends of her hair. "Where you off to in such a hurry, baby?"

"To my room," she said, hoping the ice in her voice would camouflage the fear—even as she knew it wouldn't.

Damn vamps, they could smell it with the same ease she could sense it. His grin widened and he tugged slightly. "Want some company?"

Batting his hand aside, she said, "Not hardly."

"Oh . . . so cold."

Curling her lip at him, she went to go around him. He lifted an arm, blocking her exit and caging her between his body, the door and the mass of people watching with avid interest. "Why you have to be so cold?"

She swallowed the knot in her throat. She had to say something—had to do something to get him away from her. He might not respect strength, but most of these people did. She opened her mouth to say something—*anything*—

Then, damn it, Bradley, her knight in shining armor, appeared in the doorway—just beyond Neal's shoulder. "Leave her alone, Neal."

Her little brother had shot up over the past four years, but he was still too skinny, giving him an odd, stretched out appearance. Once his body had a chance to catch up, she imagined he'd bulk up some, but she seriously hoped he didn't get much taller. He already had two inches on her.

But he was still inches shorter than Neal—and he was a human teenager, where Neal was a vampire who'd already been an adult when he was Changed. Neal shot Brad a bored glance. "I'm talking to your sister, kid, not you."

"You're not talking to her." Brad took a step forward, a harsh note entering his voice.

People who knew him would have backed away.

But this particular rec room was set aside for the adult students and faculty. Brad was a bit of a special case and had special teachers who worked with him. Not one of those teachers was here. Nobody in here had ever trained with Bradley, and not one of the people in the room had any experience with him, other than the stories they'd heard. Stories most of them probably brushed off—after all, how dangerous could a fourteen-year-old human kid be?

In Brad's case, the answer was *very dangerous*.

Ignoring Brad, Neal lifted a hand and stroked Ana's cheek. "I keep hearing how much you're into blood . . . why don't you—oomph—"

Ana felt it, a punch of psychic energy, blasting through the air. She grabbed Brad as Neal went flying backward and crashed into one of the glass-fronted media cabinets. Glass, DVDs and CDs exploded around him at the impact and he fell to the floor—seconds later he was up, moving quicker than the eye could track.

She felt the punch of Brad's power again and she shook him, distracted him for just a second, long enough for the swell of power to fade. "Brad, stop. *Now*."

He shrugged her off and squared off with the vampire. Once, whenever he used a power display like that, it would show on his face, in his eyes as he pushed his limits. The nosebleeds had stopped more than two years ago, and Ana wondered just how far those limits had expanded. She sure as hell didn't want to find out *now*, though.

"You little fuck, I'm gonna knock the shit out of you."

Ana whirled and glared at him. "The hell you will!" She might be a coward, but nobody threatened her baby brother.

He sneered at her. "Get out of my way, bitch."

From the depths of the room, people started to stir.

"Neal, back off . . . "

"Come on, man . . . "

"Backing off sounds like a damn good idea." Bradley shoved around her, once more planting his skinny butt in front of her, protecting her—damn it, *she* was supposed to protect him. It was her job, one she failed at, miserably.

The swell of psychic energy rose in the room once more and Neal grimaced as it pushed him back once more.

"Want some help?" Brad asked, a vicious smile on his face, one that made him seem far too old. Far too bitter. Far too angry.

Ana shoved between them and Brad deflected his next psychic strike—just like she'd suspected he would. He scowled at her. "Ana, get out of the way."

Behind her, she heard Neal snarl, sensed his moving—quick. Too quick.

Several things happened at once.

Voices emerged from the hall behind them, deep, angry and full of authority.

The vampire who'd been shooting pool with Duke appeared from the mess of bodies, grabbing Neal as Ana turned. Neal's hand was only inches away from her, caught in midair. The new vampire stood there, holding Neal's wrist with apparent ease while the weaker man struggled ineffectively.

"Get the fuck off of me," Neal snarled.

"No, Dominic, I think you're good right where you're at." The female voice was hard and cold, and Ana felt something inside her shrivel with fear as Kelsey Hughes came storming into the room.

The redhead paused in the door, taking in everything with one quick glance. Her husband Malachi sauntered past her and flicked a look at Neal that had the vampire's eyes going wide with apprehension. Two other instructors trailed in after him—and Duke.

Planting her hands on her hips, Kelsey demanded, "What in the hell is going on here?"

"Nothing, Ms. Hughes." Wrapping an arm around Brad, Ana pulled him against her.

Kelsey cocked a brow and glanced from Neal to the siblings. Neal still had his wrist suspended in midair and the vampire—Dominic—stood there still as a statue, like he could hold that position all night and well into morning. "Nothing. I feel several spikes in energy, there's broken glass, I walk in right as somebody's coming at you—*from behind*—and you want me to buy that line?"

Blowing out a breath, Ana said, "It's my fault—Brad came in at a bad time and he—"

"The kid did what nobody else in here had the decency to do." Dominic cut in. He let go of Neal but before the younger vampire could back away, Dominic got in his face. "You like taking swings at kids and women?"

"That *kid* attacked first," Neal snapped.

"Yeah, after he came in and found you putting your hands on his sister. Although she'd done made it clear she didn't want your hands on her."

Neal's response was cut off as a low, eerie growl whispered through the room.

Automatically, all eyes followed the sound—

To Duke, standing in the door way and staring at Neal like he'd just found his midnight snack. Kelsey shifted, casually placing her body in between the two men, blocking their view of each other. Her voice calm and cool, she said, "Neal, is that right?"

Neal opened his mouth. Snapped it close. Opened it again.

"Get out."

"Fine," he muttered. "Stupid bitch ain't worth my time anyway."

A cold smile curled Kelsey lips and she said, "I'm sorry. I wasn't clear. I don't mean leave this room. I mean, *get out*. As in out of my school."

Neal blinked. Looked from Kelsey's face to Malachi, then at Ana and Brad. "What?"

Kelsey repeated, "Get out."

"Over that bitch?"

"Nobody, and I mean *nobody* lays a hand on a woman or a child in my school for any fucking reason. Unless of course she was attacking you . . . tell me, Neal, did she attack you? Is that why you touched her?"

"You can't trust her," Neal snarled. "You can't trust her kind—she'll turn on us. She's done it once before." He jerked a chin toward Duke.

Ana's skin crawled with shame. Automatically, she tightened her arms and Brad reached up, patted her hand.

But nobody was looking at them. Or at Duke. They were staring at the exchange between Kelsey and Neal with fascination. "No, Neal. We can't trust *your* kind. You're not one of us . . . and you never were."

Neal paled. Something flashed through his eyes. "I *am* one of you. I'm here, aren't I?"

"You were brought here to train—but not to be a Hunter. You were brought here to learn control. Non-mortals can pose a danger—our job is to limit that danger. We do that through teaching, through training. *That* was why you were brought here—never think otherwise." Kelsey gave him a dismissive look and then turned her back.

Neal jerked away from Dominic and stalked across the room, placing himself in front of Kelsey. "This is fucked up, lady. I didn't hurt her—hell, I didn't hurt that little punk, either. I wouldn't hurt a kid." He sent Ana and Brad a furious look, one that scalded her and left her almost ill with all the hatred she felt coming from him.

Tearing her eyes away from him, Ana whispered to Brad, "Come on. Let's get out of here."

Brad looked like he wanted to argue, then he sighed and shoved a hand through his hair. "Okay. Maybe we can go to get a snack—I'm starving."

"That sounds like a good idea, Ana," Kelsey said, an edge to her voice. But when the witch looked at Ana, her gaze was kind, so kind and so gentle and it made Ana feel even more pathetic.

Silence fell as the brother and sister headed for the door. Kelsey lingered in the doorway, watching them with that enigmatic gaze. The witch's gaze softened as Brad passed by and she reached out, ruffled his hair. "You're a bottom-less pit these days," she teased.

The lighthearted words did nothing to ease the tension in the room. As they left, Ana breathed a little easier. Every passing step made it easier, every inch of distance helped.

Get away—she had to get away from that anger. Her shields were stronger than they had been a few years ago, but anger was always harder to shield against. Always.

As Ana and Brad disappeared from sight, Kelsey stepped back in the room. Somebody slid the door closed behind her. All around, people were staring at her. Watching with avid, intent interest and making no pretense otherwise.

Some of the people in the room would become Hunters. Many would not.

Even though they were told when they came to Excelsior that not all would join the Council, not everybody believed it. Kelsey could understand in a way. The older ones that came to them, more often not, were victims of a vampire attack, survivors of a were's bite. Their entire lives changed, and they had little understanding of why. Time and again, many of them had to leave their old lives behind—their lives, their families. Faced with a long, empty stretch of life, they latched onto anything that might give their new existence meaning.

Being a Hunter had meaning.

But that mind-set crippled them—doing it because it had *meaning* was the last reason to do it.

In more cases than she could recall, Kelsey had seen it happen. In more cases than she could recall, it was the ones who *didn't* want to be here, the ones who *didn't* want to be a Hunter that were called to it.

For some fucked-up reason, Kelsey ended up being the one dumped with the responsibility of saying *No. I'm sorry, but no, it can't be you.* Most of the instructors at the school were perfectly content to let her have that not-so-happy job.

"Are you going to make this harder than it has to be?" she asked, weary.

Neal glared at her. "I'm not making *anything* hard—you're the one throwing some kind of tantrum because that bitch can't handle her own problems."

"The bitch," Kelsey said, getting more annoyed by the second, "isn't the problem."

Neal, stupidly, thought she was referring to Brad.

Rolling his eyes, he said, "I already told you. I wouldn't hurt a kid. And I wasn't going to hurt her, either. I just wanted her to get out of the way."

"But you had your hands on her—that's what started this, isn't it? You had your hands on her, touching her, when she didn't want you touching her."

It was Duke, of all people, who spoke. Separating himself

from the crowd, he stalked toward Neal, his pale gray eyes swirling, the pupils spiking and flaring as he fought the rage inside him.

A rage that made *no* sense to Duke. Even as he prowled around the vampire, struggling against the urge to pounce, there was a saner part of his mind that kept demanding, *What in the hell is your problem*?

Ana wasn't hurt—nobody would have let it go that far. He didn't even waste time trying to convince himself that he'd be this pissed no matter who the woman had been. Of course he'd be pissed. Ready to rip a throat out.

Except he knew his reaction wouldn't be *this* extreme.

Ana—that bastard had put his hands on Ana.

"You put your hands on her—after she made it clear she didn't want you touching her. But you want us to buy that you wouldn't hurt her?" he asked quietly, pacing in a tight circle around Neal.

Neal echoed Duke's movements, keeping the shifter in his sight. Baffled, he said, "You make her sound like some kindergarten teacher, like I was going to grab her, rape her and drain her dry, just for breathing. She's not some damned innocent. She's not some helpless victim. She's not—"

"She's mortal." Duke closed the distance between them and reached out. Vamps were quick. Shifters? Quicker. Neal didn't have time to evade as Duke grabbed him and whirled. Slamming the vamp back into the wall, Duke repeated, "She's mortal—she's got psychic gifts, but her power is all in the mind. She's got no offensive powers, she's no stronger than some kindergarten teacher. She gets hurt, she'll take just as long to heal as any other mortal. You cut her, she'll bleed like any other mortal."

Neal shoved Duke back, but he was still caught in the grip of that inexplicable rage and he snarled at the younger man, flashing incisors that had already begun to lengthen. His gray eyes swirled and pinwheeled, glowing with ominous warning. Rage—hot, thick and potent, spiraled inside him, straining against his skin, fighting to tear past the confines of his self-control.

Over *her*—

Ana . . .

The man inside him struggled with it, fought to understand it. The animal inside him didn't *care*.

"Enough." The word, coolly spoken, just barely managed to penetrate the haze of fury that gripped Duke. Kelsey stepped up and laid a hand on his shoulder.

He knew what she was doing—he felt it, the calm she tried to project into him. Tried and failed. He was too fucking pissed. He had to force his hands to let go, had to force himself to step away. He dragged in a deep breath of air, but it did nothing to clear his head. The air was ripe with the scents of adrenaline, Neal's anger and the lingering trace of Ana's fear.

Neal, fangs dropped and his eyes half wild, glared at Duke. "What in the fuck is your problem?"

"Neal, I'm thinking you're the problem," Malachi said. "If I were you, I'd shut the bloody hell up."

The big vampire had been utterly silent until just a moment ago. Now he studied Duke with curious eyes, his head cocked. He had dark blue eyes, and they were usually about as easy to read as a closed book, but right now, they danced with humor.

For some reason, Duke knew the humor was directed at him, but he really didn't give a damn. "If you're expecting me to apologize, you're going to be waiting a good long while." Then he circled around them and left. At the door, he stopped and looked at Neal. He curled his lip and growled.

Malachi and Kelsey watched as he left. "It gets annoying—how often you are right," Mal said to his wife.

She just smiled. The smile died, though, as she shifted her gaze to Neal. "I believe it's best if you left now."

"I T's for the best, Brad," Ana said, sighing as she settled down on the bed beside Brad, draping an arm around his shoulders. She'd known the time was coming, but after the debacle with Neal a few weeks earlier, she'd finally admitted it to herself.

It was time to leave. "Look . . . I don't really belong here, anyway. You know it as well as I do."

"If you weren't supposed to be here, they'd make you leave. Just like they made Neal leave." He shrugged away from her embrace and climbed off the bed to pace the small room that had been her home for the past four years. "I don't want you to go."

For once, he sounded more like a kid than the miniature adult that he'd been all of his life.

"I know you don't," she said softly. "But . . . " Her words trailed off and she looked away, licking her lips and trying to figure out how to explain.

She didn't need to. Even with her shields up, even with his own, her younger brother could read her. His eyes narrowed on her face and reached out, grabbing her shoulder when she would have evaded.

That simple touch was all it took to deepen the connection and she winced as she saw the knowledge flare in his eyes. It was followed quickly by hurt. "You . . . you want to leave," he whispered. "You want to?"

Sometimes, being gifted just plain sucked. "Brad . . . "

She reached out to touch him but he jerked away, staring at her. Confused, unhappy and hurt, he shook his head. "Why? Why don't you want to be around me?"

"Oh, Brad. Honey, it's not you. *You* are the only person that's made it tolerable being here." This time, when he would have pulled back, she didn't let him. She linked their hands, taken aback by how much bigger his hands looked next to hers now. Too quick—he was growing up too quick, most of his childhood lost to pain, misery and cruelty. "I love you, you know that. I've done the best I could to take care of you after Mom died. If you needed me, you know nothing would get me away from you. But you don't *need* me, not anymore. I can't teach you anything—as far as our gifts go, you left me in the dust ages ago. I'm not putting a roof over your head, I'm not putting food in your belly—

they are." She waved her hand toward the school and forced herself to smile. "I'm not jealous, although I wish I could have done half as much for you as Excelsior has done. But I'm useless here. I'm nothing but deadweight and I can't keep being like that. I need to find something—"

She broke off, unsure of what she was trying to say.

Brad looked away, his body stiff and angry. "You can find something here."

"No. I can't. Brad, I have to find something on my own. Some place of my own . . . something that's *mine*. Something I worked for, something I earned. I'm losing myself here, baby. You've got a life laid out before you. *You* belong here—as much as Neal doesn't belong, as much as I don't, *you* do. This is your life. But it's not mine."

"Maybe that's because you won't let it be."

Ana shook her head. "That's not it. I don't have that kind of strength in me. I don't have that drive, that need. We have it, or we don't . . . and I don't have what it takes to be a Hunter."

Brad shrugged, a rough, jerky motion, but he finally looked at her. The hurt and loneliness in his eyes made her throat constrict and she could feel herself giving in. What could it hurt to stay a few more months . . . a few more years?

But then the memory of Neal's anger flashed through her mind, sizzling against her shields. He hadn't hurt Brad, and she suspected he wouldn't have. However, she couldn't say the same for herself. Neal looked at her and saw prey. She doubted he was the only one. If Neal *had* hurt her, what would it have done to Brad?

What would *Brad* have done? She had to leave, for Brad as much as for herself. Before his worry for her ended up making him do something he'd regret—or worse, something he wouldn't regret. She'd be damned if she caused him problems. He needed to focus on himself now, needed to stop worrying about her so much. Hell, maybe if she was gone, he could enjoy what little was left of his childhood instead of trying to take care of her so much.

"This is for the best," she said softly.

He swallowed convulsively, then nodded. "Will you come back? Ya know, to visit me? Can I come see you?"

"Yes. As often as I can, and as often as you want."

"Maybe . . . maybe you don't have to go far. I mean, maybe you could find a job in Huntington or something . . ."

"Maybe." But they both knew otherwise.

"I don't want you to go," Brad mumbled, ducking his head. There was a suspicious sniffle and when he looked back at her, his eyes were damp.

"I know."

He wrapped thin, bony arms around her and for a minute, she let herself pretend they were younger. For a minute, she let herself pretend she hadn't totally failed him.

"I'll miss you."

He hugged her tight and then stepped away. Smiling sadly, he said, "But you really want to get away from here, don't you?"

"Yeah. Yeah, I do. And I think I *need* to. For both of us."

Away from Excelsior. Away from Virginia. Away from people who didn't know her every shortcoming. Away from people who kept looking at her and just waiting for her to screw up again. Away from people who looked at the siblings and judged them both based on what Ana had done.

Away from Duke . . .

She shied away from that silent voice, but not quick enough. A memory flashed through her mind—those dark gray eyes, staring down at her as though nothing, no one else in the world existed. The warmth of his body. The strength.

Yes. Away from Duke—away from just another reminder of how inadequate she was.

CHAPTER 2

THE air was cool, crisp with the scents of the coming fall. Although it was still mid-August, summer was fading, and fading fast. Already the long days had gotten drastically shorter, and it wouldn't be too long before the summer sunshine was nothing but a vague memory.

Ana walked along the sidewalk in downtown Anchorage, pausing in front of a bookstore to study the display in the window. A lot of "Alaskana" books—tourism was a huge business in Alaska, something she'd figured out almost immediately. When she'd moved here a year ago, it had been in the middle of one of the coolest, wettest summers recorded, and still, tourists had been everywhere.

Just about every store, from the corner grocery to the mall on Fifth Avenue, had something for the tourists. Bookstores were no different. Most of these books, she'd seen before. The few that had caught her interest, she'd already picked up. She glanced over most of them, more interested in a decent mystery or a romantic suspense than anything else. One cover caught her eye, though, and she found herself staring at the dark rainbow of colors with something akin to fascination.

Unsolved—Mysteries of the Far North.

The cover was mostly abstract, dark reds and blues, but the faintest image of a woman's face, frozen in a horrified scream, was superimposed over the blur of colors. Something about it sent a shiver down her spine. Tearing her gaze away from it, she turned to go.

Her lunch hour was almost up, payday was still a week away—she didn't need some nonfiction crime book to add to the teetering tower of books she'd yet to read.

She made it all the way to the stoplight before she turned back. Like a nagging itch between her shoulder blades, something was demanding she go back and buy that book. Buy it. Read it.

She didn't want to buy it.

Didn't want to read it.

And Ana kept telling herself that the entire time she was walking into the store, plucking a copy from the display by the window, shelling out the fifteen and change to cover it. Even as she pushed the book into her tote, she was trying to figure out *why* she was buying it.

It wasn't like she'd ever want to read about a scorned lover taking his revenge, a burglary gone wrong—

"Spare change?"

She almost crashed into him—a man with long, unkempt hair, grimy hands, worn and threadbare clothes. He stood in front of her, staring at her with sad, sad eyes. Despair hung in the air around him, thick and clouded.

Her hand shook as she stuffed it into her pocket and pulled out a couple of ones.

"Ana!"

From across the street, she heard somebody yelling her name. Dimly, she recognized the voice, but she didn't look away from the man before her. Couldn't. Quietly, she said, "I don't have much cash . . . I'm sorry."

He smiled at her. It was a sweet smile, almost innocent,

despite the wear of years on him, despite the sadness in his eyes. "Thank you." He folded the money carefully and tucked it away. Before he walked away, he stopped in his tracks and did the weirdest damn thing.

He saluted her, back ramrod straight, shoulders back. There was something regal, something proud and confident about him in that moment.

"Ana!"

Glancing away, she looked across the street and saw Darlene Eluska, a coworker, glaring at her. Darlene glanced at the homeless man and then back at Ana, censure in her gaze.

Sheepishly, Ana shrugged. Then she looked back at the man, he was already turned, shuffling down the street with his head down and his shoulders slumped.

"Man, I can't believe you," Darlene said as Ana crossed the street. Together, they walked the block to their work. "How many times do I have to tell you? You can't go giving them all money. Most of them aren't homeless or even all that desperate."

Unwittingly, Ana glanced across the street. The old man was lost to sight now, but the sadness in his eyes, the despair she sensed hanging on him. "Oh, he was desperate, all right."

Darlene rolled her eyes. "That's not the point—you go handing out money left and right, *you'll* be the one who is desperate."

"I think I can manage without the few dollars I had on me, Darlene. He looks like he needs it more than I do."

Darlene shook her head. "You either don't get it—or you don't care." Then she sighed and pushed her dense black hair back from her face. Her round face softened with a smile as she craned her head and peered back down Fifth Avenue. "But you're right about that guy . . . he does need it more than you do. Money won't do him much good, though. Nothing's going to help him."

Something about her tone caught Ana's attention. "You sound like you know him."

"Nah. Not directly. But he's kind of a local legend. His name's Paul Beasley—*I think*. He's been around here since before I was born. Served in the air force, lived over at the base. Met this girl, fell in love with her—then she disappeared."

"Disappeared . . . ?"

Darlene nodded. "Yeah. Some of her friends tried to say he killed her, but nobody was ever able to prove it and they couldn't do anything. He . . . well, he kind of went crazy. Ended up getting discharged. I heard they shipped him back home, somewhere down in the Lower 48, but he made his way back up here again." She shrugged. "I don't know all of it, but he's been around for as long as I can remember. It's kind of sad."

S EEING him became a regular occurrence, and it wasn't one Ana was too happy with. Most of the time she only saw him from afar, the back of his head as he ducked into an alley, or that sad smile on his face as somebody pushed some money in his hand. But even those few, distant glimpses stuck with her.

As summer bled into fall and the nights got drastically shorter, it got to where she saw him usually twice a week. He rarely came in close contact with her, although there were times when she knew he saw her watching for him. It would earn her one of those sad, sweet smiles and then before she could decide whether to approach or not, he'd slip away.

Today, though, he was waiting outside the café where she'd gone to grab some tea and a scone. She'd planned on killing time at the mall, but as she caught sight of him, she lost interest in window shopping.

He stood there, staring into the window with a far-off look in his eyes.

"Hey."

At first, she didn't think he'd heard her. Then he glanced toward her, his eyes disinterested. He sighed and lifted a thin, dirty hand to the window, his fingers hovering just above the glass as though he was afraid to touch. "Marie likes pretty things."

Marie?

Ana glanced into the shop and then back at him. "Who's Marie?"

As soon as she asked, though, she could have kicked herself. Tears flooded his eyes and he started to cry. Ugly, wracking sobs that caught the attention of everybody around them. Her skin crawled as people looked from her to the crying man, then back. Attention—damn it, she hated having people looking at her.

"She's gone. Gone . . . gone . . . " he started to mumble, rocking himself.

A warning whispered in her mind and from the corner of her eye, she saw a couple of police officers glance their way. She didn't know why. But she reached out and caught his arm, tugging him along with as she walked away. He fell instep beside as easily, as trusting as a child, still crying and whispering to himself.

Putting some distance between her and the crowd gathered around them made it a little easier to breathe. Granted, not much *fun* to breathe—the guy needed a bath, desperately. It didn't make her pull away, though. She wanted to, but she couldn't. Through her shields, she could feel his pain. Her shields protected her from the worst of the impact, but they were only padding—they could absorb some of the pain. They didn't eradicate it.

Blocking it out, she patted his shoulder and said, "I'm sorry, Paul."

"You know my name." Like a switch that been thrown, he stopped crying and looked at her. Rheumy eyes blinked and then focused on her face.

Ana forced a smile. "Yeah. Somebody mentioned it to me." Uncertain what to do, what to say, but unable to just walk off, she said, "Are you okay? Do you need anything?"

"Like what?"

Ana shrugged. "I don't know. Is there anything I can do to help?"

Paul smiled, that slow, sad smile. Reaching up, he patted her cheek. "You're a nice girl. Marie said you'd try to help." Then he sighed, heaving out a harsh, heavy sigh. "But nobody can help." Glancing off to the side, he said, "No . . . no, she can't."

Automatically, Ana followed his gaze to see who he'd spoken to. Nobody—not that she'd expected to see anybody there by him. But then, as she looked back at Paul, from the corner of her eye, she saw something.

There.

Gone so quickly all she could catch was a vague impression. Young. Dark-haired, round face—made Ana think of a native, but there was no way to know for sure because the second her lashes twitched, whatever she'd seen, or who, was gone.

A shiver raced down her spine. Dragging her gaze back to Paul, she watched as the man turned away from her and headed back the way they'd come. He kept glancing off to the side and over the distance, she heard his voice.

"No, Marie. She's just a nice girl. She can't help us. Nobody can."

I F she hadn't seen that flash, whatever it was, Ana could have written the whole experience off as a lesson in weirdness, and yet another lesson in why she shouldn't go around handing out her money to anybody that appeared as though they might need it.

But she'd seen the flash, and as much as Ana wanted to discount it, she couldn't. Her skin was tight, hot, itchy, the same way she often felt just before a heavy summer downpour back in Virginia.

That night, instead of going by the Alaska Club for a workout, she headed straight home, catching the bus back out to the apartment she rented in Hillside.

It was a quiet area, close to the bus routes—damn good

thing considering she couldn't afford a car just yet. More important to her, it was quiet and the landlord was a psychic null. She couldn't get a damn thing off of him unless she actively tried, because he didn't project.

Even ungifted people tended to project and it was a fricking nuisance for somebody like Ana.

The apartment, located above a garage and complete with Internet access and a small kitchen, was perfect. Quiet, private and hers. She needed the privacy and had been trying to find a place just like this when she stumbled upon the flyer advertising the apartment.

Her landlord, Carter Hoskins, a history professor at UAA, wasn't home when she got there. The Harley was gone, and if his bike was gone in the summer, it was because he'd taken off for a few days. She was glad. He was a nice guy, but he liked to talk. Even in the best frame of mind, talking was *not* on Ana's list of things to do. The encounter with Paul earlier definitely put her frame of mind on a downward spiral.

She let herself into the room and automatically lowered her shields, checking to make sure nothing and nobody was around. It was something that had become habit. She did a quick walk-through and then dumped her stuff on the counter. Without putting anything away, without getting herself a sandwich, she sat down and booted up the secondhand laptop she'd bought from Carter a few months earlier.

The model was a little too bulky, but it ran like a dream. As Google's homepage popped up, she plugged Paul Beasley's name in the search box. If his girlfriend had disappeared and he was suspected of killing her, something would pop up on a search, she figured.

Something popped up all right.

That icy cold shiver raced down her spine as a familiar image came up under the images Google displayed just above the search results.

It was a book cover.

Unsolved—Mysteries of the Far North.

"Shit," Ana breathed out, pressing the heels of her hands

against her eye sockets. That damn book had been sitting on her bedside table calling to her ever since she'd bought it, but every time she went to pick the book up, she'd shied away from it. Lowering her hands, she stared in the direction of her bedroom.

Slowly, her gaze drifted back to the computer screen, but in the end, she got up and went for the book.

As much as she'd like to, she couldn't ignore it anymore.

SLEEP wasn't coming easily. Duke was edgy, irritable and if he didn't know better, he'd swear it was the moon. He wasn't a were, but the full moon still had a way of calling to him, to pretty much all shifters. A siren's call that wasn't easily explained.

But the full moon had been last week and there was no way it would still be having an effect on him. So it was something else tugging at him, slipping under his skin and turning his muscles into knots.

Kicking free of the sheet he had pulled up to his waist, he rolled out of bed. Knowing he couldn't stay in the room, he grabbed his jeans and headed for the door. It was spacious enough, the quarters he used when he was in residence here at Excelsior, but he felt like the walls were closing in on him.

He'd felt like this for weeks, an edgy restlessness that was only getting worse and worse with each passing day.

A run. That was what he needed.

For a shapeshifter, a good, hard run was just about a cure-all. Especially one who had to live confined inside stone walls, stuck in a place he really didn't want to be, but unable to leave for reasons he couldn't quite explain. He'd left Excelsior nearly a year ago—ironically, only a week after Ana had pulled up stakes and left. He hadn't planned on coming back anytime soon, but then he had ended up here a little over a month ago and something just wouldn't let him leave.

Without messing with shoes, he left his rooms and

headed for the stairwell. His rooms were on the third floor, and whenever he wandered back to Excelsior, the rooms were ready and waiting. It was the closest thing to home he had.

But Excelsior wasn't home, and it never would be. Not for him.

Teaching wasn't his thing, but every once in a while it was a nice break from the random patrols an unassigned Hunter did. He had no Master he'd sworn allegiance to, and that wasn't anything he saw changing. He had no lands of his own and no responsibilities.

It should be a good thing, but lately, he had to wonder if part of that wasn't the reason he was so damned restless. So edgy.

So lonely—

"Can't sleep?"

Brad Morell emerged from the shadows as Duke slipped outside. Scowling, Duke flicked a glance at the night sky and then at the youth. "School night, kid. What are you doing up?"

Brad shrugged. Although it was dark, Duke had no trouble making out the look on Brad's face. "Same reason as you, I guess. I can't sleep."

He kicked at the dirt and then glanced up at Duke, a strange look on his face. Over the past couple of years, Brad had shot up. In the past year, he'd started to fill out as well, finally growing into his arms and legs. He no longer had that long, awkward look. He was just barely fifteen, but it was all too easy to forget his age.

More often than not, he acted too damn old for his years, but in that moment, he looked like the kid he was.

Nervous. Worried.

"What's up, Brad?" Duke said, suppressing a sigh and leaning his hips against the stone wall at his back.

Brad shrugged and kicked at the dirt again.

"Brad." Duke folded his arms over his chest.

The boy glanced up at him and Duke said, "Get up here and spill it."

Brad trudged up the stairs, his hands shoved into the back pockets of a pair of baggy jeans. "You don't want to hear it," Brad warned.

Duke didn't roll his eyes, but he wanted to. He had absolutely no problem believing that he wouldn't want to hear it, considering who it was coming from. Brad only got down about a few things, and it was just Duke's luck that he'd be around for this one. "Spill," he repeated.

Brad heaved out a breath and tucked his chin against his chest. "I'm worried about Ana."

"This a specific worry or more along the lines of *I want her back here* kind of worry?" Duke asked levelly.

"Both." He folded his arms defensively across his chest and stared at the stone underneath their feet. "I do miss her. I still don't get why she couldn't try to find some place around here."

"Chances are that's not something she could explain all that easy, or she would have," Duke said, jerking a shoulder. "But it's because she needed something else . . . it doesn't have anything to do with you. Your sister loves you. I bet leaving you was pure hell on her. But I reckon she did it because she thought it was the best thing for both of you."

That, at least, he could say honestly. And he had to agree, and not just because he breathed easier when she wasn't here. Brad had never bothered trying to fit in, but before Ana had left, most people had treated him as an outsider, just because of her.

It wasn't fair to the kid and it sucked, but Duke knew Brad had to make his own choices, do his thing, without some well-meaning adult stumbling in and trying to make things better.

But since Ana had left, people stopped treating Brad so different, and he'd started making real friends—friends *his* age, too. Not just with the adults who were twice his age. Kids need friends, even special kids like Brad—*especially* special kids like Brad.

Yeah, Ana leaving had done the kid good, even though Brad wouldn't admit it. If nothing else, Ana adored her younger brother. He was the most important person in her life and there was nothing she wouldn't do for him. Absently, Duke rubbed his thumb along the scar that bisected his left pec, slashing through his nipple and ending just above his rib cage.

The wound had been caused by a silver blade. Shifters never fully healed a silver-wrought injury. This particular injury had happened while Ana stood by watching in horror, keeping Brad pressed against her so he wouldn't see.

"I know she loves me," Brad said with a scowl. Shaking his head, he said, "It's not her leaving that's bugging me, Duke. She's been gone a year. She's happier up in Alaska, I get that. I'm glad for her, even though I miss her. It's not that she left . . . it's . . . it's something else."

"Can you elaborate on the something else?" Duke asked.

"I . . . no. No, I can't." Brad's head slumped and he stared once more at his feet. "I can't. I dunno what it is, but something's going on."

Duke's skin went tight. He kept his voice calm, though, as he asked, "She in trouble?"

"No. I don't think *she* is in trouble, but somebody is. Or somebody will be."

His gut sank down toward his feet. Averting his eyes, he hoped Ana hadn't fallen back into her old mind-set, letting somebody take control and just tell her what to do, how to do it. Ana didn't much like having to make decisions and having somebody make them for her was just plain easier.

"Stop it."

Turning his head, he looked at Brad across the porch. Brad's eyes, a strange purple color, just a little more blue than Ana's gaze, met his. The worry and doubt had faded from his face and he glared at Duke like he wanted to punch him.

"Ana won't do that again," Brad said, his voice low, all but throbbing with intensity.

"I didn't say she would."

Brad sneered at him. "Damn it, you don't have to." He

tapped his forehead with a finger and sarcastically said, "Psychic, hello?"

"Hunter trainee—hello," Duke said flatly. "You got better shields than that, so use them. I'm entitled to think what I think and I don't need you probing inside my head while I'm doing it."

Mutinous, Brad glared at Duke. "She's my sister. I'm sick and tired of everybody treating her like she was some kind of monster—she fucked up, but she did it to protect me, because she loves me."

"And if she heard you swearing, she'd wash your mouth out with soap—and have my hide," Duke said. Shoving off the wall, he dragged his fingers through his hair and then stopped, looked at Brad. "I know she's your sister. I know you love her. I know you're tired of people thinking bad shit about her, but she made bad choices. She has to live with them."

"Nobody being able to let it go is why she can't live with those choices *here*." Brad turned away, staring out into the night. "I dunno why I'm even talking to you about this. You seem to get the why of it better than most people, but you can't forgive her or forget it. If you can't, they won't. You're the one who got hurt so until you let it go, nobody else will try."

He started down the stairs but on the second to the last one, he looked back at Duke. With those young but ancient eyes, he studied Duke for a long moment. "We all make mistakes and bad choices. We all have to live with consequences. But if you made the best choice you could make, knowing it was wrong, knowing it would have consequences and dealing with those consequences, wouldn't you want a second chance?"

"Nobody said she wasn't entitled to a second chance, Brad." Feeling guilty, hating it, Duke closed the distance between them and caught Brad's shoulder when the youth would have left. "I don't have some grudge against your sister. I'm not secretly hiding some hate-on for her. What's done is done and I can understand *why* even if I think she did it wrong. If you got some idea in your head that I'm responsible for her leaving, then out with it. If that's the case, I want to know so I can set things straight. I don't hate your sister and I'm not harboring some grudge."

Brad smirked. "Yes, that's the case. You're responsible for her leaving, but it's not because you hate her. We both know you don't. You are holding a grudge and we both know it. If you weren't, you would have already gone after her."

Then Brad shrugged Duke's hand off and headed back to his dorm, his shoulders slumped.

Gone after her—

Duke scowled. Getting the little psychic away from here had been nothing but one huge relief.

Liar.

There was no damned reason to go after her.

Self-delusion was a lovely thing. Let a guy keep his pride. Let a guy happily convince himself of his own version of the truth.

Setting his jaw, Duke headed off into the night, taking the opposite direction that Brad had taken. He needed that run, damn it. Now more than ever.

CHAPTER 3

A NA dreamed.
    She dreamed of a pretty young girl, her hair parted down the middle, falling down the back of a soft, gauzy white blouse cut peasant-style and embroidered along the yoke with bright flowers.

The girl had a sweet smile and when she directed it at one young man, she managed to make him blush every single time.

Her name was Marie.

She was nineteen and she was in love with an airman from Elmendorf Air Force Base. Her mother didn't know, her father didn't know, but she'd told her older sister, Beverly. Her sister was the one to help cover for her while she slipped out to meet with her boyfriend.

Caught up with the raw, tender emotion of young love, Ana felt herself getting more and more lost in the dream, unable to pull away, and unwilling to do so. It was sweet, watching them together, sweet to vicariously experience pleasure through Marie as Paul kissed her, stripped her clothes away and made love to her for the first time. Sweeter still to see the tears that burned in Paul's eyes as Marie agreed to marry him. It left a warmth in her heart, but only seconds after Paul pushed a ring onto Marie's finger, that warmth in Ana's chest turned to ice, heavy, arctic ice that threatened to push her down, down, down . . .

Marie was screaming.

Begging.

Pleading.

Dying . . .

Dying while a voice whispered, *Let me take care of you. You're mine. I have to take care of you . . . protect you . . . love you . . .*

A NA came awake, choking on her own scream, nausea roiling in her gut, vomit boiling up in her throat. She barely made it to the bathroom in time. Huddled over the cool porcelain, she emptied her gut, tears and sweat mingling on her face while images flashed through her mind.

"God."

She'd seen . . . something. It hovered just behind a veil, its malevolence just barely contained, the stink of blood and death curling out in smoky, nasty green tendrils. Reaching for her.

Once the sickness passed, she eased away from the toilet and pressed her back against the wall, staring off into nothingness. Her mind turned inward, back to the dream.

Back to Marie. Paul. The story of a missing girl and the lurid scene the book's author had depicted, Paul hunting and stalking Marie, killing her in a fit of rage and hiding her body. Like a child trying to piece together a jigsaw puzzle, Ana worked with the memories of the dream, tried to get them to align with the story she'd read in the book.

They wouldn't line up.

It didn't fit.

Useless . . .

Ana blocked the voice out and made herself focus. Yeah, her psychic gift, the only gift that could be useful in any kind of positive aspect, wasn't all that great. Without her shielding, random thoughts and images bombarded her, but she couldn't make much sense of them. It was like having five or ten radio stations blaring at top volume.

Within her shields, it was better. She could focus, pick up on individual thoughts from time to time, use the gift to pick up on whether or not somebody was lying, whether somebody was hiding something, whether there were other gifted people around.

But she'd never had any sort of cognitive psychic ability—she'd never had visions, not of past events, and not of future ones.

Her strongest ability was just to muffle psychic activity, casting the area where she was into a huge null where it seemed nothing extraordinary existed. To some extent, it even worked to blunt the instincts of some gifted people—people like Duke.

As far as Ana was concerned, it was more a burden than a gift, one that had been used to hurt people in the past. None of her decidedly limited abilities were much use in trying to figure out that dream, or why she'd had it.

"Overactive imagination," she whispered, closing her eyes and willing herself to believe it.

But it wasn't her imagination. Deep down, she knew it. Body aching, she shoved to her feet, flushed the toilet and then shuffled over to the sink. She washed her face, brushed her teeth and combed her hair and still, she felt dirty. Tainted.

And on edge.

The memory of her dream, the memory of Marie's face, danced in her mind, right at the edge of her consciousness, demanding Ana's attention. Unable to ignore it, she left the bathroom and headed to the computer.

"Just a dream." She rubbed her fingertips over her eyes, wishing she could just erase those memories from her mind that easily.

She plugged Marie Onalik's name into Google. One or two MySpace pages popped up at the top of the search results. Off the side, there were paid advertisements for

people searches, criminal background checks and the ubiq-
uitous ad, *Did you go to school with . . .*

Scrolling past those, she read the brief bits of text avail-
able under each individual result. The second to last entry to
the page made her heart skip a beat and her hands go cold.

Palmer teen goes missing.

Ana clicked on it and then heaved out a relieved sigh as a
girl's face flashed on the screen. Color photograph. Judging
just by the hairstyle, it was way too recent to be a girl who
had disappeared back in the seventies. Her focus sharpened.
Not Marie—but she couldn't click away from the page.
Couldn't. Something made her read the article in its entirety,
pity welling inside her as she read the family's impassioned
pleas, begging for information about their daughter.

"Were you ever found?" Ana asked sadly. She glanced
back at the top of the page. Ten years. The article was from
ten years ago.

She grabbed a pen and jotted the name down on a pad of
paper. She read on, uncertain exactly why—morbid curiosity
wasn't her thing. Ana was like an ostrich. She'd much rather
bury her head in the sand, even when it was something important. Or rather, especially when it was something important.

Yet she couldn't tear her attention from the computer
screen and on the second page, in the final section of the
article, she saw why.

There was Marie's name. Highlighted and linked.

Along with four other names.

*Clara Pascal's disappearance is a grim, but needed,
reminder of other missing Alaskans, mostly teens or children. Many of these crimes are still unsolved. If you have
any information on Clara's whereabouts, or information
that may help solve her case or similar cases, please contact
the Palmer Police Department or your local authorities.*

Dread filled her, dragged her down as she moved the
mouse to hover over Marie's name. Then, squeezing her
eyes closed, she clicked. She didn't want to see.

If the article had any pictures of the long-missing Marie,
Ana didn't want to see them. She didn't *want* to know if

the woman she'd dreamed about was Marie. Because if the woman's face looked anything like what she'd seen in her hazed, unclear dreams, Ana didn't know what she'd do.

You don't have *to do anything.*

She swallowed. Tried to believe that. She didn't *have* to. Not really. She wasn't a Hunter. Marie, no matter what had happened, was dead and nothing Ana did would change that fact.

She didn't *have* to do anything, did she? After all, the girl had most likely been dead for thirty years.

Setting her shoulders, she took a deep breath and made herself open her eyes.

But a weight dropped down on her, crushing the air from her lungs, as she stared into the face of Marie Onalik.

In the back of her mind, she heard a voice. Crying, pleading, begging.

Help me, please . . . oh, God . . . somebody please help.

"A NA Morell, amateur sleuth, on the case," she muttered, hiking her bag up on her shoulder as she plodded along the side of the road, checking the addresses. Her skin buzzed and she glanced out of the corner of her eye to the houses across the street. Nice houses. Her rented apartment in Hillside was nice, way nice, but these houses made Hillside look like the slums.

Gleaming oak doors, heavy windowpanes of etched glasses. Manicured lawns, riotous bursts of flowers. Two- or three-car garages and the cars parked in some of the driveways were of the Hummer, Mercedes or BMW variety. *Nice* with a capital *N*.

She was about as out of place here as she had been back at Excelsior, completely out of her depth, but she wasn't turning back. She couldn't because for the past three days when she tried to sleep, her dreams were haunted with the plaintive cry of *Help me, please . . . oh, God . . . somebody please help.* Not exactly a soft, pretty little tune to fall asleep to.

If she wanted to sleep decently anytime in the near future,

then she needed to at least try to figure out what had happened
to Marie. Try to understand why the face of a dead woman
was haunting her every waking and sleeping thought.

Finally, she reached her destination and she shifted her
backpack, holding it on her shoulder as she stared at the
house before her. It wasn't as big as some of the others,
constructed of mellow gold logs and lots of windows. Situated on the mountainside just outside of Chugach State
Park, the house faced out over Cook Inlet.

There was a tricycle just beside the walk, painted a
bright, vivid pink with a purple seat. It had a nameplate on
it—*Marie*. Her skin crawled, her throat knotted up and she
froze in her tracks, staring at the name tag and struggling
to breathe.

Lock it down, girl. She took a minute to level out her
breathing and focus. More to calm herself than anything,
she bolstered her shields and went through one of the mental exercises that had been drilled into her head. *Nothing
in. Nothing out.*

Her normal shields were pretty solid, but they were
designed to let some things filter through, the kind of things
a psychic started to rely on, without even realizing it. With
her normal shields, she was just a little more attuned to
things, like hypersensitive instincts.

But right now, she didn't want that. She didn't want
anything filtering in or out. Not until she got the lay of the
land, so to speak. She wouldn't broadcast anything, and she
wouldn't pick anything up. Not unless she chose to, and right
now, she definitely didn't choose. Not when she was getting
ready to approach the family of a murdered young woman.

Tearing her gaze away from the tricycle, Ana forced
herself to take a step. One. Two. Three. Once she reached
the porch, she didn't slow and try to prepare herself, didn't
take two seconds to brush her hair back from her face or
straighten her clothes. If she paused for even a second, she
was going to take off running.

She pressed the doorbell, hearing it echo through the
house behind a door inlaid with lovely panels of stained

glass. Through the glass, she caught a distorted shadow and she pasted a smile on her face.

The door opened and Ana's smile fell away as she found herself gazing into a disturbingly familiar pair of brown eyes. The woman gave Ana a polite smile and asked, "May I help you?"

Her smile faded as Ana stood there, unable to speak. Lines appeared next to the woman's eyes, bracketed her mouth and she went to shut the door.

Desperate, Ana moved, lifting a hand and reaching out, touching the woman's hand. "I'm here about Marie Onalik. Your sister."

The woman's eyes widened. Tears appeared.

Pain arced, slamming against Ana's shields. She jerked her hand away, but not quick enough. Grief and anger slammed into Ana's shields with gale force, threatening to blast her shielding to smithereens. So much for nothing in—*stupid. You shouldn't have touched her!*

Physical contact made it worse.

Locking her knees, she battled through the outside forces of pain and grief, blocking them out. She slapped up an extra shield, this one so thick and heavy, it was like she'd locked herself in a crypt buried deep below the earth's surface. Blinded, deafened. Psychically speaking, at least. A werewolf the size of Bigfoot could come up behind her now and unless heard with her ears, she'd never know—not buried under this many shields.

She couldn't have that pain filter through again. Not if she wanted to get through this without looking like a nutcase.

"Who are you?" Beverly Onalik Hartwick demanded. "Another wannabe writer wanting to sell some macabre story about my sister's disappearance, how the boy she loved went crazy with jealousy and killed her?"

"No. That's not what happened." Ana shook her head.

Beverly snorted. "How would you know? How old are you? Twenty? Twenty-one? My sister's been missing since 1974—there's no way you can know what happened to a woman that disappeared before you were born."

Forcing a smile, Ana said, "I know. It's just . . . " She licked her lips and took a breath. She was doing this all wrong. Completely, totally, all wrong. "Look, I've met Paul Beasley. I know he used to date your sister, but I don't think . . . "

Beverly's angry glare faded. She studied Ana's face and then slowly, a sad smile came. "You don't think Paul had anything to do with it, do you? That what you want to say?"

"Yes." Ana swallowed the knot in her throat.

Sighing, Beverly stepped back and gestured for Ana to come inside. "I can talk for a few minutes. I watch my granddaughter during the day and she's down for a nap. Once she wakes up, you'll have to leave." She met Ana's eyes squarely. "My daughter was four when Marie disappeared but she still remembers her aunt. She hurt for a very long time over losing her—gave Marie's name to her daughter. I won't have them upset over this."

"I don't want to upset anybody." Following Beverly into a large, open living room, Ana tucked her hands into her pockets and said, "I just wanted to ask a few questions, that's all."

"To what purpose?" Beverly asked sadly. "It's been more than thirty years. She's not still alive . . . I know that. She won't ever come back and I doubt I'll ever know what happened, at least not in this life. What good will it do to ask questions?"

"I don't really know. I just feel like I need to ask them," Ana replied honestly.

Beverly settled down at a breakfast bar and gestured to the seat next to her. "I don't really know how much I can tell you, but if it's something I can answer, I will." She waited a beat and then said, "I won't be offering you a drink. I'm sorry, but I'd rather you just ask your questions and leave."

Ana opened her mouth, but she still wasn't sure what exactly she should ask. What she should say. What she needed to know. Before she had any luck figuring that little puzzle out, she heard footsteps. Automatically, she looked up as a tall man, balding and whip-thin, entered the room.

He came to an abrupt stop when he saw her, a puzzled

smile on his face. "Hello." He glanced at Beverly and said, "I'm sorry . . . I didn't know we were expecting company."

Beverly smiled at him, but it was strained. "Kyle, I'm sorry . . . we didn't interrupt you, did we?"

"No." He smiled at Beverly and then looked back at Ana, curiosity in his gaze.

Ana didn't know what to say. Fortunately, Beverly did. She gave Ana another smile, this one a little more relaxed. "This is . . . oh, dear, I'm sorry, I forgot your name."

"It's Ana."

Beverly looked back at her husband. "This is Ana. She's a tourist and she'd taken a break outside, admiring the view. I saw her while I was checking the mail and we got to chatting. She mentioned some of the beadwork she'd seen down at the museum and I ended up inviting her inside to see some of Mom's beadwork." She gestured toward the living room as she did so.

Ana glanced that way and saw a beaded belt in a display case on the wall. A baby belt—she knew what it was called because she'd been to the Alaska Native Heritage Center and she'd seen some of the work down there. She'd enjoyed looking at the different types of art enough to do a little bit of research.

Thank God.

Without missing a beat, she smiled and said, "It's lovely work. I can't imagine how much time goes into crafting the belts. I think I read somewhere that women here used to work on them for months—it was almost like a trousseau."

"Oh, yes," Beverly said, beaming. "My mother spent weeks and weeks working on that one. And they still do make them. In some of the smaller villages, especially. Women use the belts kind of like a papoose."

"Be careful, Ana. My Beverly could talk for hours about this subject. I'm Kyle, by the way, Beverly's husband."

"It's nice to meet you."

He nodded, an absent look on his face. "I just came to get some more coffee. I've got to get back to work."

While he poured himself a cup, Beverly chattered on, about the belt her mother had made, about her own attempts. She kept it up until his footsteps faded down the hall and they heard a door shut somewhere in the house. Beverly heaved out a breath and gave Ana a grateful look.

"Thank you. I'm sorry, but I just felt lying seemed best. I was so upset after that book came out. I was depressed for weeks and I didn't want Kyle . . . well . . . " She sighed and shook her head, brushing her hair back from her face. "Kyle shouldn't have to keep picking up the pieces each time I fall apart."

"But isn't that what he's there for?" A sympathetic smile curled Ana's lips even as a ribbon of envy curled through her. She knew what it was like to fall apart, but she didn't know what it was like to have somebody there to help hold her together, to help her pick up the pieces. "You'd do the same thing for him, I imagine."

"Of course I would." Beverly smiled. "And yes, I imagine that's one of the benefits of being married, having somebody you love living your life with you—so you can share the burdens. Still, this burden just keeps getting heavier and heavier, not easier. I don't want him to keep worrying about me so."

"You didn't want him to know that I'm here asking about your sister. You don't want him upset." She shoved the envy aside.

"No. No, I don't." Beverly braced her elbows against the table. Her dark eyes, cool and direct, bored into Ana's. "Please don't make me regret talking to you. Please don't make me regret lying to my husband."

*S*HE *liked to go hiking up in the Mat-Su Valley. Loved the glacier.*

Everything else that had been said had fallen on mostly deaf ears, and Ana doubted if she could have recalled the conversation with any credibility, because as soon as she'd heard the words *Mat-Su Valley*, that nagging, impatient demand had flared to vibrant, hot life.

The valley. Something had happened in the valley, and

Ana was going to have to go there. Which was why she took two personal days, why she shelled out a ridiculous amount of money to rent a car for the weekend and why she was driving north on Thursday morning instead of catching a bus to her job.

Four days. She'd give it four days and see if she figured anything out.

Off in the distance, mountains rose into the sky, tall and green, vibrant against a sky so blue, it hurt to look at it. Along the roadside, the skeletal remains of trees jutted upward, the remnants of an earthquake that had hit Alaska decades earlier.

Somebody had told Ana the stands of dead trees were called ghost forests. When the 1964 earthquake hit, huge areas of land dropped below the sea level, leaving the trees' roots submersed in saltwater from the ocean, killing them.

They were eerily beautiful but today, for some reason, they took on a more macabre slant and Ana found herself working to *not* look at the trees. She didn't want to see them. Or the mountains, either.

Just focus on the road. Focus on whatever lies ahead and whatever you're getting into.

D UKE was going out of his damned mind.
       Edgy.

Itchy.

Restless.

It had gotten worse after the run-in with Brad a few days earlier and all he wanted to do was head out again. Go back on patrol for a few more months. Just climb on his bike and ride out, maybe head north up the coastline this time. Bounce around New England for a while.

A lot of the Hunters without formal territories had a tendency to just roam, looking for trouble in areas where no Master controlled things.

Sometimes, it was damned monotonous, but it kept him busy. Plus, if he was out on patrol, sooner or later, he would come across trouble. Lately, he was strung so tight, trouble was just what he needed.

A good fight just might clear his head a little.

He couldn't leave, though.

It wasn't that anybody would stop him. He just *couldn't* leave. Whatever it was that kept him from leaving was some mess of his own, but he couldn't figure out what in the hell the problem was.

How he was supposed to handle it.

One thing was sure, he had to figure that answer out. Excelsior was supposed to be where he came when he needed downtime. Not home, really. But the closest thing to home he had.

A safe haven. Quiet. Controlled. A place where none of them had to live behind the normal personas that they projected to the mortal world. Where they could just be who they were and not worry about anything else.

He loved coming back here and didn't even mind all that much when they started drafting him into helping the regular instructors. For the most part, he felt at peace here, even if he did still find himself looking for Ana Morell, a fucking year after she'd left.

But the peace he'd needed to find, hoped to find, expected to find, had eluded him this trip, and he was about to climb out of his skin just from how fucking edgy he was. It was like the night of the full moon, only worse, and it only affected him.

He stormed out of his rooms with a scowl, his mood downright toxic. A couple of the people he passed by took one look at his face and cut a wide berth around him. He knew it and he didn't care. He wasn't on rotation to teach today, and he'd steer clear of the school itself and anyplace where he'd come in contact with the students, but he'd be damned if he stayed inside his room another minute.

He had some vague idea in mind about the gym. Maybe he could find a sparring partner and work some of this tension off . . .

But his feet led him elsewhere. To the lower levels under the main school, to an area nobody but the teachers and

Hunters ever saw. He found himself in Kelsey Hughes's office, her *real* office, not the one she used on the rare occasion she had to be headmistress for the mortal world.

This room, while definitely an office, had things that just wouldn't fit into the normal persona Kelsey projected to the mortal world. A sword hung over her chair, clearly old, painstakingly cared for. Other weapons and artifacts adorned the walls. Bookshelves lined the walls, holding ancient, hand-bound books, protected from dust and carelessness by gleaming glass fronts. Those books held a written account of the history of the Hunters, going back for centuries. A great deal of them were written in languages that hadn't been spoken in centuries.

It was a soothing room, though, or at least it normally seemed that way.

Not so much today.

In the quiet, empty office, he paced back and forth until he wouldn't have been surprised to see a path worn through the carpet.

"Kelsey's not in right now. She's got a class."

Glancing up, he met Cori Marcum's gaze. She lingered in the doorway, eying him warily. "I can see she isn't here, thanks."

"She . . . ah . . . she may not be back tonight."

He bit back a pithy remark and just nodded. She frowned at him and then left in silence. Too *much* silence, that deafening silence that weighed down on a man and threatened to drive him nuts. The skin along his spine itched and he could feel his muscles twitching with the urge to shift. Shift and run.

Stopping in his tracks, he pressed the heels of his hands to his eyes and swore. "What in the hell is going on?"

Fuck. He could *hear* the damn growl in his throat. Storming across the room, he jerked open the door to the restroom and crossed to the sink. He paused, staring at his reflection in the mirror.

His eyes glowed, swirled, but he didn't need to see that little sign to know how precarious his control was just then.

He could feel it, feel the beast lurking just under the surface of his skin, lurking too close, desperate to be let loose.

Turning the cold water, he bent over the sink and splashed it on his face.

He turned off the water and stood there, head lowered. He reached for focus. He reached for calm. Focus, calm; they weren't coming too easily for him.

"Get it under control."

Of course, it would help if he could figure out what *it* was. If he knew what the hell was wrong and why he was so keyed up—

In that second, the phone in Kelsey's office rang. Slowly, Duke straightened from over the sink. Slowly, he turned his head and stared back into the office.

Ring.

Ring.

Ring.

It was an old-fashioned sort of phone, the kind with a rotary dial, no extra lines. About as simple as a phone could get, and nothing computerized to it. Witches and technology didn't mix all that well for the most part, and Kelsey was worse than most.

Cori appeared in the door but stopped as Duke started toward the phone. "I can get that . . . " she offered, but her voice trailed off.

Duke didn't even hear her speak. For some reason, the damned ringing had him utterly fascinated. All the tension in his body spiked as he reached for the phone. Lifting it, he held it, and simply waited.

"Ahhhh . . . hello?"

He closed his eyes. At the sound of her voice, that caged, restless, edgy anger melted away, replaced by a narrow-minded focus that Duke recognized all too well. "Ana."

There was a long hesitation before she replied, "Duke?"

"Why are you calling?"

The sound of his voice, harsh and gruff, had the dual effects of making Ana flinch and forcing her to lock her knees just to keep from wilting. *Duke* . . . She closed her eyes and there it was, his image springing to life as though it had been painted on the inside of her eyelids.

Duke—she hadn't seen him, hadn't spoken to him in more than a year.

Taking a deep breath, she opened her eyes. It didn't help. Her belly was hot and tight, her nerves scrambling. On the inside, she was a mess. But he didn't need to know that—he wasn't here. He couldn't see how he affected her, couldn't smell it. As long as she didn't let it show in her voice, she was fine.

She made herself look out the window of the bed-and-breakfast, out into the mountains. It was a beautiful view—beautiful, and a stark reminder of why she'd called Excelsior.

If Ana could disconnect from the dark chaos rioting through her, she would have probably been struck silent just by the beauty. But she couldn't disconnect and when she stared out the window at the mountains towering into the clear blue sky, she felt chilled to the bone.

Something was wrong here.

Very wrong.

Damn it, just tell him that. Why did it matter that it was Duke that answered the phone and not Kelsey? Logically? It didn't matter. But logic never had much to do with what happened to her when she heard his voice, when she thought of him, when she saw the sexy shapeshifter.

She swallowed again, her mouth dry. "Is . . . ah . . . is Kelsey there? It's kind of important."

"She's not here. Why are you calling?"

"Is her assistant Cori around?"

"Why are you calling?" he said for the third time and this time, she heard an edge creeping into his voice.

Ana pinched the bridge of her nose and sighed. *You can't back out now . . . you're already involved and you can't let this go until you do something—just tell him.* She blew out a harsh breath. "There's something wrong up here. I don't know what it is and even if I did, I'm not exactly qualified to deal with it."

"Up here—you still in Alaska?"

She frowned. *How do you know that?* But instead of asking, she said, "Yes."

"Going to have a problem getting much help up there. Especially in the summer. Vamps can't handle the daylight. Most of the witches get their senses scrambled that far north and weres don't like the poles."

"We don't have much summer left." Ana caught a lock of her hair. Without thinking, she started to twirl it. "Somebody needs to come up here, Duke."

He grunted. "You're somebody. You're up there. The poles won't mess with psychic talent."

Her jaw dropped. "Uh . . . Duke, I'm not a Hunter. I just feel like something is off."

"Then deal with it, princess. Kelsey's not here to help you figure it out. Hell, if it was *that* bad, somebody would already have felt the need to trot on up there and check things out."

The condescension in his voice cut, and it cut deep, but she could deal with it. He had every right to dislike her, every right not to want to talk with her, every right to avoid having anything to do with her.

But she wasn't going to let his problems keep her from getting help up here. Narrowing her eyes, she said, "Wow, isn't that an admirable attitude for a Hunter to have?"

"You know all about admirable traits, don't you, princess?"

Then he hung up the phone.

Ana swallowed and lowered the handset, staring at it in dazed disbelief for a minute before hanging up. *Deal with it.*

"I don't know *how* to deal with it."

Reluctantly, she lifted her gaze and once more focused on the mountains, staring at their pristine, rugged beauty. Her throat was dry. Painfully dry. Rubbing the back of her hand over her mouth, she took one step toward the window, then another.

It was a warm day, hovering in the mid-eighties outside but she felt chilled. Lifting a hand to the glass, she closed her eyes and rested her brow against the window. *Deal with it.*

"I don't know how," she whispered.

A chill raced down her spine. She cracked open one eye and stared at the book lying on the bed. *Unsolved— Mysteries of the Far North.*

She couldn't look at that cover now without seeing Marie's face. Couldn't lay her head down to sleep without hearing a scream.

I don't know how to deal with it . . .

Straightening, she turned and picked up the book. Stared at the cover. "You'd better learn."

Duke slammed the phone down and stalked out of Kelsey's office. Disbelief burned inside him, side by side with denial. On some level, he knew what he had to do. Hell, some part of him had known this was coming all damn day. In an abstract sense, at least. This was what he'd been waiting for.

Ana—

Cori looked up from her desk. "Who was it?" she asked.

"Somebody looking for Kelsey."

Cori's lashes flickered. "I . . . ah . . . I heard you say Ana . . . did she say what she wanted?"

"I'll handle it," he snapped.

Her pale blue eyes narrowed. "Duke, that's my job."

Cocking his head, he studied the slender vampire as she came out from behind her desk to stand beside it, her hands knotted in small fists. Her throat worked as she swallowed and he could scent the nervousness coming off of her.

"I'll take care of it," he said again, trying to keep the edge out of his voice. He'd already been a fucking bastard to Ana. He didn't need to repeat it.

"Duke—"

He ignored her. He could deliver the message to Kelsey just fine.

Deliver the message and then get the hell out of dodge. Kelsey could handle this mess, figure out who to send out to Alaska, then Duke could just get the hell out of dodge and try once more to work on forgetting all about Analise Morell.

CHAPTER 4

"Y ou're getting your ass on a plane, that's what you're doing. That's the only thing you're doing, so deal with it," Kelsey said, storming into her office. She jerked the band from her ponytail as she settled behind her desk.

"Now, if you don't mind, the paperwork went and made like bunnies in the night, multiplying. I've got work to do, and you've got packing to do." A pair of gold-framed glasses rested on the top of a stack of file folders. She gave them a look of acute dislike and then took the glasses and slipped them on. Then she combed her fingers through her red-gold curls and reached for the top file.

Pack? Duke glared at her, unable to believe what she was telling him. Well, not true—he *could* believe it. He just didn't want to.

When she looked back at him, the irritation she felt was written all over her face, glinting in her eyes. "You're still standing there, Duke. Get packed."

"I'm not getting on a plane." *Getting my ass on a plane? The hell I am.*

Kelsey narrowed her eyes. "You know, I get the feeling

you thought that was a request. It wasn't. It's an order, Duke. Get packed, get to the airport. I'll have a ticket waiting for you."

"Why in the hell am I going?" He already knew the answer, though. Because he had to. It had been pulling at him from the time he got out of bed, and now that he knew *where* he needed to be, it was like some fiery fist had a hold on his gut, dragging him along while he stood with his heels planted in the dirt and fought back.

"You're going because you took the call," she replied, her voice level. "And I'm not talking about the damn telephone . . . although, Duke, stay the hell out of my office."

Clenching his jaw, he glared at the witch. He was pissed, he was wrong, he *was* going to Alaska and he fucking hated all three. Worse, though, was the fact that he was going to have to see Ana.

Shit. He didn't want to see her, look into those soft purple eyes and let her tangle him up inside again. He was still trying to undo the knots from the night they'd first met and it had been years. Years since she'd played him for a fool and led him into a trap that could have killed him.

At the same time, though, there was a huge part of him that was almost desperate to see her again.

Frustrated rage twisted through him; bitter reluctance lay on the back of his tongue. Through clenched teeth, he said, "I don't like this."

"Really? I hadn't noticed." Kelsey gave him a mockingly sympathetic smile. Then she shrugged and leaned back in her chair, staring at him over the desk and its neat stacks of file and paperwork. "I don't much care if you like it or not, but it's what you have to do . . . and you know it. I can feel it."

"You wouldn't if you'd keep out of my thoughts," he snapped.

"I'm not in your thoughts—I do emotions, pal. Not thoughts, and you know it. And I don't have to go reading anything to feel the urgency on you—you're practically broadcasting. You might as well have a neon sign over your head that reads Hunter on Call—Stay Out of My Way."

Duke was silent.

"Duke, you're fighting the inevitable." Kelsey sighed and slipped her glasses off. "Look, even aside from the obvious, you need to be on a plane. You're one of the few that *can* do this."

He folded his arms over his chest and glared at the sword that hung over her desk. "Other Hunters can manage going that far north."

"In the winter, yeah, a vamp could handle it. But the poles are hell on witches . . . trust me, I know. I can handle it, but it's not like I'm free to head north for a while. Not too many other witches free who could cope up there, I can guarantee that. I've been to Alaska and it's like trying to focus on one grain of sand in the middle of a sandstorm. Weres have control issues that far north—something about the polarity, but I'm not a science-minded type and I don't need to understand the technical details. Were and the poles just don't mix."

Their gazes locked and Duke tried not to let the helpless anger show on his face.

She knew though. Even if she didn't see it on his face, she knew.

"You're a natural shifter, Duke. You might feel a little more on edge up there, but you can handle it." With a smirk, she added, "I don't think it's *Alaska* that's the problem, though."

Hell, yeah. She definitely knew. Flushing, he focused on his feet. *Ana*—

A problem—damn straight. Ana was a fucking problem.

Kelsey kicked her legs up, rested her booted feet on the desk. "Ana's the problem," she said quietly, echoing his thoughts with eerie precision.

"I think you can handle it, but if you have doubts . . . " She let her voice trail off and pursed her lips thoughtfully. "There *are* other shifters, I suppose. Or I could talk to the witches, see who is free and see if any of them have experience that far north. Some of the witches *can* function there, it just takes time, practice, some experience is nice. Hmmmm."

A sly smile curved her mouth. "I think Grady could handle it. He was born in northern Michigan. Yes, I think Grady could handle things just fine."

Grady—

A mental image of the witch flashed through his mind. The black man was a nice guy and under normal circumstances, Duke would definitely agree that Grady could handle a few weeks in a place where his gift might become unpredictable. Especially if he'd grown up in a similar environment—he would be used to dealing with the poles.

Fine, send him. The words burned on his tongue.

"The hell he will," he snarled.

Kelsey gave him an innocent look. "Oh, I don't know, Duke. He's on friendly terms with Ana, too—"

Duke growled.

Kelsey laughed. "Well, unless you want me to send Grady, then you'd better get packing. You wasted enough time fighting this already, my friend."

WELL, *there goes yet another day of complete and total failure,* Ana thought. Dismally, she trudged up the steps that led to the private entrance of her room. The owners of the bed-and-breakfast were rarely about. She'd met them upon checking in, run into the husband briefly the past morning over a simple breakfast buffet of cereal, doughnuts and pastries.

Other than that, she hadn't seen them and she had to admit, she was glad. There was no way she could manage any kind of polite small talk just then. Not that small talk was her favorite way to spend time, anyway.

So, what did you do today, Ms. Morell?

Well, I went hiking on a few trails, tried to figure out just what in the hell is going on here. Tell me, have you noticed anything unusual going on? Like . . . oh, say . . . something downright evil, like murder, rape and torture?

Smirking, she said, "Yeah, that's certain to open some

doors for you. Doors to the nearest mental institution." She sighed and dug the key out of her pocket.

She wanted a long, hot bath in the claw-footed bathtub. It was getting close to sunset and the bathtub was situated under a window that faced the west. Ana could sit and soak and watch the sun set, but it was a luxury she wasn't going to take. She was running out of time. She'd spent the past two and a half days prowling around the Mat-Su Valley, looking for God only knows what, for God only knows who.

Wasting her time.

She didn't have that much time left to waste, either. Tomorrow was Sunday and she had to check out of the B and B and head back to Anchorage. Monday, she had to be back at work. So instead of sinking into a tub of water to relax, she took a quick shower, brushed her teeth and then collapsed onto the bed.

She fell asleep on the bed, too tired to even crawl under the covers.

And she awoke cowering on the floor by the wall, holding herself and rocking.

The coppery taste of fear lay heavy on her tongue and she swallowed back the bile boiling up in her throat.

A girl's face lingered in her mind, her lifeless, dark eyes staring upward, frozen in death. Her body had been naked, bruised by brutal hands, bite marks peppered over her breasts and thighs. Blood and semen stained her thighs.

She was dead.

But it wasn't Marie.

DUKE didn't like flying.

He *hated* it.

It didn't help that Kelsey and Cori hadn't been able to find a nonstop flight from Virginia to Anchorage. He'd flown into Minneapolis late and spent a miserable night in a hotel while waiting for the 10:20 flight to Anchorage.

Unable to sleep, he'd spent the entire night thinking about Ana. When morning came, he had been frustrated, exhausted and irritated beyond all belief. Anxious to get this over with, he hadn't dreaded climbing on the plane until he actually settled down in the seat.

Now an hour into the flight, he was wishing for solid ground, grass under his feet and silence. Someplace where he could run, run until he'd exhausted himself.

The first-class section of the plane might boast wider seats and abundant leg room. It might include pleasant, attentive staff and a discerning menu. But none of that was going to do a damn thing to change the fact that he hated flying. Fuck, he was already on edge because of Ana. Spending the day on a plane was the last thing he needed.

"Drink?"

He tore his gaze away from the seat in front of him and focused on the flight attendant. She gave him a friendly smile, flirtatious and inviting. He glanced at the cart in front of her, and decided, no. Getting on a plane wasn't the *last* thing he needed.

Getting on a plane and getting drunk was the last thing he needed.

Despite knowing it wasn't the wisest course of action, he debated on whether or not to get some whiskey. The burn of it might ease some of the tension inside him.

It wouldn't last, though. Shifters just burned through it too quick. Although he could spend the next eight hours getting drunk on the Council's tab, anything that was going to screw with his control was something he had to avoid.

He shook his head and focused once more on the back of the seat in front of him. Arms crossed over his chest, legs stretched out in front of him, he stared straight ahead. Straight ahead, because he didn't want to risk catching sight of one of the windows. Damned planes. Too confining, too noisy—*too fucking high in the air.*

"I don't much like flying, either."

Duke didn't bother glancing at the woman sitting next

to him. If he did that, he might see the window. See out of it. See the ground way too far below.

Not one to take a hint, the woman leaned in, pressing her breasts against his bicep as she laid a hand on his arm. From the corner of his eye, he could see her face and the mask of concern, but he could also smell her—smell her interest, not specifically in him, though. Just a fling.

"The trick is to find something else to think about," she said. "So you don't worry. There's nothing really to worry about, you know. Air travel is so much safer than car travel."

Safer . . . yeah, as long as they stayed in the air. He could survive a car wreck, but even a shifter wasn't going to be able to make it if the plane suddenly went crashing down to earth.

It didn't really *matter* in his mind that it wasn't a likely possibility.

Didn't matter that he'd flown hundreds of times and landed safely each time.

He'd used to hope that serving in the army might help his problem with flying, but it hadn't. The only thing frequent flying had done was just make damn sure he had to come face-to-face with his fear on a regular basis.

"It's going to be a long flight."

Duke cut his eyes over to the woman next to him and immediately wished he hadn't. Beyond her artfully tousled and streaked bronzed hair, he'd seen blue sky and fat, puffy clouds. *Too damned high*—

Jerking his eyes back to the front, he stared at the seat in front of him and slumped deeper in the seat.

She glanced behind her and then slid down the thin panel, blocking the view of the window. "There. That should help." She leaned in a little closer. The hand on his arm slid down to rest on his thigh, a few inches above his knee. With her lips only an inch from his ear, she whispered, "Why don't we try to keep each other distracted?"

He slanted another look in her direction. Slowly, he took a deep breath, taking in her scent. Female. A little heavier on the perfume than he liked. Still, soft . . . warm . . . definitely female. He caught the trace of another scent on her, though—a guy's. It had a feel to it, a settled-in feel. Somebody she came in contact with regularly. *Close* contact.

He smirked and glanced down at the hand on his leg. Her left hand. There wasn't a ring there now, but there had been. Recently. He could see the paler strip of skin where the band had rested. Chances were, it was tucked somewhere inside her purse or something

"Very considerate of you . . . sure your husband won't mind?"

Then he caught her wrist and guided it back to her own lap. Ignoring the look of disbelief on her face, he folded his arms over his chest, closed his eyes and feigned sleep.

He wasn't about to sleep, though.

The woman was right about one thing, though—he did need to find something else to think about, something else to focus on. Like the fact that shortly after he landed, he was going to have to track down Ana and apologize for being an ass. And he was going to have to find some way to work with her for a little while.

Close contact with Ana Morell—something he'd avoided like the plague for five years.

Shit, the last time he'd been in *close* contact with her, he'd been just a breath away from being about as close to a woman as a man could get. So fucking close the scent of her wet pussy had flooded his head, so close her tight nipples had pressed into his chest as he arched her head back and kissed her. With her skirt shoved to her waist, the only thing that had separated them had been a pair of panties and his jeans. Too many times, he'd found himself dreaming of that night, but the pathetic part was that only half of the dreams were nightmares.

The rest of them were the sort of dream that brought him awake on the knife's edge of desire, his cock aching and his balls burning. Too many dreams where he wished he'd at least had the chance to bury his dick inside that soft, pale body before she sold him down the river.

She might have sold you down the river, but if it wasn't for her, you wouldn't have gotten out of that hellhole alive.

It was a familiar voice, one that had whispered the same thing in his mind over and over. The voice of his conscience? Or the voice of his libido? Duke didn't know, didn't care, wished it would just shut the hell up.

One thing was certain, he wasn't ever going to get that damned close to Ana ever again. She'd betrayed him, humiliated him, *hurt*—

No.

One hand closed into a fist. She hadn't *hurt* him.

He'd have to care about her in order for to hurt him on any level other than physical. And he didn't care about her.

She might have caused him physical pain, might have been behind some of the most hellacious moments of his life, but it was all physical. All of it. She couldn't hurt him on a deeper level because he didn't care about her.

He didn't.

CHAPTER 5

L ATE Sunday night, with her checking account a few hundred dollars lighter, Ana returned the rental and caught the bus back to Hillside. Nothing. She'd accomplished exactly nothing, other than wasting money. She was careful with finances and she hadn't spent anything she couldn't afford to lose, but there was no way she could keep this up. She'd be completely broke in a couple of months and she could just say adios to the idea of trying to buy a car in the spring.

You'll make it work. She wanted to give herself a better mental pep talk, but she was too damned tired and even on the best of days, Ana was not an optimist. Stubborn, yes. Optimistic, no.

The ride across town took too long. When the bus finally arrived at her stop, she was the only one to exit and she breathed a sigh of relief as she stepped out into the cool night air. Riding the bus was cheaper on the wallet and better on the environment, but she hated being closed in with a bunch of strangers. She kept her normal shields up but even through those shields, it made her skin itch and her head throb.

She needed a break.

Needed some peace and quiet to clear her head.

A few hours earlier, on the drive back to Anchorage, she'd swung by Eklutna Lake, looking to do just that—ease her raw nerves. She'd walked the quiet paths, listened to kids playing down on the lake's edge and let her tired brain rest.

As sore as her body had been, as much as she wanted the comfort of her bed, she had needed to soothe ragged edges of her mind more. After her miserable attempts at playing psychic Nancy Drew, she'd desperately needed it.

But now it was like she hadn't ever had that quiet time.

And of course, she didn't really have much time to unwind since she had to be back at work in the morning. She hitched her purse higher up on her shoulder and took the handle of her small carry-on, wheeling it along behind her as she walked the two blocks home.

Her muscles strained and screamed at her with every step. Too much walking and hiking. Ana was active enough, something that had been drummed into her head back at Excelsior. But being able to run a couple of miles on the treadmill and some strength training on the weights wasn't enough to prepare her body for the past few days.

With her eyes and her heart heavy, she turned down the gravel drive and trudged toward her apartment. She kicked a small rock and sent it flying. Absently, she lowered her gaze, watched as it came to a stop a few inches away. Kicked it again. Again—

A pair of booted feet appeared in her line of vision and a hand caught her arm. Hissing out a breath, she reacted instinctively, jabbing toward the neck with her free hand and lifting her foot. But before she could smash it down on the man's instep, he moved.

Moved too quick—

She found herself whirled around, her back pressed up against a hard male body. Panic welled.

"Ana!"

That voice—

She stilled, sucked in a breath. As she did, the panic

inside her started to ease, her body relaxed, before she even realized why.

It took a minute for her head to catch up.

She could smell him . . . and she knew that smell.

Licking her lips, she whispered, "Duke?"

He let her go, quick, as though he couldn't stand to have his hands on her, and she figured he probably couldn't. Instinctively, she tightened her shields, unwilling to pick anything up from him. Even if she deserved to have his disgust filling her head, she'd rather not, thanks very much. Edging away, she turned and looked at him.

The sight of him hit her straight in her core, a punch of heat that left her legs weak and her skin tight and itchy. She let go of her carry-on and folded her arms across her middle. "What are you doing here?"

"Whatever in the hell the problem is, it isn't important enough to keep you from taking off for a weekend?" He glanced down at the carry-on and then up at her face.

Ana narrowed her eyes. "You're the damn Hunter, not me. Playing avenging angel, guardian angel, that's *your* business, not mine." Exhaustion, unrequited lust and fear were sheer hell on a person's willpower, she realized, clamping her mouth shut before she could say anything else.

"So you don't see an issue with calling across the country and claiming there's some sort of problem and then just disappearing for a weekend getaway?" he drawled, his voice caustic.

"You told me to handle it myself, if I recall correctly." She almost said something else, but decided against it. Almost told him that she'd tried and utterly failed.

It didn't matter. He was here now; he could handle it. Hooray for him. No reason for her to sink another couple hundred dollars into this mess, no reason to take off personal time and try to handle something that was way beyond her reach, no reason to lay awake at night, afraid to sleep because she feared the nightmares.

Let him deal with this bullshit. That's what he was supposed to do.

Aren't you feeling bitchy today? she thought darkly. Without another word, she grabbed the handle of her carry-on and headed toward the staircase by the garage door.

"Yeah, taking off when things get dicey, that's your way of handling things," he said, sardonically, following along behind her.

Too close, too. She could feel him, feel that big, warm body, the heat he put off, shadowing along close enough that if he just lifted a hand, he'd touch her. Halfway up the steps, she stopped and shot him a narrow look over her shoulder. "What are you doing?"

"Following you. What are you doing?"

"I'm going to my apartment. I'm tired. I want to take a shower and go to bed."

He glanced over her shoulder toward the door at the top of the stairs. "Sorry, princess, but you got some explaining to do before you can go to bed."

"Explaining." Ana sighed and then started back up the steps. She'd already tried explaining to him and he'd mocked her, laughed at her. Told her to handle it herself and she'd tried, failed miserably and now he was here. Hell, that had likely been his plan all along—get her worked up and then show up in the flesh and save the day.

Of course, she doubted he really would have expected her to actually *try* to handle it. Abruptly, she was pissed. Not just irritated, not just tired and grouchy, and not just edgy because she felt so damned guilty for what she'd done to him. She'd made huge mistakes in her life, but damn it, she'd done her best to rectify them, and she was sick and damned tired of having to pay for it in their eyes.

Seething, she stormed up the rest of the stairs and jammed her key into the lock, undoing the lock with a vicious twist of her wrist.

He followed her inside and she shot him a dirty look as he dropped down on the couch, settling down with lazy, feline grace.

"Make yourself at home," she drawled. She left the

carry-on by the door and shut it, turning the lock on the doorknob and then the deadbolt.

"Those locks suck," he said, flicking a glance at her door.

"I'll make a note of it." Crossing her arms over her chest, she glared at him. "Whatever you need me to explain, fine. Ask away so I can explain and get your ass out of my home."

A grin curled his lips. "Ana, you're swearing. What's got you so pissed?"

"I'm not pissed," she lied.

"You know, even if you did do some kind of number on my instincts, I don't know why in the hell I ever fell for any of your lines," he mused, shaking his head. "You're a lousy liar."

"I didn't hand you *lines*."

Then, as something flashed through his eyes, she wished she hadn't said a word.

The last thing she needed to do was think about ancient history, not when he was here. Not when he was so close. Not when he could smell every subtle change in her body, whether it was because she told a little white lie, or because her body went all hot and achy with need, getting worse with very damn second he was there.

"Didn't you?" He came off the couch and paced toward her, that big, hard body all fluid, sexy grace and long, powerful muscles. His golden hair fell around his face and his gray eyes glittered in the dim light.

"You fed me all sorts of lines, and then I get a knife shoved into my chest and I wake up and find out the pretty blonde princess who had me twisted up inside was the puppet of a fucking psycho. Maybe that's the difference . . . when somebody's pulling your strings you do just as you're told. Did Cat tell you to get hot for me? Is that why you seemed to want me so bad?"

Stop it. Duke stared at her, watched as the blood drained from her face, leaving her pale, her haunted, dark purple eyes all but black.

Stop.

Cat was dead. She didn't fucking matter anymore, and

if Ana was any kind of threat to them, every single last Hunter around would know. She'd be watched—or already dead. She wasn't a threat and he knew it. At least not *that* kind of threat. Not anymore.

The kind of threat she posed to *him* was a different story, but one didn't really have anything to do with the other.

She'd screwed up and even Duke wasn't so blind to the fact that she had tried to make amends. She was guilty, never claimed otherwise, didn't offer excuses or any other lame shit to try to help explain away what she'd done. Even the more plausible reason—her fear for her brother, she never used that card.

If it was anybody but Ana, he probably even could have found some reluctant admiration.

But with Ana . . .

Even as he told himself to stop, to back away, find out what he needed to know and get the hell away from her, he couldn't. Even as he lifted a hand to touch her, curling it around her neck and tugging her close, he told himself to quit and he couldn't. "No answer, Ana?" he whispered, rubbing his thumb across her full lower lip.

Let it go—none of that matters.

Except it did. It *did* matter, why she'd all but melted in his arms, melted around him, over him, so damned hot she'd almost burned him. Had she really wanted him? Or had it been because she had psycho bitch pulling her strings? How deep had Cat's control on Ana gone?

She shook, her body all but vibrating. She was afraid, he could scent it on her, but it wasn't just fear. His lids drooped over his eyes, a growl rumbling in his chest, as he realized he had his answer right there.

Ana didn't have to say a damn thing.

She wanted him. All but burned with it.

That realization could have laid him out flat. Stunned, trying to adjust to it, he stared down at her. She returned his stare, watching him from carefully blank eyes. Those eyes didn't reveal anything, but her body was a different story.

Want.

Need.

Longing . . .

It was the last one that really floored him. Longing . . . something that went deeper than desire, deeper than need.

He scented it on her. It was enough to make his mouth water and his cock swell. It was enough to have his heart aching, for reasons he didn't entirely understand. Enough to make him want to haul her against him and finish the dance they'd started five years earlier. He didn't, though.

Because of her fear. He didn't like her being afraid of him. Heat—he just wanted to smell heat coming off of her, the heat, the desire . . . the longing.

"You're hot now," he whispered, lowering his head until his lips hovered just a breath away from hers. "I can smell it, almost taste it. Why are you so hot, princess?"

"Leave me alone, Duke."

He should. He knew he should. He needed to back away, get the hell away from her, before the anger took control again, before the hunger burning inside him flared too hot for him to handle, before it spilled out onto them and scorched them both. Instead, he dipped his head and nuzzled her neck, breathed in the soft, warm scent of her. She smelled of lavender, soft and subtle, something that clung to her hair and skin.

"You know something that's eaten me up for the past five years?" he whispered, raking his teeth along the curve of her neck. "Five years ago, I had you this close . . . this close to heaven and I would have done just about anything to get inside you. This close . . . and then I realize I'm closer to hell than I am to heaven—and I never even had the chance to fuck you. If you were going to send me to hell, Ana, you could have at least given me a send-off."

"Duke . . . don't."

"Why not?" He straightened, staring down at her averted face. He toyed with the top button of her shirt and wondered what she'd do, how she'd react if he bent his head and tore the buttons off with his teeth. "Why shouldn't I touch you? You want me. You can't lie about that."

She reached up and caught his wrist and shoved him away.

He let her, although he was tempted not to. And when she stepped back, he let her, even though he didn't want to.

"Why shouldn't I touch you?" he asked again, his voice low, harsh with the hunger tearing into him.

"You hate me. I can't blame you for that, but I'm not going to sleep with a guy that hates me."

Cocking his head, he studied her face. His anger, the blinding anger that he had lived with for years began to fade as he caught scent of something else. Something besides desire and longing, something other than fear and hesitation.

It bothered him, that faint, almost hidden scent. Bothered him even more than her fear. It was acrid, sharp—almost like pain. Like she was hurt. Hurt—because she thought he hated her?

"I don't hate you."

She snorted and backed away from him, circling away warily and watching him like she didn't quite trust him. "Yeah, sure you don't. And you aren't pissed off at me anymore, either." She backed away from him, keeping her eyes on his face until she had put the width of the room between them.

He frowned at her. He didn't like her being afraid of him. Wary, that was fine. It didn't bother him, but actual fear, he didn't like it. And he didn't like knowing he'd done something to hurt her.

Sucker—she suckered you in once and you're going to let her do it again?

Blocking out that voice, he hopped up and settled on the counter behind him, watching as she curled up on the couch. She was about as far away from him as she could be without leaving the room.

"I don't hate you," he said again. He wondered at it, how easily he could say it and mean it. For a long time, he hadn't let himself think about whether or not he hated the pretty blonde that had been responsible for putting him through hell, afraid to let himself think about the answer because he'd feared it.

Hate was an ugly emotion, one that threatened a man's control, and to a man like Duke, control meant everything.

Looking at her made it hard to think, though, and he focused his gaze on the floor instead, staring at the warm gleaming wood as he made himself think back, made himself remember.

"I'm not going to lie to you and say I'm cool with what happened, but I get why you made the choices you made. I don't agree with them, but they make sense." He glanced at her from under his lashes, watched the surprise flicker across her face. "I've already wasted enough energy being pissed at you over the past few years. But I don't think I ever hated you. I dunno, maybe I'm too damn lazy to waste that much energy on something that's done and over with."

"Fine. You don't hate me. You'll just distrust me and anything I say or do for the rest of your life," she said, averting her gaze.

She took off her shoes, dropping the thick-soled hiking boots by the couch and then focusing on her socks, paying a lot more attention to the simple task than what was really needed. Duke watched her, watched as she settled back against the couch and reached up, toying with the top button of her shirt.

An unconscious action, Duke suspected, but still, he couldn't quit staring at her slender fingers and wishing she'd undo that button. Then the next one. And the next . . . he wanted her. Wanted to see her strip out of her shirt, her jeans, her bra and panties, to see her naked in front of him.

He wanted her—just as he had for the past five years, but for some reason, it no longer pissed him off quite so much. No—not *some* reason. That made it seem indefinable, like he didn't quite understand the change. But he did. It was because he knew the truth, or at least some of it now. Because he'd finally made himself ask the question that had haunted him for so long.

She had wanted him that night. It hadn't been a lie,

hadn't been a show to sucker him in. She'd wanted him then, and she wanted him now.

Plus, as much as he hated to acknowledge it, knowing that she'd suffered thinking he hated her . . . that meant something, right? Maybe it even meant—hell, he didn't know. Maybe it meant she felt something. Maybe there was just the slightest chance that she was as hung up on him as he was on her. Maybe he wasn't the only one walking around with a tangled, twisted mess trapped inside.

Shit. This was too confusing. Way too confusing.

"If I distrusted you, I would have hung up the phone when you called," he said flatly, slipping off the bar and stalking around the counter into the kitchen. It was small, too confining, but he needed something to eat. Something besides lousy airport food or a hamburger. Jerking open the refrigerator, he stared inside.

"Why are you here?"

He glanced into the living room as Ana rose from the couch, still watching him with shuttered eyes.

The first night he'd met her, those purple eyes had been like windows into her soul, showing her every last emotion—it had been endearing that first night, seeing the desire and the nervousness warring within her. Then the rug was jerked out from under him and he'd ended up struggling for his life, and he figured it had all been an act.

Now he was realizing it hadn't been an act. But things had changed—she'd learned to hide her emotions better.

He hoped she'd gotten better control over her gifts, too. One of those gifts had caused them a lot of trouble and it was one that would wreak havoc on his instincts.

Although sometimes he had to wonder if she'd clouded his instincts as much as he wanted to believe. He'd been thinking with his dick from the moment he laid eyes on her.

Hell, she wasn't the only one who'd fucked up that night. He had, too.

Of course, if he hadn't gone with her . . .

He shied away from that. It was something else he hadn't let himself think about, and he wasn't going to change that now. Tearing his gaze away from her, he looked back into the refrigerator, studying the rather bare shelves.

Behind him, Ana sighed, exasperated. "Are you going to answer me? Why are you here?"

"I'm here because you called."

"Why you?"

He took his time answering, taking a few containers from the shelves and peeking inside. A few, he set on the counter, a couple, he put back on the shelves. One he tossed into the trash can alongside the wall—he didn't even need to look inside that one. Whatever it had been, it was now science-fair material. "Apparently I was the best candidate."

"I bet that went over swimmingly."

Duke shrugged and pulled the lid from the first container. Buffalo wings. Some salad in another container and then a third one held banana pudding. Yum. Glancing up at Ana, he said, "I need to eat."

She glanced at the counter and then back at him. "I never would have guessed."

"You went and turned into a smart-ass," he said, still waiting. "Do you mind?"

Ana frowned. "If you need to eat, then why do you care if I mind?"

"Do you mind?" he repeated.

"No. I don't mind. Eat. Please. Eat and then do whatever in the hell you need to do so you can leave me alone."

"Whatever in the hell I need—I'll remember that." But first, he really needed to eat.

"You hungry?" he asked as he started in on the wings—excellent, even if they were cold. Spice and flavor, not just heat.

"No."

"Did you already eat?" he asked as he popped open the lid on the salad.

"No. Just not hungry."

Before he could look for any salad dressing, Ana was going through her refrigerator. She offered him two bottles and he took the blue cheese. He could have done without the salad, but when he was that hungry, food was food. The pudding was homemade, filled with chunks of bananas and vanilla wafers. The first taste had him grunting with approval. He took another bite and studied her from under his lashes. "You don't eat enough."

"I eat just fine. Look, can we—" The phone rang, interrupting her. She frowned, glanced at it as though a little startled.

"Hello?"

Even though Ana had been the one to answer, Duke had no trouble recognizing Kelsey's voice. He grinned. He should have known she'd be checking up on him. He listened to the conversation as he polished off the pudding.

"Yes, he's here." Ana's gaze slid in his direction then bounced away.

"Good." Kelsey released a pent-up breath. "I wanted to make sure he didn't bolt at the airport. I'd meant to call, let you know he was coming, but I got sidetracked."

"Why would he have bolted at the airport?"

Duke felt blood rush up to his cheeks as Kelsey cheerfully chirped, "Oh, he's got this thing with flying."

"A thing about flying?" Ana repeated. "What kind of thing?"

"Scares him to death, if I'm guessing right. But that's beside the point. I just wanted to make sure he got there okay and you two had hooked up."

Kelsey, you're evil, he thought, glaring at the phone as Ana glanced at him. He caught a flash of amusement in her eyes as she studied him. She looked like she was trying to decide if she wanted to laugh or not. "He's here right now. We haven't had a chance to talk or anything, though. I just got home."

"That's fine. Duke can handle things. I've got to go. It's pretty late here."

Silence stretched out between them as Ana hung up the phone. She glanced at him, then away. Looked back and this time, she looked like she wanted to say something, but then she looked away again.

She kept that up for about thirty seconds before Duke's temper snapped.

"What?" he demanded after she opened and closed her mouth before saying anything for the fifth time.

"Ah . . . she said you . . . uh . . . well, you don't like to fly?"

Duke snorted. No, that wasn't what Kelsey had said. That would have been too polite. Kelsey had a mischievous streak a mile wide. "That wasn't exactly what she'd said, now was it?"

"Well, no. Not exactly." She blinked, then stared at him like he'd suddenly sprouted an extra head. "She said you were afraid of flying."

Jamming his hands into his pockets, he stared right back. "I'm not afraid of flying—I'm afraid of being trapped inside a tin can that could come crashing down to earth at any given time. Going out in a blaze is just fine, as long as I'm not strapped into some chair and hurtling toward the earth at a thousand miles a second."

"Air travel is ridiculously safe, Duke." Her mouth was a straight, unsmiling line, but he could see the corners of her pretty pink lips quirking as though she had to fight the urge to smile—or laugh.

He scowled and dumped the bowl on the counter. "Laugh away, Ana."

"I'm not laughing," she said.

Only because she was fighting it. But it didn't bother him as much as he would have thought. Maybe it was because when she was fighting not to laugh, that blank emptiness in her eyes faded away.

Edging around him, she took the empty bowl and gathered up the rest of the dishes.

He ran his tongue along his teeth, watching her as she dumped the dishes in the sink.

Whatever in the hell you need—she told him to do whatever in the hell he needed. Bad words to say to a man, he figured. He stared at the back of her head as she ran some water over the dishes. The smell of apple-scented soap filled the air; a few stray bubbles drifting upward as she washed the bowls.

Her hair had gotten longer, hanging halfway down her back. She'd braided it. Closing the distance between them, he reached out and tugged the band from the end. He tossed it onto the counter and started to comb his hands through her hair. She went still under his touch.

"What are you doing?" she asked, her voice shaking.

He rested his hands on her waist, held her steady as he leaned into her, nestling his cock against her denim-covered backside. "You told me to do whatever I need. I think I need to do you."

She stood stiff, straight, unyielding as he reached around and sought out the buttons of her shirt, freeing one then another, then another until the simple white cloth parted, revealing a slim strip of pale flesh.

"I'm not going to sleep with a man who can't stand me," she said.

"We've already covered this, baby. If I couldn't stand you, I wouldn't get hard just hearing your voice." Leaving the shirt hanging on her, unbuttoned down the front, he rested his hands on her shoulders and listened to her breath catch in her throat. "I get hard when I hear your voice, when I think about you, when I see you, when I walk through a room and smell you. Hell, even watching you trying not to laugh about me and planes is enough to make me hard."

He slid his hands around her and reached up, cupping her small, silk-covered breasts in his hands. "And I don't plan on doing much sleeping just yet." No, the only thing he planned on doing in the next couple of hours was fucking her. He had to.

Whatever Ana sensed wrong around here, it wasn't so choking, so pressing that it had his skin crawling. He couldn't really feel much of anything, beyond her.

So that meant it could wait.

She couldn't.

Just then, he wasn't aware of anything but his need to have her. Finally have her, finally give in to the urge he'd been fighting for too damn long. This obsession he had with her, it wasn't going to get better until he dealt with it and dealing with it meant having her. Taking what she'd promised him years earlier.

"You didn't come here for this," she whispered.

Actually, Duke suspected he had. No, not entirely. He had a job to do, and he'd do it. But if that was all that mattered, he wouldn't have felt so drawn to make his way to her house and sit outside while he waited for her to arrive. He could have left, at any time, and just prowled around until something in his gut woke and called him to action.

But he'd come here. To her.

And for this.

"I did come for this," he said gruffly, plumping her breasts together and staring down, fascinated by the sight of his hands on her body.

Duke's skin was gold, naturally so. By contrast, Ana's breasts looked snowy white against his hands, creamy and warm, the scent of lavender rising stronger on the air. "I came for this and if I had half a brain, I would have done this years ago. You're inside my skin, Ana, and that's not going to change until I have what it is you promised me five years ago. What you promised *us*."

A sigh shuddered out of her. "Duke, this isn't a good idea."

"Yes. It is." He let go of her, rested his hands on the counter beside her. He wanted her, and he had every intention of having her—but he wouldn't force it on her. Gripping the counter, he dipped his head and whispered, "You wanted me five years ago, didn't you?"

He had to know, had to hear the answer from her, even though his body already knew.

Her answer, when it came, was soft and hesitant. "Yes."

Duke flexed his hands and just barely managed to swallow a pleased growl. "You wanted me, the same as I wanted you. You want me now . . . the same as I want you now. It's not going away, Ana, and you know it. We might as well deal with it. But if you can't handle that, then you tell me now. Tell me, and I'll give you some room, give you a little more time."

Handle it?

Hell, no, she couldn't handle it. She couldn't handle *him*. She'd never been able to handle him, not even when she'd spied him across the crowded bar five years earlier and known what she had to do.

She'd chosen him—on purpose, because she'd recognized what he was. If one of his kind went missing, it would be noticed. Somebody would come looking for him, and maybe, just maybe, it would be somebody who could handle Cat.

It had been a calculated, cold decision—one she'd made for a couple of reasons. She couldn't keep doing what Cat wanted of her and stay sane. She couldn't become the monster that Cat was. And she had to get her brother away from Cat before it was too late. It had been a desperate gamble, a desperate plan.

It had worked, all too well.

"Ana?" His breath was warm against her neck, his mouth hot and silken as it glided over her skin. "You going to run away, princess?"

She wanted to. This was a bad, bad, *bad* idea and she knew it. Duke wanted to fuck her, because he hadn't been able to do it that night. That was his way of "dealing" with it. It wasn't the way she needed to do it, though, and if she gave in, it was going to leave a scar on her.

What was one more?

Taking a deep breath, she reached up and freed the front clasp of her bra.

Behind her, Duke blew out a harsh breath, a sound that was low and rough and sexy. It had her knees weak. But then he went to draw her shirt away and she stiffened, reaching up and holding it in place.

"Ana?"

"The shirt . . . I . . . I want to leave it on."

He dipped his head and nuzzled her neck. "Shy, princess?"

"Yes . . . no." Geez, how did she tell him that she had

enough scars on her back to rival the ones on his chest? Not exactly titillating talk. "Can I just keep the shirt on?"

He kissed her, an openmouthed, hot kiss that she felt clear down to her toes. "For now." He toyed with the waistband of her jeans and murmured, "What about these? Because, Ana, we really need to lose these."

"I—uh—okay." It was about the best she could do without whimpering.

Another hot, soft kiss, this one on her shoulder, his heat scalding her even through the white cotton of her shirt. "Put your hands on the counter."

She did, locking her knees in an attempt to keep her legs from shaking under her. Blood roared in her ears, pounded and pulsed in tandem with the ache in her sex. She was hot, embarrassingly wet already and when he stripped her jeans and panties away, she gasped as cool air kissed the hot flesh between her thighs.

"You're wet for me," he whispered. "I smell it. Spread your legs for me."

She whimpered, her breath catching in her throat when he reached down between her thighs, stroking her slick folds with his fingertips.

"You're tight." His voice had dropped to a low growl, so rough it was almost unintelligible. He pushed one finger inside her and Ana's knees buckled under her, her breath caught in her throat—couldn't breathe, couldn't breathe. He stroked deeper, his rough fingertip rasping over swollen tissues. Shaking, she sagged forward, letting the counter take more of her weight. Duke growled, stroking his other hand down her hip.

He said something, but Ana couldn't understand his words. Nothing made sense, nothing connected—nothing even existed except for his hands on her body, the slow, easy glide of his finger in, out of her sex—nothing—

She came, harsh and sudden, sagging against the counter. She whimpered, letting the counter take all of her weight, pressing her flaming face to the cool surface. Her breasts pressed flat against it, her shirt and bra clung to her damp body, and her sweaty hair lay in a tangle over her shoulders and face, blocking the world out.

Unable to think past the roar of blood in her ears, she drifted, half caught in a daze, only dimly aware that Duke was no longer touching her. A harsh, rasping sound, oddly loud. The whisper of cloth, a dull thud. Lifting her lashes, she tried to look behind her, but her hair was in the way. She went to brush it out of the way and Duke caught her wrist. "Be still," he muttered, pressing her wrist to the counter, holding it there.

He nudged her thighs apart and she gulped as something pressed against her buttocks. He was naked—naked, and oh . . . oh, shit—

The head of his cock, thick, full and hard, nudged against her entrance. Panicking, she tried to close her thighs but he shifted, using his knees to keep her open. She cried out as he pressed against her, forcing her to yield. Thick—burning hot, scorching—stretching.

Ana keened as he filled her, driving deep, deeper. Pain flared, sharp and bright and she twisted, trying to escape. Tears welled in her eyes and she squeezed them shut, tried to muffle her sob against the counter.

But he heard. Half lost, the soft, panicked cry penetrated Duke's lust-fogged brain, slapping against him like an icy wave. His nostrils flared, catching the scent of pain, fear—*Ana*. Fuck, was he . . . ? He was—he was hurting her.

Damn it, damn it, damn it—he made himself stop, half of his aching length buried inside her snug heat. Sucking in a deep breath, he gathered her hair in his hand and pushed it aside, trying to see her face. She hid from him, shifting so that he could barely see her profile.

But she couldn't keep him from seeing the tears.

"Ana?"

The silken wet sheath convulsed around him and Duke shuddered against the need to thrust, to ride that soft body and empty himself, but just fucking her—was that all he really wanted? No—hell, no, that wasn't all he wanted. He wanted her to moan, to whisper his name and come for him.

But he was moving too quick. She wasn't ready—although, damn it to hell, she fucking *felt* ready, hot and soft as butter, melting all around him, sweet, tight and slick.

Too tight—somewhere in the back of his mind, an alarm sounded, but he blocked it out. Bending over her, he braced his elbows on the counter on either side of her body, careful to keep from moving his lower body. He skimmed his lips over her cheek and whispered her name.

She didn't respond.

Laying his hand on her hip, he stroked upward, brushing her shirt away so he could caress the outer curve of her breast. He tried to tug the offending material away but she gasped and hunched her shoulders. "Shh . . . okay. It's okay," he whispered. Even though he wanted that damned shirt off, he let go. Gathering her hair, he pushed it over her other shoulder and lowered his lips, kissing, biting her neck gently. She shuddered . . . and then oh so slightly tilted her head to the side. That small encouragement was all he needed. Duke set his teeth in the curve where neck and shoulder joined and bit her, lightly. Ana gasped and shifted under him, raising her upper body a scant inch off the counter. He slid a hand under her, shoved the shirt away so he could palm her breasts, tug on her small, stiff nipples. She arched against him and moaned under her breath.

Slowly, he moved his hips, nudging another inch of his length inside her. Instantly, she tensed. Tight—

Too fucking tight—That alarm in the back of his head was screaming now. He gritted his teeth as her sweet pussy clenched around him and then he made himself step away. It was sheer agony, leaving the slick, wet glove of her pussy and his body was raging at him. She whimpered, her body shuddering. He crowded up against her, cuddling his cock against the soft curve of her ass.

"Ana."

She darted a quick look at him over her shoulder and when she would have looked away, he caught her face, craning her neck around until their gazes locked. "How long?" he demanded as he wrapped his free arm around her waist.

Her lashes lowered, shielding her gaze. A growl slipped past his lips before he could stop it.

"How long?" he asked again, sliding his hand down and cupping her heat in his hand.

She didn't answer.

Duke swore and let go, but only long enough to make her turn and face him. She tried to go around him, but he brought an arm up, caging her in. He tangled his hand in her hair, tugging her head back and forcing her to look at him. "How long, Ana? A few months? A few years . . . *ever*?"

She stared at him, her dark purple eyes all but black in her face. She caught her lower lip between her teeth and Duke groaned, dipped his head and kissing her until she opened, until she stopped biting her lip and kissed him back. Then he caught that lower lip between his teeth, shuddering as he bit down.

"Tell me, damn it," he rasped against her mouth. "How long?"

He wasn't sure she'd answer. He started to think it might be better if she didn't. But then she sighed, a shaky, unsteady sound. "Never."

Never—

For him, yeah, he was damned glad she'd answered. But maybe not the best thing for her.

Cupping her chin in his hand, he stared into her eyes, fighting the animal that lurked just under his skin. "Do I stop? This is your one chance, Ana. Tell me to stop and then get the hell away from me before I lose it."

She gulped and stared at him, a look on her face that was caught between terror and fascination.

"Do I stop?" he demanded again.

Ana licked her lips and then whispered, "No." It was quiet, all but soundless.

His control fell away in broken shards and he turned her

back around, bent his knees and reached between them, aligning the head of his cock to the mouth of her pussy. "This will hurt . . . I'm sorry," he rasped.

Was he lying? He didn't know—*liar*!

He wasn't sorry. Not at all. Not as he sank his aching cock inside her, keeping that fucking shirt fisted in his hand, out of the way so he could watch as he—*finally*—took Analise Morell. Even when she twisted and tensed against him, even when she whimpered softly and tensed up, her body fighting his invasion. Even when he scented her tears. He wasn't sorry—

She whimpered his name, shuddered and arched her back, trying to twist away from his possession until he caught her in his arms and spun, turning from the counter and going to his knees. He took her with him, forced her thighs wide and braced his hands on her hips as he tunneled deep, forcing his way past the resistance of her virgin pussy, deep, deep, until he'd seated his entire length inside her.

She was crying when he was done, shaking, her soft, slender body undulating, fighting to accept his possession, fighting to reject it. Duke sucked in huge gulps of air, waging his own battle—the battle to ride her, hard and fast, to sate that hunger that had burned within him for far too long—and the need to stroke, sooth and ease.

Dipping his head, he pressed a kiss to her spine. Felt something—something that disturbed him enough that it shook some of the lust from his brain. Ana lay with her torso against the floor, whimpering and shaking, completely distracted and unaware as he caught the hem of her shirt and pushed it up. Baring her lower back, and the numerous long, thin scars that marred her flesh.

Fury leaped inside him, but he thrashed it down. *Not now*—gritting his teeth, he battled the anger back and let the shirt fall back into place. Dipping his head, he trailed his lips over her back, feeling one scar, then another, another.

She knelt before him, unaware. Ana moaned raggedly and rolled her hips. It was too much—

Duke swore and gripped her hips, held her steady as he started to ride her. Slow. He battled the beast inside and won, taking her slow and easy, taking the time to tease and caress, kissing her hidden scars, reaching around and under her, petting the slick wet flesh that stretched so tight around him, then seeking out her clit and stroking it. She stiffened and Duke's eyes damned near crossed as her pussy convulsed around him.

"Like that?" he rasped, tugging on the hard bud. She wailed out his name and he grinned, hot, savage satisfaction jolting through him.

She shoved her ass back against him and then rocked forward, rubbing against his fingers. He reached down and caught her wrist, guiding her hand between her thighs. She tensed and the scent of her body changed, spiked— sharp with embarrassment, hot with need. "Touch yourself, Ana."

She whimpered but did just that. Duke splayed his hands across her hips and held her steady. "I'm done waiting now," he rasped.

And he was—before another second passed, he was riding her hard, shafting her deep. She screamed, a sound caught between pleasure and pain, but he didn't stop. Didn't slow. Even after she came, clenching down around him like a silken fist, he didn't stop. She convulsed and twisted and shuddered underneath him and still, he didn't slow. Hunger burned inside him, the deep ache of hunger suppressed for so long that finally yielding to it was almost as painful as refusing it.

She wilted underneath him, sagging to the floor. Duke rumbled out her name and moved with her, sprawling atop her body, bracing one elbow on the ground beside her and grasping her thigh with his other, holding her open. Her scent surrounded him, sank into his pores, flooded him. The low, husky moans echoed through his head and each time he drove his dick into her pussy, she clenched around him.

She came again, vising down around him, milking him, clenching . . . squeezing . . . he roared, the animal inside him tearing free just long enough to make him bend his head, long enough to have him setting his teeth against her shoulder, biting her through her shirt—marking her.

Power flared, danced along his spine, threatened to emerge. Growling, he bit down harder and came, came so fucking hard, his body gave out on him and he collapsed on top of her, crushing her slender body into the hard, unyielding floor.

CHAPTER 6

"I've hurt you." He should say he was sorry, but Duke knew he couldn't do it, not without lying to her. He couldn't have this, couldn't be the first man to touch her, without bringing the pain. He couldn't say he was sorry and as he pulled away from her and sat up, staring down at her still-quivering body, all he could feel was a gut-deep sense of satisfaction.

Sighing, he reached out and traced her shoulder, eying the torn cloth and through it, the indentations of his teeth, checking for bruising. The skin wasn't broken and it didn't look like she was going to bruise, but for some seriously strange reason, he wasn't happy about that. He wanted to see his mark on her. Wanted it so bad he could taste it.

Taste *her*.

Yeah, that primitive instinct to mark her wasn't at all helped by the fact that he could still taste her, still feel her. It didn't help that her scent covered him. Didn't help that he could feel each breath that shuddered out of her lungs as clearly as he could feel his own chest rise and fall.

"Ana."

She stirred, and through the curtain of her hair, he caught a glimpse of her eyes, but she didn't respond. All she did was sigh and squirm against the floor. Goosebumps broke out along her flesh and he blew out a breath. Working his arms underneath her, he brought her against his chest and rose, striding out of the kitchen and down the hall. He hadn't exactly taken a tour earlier, but the apartment wasn't big. Finding her bedroom took all of twenty seconds.

The room was small, the bed a double that was barely going to be big enough for the two of them. He shifted and managed to flip the top blanket down, placing her inside the bed and then sliding in alongside her. She stiffened, her lashes lifting to stare up at him, bemused. He nuzzled her neck, licked her. "You're trying to fall asleep on me."

She slicked her tongue across her lips. "Sorry."

But already her lashes were drooping. Before she could drift back into sleep, he laid a hand on her belly. "Ana."

She blinked, gave him the wide-eyed stare of a woman struggling to remain awake.

"I hurt you." Watching her face, he grazed his fingertips across the curls between her thighs.

Confusion flickered in the dark purple of her eyes. Then she blushed. "I'm fine."

She averted her head but Duke caught her chin and made her look at him. The blush on her cheeks deepened, crept down her neck, down to the tops of her breasts. He tore his gaze away from her chest—if he kept watching to see just how low that adorable blush would go, he'd be a slobbering maniac in a matter of seconds.

No—he needed to talk for a few seconds. Talk, not fuck her again. "Why, Ana?"

The purple of her eyes flashed jewel-bright and she squirmed to the left, as though she'd roll away from him. He took care of that problem by rolling on top of her. The soft cushion of her belly cradled his cock and instinctively, he rocked against her once.

Why me?

Why did you let me?

Why haven't you been with a guy before?
When can I fuck you again?
He wanted to ask all of those questions, wanted an answer to all. But all he could manage was, "Why?"

"Does it matter?"

He buried his face in the curve of her neck and kissed her. "It matters—or I wouldn't ask." *Please don't let this be some sort of apology—*

Because, hell, if it was, Duke was pretty fucking sure he was going to owe *her.* And that he'd need to get his head examined. It had been worth it—the five years of sexual frustration, all those nights he spent dreaming about her, the days he'd spent getting tortured, it had all been worth it for this moment, to feel her lying underneath him, to hear her whimper his name as he brought her to climax and to sink his cock into that virgin pussy and know that he was the first. The only.

"Why, Ana?"

She tucked her chin against her chest, closing her eyes. "You ask impossible questions."

"No. I asked a simple one . . . why? Because of what happened?"

Her eyes flew wide and she flinched. Working her hands between them, she shoved against his chest and snapped, "Get the hell off of me."

"No." He dipped his head and nipped her lip, shuddering as he caught just a little more of her taste. "Is that why?"

She lay beneath him, stiff and rigid, unyielding even when he shifted lower and caught one pink nipple in his mouth. "I'm not a whore," she whispered, her voice breaking in the middle.

"No. I never thought you were." He licked her again, tracing the distended peak with his tongue before resting his chin between her breasts and staring up at her. "Why would you say that?"

"If I'm doing this as some way of making amends, then this was some kind of payment—and that would make me a whore." She closed her eyes, turned her head. Her hands, clenched into small fists, separated them.

Duke just couldn't have that. He needed to feel her. All of her. Catching her wrists in his hands, he brought them up by her head. Staring down into her shuttered eyes, he realized he'd hurt her—again. But this time, he was sorry. Sorry enough that it knotted his gut and left a bad taste in his mouth. Dipping his head, he rubbed his cheek against hers.

"Sorry, princess." He murmured the words against her lips and used his hands to stroke her rigid body until she started to relax, until her body welcomed his again.

Rising up on his elbows, he stared down at her. His gaze lingered on her mouth, that pretty pink bow. Unable to resist, he traced her lips with his finger. She shivered and her eyes darkened.

Duke gritted his teeth as her response sent another flare of heat coursing through him. *Focus. You were talking, remember?*

Yeah, he remembered. But he'd always viewed talking as a waste of time.

Jerking his attention back on track, he studied her face. "So it's not because of that. But why, Ana? You went all this time . . . why me? Why now?"

She blushed and looked away.

Catching her chin, he guided her face back to his. Quietly, he said, "If it didn't matter to me, I wouldn't ask."

She was quiet, quiet for so long, he didn't think she was going to give him the answer he needed. But then finally, she sighed. Her gaze fell away from his, self-conscious and nervous. "Why do you think?"

"Because you want me . . . do you want like I want, Ana?" he whispered against her lips. He kissed her, taking it deep even as common sense whispered he should stop. She didn't need this again, even if he was craving her. "Crave like I crave . . . need like I need?"

"You don't need me."

"You're wrong." He settled his hips against hers, nudged the slick wet heat with the head of his cock. "I need like you couldn't even begin to imagine . . . wrap your legs around me."

Her lashes lifted. She stared into his eyes and Duke wondered if she'd tell him no. If she did, he'd stop. He could—even though he needed her like he needed air, he could stop. But all she did was wiggle beneath him, her movements slow, awkward in a way that wrenched his heart. Then she wrapped her legs around his hips, and he shuddered as the head of his cock rubbed against her slick folds.

He sank inside her, taking it slowly this time, giving her one slight inch at a time, watching her face and easing back any time he glimpsed pain in her gaze. "Ana . . . " He closed his eyes and growled her name as she arched up.

He slid deeper.

She cried out and he swore, stiffened above her. Eyes flying open, he stared at her face. "Am I hurting you?"

She shuddered, whimpered. "Yes . . . " But then she tightened her thighs around his hips. "Please don't stop."

Stop—hell, no, he wouldn't stop. Not when she moved against him like that, not when she slid her hands up his chest and tangled her fingers in his hair. Not when she sobbed out his name and tugged his face down to hers, pressing her mouth to his and moaning as he kissed her.

Stop—no, he couldn't stop with her.

She'd gotten under his skin, settled there years earlier until she was a part of him, every bit as much a part of him as the beast that lurked just under the surface. Every bit as much a part of him as the color of his eyes or his hair. Tangled up inside him, confusing the hell out of him as he swung between obsession, need and hurt.

Bracing his weight above her, he tugged her shirt off. He needed her naked. Needed nothing separating his hands from her flesh. She let him this time, and they left the shirt lying under her in a tangle. He stroked a hand down her side, rubbed his index finger over one thin scar, watching her closely.

Her eyes widened and she tensed.

"No," he muttered. Dipping his head, he kissed her, hard and quick. He cupped her ass in his hand and lifted her, tucking her more fully against him. "Mine. You gave yourself to me, Ana . . . you're mine."

His . . .

Scars, fears, sad violet eyes, soft silken skin . . . all of her. She was his.

S HE awoke alone.
      For a minute, she lay there, drained, so full of stunned disbelief, she couldn't think past it.

Duke.

His scent covered her sheets, permeated her skin. There was no way she'd dreamed what had happened a few hours ago, but still, she couldn't wrap her mind around it. Couldn't believe—

"I'm making breakfast."

His voice, pitched low, drifted through the wall. Mouth dry, she stared toward the door. She couldn't see him, couldn't hear anything other than a faint sizzle coming from the kitchen, but he'd heard her, knew she was awake.

Breakfast.

Duke was making breakfast.

Duke was *here*.

Swallowing, she glanced toward the foot of the bed, spying the plain T-shirt she usually wore on summer nights. Pain sliced through her as she stood up. The muscles in her thighs ached and with every move, they screamed at her. Sensing his approach, she grabbed the shirt but he appeared before she managed to tug it on. She stood there in front of him with the shirt pressed to her breasts and feeling like a fool.

He didn't come toward her, just stood there, bare-chested, one shoulder braced against the wall. "You're sore," he said quietly.

She shrugged. "I'll be okay."

He nodded and then shoved off the wall, crossed the floor to stand before her. She tensed as he laid a hand on her shoulder, tugging. "Duke—"

"I know about the scars, Ana. I felt them last night." *And saw every damn last one of them when I woke up*, he thought, still burning with fury. Ten scars. Ten times, she'd been sliced up with a knife. He didn't need to ask to know who'd been holding the blade.

She blushed and looked away, humiliation hanging around her like a cloak. She stood malleable in his hands and this time, when he tugged for her to turn, she did so. Her head hung low, her long pale hair hiding her face from him. He could hear each ragged, uneven breath, and it was like a shard in his heart.

"Cat," he said flatly.

She swallowed and nodded. Carefully, he traced one finger over the longest one. "Why?"

"Because she could."

A growl rumbled out of him and his skin itched, burned hot. The animal inside him screamed. Wanted *out*. Wanted blood. But the bitch was dead. Gently, he pressed his lips to first one scar, then another, then another. When he'd kissed every last one, he straightened and tugged her back against him, wrapping his arms tight around her. "Don't hide them from me," he said quietly.

She didn't respond.

Blowing out a breath, he skimmed his hands up over her arms and made himself take a step back. Then another. Made himself stand still as she fumbled with the shirt she held and tugged it on. But she didn't turn to face him until he made her. "I don't want you hiding from me," he said, trying to keep the edge out of his voice. "I don't like it."

"I'm not hiding—"

"Yes, you are. That's why you didn't want me taking your shirt off—you didn't want me seeing the scars."

She swallowed and licked her lips. "They're ugly, Duke."

"No." He flicked a glance at his chest, studied his own scars. Some of them were puckered and tight, others were long slender slices similar to the ones Ana had on her back. The scars he had from psycho bitch had all been done within a matter of days. Cat had tortured him and enjoyed every last second of it, but his abuse at her hands had been short-lived.

But without her saying a word, Duke knew it wasn't the same with Ana.

"If you can look at my scars without flinching, I can do the same to you." He brought her up against him, caught a hand and guided it to his chest. "If you can touch mine and still want me, I can touch yours . . . and still want you."

He slipped a hand under her shirt, tracing the scars. Then he nudged his hips against her belly and rasped, "And I definitely want you." He caught her mouth with his, kissed her until she was rocking against him, shuddering in his arms.

Stop. Stop it or you won't be able to.

He stopped. Barely. Gritted his teeth and made himself take a step back. Then another. Distance. He needed some distance. That was the key. He settled by the wall near the door and tried not to think about those sweet, warm curves and soft, white skin.

Of course, it would be easier if he wasn't staring at all those sweet curves and soft skin. Tearing his gaze away, he glanced toward the kitchen.

"Come out here and eat. We need to talk . . . " His gaze flicked over her, taking in every single inch from the top of her head to her feet. "And if you stand there looking at me like that for too much longer, I'm going fuck you again."

Ana's heart fluttered in her chest and her mouth went dry. He wanted her, scars and all. "I . . . ah . . . I'm fine with that."

Duke cocked a brow. He pushed off the wall and stalked toward her, his body a beautiful work of golden skin, sinewy muscle and feline grace.

"No. You're not." He laid a hand on her belly, held her eyes as he slid his fingers down, pushing just the tip of one inside her sex.

Ana flinched and stiffened. Blood rushed to her cheeks as he pulled his hand away and lifted his fingers to his lips, watched her as he licked them. "You're not fine. You're sore. And as much as I want to, if we have sex again right now, it's going to hurt you, probably worse than before. I don't want to hurt you this time."

He rubbed his lips across hers and whispered, "Come out here where we can talk."

"I . . . ah, I need to go to the bathroom." Brush her teeth, her hair, wash her face—get a fucking *grip*.

"Okay. Then come out. Talk to me."

S HE emerged from the bathroom nearly ten minutes later. Duke watched her from the corner of his eye as she slipped into the small kitchen. Two more minutes and he had been ready to go get her himself.

Her hair was neatly combed, twisted up into a knot on her head and secured with some sort of clip. He could smell soap, water and toothpaste—and himself, his scent, permeating her skin. Unable to stop it, he smiled. He liked the way she smelled with their scents merged.

"What . . . ah . . . what exactly do you need me to tell you?"

He flicked a glance up and then looked back down at the skillet, eying the eggs he had sizzling in there. There was a plateful of bacon already done. Some eggs for her, butter up the toast, then they could sit down and eat.

"I'm not going to ask right now," he said carefully, resisting the urge to do just that. "But soon, you're going to explain to me about those scars on your back."

Ana blushed. "I don't like to talk about that."

"Ana."

Her eyes met his and then darted away. Sighing, she said, "Fine. Just . . . just not now, okay?"

"Good enough. We got other things we need to talk about, anyway. How do you take your eggs?"

She blinked. "That's what we need to talk about?"

"No," he said, flipping the eggs and letting them sizzle for a few seconds. "But we need to eat and we might as well eat while we talk. Over easy work for you? Scrambled?"

"It doesn't matter."

He watched as she shifted on the stool, flinching, then blushing as she realized he was watching her. "How sore are you?"

She lifted a shoulder. "Not too bad."

"Good." He slid his eggs onto his plate and then cracked open two more. "Two enough?"

"Two is too much," she said, wrinkling her nose.

"I'll eat what you don't." He was fucking *starving*. Sex, stress, they burned through his resources quicker and a shifter's metabolism was through the roof anyway.

"Okay. I don't have much time anyway . . . I need to get to work."

He frowned. "Take the day off."

"I can't. I took two days off last week."

"I need you with me right now."

He finished her eggs and dished her up a plate, four slices of bacon and the two eggs. Slathering some butter on the toast, he added it to her plate and pushed it across the counter to her. "Eat."

She ate less than one egg. One piece of bacon. Two bites of toast. Then she tried to slide the plate across to him. Duke scowled. "Eat more."

"I have to shower still." Ana shook her head and glanced at the clock. "What . . . what do you need me to tell you? The bus leaves in less than an hour, so I've got to hurry."

"Take the day off."

Exasperated, she blew out a breath. "I *can't*. I already took two days off last week trying to . . . " Breaking off in midsentence, she shook her head. "Look, I'll leave you my cell number. After I shower, I'll have about twenty minutes before I have to leave."

"Two days off trying to do what?"

She gave him a baleful stare. "Nothing, Duke." She slid off the stool and winced, ignoring the way his eyes lingered on her body, drifting low and settling on her hips. "I'm going to take a shower."

He caught up with her before she'd taken three steps. Caging her up against the counter, he said, "Two days doing what?"

She shoved against him. "Damn it, Duke, I've got a job to get ready for."

"Answer me and I'll leave you to it," he replied easily.

His lips brushed against her cheek and she averted her face, but he wasn't too put off. All he did was nuzzle her neck, nip on her earlobe as he waited for an answer.

"I did just what you told me to do, Duke—or at least, I *tried*," she finally said, shoving against his chest and trying to twist away from him. He let her get one step and then he caught her arm, spinning her around and tugging her back against him.

"What did I tell you to do?" he asked.

"You told me to *handle* it." She curled her lip at him and added, "So I tried. And won't you just be surprised to know that I totally and completely failed."

She jerked her arm away and this time, surprisingly, he let her and he didn't try to follow her, either.

DUKE watched her disappear into the bathroom and then he swore, scrubbing a hand over his face. Stubble scratched against his palm.

Closing his eyes, he thought back and mentally played back his conversation with her from a few days earlier.

Something's wrong up here.

Handle it yourself, princess.

He hadn't been serious. Granted, he hadn't put much weight in what she said. He'd planned on passing the message to Kelsey and then disappearing, getting a lot of distance between himself and any reminder of Analise Morell—or at least he had tried to convince himself into thinking that.

Kelsey had other plans, and Duke was honest enough with himself that he would have ended up here sooner or later anyway. He might have tried to pass it off as curiosity, but Ana had been under his skin too long and he wouldn't have been able to stay away.

He spent the past few years deluding himself about how he felt over her. He'd convinced himself that it was distrust, dislike, even hostility that kept him so on edge around her.

Those days were over.

All it had taken was feeling her body pressed against

his again, tasting her soft, pretty mouth. Knowing that
she'd wanted him—*still* wanted him. Seeing the sadness
in her eyes. Even before he'd seen the scars on her body,
he'd been lost.

You are so fucked, he thought miserably.

Shit.

You told me to handle *it. So I tried. And won't you just
be surprised to know that I totally and completely failed.*

Shit. Shit. *Shit.* He'd told her to handle it, but he hadn't
expected her to try.

Ana had some limited psychic abilities, but nothing she'd
ever managed to use in much of an offensive manner. Even
the way she used her gift to block out the presence of others
was more of a chameleon trick than anything else. She hid
herself, and their bad luck was that she couldn't isolate her gift
and it spread out across huge swaths of land, sometimes miles.
Her way of controlling it was just to lock the gift down.

Up against some of the things the Hunters had to face,
she was all but helpless. A growl vibrated out of his chest
as he thought about what could have happened.

Her instincts were better than a mortal's. As required of
all students at Excelsior, she'd learned basic fighting and
self-defense skills, but just the basics. None of it would do
her much good against something more than mortal.

Handling messes was *his* area, not hers. Never mind his
random moments of stupidity. He wanted to storm into the
bathroom and yell at her. She should have known better—

So should you.

He stopped in his tracks and scowled, shoving a hand
through his hair. Yeah, he should have known better. Ana
had made some serious errors in judgment in past years,
but she'd done it for the right reasons—if doing the wrong
thing could ever be for a right reason. To protect her brother.
It took a spine of steel to live with a monster like Cat and
come through with any semblance of sanity. Ana had lived
with the monster for years, even though she could have run.
Lived in a place where she'd been tortured, and she'd done
so without letting Cat break her.

How bad, he wondered. How bad had it gotten? He wanted to know, but now wasn't the time to push.

She'd stayed, because she wanted to keep her brother safe.

A spine of steel, a good heart—shit, yeah, he should have known better.

He glanced toward the bathroom and then turned back, studying the living room. Without a qualm, he crossed the room and settled down on the floor by her overnight bag. Tucked inside the interior pocket, he found a file folder full of copied newspaper articles and neatly made notes.

He'd only managed to get through the first page of notes, though, before he heard the bathroom door open. He flipped over to the next page and kept reading as Ana came padding out of the bathroom. She stopped in the doorway and he glanced up, met her gaze.

"What are you doing?"

He looked pointedly at the file open on the floor in front of him. "It looks like I'm reading."

"Yes. It does look like you're reading. Its looks like you're reading *my* stuff."

Quirking a brow, he said, "This is why you called me, right?"

"Yes." She crouched down beside him and smoothed down the long skirt she wore. It pooled on the floor around her and absently, he caught some of the silky fabric between his thumb and forefinger, stroking it. "You know, I don't much care for having somebody go through my things without asking."

Duke shrugged. "Asking takes time. I'm not big on wasting it." He lifted one of the copied articles. "Who is this?"

She didn't bother looking at the image on the paper. Sighing, she straightened and moved over to the couch. "Her name is Marie. She disappeared from here back in the seventies."

Duke frowned. Hell, he'd thought it looked kind of old. But not *that* old. "I'm not exactly the *Cold Case* files type of help you might need, Ana. Going to be hard for me to find a trail that's more than thirty years old."

"It's not just her," Ana said, her voice faint. She put on a pair of sandals, taking her time with each buckle. "There's something else going on—I don't know if it's connected to her, if it *is* her, or what. I just know there's something weird going on."

Duke blew out a breath and then brought up a hand, pinched the bridge of his nose. "Ana, I don't know if you know how this works or not . . . when there's something weird, *our* kind of weird, going on, we feel it. It's kind of like a magnetic pull. We feel it. I'm not feeling it here."

Ana opened her mouth, but then closed it. Her gaze lowered to her hands and he watched as she rubbed her palms together. "Maybe you should give it a little bit of time."

"It's not like I'm just going to walk around for a couple hours and then disappear. I'm going to hang around a while, see what happens," he said, grimacing. He gathered up the folder, all the loose articles and the book he had yet to look at. Tucking them back inside her carry-on, he zipped it closed and then rose. "Just don't expect much of anything, okay?"

Ana laughed. "I stopped expecting much of anything a long time ago." She sighed and smoothed her hands back over her hair. "I need to get to work."

He watched as she moved around the house, gathering up her purse, a lunch box. She stopped by the counter and jotted something on a notepad. "Here's my cell phone if you need it," she said softly.

"Ana, I can't do much of anything but walk around this city and hope something pops. You're the connection here—if something is going to pop, it's going to have to do with you."

"Duke . . ."

"Fine." He scowled. "Go punch a clock. Have fun with it. I'll try to muddle my way through this on my own." Turning his back, he stared out the window at the green mountains.

Behind him, he could hear her moving around, heard the quiet click of locks, the door as it opened. He tensed, ready for the door to shut.

"It's not that I have fun punching that clock, Duke. I like my job well enough—and I need it. I don't have some clandestine, uber-rich assembly of superheroes around to pick up my tab. But if I thought I could help, I would."

Duke shot her a narrow glance. "Hell, Ana. It's not like anybody made you leave Virginia. You chose to come here. If money's the issue—"

"It's not . . . or at least, that's not all of it. You don't get it. I'm *not* extraordinary, Duke." A sad, bitter smile formed on her lips, wobbled and then fell away. "I'm not. My mother was telekinetic. My brother is one of the most powerful psychics the Council has ever seen . . . and he's still a kid. Me? I've got a weird gift that doesn't really do me a damn bit of good, and that's it. I'm *not* extraordinary. I'm not going to lead an extraordinary life. But that doesn't mean I can't have a life. That doesn't mean I can't take care of myself. It doesn't mean I have to be a burden to others—not anymore."

Ana shut the door behind her and headed down the stairs before she could say anything else. It's not like there was really that much to say anyway. Right now, she had nothing that could help him and taking a day off wouldn't be doing her job any favors. She needed the job. It was nothing less than the truth.

She needed the job.

She *liked* her job.

She liked doing something nice and normal, after a lifetime of everything *but* normal. She liked knowing where she was supposed to be on any given day and she liked knowing she could take care of herself.

It might sound mundane, but she needed it.

Still, as she strode away from the apartment, and Duke, some part of her wanted to stay.

Some part of her wanted to be there with him, find some way to help. Some way to prove she could be more than just a liability.

CHAPTER 7

A NA wasn't too keen on giving him the hand he needed, but he hadn't come up here just to sit in her apartment and wait for lightning to strike. If she said she felt something off, then he needed to at least see if he couldn't find it on his own.

So he used her shower, changed into a pair of jeans and a clean T-shirt. Then he picked up the mess he'd made in her kitchen before taking a few minutes to get online with her laptop. He pulled up a map on Google and studied it, making notes of the main roads, the parks—and damn, were there a lot of parks. Most of the eastern part of the city bordered a huge state park. He glanced out at Ana's window to the east, eying the green mountains spearing up into the sky.

The mountains—a good a place to start as any, he figured. Since he really didn't have a destination in mind, he may as well pick one that might be relatively private. He could use a run. Burn off some of the tension lingering inside him, empty his mind and just see what happened.

Of course, he was going to have a hard time emptying his mind since every few minutes, he found himself thinking about Ana and the way she'd looked at him, those purple eyes somber and sad.

Duke scowled as he locked the door behind him a good hour after she'd left. He jogged down the steps and headed down the drive, turning right. Up ahead, he could see mountains, and more, he could smell them. Wild and green. Even though he was trapped in a decent-sized city, he wasn't overwhelmed by the stink of car fumes, exhaust and humanity. He could breathe.

It was a beautiful land. It hadn't taken him more than five seconds to realize that, and he'd had a lot more than five seconds to kill the day before while he found his way to the address Kelsey had given him, and while he waited for Ana to show up.

Beautiful, quiet, serene. Duke didn't think he'd ever been any place quite like Alaska before. So wild, so open. Kind of sucked that most of the people he knew wouldn't ever be able to do more than visit for a day or two. Some of the witches might adjust okay, but the were-creatures and vampires were pretty much out of luck.

Kelsey had mentioned something about the stronger pull from the poles, polarity, something—sounded a lot more technical than he really cared to get—that affected a were's control. Were-creatures were all about control—they had to be. Vampires didn't have any problems being close to the poles, but they were territorial creatures and any vamp that settled here would either have to all but hide out during the summer months or relocate. Those territorial instincts weren't going to take to yearly migrations.

Of course, if some feral vamps ventured here during the winter months . . . damn. Duke winced even thinking about it. They needed somebody up here—

"Somebody?" he muttered. He shoved a hand through his hair, brooding. Yeah. Somebody probably should be up here, but it wasn't like there was a huge pool of people to pull from. He could just see himself mentioning it to Kelsey, too. She'd probably throw Grady in his face again.

"Like hell."

He didn't want some Hunter settling down here. He especially didn't want *Grady* settling down here. Not if this was where Ana was making her home.

Without realizing it, he started walking down the sidewalk at a fast pace, desperate to leave the city behind.

Eventually, the sidewalk stopped, he saw fewer people on the roadside and the cars came by only sporadically. Then he started to run.

His thoughts tangled inside him, twisted him into knots. Memories of last night slipped up to tease and taunt him. The way she'd felt against him. How she'd gasped his name. The way her body heated when he touched. The scars on her back. The faster he ran, the faster he needed to run and soon, he'd left the city behind and was climbing, up, up, up, following a steep, twisting road, his booted feet all but soundless.

Why?

Why do you think?

Because you want me . . . do you want like I want, Ana? Crave like I crave . . . need like I need?

Her nails digging into his flesh. The way she gasped when he sank his teeth into her shoulder, her entire body clenching and shuddering under his.

The thin ridge of scars he'd felt under his hands. *I know about the scars, Ana. I felt them last night.* The humiliation he'd seen in her eyes.

But soon, you're going to explain to me about those scars on your back.

I don't like to talk about that. Sad eyes, lingering on his for just a moment and then looking away as though she couldn't bear for him to know.

The way she curled into him as she slept, and the way she blushed when he looked at her.

I'm not *extraordinary, Duke.*

She really believed that.

Hell, even when he'd wanted to hate her, he'd been amazed by her. She'd stayed in hell because she wanted to protect her brother. How many teenaged girls would do that? Stay in a place where they weren't just mistreated, but *tortured*?

I'm not *extraordinary. I'm not going to lead an extraordinary life. But that doesn't mean I can't have a life.*

"A life," he muttered, coming to a stop just at the bend in the road. Exactly what did she want to find in this *life*?

Blowing out a breath, he moved to the edge of the winding gravel road, staring down on over the mountain. How long had he been running . . . ? Long enough that he'd started to sweat, long enough that the muscles in his body had loosened, relaxed—but not long enough that he'd taken the edge off.

His head was a fucking mess and it was because of Ana.

Pressing the heels of his hands against his eyes, he swore. "You can't do the damn job if you can't get your mind off of her."

She'd always done this to him, left him edgy, confused and twisted up inside. It was a huge part of why he'd always steered clear of her back in Virginia. There had been times when he'd avoided returning home just because he didn't want to see her and deal with that turmoil. Right now, he needed to deal with it, though. If he didn't, he wasn't going to find any peace inside his head, and if he couldn't level out, he wasn't going to do anybody any good.

Too bad he couldn't seem to figure out how to get level. What in the hell did it matter if she seemed just fine with punching a time clock, living a mortal's life?

"She *is* mortal, you dumb cat."

Gifted, yeah, but still mortal. She was in a position to make the call about whether she wanted to live out in the mortal world or try to use her gift. She hadn't ever been called to serve, but there were other ways to use a gift besides being a Hunter. She'd made her choice.

Hell, before the choice had been taken away from him, Duke had been perfectly content himself to live a nice, normal life. He'd kept his secrets, guarded them well, and he'd been just fine doing that. No reason he couldn't have kept doing that if life hadn't gone and taken a sharp right turn on him.

A real home. Maybe a family. Somebody there at night—nothing wrong with wanting that . . .

A growl rolled out of his chest. Is *that* what she was looking for?

This life Ana wanted, did it include some normal guy? A guy who'd never really understand the choices she'd made, the life she'd lived, all the mistakes and heartaches and losses . . .

Hot, potent rage sank into him, claws and teeth bared. *Mine—*

Off in the distance there was the low rumble of a car engine. Swearing, Duke looked down the road. Then, with an impulsive grin, he moved, jumping off the road. It sloped down at a sharp angle and he landed in a crouch, his knees flexed, one hand resting on the earth.

Up on the road, a car drove by, leaving a cloud of dust in its wake. Duke lingered for a second, waiting until the car's engine faded and then he focused. East—he needed to head farther east. Away from the town. Away from the roads, from the humans, from everything. East into the mountains.

He needed to run, *really* run. The kind of running he couldn't do on two feet, and the kind of running that he couldn't do where human eyes could see. His skin, tight and itchy from all the tension pent up inside him, began to heat but he didn't give in yet. Not until he was sure. Not until he was alone.

A NA glanced at the clock on her desk and then focused on the voice on the other end of the line. One of her boss's more difficult customers, the club owner was pissed off because the IRS was investigating him and he wanted to know why.

"I'm sorry, Mr. Woolsey, but I can't answer those questions. Yes . . . yes, he'd be happy to discuss this with you . . . " She winced as he once more started to yell.

By the time she got off the phone, she had a raging headache. She knew it wasn't all from Lawrence Woolsey, though. She hadn't slept enough over the weekend and last night, instead of catching up on sleep . . . Duke.

Her mouth went dry even thinking about him, and despite the headache pounding behind her eyes, she smiled.

"You look like *you* had a good weekend."

Ana jerked her head up and blushed when she realized Darlene was staring at her. There was a wide grin on the other woman's face and a teasing light in her eyes. "Ah . . . it was interesting," Ana hedged.

She couldn't call it good.

Not even the parts involving Duke.

Well, maybe a few . . .

She clenched her knees together as a pang of longing struck. Yes, there were definitely a few parts involving Duke that could be described as *good*. Fantastic. Unbelievable, even. She licked her lips and forced a smile for Darlene's sake. "Interesting, but I'm kind of glad it's over."

Liar.

She scowled inwardly. She *was* glad it was over. She was glad Duke was here, even though as of yet, he couldn't feel much of a need to be here. She was glad. She didn't have to keep worrying about her gut-deep premonitions of doom. There was a Hunter here, somebody who could handle things. So she didn't have to. She didn't *want* to. She didn't know how, and even if she did, it wasn't her calling.

Yet, still . . .

" . . . Okay?"

A hand touched her arm. Startled, Ana looked up and met Darlene's concerned gaze. "I'm sorry. My mind's wandering."

Cocking a black brow, Darlene said, "Yeah, I noticed. I'm kind of curious just how far it's wandering. One minute, you look like the proverbial cat that ate the cream and then you look like you lost your best friend." She propped a hip on Ana's desk and waited.

Ana didn't flinch under that heavy stare. Darlene, as insightful as she was, couldn't see clear through to Ana's soul. After spending years with people who could do just that and more, it didn't take much to keep a blank expression, to keep Darlene from seeing anything too deep.

"Darlene, I'm fine. I just had a crazy weekend—I've got a lot on my mind."

Understatement of the century.

"W HAT do you want me to do?"

People walking by the poorly dressed man either ignored him or found a way to stare at him without being too obvious about it.

Paul barely noticed. With tear-filled, rheumy eyes, he shook his head and whispered, "I can't leave. My memories live here." Memories—faded, worn, but all he had to keep him company throughout endless days and nights.

It was a hot day, especially for the city of Anchorage, the mercury pushing up near ninety. Even though it was August, it usually didn't get quite this hot, quite this humid here. But as a businessman edged around Paul, just a few inches away, an icy chill raced down his spine—cold, like somebody had replaced his blood with ice water. Picking up his pace, the businessman got away as quickly as he could.

Behind him, Paul stared at him stricken and then once more focused on the empty air in front of him. "Are . . . are you okay? Did he hurt you?"

Marie smiled at him. Her image was wavery, transparent. But she looked beautiful to him. Beautiful, the same now as she'd looked when they'd met. A long time ago. Too long. "*I'm fine, Paul. I didn't even feel it. Now come on, listen to me. I want you to leave here. Leave now.*"

"I can't." His face crumpled, but he managed to keep from crying. "I just can't, Marie. This is where you are. If I leave, you won't be there with me, will you?"

Ghosts could cry. Paul had seen her cry often through the years, but this was worse, because this was his fault. She'd asked him for one thing, and he couldn't do it. But he couldn't leave her. Couldn't leave, couldn't . . .

"*It's not leaving me, Paul. It's protecting yourself. Something bad is going to happen. I can feel it.*"

She shivered, the air around her turning icy. It didn't go unnoticed by others, although most of them just walked faster, hurried by, unwilling to look at Paul, unwilling to try to see what he was staring at, and none of them wanted to think about why it seemed a good thirty degrees cooler around him.

"I can't leave. I'm sorry. I just can't."

Then he smiled, desperate to chase the sadness from her eyes. Digging into his pocket, he pulled out a carefully folded piece of paper. "I found some paper today. Paper and pencils. Somebody left them at Earthquake Park. I drew a picture of you. Of us . . . "

He showed it to Marie, to the woman nobody could see but him. And all around them, people pretended as though they couldn't see the man who stood before them, talking to thin air.

S ITTING on the narrow landing, perched on the edge of the top step, Duke rested his elbows on his knees and waited. In the back of his mind, he could hear seconds ticking away.

Ana wasn't home.

It was nearly nine o'clock and she wasn't home.

The sun was still burning high in the sky, and while that was enough to confuse his internal clock, he'd been checking the time every hour, on the hour since six. That was when he figured she'd be home.

And she wasn't.

He'd tried calling the cell number she'd left with him, but it had gone into voice mail, and so far, she hadn't returned any of his messages.

Up on the hill, he could hear the sound of the bus approaching, but this time, he didn't get up, didn't jog down the steps. He'd done that every single time a bus drove down the street and there were a decent amount of buses. He was starting to feel a little stupid—and a lot irritated.

No damn reason she couldn't have called. None.

Then there was a voice that countered back, *Maybe she didn't think about it.*

Except Duke wasn't too impressed with *that* answer. There was no reason she *shouldn't* think about it, as far as he was concerned. He was here because she sent word back that there was some vague sort of trouble. Of course he was going to be want to stay on top of things—on top of her—

"Damn it, stop thinking with your dick," he muttered, scrubbing his hands over his face. And listening. Even though he made himself wait on the stairs this time, he was listening as the bus slowed down. Listening to the faint sound of voices a few hundred feet away.

Listening closely enough that he recognized Ana's voice. " . . . Do you?"

There was the sound of male laughter and then a new voice, "Of course not."

Ana said something else, but Duke barely registered it. She was here. Shooting to his feet, he started to leap over the railing, only to freeze and squeeze his eyes closed. *Way to blend, you stupid cat.*

With a scowl, he held himself back and jogged down the steps. By the time she appeared in view, he'd already made it up the driveway. She came to an abrupt stop when she saw him. Something flashed in her eyes. He heard the faint sound of her heart as it skipped a few beats and then fell into a regular, but fast rhythm. The scent of vanilla, lavender and woman heated, warmed, and he had an urge to dip his head and press his lip to her neck, just to breathe her in.

Instead, he hooked his thumbs in his pockets and stared at her. Flicked a glance to the man at her side and then focused back on her. Tried *not* to focus on the close-fitting shirt, sleeveless and veeing down between her breasts— that definitely wasn't what she'd been wearing when she left the house that morning. It was paired with some short skirt-looking thing and tennis shoes.

Ana frowned at him, but as the man next to her glanced her way, the frown disappeared. "Hi, Duke. I was just telling my landlord that I was probably going to have company for a few days."

He glanced back at the man standing next to her. Close to Duke's height, but taller by an inch or so, lean and fit. Hair going silver at the temples, some lines fanning out from his eyes. Duke took note of everything, including the fact that the guy's pheromone level was seriously spiked. Landlord—yeah, and if the guy was happy to leave it at that, Duke ate Meow Mix for breakfast.

The man smiled and stuck out a hand. "Duke? So you're the company? Carter Hoskins."

He flicked a glance at the man's offered hand. *Blend . . . remember?* Slowly, he accepted and shook and then looked back at Ana. "I was getting worried." *Getting pissed is more like it.* Wasn't getting any better, either, watching the way her landlord kept looking at her.

She shrugged. "I'm sorry. Guess I should have called. I usually go by the Alaska Club after work so I can get a workout in a few nights a week." She gestured at her clothes and shrugged.

"We ran into each other leaving," Carter said. "Tried to talk her into getting a bite with me. Eating alone after a while gets kind of boring."

"I bet." Duke didn't bother looking at the man.

Ana's eyes narrowed. Then she looked away from Duke and smiled at Carter. It was a real smile, he noticed, and his irritation spiked even more. She hardly ever smiled at him and when she did, it was that nervous, hesitant curl of her lips like she didn't really want to smile period. Or like she was afraid to. Or like she didn't think she deserved to.

But she was smiling at this guy. A friendly, open smile that Duke was pretty sure he'd never seen—at least not one he'd ever seen directed at *his* way.

"I'm sorry, Carter. It's just been a long couple of days and with Duke being here . . . "

"Hey, it's not a problem." Carter waved it off and focused on Duke again. "Ana doesn't much like to talk about herself. Are you a friend? Family?"

Duke heard the unspoken question, even though it seemed to pass right over Ana's head. She started up the walkway and said, "Duke's a—"

"Friend," he interjected, unsure exactly what she was going to say, although he could tell what this Carter guy *wanted* her to say—or rather, what he wanted her *not* to say.

Their eyes locked. Carter's brows lifted and then he smiled, shook his head. "Well, I hope you enjoy your trip to Alaska, Duke. Ana, you have a nice night."

As he headed toward the main house, Duke just barely resisted the urge to bare his teeth at the man. Shit, he'd gone and developed a possessive streak a mile wide. But then he looked back at Ana as she glanced over her shoulder at him. That look, the frown on her soft mouth, the sadness that seemed so much a part of her, was enough to drive the air out of his lungs. Her gaze met his, and then she looked away, heading toward her apartment.

Leaving him to stand there and stare at her. Brood. No. He hadn't gone and developed a possessive streak when it came to her. He'd always had one.

Neal. Dominic. A half dozen other faces flashed through his mind. Some of the men had wanted her just on a physical level—like Neal. Use her, hurt her if he could, because she was just prey. Then some of them, like Dominic, had a more serious interest, but even that had put Duke's teeth on edge.

He caught up with her just before she reached the door, standing close behind her as she opened it. He felt a pair of eyes on the back of his neck, and as he followed her into the apartment, he glanced back. Saw the landlord staring out a window and watching them. It was harder to suppress the snarl the second time around, but he managed it.

But once the door shut behind them, Duke didn't bother suppressing anymore. He followed Ana through the apartment, staying just a breath behind her. She shot him a nervous look over her shoulder as she stopped, putting her purse and a duffel on the counter.

"What . . . " Ana licked her lips. Her voice was a pathetic, embarrassing squeak and clearing her throat didn't help at all. "Is something wrong?"

He didn't respond. Instead, he dipped his head and nuzzled her neck. She hunched her shoulder and tried to ease away. "I need to take a shower, Duke."

"Later," he muttered, raking his teeth along her skin.

"Duke, I just left the gym. I'm hot, I'm sweaty—"

He brought up a hand and pressed it against her belly, urging her back against him. "You taste delicious," he rasped. His voice was a low, hoarse growl and even if she hadn't already been weak-kneed, that would have done it.

He nudged a leg between her thighs and rested a hand on her hip before slipping it down to toy with the hem of the skirted shorts she'd worn for her workout. He tugged it up and then grunted, straightening away. She could feel the heat of his gaze moving over as he studied her workout clothes.

She turned and rested a hand against his chest, but whatever she'd planned on saying dried up on her tongue as he went to his knees in front of her and leaned forward, pressing his mouth to her stomach. He made quick work of the shorts and under a minute, he had her standing in front of him wearing nothing but the sport tank. "If I hadn't been here, would you have eaten with him?" he asked, his voice harsh.

Dazed, Ana blinked and stared down at him. "Huh?"

"Your landlord. Were you going to eat with him?"

She frowned. Tried to think. Eat. Landlord . . . oh. Yeah. Carter. Dinner. Yeah, she remembered. Blood rushed to her cheeks and she tried not to squirm as he lifted his head and stared up at her. "I don't know. Probably not. He likes to talk too much."

"Talking can be a total waste of time. Better things to do with my mouth." Then he proved it, leaning in, pressing his mouth against her and licking her.

Ana slapped her hands against the counter behind and braced herself. Her knees wobbled, threatened to give and she locked them. He growled at her and pushed her thighs wider.

"Duke, I'm going to fall." Her head spun and she clutched at the counter.

"I won't let you fall," he muttered against her. "Wanna taste, Ana. Fuck, you're sweet . . ."

He lapped at her flesh like a cat, tonguing her clit and then sucking on it. True to his word, when she wobbled on her feet, he caught her hips in his hands and steadied her, easing her back and up onto the counter. She slumped backward, her head banging against the cabinet at her back, but she didn't care. Curling her fingers into his hair, she stared down at him and shuddered as he parted her flesh with his tongue and then pushed inside.

She cried out, heat unfurling through her, licking at her flesh, drawing her body tight, tighter. "How sore are you?"

She flinched as he circled her entrance with one rough fingertip, pushing just a little inside.

He pulled his hand back and then pressed his mouth to her. "Still sore, baby . . . I'm sorry . . ."

He kissed her. Soft. Gentle. Teasing. Pushing, working her closer and closer, using nothing but his tongue and his lips. She shuddered, moaned. Fisted her hands in his hair as she rocked and wiggled and moved against him. "Please, please, please, please . . ." she whimpered, barely even aware she was talking.

Duke growled against her flesh and caught her clit between his teeth. Tugged gently.

She saw stars. Real? Imagined? Who knows? Slamming her head back against the cabinet, she bit her lip to keep from crying out as she came. Duke remained between her spread thighs, licking and lapping at her flesh until she finally sagged backward. Then he stood and wrapped his arms around her, tucked her up against him.

He was still fully clothed. Jeans. T-shirt. Through the denim, she could feel his cock, throbbing and hard, pulsating against her. "What about . . . ?"

"You're sore," he whispered, pressing his lips to her shoulder.

Yes. She was. "I'm not that sore," she said, reaching

between them and running the back of her hand over his erection.

"You would be." He went to pull away.

His breath hissed out between his teeth as she slipped her fingers inside the waistband of his jeans. "Ana . . . "

She pulled her hand back and inched down off the counter. Holding his eyes, she reached for the waistband of her tank and stripped it off. It fell to the floor as she went to her knees in front of him. His eyes flashed, the pale gray swirling, glowing.

As she unzipped his jeans, he growled. When she leaned and pressed her lips to the rounded, blunt tip of his penis, he groaned.

When she licked on him, sucked on him and fumbled her way through, he threaded a hand through her hair and guided her until she found her rhythm.

"Fuck, that's sweet . . . damn it, Ana . . . fuck, your mouth . . . yeah . . . "

He muttered, growled and groaned, talking her through, although it reached a point to where his words became too rough, too guttural for her to understand them.

When he came in her mouth, he made a sound caught between a shout and a growl.

Then he sank down to the floor in front of her, pulled her close and purred.

"You purred," she said an hour later over a haphazard meal of boxed macaroni, sandwiches, salad and pudding cups. Blood rushed to her cheeks as he glanced up at her over the rim of a glass and grinned.

That smile had a decidedly feline slant to it. His lashes drooped low over his eyes and he lowered the glass, leaned over the narrow counter that separated them and covered her lips with his. "You stroke a cat the right way, he's gonna purr," he teased, licking her lower lip. "You can make me purr any day of the week, darlin'."

He settled back on the stool and she focused on her

sandwich, but her mouth was so damned dry, she might as well have been eating sawdust. She was starving, she realized, but even though she had already plowed through half the sandwich, it had no taste. It eased the ache in her belly, and that was enough.

Starving, and thirsty. She went through two glasses of iced tea before the thirst slaked and glanced up to find Duke watching her with a grin. Self-consciously, she touched her fingers to her lips. "What, do I have mustard on my chin or something?"

"No . . . you're smiling." His smile faded. He didn't move, but somehow everything about him changed. Went dark and grim. In a level, flat voice, he said, "You smiled at that guy earlier and I wanted to punch him."

"Guy? What guy?"

Duke jerked his head toward the window. Through the blinds, she could see the lights from Carter's house. "Your landlord."

She blinked. "Why did you want to punch Carter?"

"Because you smiled at him." He wasn't looking at her.

He was staring at his hands, she realized, flexing them, clenching them into fists and then relaxing them again. Over and over.

"You don't smile much, Ana," he said softly. His gaze cut to hers and he added, "At least, not around me."

Ana squirmed on the barstool. "I . . . "

Shaking his head, he said, "You don't need to say anything or explain it. I know why you don't smile. Or at least I think I do. You don't feel safe. You feel too guilty. Or you don't feel like you should let yourself be happy—even long enough to smile." He waited half a beat and then asked, "So which is it? Or is it all of those reasons?"

Those gray eyes, they saw too much. Even if he didn't have a witch's ability to feel or sense emotions, even if he didn't have any telepathy or the mental gifts a lot of vampires had, he saw too much. Tucking her chin against her chest, she focused on her plate. Her sandwich was gone, she realized, absently. No, not just the sandwich, but all of her food. The sandwich, the bland macaroni and cheese that he'd jazzed up a little with some canned tomatoes and red chilies and extra cheddar, her salad and the pudding cup. Her belly was nice and full, satisfied. It wasn't sitting like a stone in her belly, either.

"So which is it, Ana?"

There was nothing accusatory in his voice, but still, she felt defensive, wrapping her arms around her middle and fighting the urge to get up, walk away. She hated confrontation. "I'm sorry."

He cocked a brow at her. "For what . . . not smiling at me? People smile when they are happy. You and me, we haven't exactly had a whole lot of chances to be happy around each other, have we?"

"Duke . . . "

He slid off the stool and came to stand behind her as she fumbled for words, not even sure what she wanted to say.

"Maybe we should go ahead and have this out." He laid his hands on her shoulders and from the corner of her eyes, she could see them flex, then felt them curl and tighten. "We both got shit inside us that we need to get rid of. If I want to see you smiling at me instead of your fucking landlord, we need this out of the way."

He turned her around on the barstool and she felt the weight of his stare bearing down on her. She didn't want to look at him. Didn't want to hear whatever he had to say—it was going to hurt—

A long-fingered hand cupped her chin and he tipped her head back. "I don't like your methods, Ana. I don't like how you let a monster use you."

She flinched even as he stroked a thumb over her lip. Yeah. It was going to hurt.

But . . . it didn't. Instead of yelling at her, instead of demanding a damn thing from her, what he did was dip his head and nuzzle her neck as he whispered, "But part of me understands why you did it. You wanted to protect Brad, and you wanted to live. I'm a big fan of surviving myself, so even if I don't care for the route you chose, I can understand it."

She blinked, fighting the tears that burned in her eyes. She gulped, trying to breathe past the knot in her throat. He curled a hand over the back of her neck and kissed her while she sat there, too frozen to move, because if she moved, she was going to shatter. Splinter into a million pieces.

"You should hate me for what I did." Her hand shook as she reached up and traced the scars on his chest through his T-shirt. She didn't have to see the scars to know where they were—the pattern was emblazoned on her mind. She saw it when she tried to sleep and her dreams were plagued by the blood he'd shed. Blood he'd shed because of her cowardice. "You could have died. I know that. I knew it even when I took you to her that you could die. But Brad . . . " Unable to find the right words, she just whispered, "You should hate me."

He reached up and curled a hand over hers, pressed it flat against one of the scars. She could feel the ridged flesh under the cotton.

"Yeah. And I figure I would have died if you hadn't gotten it into your head otherwise. We know what Cat wanted with me. Until she knew about my connection to Kendall, all she wanted from me was as much pain and blood as she could get before she got impatient and just killed me. You knew it was coming and so did I. You could have just stayed away and let her do what she wanted, but you didn't."

"Don't make it sound like I was doing anything heroic, damn it. I *chose* to take you to her for a reason. She didn't care if I brought her a mortal man, a vamp, a shapeshifter. She just wanted a man. I knew what you were, and I knew it before I went up to you in that bar. I didn't figure it out after the fact or anything like that, even though I know that's what Kelsey, Kendall and a bunch of people think. They're wrong—I knew what you were the second I saw you. That's why I *chose* you. I knew if you went missing, people would take notice."

"People . . . as in my people. The Hunters," he said slowly.

"Yes." She wanted to hide. Instead she stared into his eyes and waited for the condemnation.

"Did you have any idea what might happen to you if I ended up dead?"

"Yes." She almost told him she'd expected it to happen no matter what. But for some reason, she doubted that was the best thing to tell him right now.

"If Cat had found out . . . " Duke stopped in midsentence and took a slow, deep breath. His eyes, glowing and hot, locked on her face and he shook his head. "That was a damned stupid way to get our attention. Why didn't you just lay it out to me that night? If you knew what I was—"

"And leave Brad alone there?" Ana interrupted. She pressed against his chest. She needed to move, couldn't hardly breathe. "I couldn't do it that way—if I left him alone and didn't come back one night, she would have hurt Brad."

"She would have tried. Ana, that brother of yours is more capable than you think. Even back then he was."

"He's a kid," she said, her voice cold and harsh. "Just a kid. I was supposed to take care of him and nothing was going to stop me."

Her hands shook as she reached for the waistband of her tank-styled pajama top, shook so bad as she stripped it off it was a miracle she even managed it. Turning away from him, she gathered her hair in her hand and exposed her back. "You wanted to know about the scars. I'll tell you. I got some of them because Cat wanted me aware of just what might happen if she ever suspected that I was trying to get help. Even in the most circumstantial way."

She reached up and brushed her fingers over one of the marks higher up on her back, shivering as she remembered the pain. It hadn't been the first time Cat had cut her, but it had been the worst. Worst, because she had threatened to do the same to Brad.

Ana shook as she remembered the pleasure she could feel coming off the vampire as Cat used the knife to draw blood. "I tried once, to get help. There was this guy, a werewolf, I think. Older, had a kind smile. Made me think of a big teddy bear. He was in the area and I snuck away from

Cat, found him and talked to him. He wasn't a Hunter, but I'd hoped he knew . . . "

She stopped and took a breath. Shivering, she drew her shirt back on and turned to face Duke. "I'd hoped he could find a way to get word to somebody. Cat knew. I don't know how. She was psychic, but I never really understood just what kind of psychic skill she had. It doesn't matter, either. She knew what I'd done . . . and she tracked the man down that very night and killed him. Then she came back and made the first cut on my back. Every so often, she'd do it again and remind me that the scars on my back would seem like a paper cut compared to what she'd do to Brad."

Duke was staring at her, his eyes unreadable. She could feel his anger though, humming just above her shields, scalding and hot. She licked her lips and took a deep breath, braced herself.

"Then one night, a few nights before we met, she had me bring a guy to her. She killed him. Right in front of me. And I knew I couldn't keep doing it. I felt it when you and Kendall arrived. I made up my mind what I was going to do and I did it. I knew what could happen, to you. To me. But none of it mattered if it meant getting somebody there who could help Brad. Get him away from her before she got to him like she did to me."

"She didn't get to you, Ana."

"Didn't she? I brought you to her. I brought that other guy. Hell, I brought men to her just so she could screw them and feed from them—even if she didn't really hurt them, it doesn't make right. I knew how crazy she was and I still did it."

"You did it for your brother, baby. To keep her from hurting him, from hurting you." He pulled her against him.

She fought at first but then she sagged, letting him take her weight. "I knew you could end up dying, but I couldn't let that stop me."

"I know." He nuzzled her neck, stroked a soothing hand down her back. "Shhhh . . . it's okay."

But Ana didn't want him soothing her—she wanted him

mad. She wanted him as mad about the choices she made as she was. Mad and disgusted at how weak she was. Shoving against his chest, she glared at him and said, "Okay? She could have killed you—I wouldn't have been able to stop her. But it's *okay*."

"She didn't kill me."

"That's because she didn't really try," Ana snarled.

He lifted a shoulder in a shrug. "She didn't not try, either. You and me both know I wouldn't have lasted more than a couple of days if it wasn't for you. I was halfway dead by the time Kendall showed up, and I would have been all the way dead before that if you hadn't kept intervening. We know that she would have killed me before Kendall managed to find me, if you hadn't placed yourself out in the open, then led them to me. You didn't let that happen, Ana. I'm not dead. Brad's safe. So are you. So yes. It's okay."

"It's *not* okay," she shouted. "You know why I didn't want her killing you. You were Brad's way out. *My* way out. I wasn't going to lose that chance." She jerked back, tried to get away from the sympathy, the understanding she saw on his face, tried to break away, but he didn't let her.

"Damn it, you weren't the first guy I led to her. Didn't you hear that part? There were others—most of them she just fucked and fed from, then she let them go. Couldn't go catching too much attention—she was crazy, but she was smart."

Her breath hitched in her throat as she remembered the night that had all but broken her. The night she'd seen a man cut down in front of her, like he was less than nothing. "The guy I brought home a few days before I found you, he wasn't so lucky. He didn't get away."

Duke narrowed his eyes. "Don't go trying to get me pissed off, Ana. I'm not some idealistic fool. No, I'm not seeing too much heroism involved in you leading me off into a fucking trap." He reached out, threaded a hand through her hair and held her steady when she would have pulled away. Dipping his head, he watched her from just a whisper away. Close. So close she could feel the soft kiss of his breath against her flesh. "I don't idealize what happened. Neither do you . . . I could have died. And it's just as likely *you* could have died. Kendall wanted to kill you."

She flinched, even though it was nothing less than the truth.

The hand in her hair flexed and then he lowered it to her neck, kneading the tight muscles there. "She wanted to kill you . . . and you know it. You would have let her do it, if it helped your little brother. You were scared to death. Scared of her. Scared of Cat. Scared of me."

"I'm a damned coward, Duke. I'm scared of everything. Hell, half the time Brad scares me." She blushed hot with shame.

He shrugged. "Considering what I've seen the kid do with his mind alone, only an idiot wouldn't have a few of those moments around Brad." Then he sighed. "There's a difference between being scared and being a coward, Ana. I don't like how you caved for Cat instead of fighting . . . but if you'd fought her, she would have killed you. And possibly Brad."

A grim look tightened his features and the air around them blasted hot. It shuddered and heaved with suppressed power as she watched, fascinated. He gritted his teeth and snarled, battling back some deep, ugly rage. The kind of rage that threatened a shifter's self-control.

She could feel it, the power of his beast lurking just under his skin. It glittered in the depths of his eyes as he caught her face in his hands and arched her head back.

"I hate what that bitch did to me," he rasped. "I have nightmares, where I'm still stuck in that hole, waiting to die, trapped as she comes after me with a silver knife and uses it on my chest like it's arts and crafts hour. But as much as I hate her for that . . . it's worse when I think about her doing something like that to you."

"I didn't know." His eyes glowed and even though she knew he wouldn't hurt her, her heart stopped when the gray of his eyes swirled, like dark clouds in a thunderstorm. His pupils bled from round to elliptical, slitted like a cat's. His powerful body shuddered. His hands flexed as he skimmed them up over her back. "Fuck, you got any idea how sick I get, thinking about these scars? I didn't know."

She wanted to pull away. Wanted to kiss and soothe and stroke him, although she didn't entirely understand why he was so angry. "You couldn't know. I never told anybody."

"But I should have known," he rasped. He nudged her in his arms, made her turn. Her breath hitched in her throat as he tore her shirt, tearing it apart with his hands. "Damn, somebody should have. Why didn't you tell anybody what she did to you?"

"There was no reason to."

"The hell there wasn't." His voice took on a hard edge and he demanded, "What else did she do to you?"

"Nothing."

"Don't lie to me," he rasped. He hauled her back against him and she shivered at the feel of him pressed so close. "I know she hit you—I remembered seeing it. How often did things like that happen?"

"Duke—"

"Now, Ana."

He was so mad, she could feel the heat of it in the air all around them. Tell him *now*? For some reason, she didn't think that was a good idea. Licking her lips, she said, "Why? What does it matter now?"

He licked one scar, the longest one. That had been the first one. It started just below the nape of her neck and ran eight inches along her spine. Cat had laughed when she did it. *Just think, Analise. Go just a little too deep, and you're paralyzed. Going to be harder to protect that sweet baby brother from the likes of me if you can't get out of a damned bed . . . you won't be screwing up again on me, now will you?*

Cat's favorite perversion had been to break the unbreakable, to break good, decent people, like Ana's mother had been. Like Duke. But the first time Cat had sent her out to bring back a man, Ana had brought somebody far too flawed in Cat's eyes. A thug, somebody who stank of drugs, blood and money. Already corrupt, and already a coward, he'd broken for Cat, all right. Too easily—she'd been so disgusted with the man, she hadn't even fed from him.

Then she had taken her anger out on Ana.

"They matter," he whispered, his voice guttural. "Tell me."

"Some of them happened because I didn't do what she wanted," she said on a shaky sigh. "So she did that to remind me what would happen if I failed to obey her again. As afraid as I was, I was more afraid of not being there for Brad . . . and she knew it."

"That's how she kept you in line."

Ana shrugged, staring at the counter in front of her. "It wasn't so much about keeping me in line. It's not like I ever really tried to run, never tried to stand up to her. But when I did anything less than what she demanded, she reminded me of the cost of failure. I couldn't let her hurt Brad."

Duke's hand flexed on her back, fingers spreading wide. Then, carefully, he turned her back around and eased her body against his. His eyes glowed as he stared down at her, so alien set against his mortal skin, but it didn't bother her.

"So you let her hurt you." A low rumble of noise escaped him and then he closed his eyes, lowered his head. His long, lean body shuddered and when he lifted his head to look at her again, his eyes were once more human. Or at least they appeared to be.

She could still glimpse that wild, primal power in him, feel it dancing along her skin.

She swallowed as she stared up at him, trying to understand everything she sensed coming from him. It was like she was in the middle of a room, with ten different radio stations blasting at her. Nothing made sense, nothing connected.

Desperate for relief, she slammed additional shields up. She didn't think anything from the outside was leaking in on her, but right now, she couldn't be sure. She wasn't sure of anything, other than the fact that Duke, once again, had managed to rock the foundation of her world.

Her heart stuttered and tripped along within her chest and her lungs felt tight. When he reached up and pushed his hand into her hair, she felt tears sting her eyes.

She didn't even know why.

Then he dipped his head and rubbed his lips across her shoulder. "Are you hiding from me again, Ana?"

"Hiding?" she asked, after licking her dry lips. It was a miracle she could even talk. Her throat felt like the damned Sahara.

"You're pulling back." The words were a low, frustrated growl. "I felt it. Just now."

"I'm not pulling back." She lifted her head and looked at him, held his gaze. "You're just . . . my head's too full, Duke. I'm having a hard time telling where I end and you begin. I can't have shaky control. I reinforced my shielding, that's all."

Lids drooping low over his eyes, he tugged on her hair, arched her head farther back. "Okay. I don't like it. But okay. Just don't hide from me."

Hide? Half hysterical, she wondered whether it was even possible to hide from him.

But she didn't say that out loud. Instead, she just leaned in and pressed her lips against his throat. So many times, she'd wanted to touch him. By some weird twist of fate, now she had the chance.

His arms came up, surrounded her. Sighing, Ana cuddled against him.

"You really should hate me," she whispered absently.

"No. I really shouldn't."

CHAPTER 8

I T pulled him from his dreams.

That low, deep burn, gnawing at his gut, teasing the beast that lay just below the surface. *Run,* the cougar whispered. *Run. Hunt. There's prey . . .*

Emerging out of sleep, Duke rolled out of the bed silently and stood, staring out into the night with his head cocked. Hands curled into loose fists at his sides.

Run. Prey.

He cast one lingering look at Ana. She was asleep, lying on her belly facing away from him. Her silvery blonde hair lay in a tangle around her head and shoulders, hiding her face, hiding the scars on her back. He didn't bother waking her as he slipped out of the bedroom. Barely even thought to pause in the living room to gather up his clothes.

Walking bare-assed down the street wouldn't much bother him, but if he got his butt arrested, it would interfere and Duke didn't want interferences.

Run. Hunt. Blood . . . there's so much blood. No time. No time.

The whispering voice grew louder with each second

and Duke was all but growling as he emerged from Ana's apartment. No. No time at all. The air was thick with blood, even though the death came from miles away.

Even his altered senses couldn't truly scent the blood, not yet. He felt it, felt it in his bones. Sensed the pain. Sensed the blood. Sensed the death.

The earth was heavy with it. Shuddering and scream-ing in denial. Weeping. Blood had been spilled. Innocence destroyed. Life lost.

Too late. The cry for help had come too late and now a life had been lost.

Where . . . when . . . *why*? Why was he too late?

D UKE wasn't there when she woke.
     Ana blinked gritty eyes and rubbed them with the heels of her hands before lowering them to stare at the empty bed for a few more seconds. He didn't magically appear and she blew out a harsh breath. Climbing out of bed, she headed into the kitchen.

He wasn't in there, either, but she'd already known that.

Even with her shields up fast and tight, there was a tin-gling, razor's edge awareness of Duke. How he watched her, how he moved, how he breathed. If he was anywhere in the apartment, she'd feel it.

No, he'd managed to slip away in utter silence, without waking her as he left. Ana wasn't the easiest of sleepers. Too many years of sleeping with one eye shut and the other on Brad, she rarely slept well when there were others around. This was the second night in a row that she'd managed to eke out a decent night's rest in the presence of another.

She'd slept well enough, but she didn't feel all that great. Not sick, exactly, despite the headache that pounded behind her eyes, throbbed at the base of her skull. Her skin felt tight and itchy and there was a vague sense of restless-ness pulling at her. It tugged and twisted at her conscious thoughts as she got ready for work. Breakfast, shower, clothes, all of it done quickly and without much thought. Good thing, because she was having a hard time concentrating, and that was a bad thing.

Her shields felt off. Pressed in, somehow. Like an unseen hand was pushing down on them. Her headache probably had something to do with the problem with her shields, she realized as she slipped out of the house and saw Carter heading toward his bike.

Thoughts whispered along her skin. Nothing defined, nothing concrete—she couldn't even make sense of them, but they were Carter's thoughts. She recognized the feel of them.

"Not good," she muttered to herself. He was a psychic null—between that and her own shields, she shouldn't pick up anything from him. The only way for her to pick up clear thoughts was through close physical contact or a close bond. Without that, all she could pick up were those annoying whispers. Her shields were meant to keep those whispers *out* and her own thoughts, and her gift, locked inside her head.

Unshielded, her psychic skills did nothing but annoy her. Being surrounded by whispers and unable to make heads or tails out of them without physical contact—very annoying.

She used the short walk to the bus stop to bolster her shields and try to figure out why they'd slipped enough for outside thought to filter in. Didn't make sense. Once she'd learned how to really shield, it had come easily, like breathing. Those annoying whispers faded into blissful silence and her "blocking" no longer affected those around her.

Nothing in. Nothing out—and it had been the *nothing in* part that had been harder to learn, harder to control.

The bus groaned to a stop in front of her and she climbed on absently, settling in a vacant seat near the front and staring outside. If her shields had slipped during the night, had she unconsciously used her other gift?

Ana cut that line of thinking off before she could even really start. It hadn't happened. If she'd been blocking, she would have felt it, sensed it. The blocking was more a chameleon trick than anything else, an instinctive, passive sort of defense. It made her blend in, kept her psychic gift from showing to others unless she was actively using it.

Gifted people, mortal and non-mortal, tended to recognize each other. They felt different, and to the altered senses of a vamp or shapeshifter, they smelled different.

Being a chameleon didn't seem a bad thing in Ana's mind, but she had a hard time limiting her range and it ended up paling out the traits of others. It was why Cat had exploited her back when she'd been younger. Ana's gift had kept Cat from showing up on the Hunters' radar.

Because of that, Ana didn't allow herself to use the gift. She kept it locked down good and tight. Even though no active Hunters lived in Alaska, and few gifted individuals, keeping it lashed down just seemed best.

Locked down, good and tight, behind the same shields that kept outside stimuli from tripping up her psychic gift.

Except those shields were slipping.

Irritated, distracted and a little worried, she nibbled on her lower lip and wondered what had happened. Building shields was a mental exercise. As simplistic as it might seem, shields were established with a slow, annoyingly necessary mental trick—the visualized building of a mental wall. Building that wall was something that could take a psychic weeks to finish. Sometimes months.

Ana's wall was "made" of creek stone, and it was an image she could bring to mind effortlessly, easily. As the bus rumbled along its route toward downtown Anchorage, she did a mental examination of her wall, searching for chinks, missing stones and weak spots.

What she found was a place where the wall bowed in, just the slightest curve. Like somebody had leaned in and pushed. It needed to be fixed—now that she had "seen" it, she could feel the weakness, could feel where whispers of thought managed to filter through minute cracks she couldn't even sense.

But she couldn't take the time away right now to do it—

zoning out in public for extended periods of time wasn't what she'd call a wise move. So instead of rebuilding that part of her shield, she did a quick fix. Envisioning a big boulder, right at the spot where her shield bowed in. Crude and it wouldn't work in the long run, but it would get her through the day.

And it only took a few minutes, as opposed to the days, weeks or months that building elaborate shields could take. It wasn't particularly strenuous or tiring, either. Still, when she climbed off the bus at her stop on West Fifth Avenue, she was hot, sweaty and out of breath.

She riffled through her bag until she found a clip and then she twisted her hair up off her neck. The kiss of cool air felt good and she let herself enjoy it for a minute, let her breathing level out and her pulse calm.

The break didn't last long, though. She had to get to work. Automatically, she looked around for Paul. The area by the mall seemed to be a favorite.

He wasn't there. With a mental shrug, she headed toward work. She was going to have to work through lunch, try to get done early. Her boss was laid-back, especially since they were right in between the major tax days of the year. If she finished up, she'd ask to leave early. Hopefully, she could do just that. She needed some peace and quiet to fix the weakness in her shields.

With Duke here, she couldn't risk having anything off. Even though she knew nothing had happened with her blocking, if those shields slipped and too much outside stimuli bombarded her, it would be too easy, too natural, to slip back into old habits.

That wasn't anything she wanted to risk. She didn't want to affect his judgments or instincts in any way.

Ana worked straight through the morning, although keeping her mind focused on work was another exercise in frustration. Her head just wasn't into working today, or much of anything else that required focus, probably. She finally fell into a rhythm, though, waving off Darlene's invitation to lunch, returning phone calls, copying and mailing out paperwork, dealing with email, the thousand and one small details that fell under her job description. It looked like she just might finish in time to cut out a good two hours early.

"Ana!"

She looked up and found Darlene standing in front of her desk. The other woman's eyes were stark in her face and even through her shields, she could feel the buzz of anxiety coming off of Darlene. "Hey . . . I thought you'd already left for lunch."

Darlene rolled her eyes. "Ana, I swear, you've got tunnel vision when you're working. I've been back for a couple of hours. It's almost three."

Three? Ana glanced at her watched and winced. Damn. Two fifty-two. So much for getting home by three thirty. She sighed and leaned back, straightening up her desk automatically as she looked back at Darlene. "Everything okay?"

"No, it's not. Man, you're not going to believe what I just heard." Darlene gestured impatiently and said, "Come on."

Ana shook her head and focused on the mess of papers in front of her. Jumbled piles of receipts that she needed to straighten out, mileage logs that needed to be tallied. "Something's come up and I've got to leave early."

"It's about Paul."

Slowly, she lifted her gaze and looked at Darlene. "Paul . . . as in the homeless guy?"

Darlene snorted. "Yeah, as in the homeless guy that I see you slipping money to once or twice a week. *That* Paul."

"What about him?"

She made an impatient face and curled her fingers again. "Come on . . . it's been on the news for the past fifteen minutes."

"Darlene."

"Fine, fine." She rolled her eyes and pushed midnight dark hair back from her face. "He's dead, sweetie."

"Dead . . . " Ana felt the breath inside her lungs freeze, lock tight. "Dead?"

Darlene nodded, her face troubled. "I saw something on the news this morning about how the police were investigating a possible double murder and they just confirmed it was him. It looks like he killed a girl . . . I saw her picture. She looked a lot like that girlfriend people said he killed back in the seventies. A *lot* like her."

Wrong. Wrong. Wrong.

Ana took a deep breath and eased back from the chair, took a few seconds to make sure nothing she felt on the inside was reflected in her face, the way she walked, the way she spoke. In silence, she followed Darlene back to the break room.

The TV was on, a bright red banner along the bottom declaring, *Breaking News . . . Local man believed to have murdered girl, then self.*

Wrong. Wrong. Wrong.

That wasn't right. Ana didn't know exactly why she was so certain, but she knew, as well as she knew her own name, she knew they were wrong. Paul wasn't a killer. He couldn't hurt anybody.

But somebody had hurt him.

Her gut went watery and she had to lock her knees just to stay upright. Next to her, Darlene stood with her arms crossed over her chest and her eyes locked on the TV screen. "Oh, man, girl . . . I told you that you shouldn't be talking to him. Crazy. Man was crazy. I knew he was, but he seemed so harmless."

Ana bit back her instinctive reply and just remained silent, watching as the cameraman zoomed in on a small, ramshackle-looking house. Something about the sight of it made the hair on the back of her neck stand on end.

"I haven't seen the house before, but I know the area. It's out a little past Potter's Marsh, just off the old Seward Highway. The bodies were found a few hours after midnight. Somebody made an anonymous call." Darlene swiped the back of her hand over her mouth and continued to stare, mesmerized, at the TV.

Potter's Marsh. Absently, she reached up and rubbed the tight muscles at the base of her neck. Inside, she flinched as Marie's face flashed across the picture.

"Back in 1973, Beasley was arrested on suspicion of killing his girlfriend, Marie Onalik. There was a lack of evidence to hold him, however, and he was released," the reporter stated.

Now the screen was spliced in two and on the other side, another female's face. *"While authorities haven't confirmed it, our sources report that the family of missing teen, Candice Randall, has been contacted. Our sources also confirm the family was seen entering the police department. Randall, an eighteen–year-old freshman who attends the University of Alaska, was reported missing by her roommate early Friday morning."*

Blood roared in Ana's ears and she reached out, grabbed the back of a nearby chair as her head started to spin. The resemblance between Candice and Marie was unmistakable.

"What are they doing plastering her face on the TV if they don't even know it's her?" Darlene demanded. "God, can you imagine how sick her parents must be?"

Ana was only half aware of Darlene, though. She couldn't seem to focus on anything but the two images on the screen. *Candice Randall*—two days missing. Two days.

You are so completely useless. Ana stared dry-eyed at the TV, at the young woman's face.

Candice.

Ana knew her face. She'd dreamed about that girl only days ago. *Two* days ago.

A hand touched her arm and Ana, without thinking, grabbed it and squeezed, pressing down on the sensitive area between the thumb and forefinger. Darlene yelped and jerked. The sound of her friend's voice had Ana relaxing her hold and she blushed bright red, watching as Darlene cradled her hand to her chest.

"Geez, Ana. Jumpy much?"

Wincing, she said, "I'm sorry, Darlene." Rubbing her

sweaty palms together, she took a few steps back. Distance. Shit. Needed some distance. "Yeah, I guess I'm pretty jumpy right now."

"No shit." Darlene wiggled her fingers. Then, with a slow, reluctant smile, she met Ana's gaze. "You need to show me how you did that. That was kind of cool."

Ana shrugged. "They've got tae kwon do at the Y. I think they offer it at the Alaska Club, too. That's all it is. I took it in . . . college." Not exactly a lie. She *had* taken college courses back at Excelsior.

Licking her lips, she glanced at the TV once more. She needed to get out of here. As in *now*. She'd thought her focus was off a few minutes ago, but this was so much worse. "I think I'm going to check with Gary, see if he'll let me head on home. I'm pretty much done and I can come in a little early tomorrow and finish up."

"Probably not a bad idea. You're looking a little green around the gills." Darlene reached up and rubbed Ana's shoulder. "It's okay, you know. You're not hurt. But you know you need to be more careful. All that kung fu martial arts stuff doesn't do much against a gun or a knife."

Hurt? Kung fu? Ana squinted at Darlene, unsure what she was getting at. When it finally dawned on her, she gave her friend a wan smile. If Darlene wanted to think that Ana was all shook up because she was imagining herself in the place of the slain girl pictured on TV, let her. Ana didn't have the presence of mind just then to convince her friend otherwise, and nor the time. She needed to get out.

Get away.

F ROM halfway up the steps, he caught the faint sound of a heartbeat. Duke could smell the lingering scent of her skin as he reached the landing. It was early—he hadn't expected to find her home. Had thought he'd have an hour or two, at least, to cool down, get his head straight.

Figure out another fucking explanation besides the one that had his gut all in a tangle. She wouldn't be doing it—

not with him here. She knew it was too fucking dangerous. Besides, he'd feel it, right? Or he should at least feel enough to realize something was off—

You didn't then. Back then, the only thing he could remember feeling was how much he wanted to feel Ana. Naked, open, begging for him.

Damn it, he'd needed a few hours to think things through. "You're not going to get it," he muttered, rubbing the back of his neck.

Without another thought toward cooling down or thinking things through, he opened the door and just barely managed to keep from slamming it behind him. He closed it quietly and stood there, scanning the living room and kitchen area. Empty.

Frustrated, he prowled through the small apartment, ears pricked as he listened.

It was damn quiet, but she was here. He heard her heart beat—

—coming from behind a closet door?

For one moment, ugly fear surfaced. Crossing the living room, he jerked open the door. Heart slamming in his throat, he looked inside. Ana . . . and she was fine.

Scrubbing a hand over his eyes, he took a second, forcing a breath past the knot in his throat. Then he crouched down in front of her. Her eyes were fixed, blank, staring straight ahead.

Meditating? Biting back a curse, he settled in the hall on the floor, bracing his back against the wall and watching her.

She didn't move. Didn't blink. Barely even seemed to breathe. If Duke hadn't been around psychics back at the school, he'd be getting seriously freaked. As it was, he just barely had enough control to sit there quietly instead of trying to nudge her out of the trance state.

Twenty minutes passed. Thirty. She was sweating now, and her heart beat faster, and her breathing became more and more labored. At forty-five minutes, the sweat beading on her brow started to roll down her face, into her eyes, rolling off her nose and chin to drip onto her shirt or the floor beneath her. Duke waited, his hands opening and closing into fists, his skin tight and itchy.

He almost left.

That was what he should do.

He needed to get out into the streets and prowl around—

No. No, he didn't, because there was nothing to find. There was no killer to find, because he'd taken his own life. No job for him to do. Nothing to keep him here—not a damn *fucking* thing he could do. But he could have.

Could have, and that was the bitch.

He could have done something to help that girl, help her before some bastard suffered a psychotic episode and targeted the girl. He should have done something, should have known—

Lost in his own thoughts, he didn't see the gradual change take place on Ana's face. Didn't see her eyes lighten from near black to violet, didn't see the return of color to her cheeks, or the way her body sagged as she came drifting back to awareness.

It wasn't until he heard her take a deep, harsh breath that he realized she was coming out of it. He drew up a knee, braced his elbow on it and stared at her.

She reached up and passed a hand over her damp hair. Grimacing, she reached for the towel at her side. As she mopped the sweat from her brow and neck, she frowned at him. "Hi. How long have you been there?"

"Close to an hour. How long have you been in there?" he asked, gesturing toward the closet. "And why the closet?"

"It's quieter. Darker." She shrugged. "I focus better when I've got nothing around to distract me."

He nodded and lowered his eyes, studying the carpet. The helpless anger in his gut seethed, an ugly, nasty poison. Driving him insane. A girl dead, because he hadn't felt the call to act. Try as he might, he could only figure out one plausible explanation.

He hated to let himself think it. Hated that he was sitting there, staring at her and wondering.

But it was the only thing that made sense.

"Are you blocking things, Ana?"

She didn't look startled. That was the first thing he noticed. Just resigned.

The second thing he noticed was that all of a sudden, she was afraid. Very afraid. Although the calm expression on her face didn't waver, he could feel her fear. It hung in the air around her like a summer storm, thick and choking. It made him edgy and it showed in his voice as he demanded, "Are you?"

She shot him a look. Pushing slowly to her feet, she rested a hand on the doorjamb of the closet and frowned. "Why?"

Duke came to his feet as well and closed the distance between them. Leaning in, he whispered into her ear, "Because a girl died last night and I didn't know a damn thing about it until this morning."

"People die all the time. You don't feel every death," she said, her voice wooden.

"But I would have felt this one . . . and I think you know it. I *should* have felt this one. She was raped. Beaten. Tortured. The kind of thing that draws my kind in like moths to flame. I should have sensed it, sensed *her* and helped her before it was too late. But I didn't. Why didn't I feel anything, Ana?"

She brushed by him, keeping a careful distance between them. Out in the hallway, she glanced at him over her shoulder. "I don't know."

"Is it you?"

She stopped, staring straight ahead. When she didn't answer, he circled around and stopped in front of her, watching her. She'd changed clothes at some point in the day, unless of course she'd worn those skimpy shorts and a thin tank over braless breasts to work. The tank was damp now, clinging to her sweat-slicked flesh, outlining hard, tight nipples.

His mouth was watering but he wouldn't let himself reach and touch. Right now, he didn't trust himself. He needed to hear her say it, needed her to tell him he was wrong.

You going to believe her? some bitter inner voice demanded.

Duke didn't know. But he needed the answer.

"Ana . . . is it you? You blocking things out again?" he whispered again, skimming his fingers along her shoulder.

"No." She shivered and brought her arms up, crossing them over her chest. From the corner of her eye, she watched him and he could see nerves and fear jumping in that gaze.

"You sure?"

A terse nod.

He smirked and said, "You don't look too sure. You look kind of nervous. Guilty. Worried. If you aren't doing anything, why are you feeling nervous, guilty or worried? If nothing's wrong, how come you're hiding in a closet in the middle of the day?"

"I wasn't *hiding*," she said, her eyes narrowing. "I was in there working on my shields and I needed someplace dark and quiet. A closet is about the best I'm going to get for dark and quiet."

"Why in the middle of the day?"

"Because it couldn't wait." She turned away from him and sighed, reaching up to link her hands behind her neck. She twisted her head one way, then the other, working out the kinks that came from sitting too still for too long. "I woke up this morning feeling like something was off, but I couldn't explain what. Still can't. My shields feel weird, but they aren't broken. It's like they've been dented, but if I was doing a broadcast block all over the place, my shields wouldn't be viable at all."

"If you've got a weak spot, that can be a problem. You can't be sure you're not bleeding through."

Ana gave him a withering look. "I know how psychic shielding works, Duke. Better than you. It's not the kind of weak spot that would let me go around broadcasting a block. Besides, I can *feel* it when I'm doing it, or at least I sense it trying to come to life in me and it hasn't happened."

"At all. You haven't done any blocking. At all."

The doubt in his words stung. She'd be damned if she let him see, though. Mentally, she squared her shoulders.

"No. I haven't."

That much, she was confident of. Despite her knee-jerk

instinct earlier, wondering if she had been slipping, Ana knew better. Her chameleon trick wasn't the most active power, but it was the one she had the best control over—she was either blocking, or not. There was no in-between. It was too unpredictable, too much potential to cause harm—controlling it was her only option.

Duke continued to study her, his eyes hooded and grim. He'd pulled his dark, golden blond hair back into a queue at his nape, leaving the stark, masculine lines of his face unframed. His mouth was a harsh, unsmiling line.

Hard to believe this was the same guy that had cuddled up against her last night, kissing the scars on her back and holding her close as she slept. Instinctively, she withdrew. The cold, angry man in front of her was the man she'd dealt with in the years before she left Excelsior. It was no less than what she'd expected when he'd shown up here in Anchorage, but this wasn't who'd she spent the past two days with.

It hurt. Like a punch right square in the gut, it hurt. But it only got worse when he sighed and reached up, rubbing at the back of his neck. "Something's not right, Ana."

"I'm quite certain that's what I told you when I called Excelsior," she said icily.

He frowned. "That's not what I was meant. Yeah, I realize something's going on up here, but what I wasn't expecting was a big, gaping void. Even before the Council recruited me, I could feel disturbances—with a big disturbance last night—I should have felt it, and I didn't. That's not right."

Some of the tension spiking the air around him eased, but when he reached out to touch her, she deliberately took one slow step backward. She needed that distance just then.

His lashes flickered and a muscle jerked in his jaw.

Keeping her voice flat, she said, "I need a shower."

Actually, what she really needed was to get her head examined.

Without waiting another second, she brushed past him and locked herself in the bathroom. She hadn't seen this coming, and while she was surprised as hell that neither of them had sensed any sort of upheaval last night—especially

Duke—what really caught her by surprise was the fact that he seemed to think she had somehow interfered.

What did you expect?

The guy that had been waiting for her two days ago, hard, cool and distrustful—that man she would have expected this from. But from the man who'd held her through the night, it came as more of a surprise.

He's the same man. You slept with him—that doesn't change anything.

Logically, she knew that. It just . . . well, it felt like things had changed.

Standing in front of the mirror, she stared at her reflection as she reached up for the band that held her hair. She tugged it loose and dropped it on the countertop, watching as her pale blonde hair floated down to her shoulders. Her scalp was still wet with sweat, her damp clothes clinging to her body.

She was cold. Cold all the way to the bone, but it had nothing to do with the sweat drying on her flesh. Cold and humiliated, sick with it.

She'd slept with him, even knowing it was a mistake, she'd slept with him. She'd told herself she hadn't expected anything from it, other than pleasure, other than finally having something she'd been wanting, needing, craving for years.

She was a fool, though. An idealistic fool, and that didn't set very well. Somewhere, deep inside, she'd expected something . . . or at least *hoped*.

Duke had just made it painfully clear that she wasn't to be trusted, though. He couldn't have made it clearer than if he'd dragged her back to Excelsior and put her under lock and key.

"What did you expect?"

SHE emerged from the bathroom an ice princess.
    Duke was familiar with the ice princess. She'd made her presence known shortly after arriving at Excelsior five years earlier and she was the woman most of the people at

the school knew. Cool, distant, unaffected by damn near everything around her.

He fucking *hated* that ice princess routine. He hadn't realized just how much he hated it until now.

He sat at the breakfast bar, her laptop open in front of him, but the news articles he'd pulled up couldn't hold his attention. After she'd disappeared into the bathroom, he'd almost gone in after her, and now he wished he would have.

She'd used that time to rebuild the walls between them, and while he understood, mostly, he'd be damned if he let her pull back like that. He'd spent the past five years living with those walls in between them, and he'd been content with it. It had been easier.

He wasn't interested in easy anymore. Not if it kept him from her.

She was hurt—he understood that, too. Once he could manage to speak without snarling or grunting like a fucking caveman, he'd apologize. He had to get the anger under control first. It was clouding his head, interfering with his thoughts. If he had tried to cool down earlier, taken a few minutes to think things through while he sat on his ass and waited for her to come out of the trance, he could have avoided hurting her—a fact he was seriously kicking himself over.

It didn't make sense that Ana would call for somebody to come and help, and then interfere. No logic to it. One thing Ana had in spades was logic.

So the natural conclusion, now that he'd thought it through, was that Ana hadn't done anything. Something else had kept him from sensing what had happened last night, but he didn't like the implications there, either.

As she walked past, she glanced at her open laptop and then at him. He smiled, but he knew it looked every bit as fake as it felt. "I'm trying to see what information I can find out about the man who killed that girl."

She lifted a brow. "Then I'd suggest you start trying to find who killed her, and I don't think you'll find the answers on who did it anywhere on my laptop."

Unspoken were the words, *Get out.*

Want me gone? Tough luck, sweetheart. I ain't going anywhere. But instead of telling her that, he just leaned back on the barstool and said, "I don't need to go digging for those answers. After he killed her, he killed himself. I'm looking up stuff about him."

Ana sneered. Curled her lip at him and sneered. It was so fucking out of character, that for a minute, all he could do was sit there and stare—and think about grabbing her, hauling her into his lap and kissing that look off her soft, pretty mouth.

Instead, he laid his hands on his thighs, opened, closed, flexed. The itching didn't fade, and neither did the need to touch her. Hell, all it did was get worse. The longer he looked at her, the more he needed to touch her. All the blood in his head drained south until his damned dick was as hard as a pike.

Her words, though, served as an effective bucket of cold water. "I don't care what the paper said, what reports say, what the police will say. *He* didn't kill that girl." She edged past him into the kitchen, keeping that careful, cautious distance between them, and Duke saw red.

Coming up off the barstool, he stalked after her. She went to open a cabinet and he slammed a hand on it, shutting it. She stiffened, her breath hitching in her throat as she shot a look at him over her shoulder.

"Do you mind?" she said coolly.

"Explain."

She turned around in his arms, staring at him as though he'd lost his mind. "Explain what? I'm thirsty. I'd like a drink of water. You're in my way. Do you mind?" As she spoke, she arched away, trying to increase the distance between them.

Screw getting his head on straight. He banded an arm around her waist and hauled her up against him.

"Stop pulling away from me."

Ana squirmed, shoved against his chest. For about fifteen seconds. Then she went stiff and stared straight ahead. "Let me go, Duke."

"Not happening." He caught her face in his hands, cradled it and gently, but inexorably, forced her to look at him. "I'm sorry. Okay? I didn't mean to hurt you and I'm sorry. I didn't have any reason—"

She tensed. "Bullshit. You have plenty of reasons not to trust me and I understand them all perfectly well. *Perfectly* well. You reacted just the way any other Hunter would have and I'd be a fool to expect otherwise."

"I'm not just any Hunter," he said softly. Yeah, any other Hunter would probably instinctively doubt her.

She just stared at him.

He could still feel her hurt. Actually *feel* it, like a knife piercing his heart. It hurt . . . her pain hurt him, infuriated him. "I'm sorry," he whispered, dipping his head to brush his lips across her cheek. "I had *no* reason, Ana. I was acting on instinct and anger. I'm fucking pissed right now, frustrated as hell and I don't handle it well. That doesn't give me a reason to take it out on you, and that's exactly what I did. I'm sorry."

"Fine. You're sorry." The words were hollow, empty.

"It won't happen again."

"Yes, it will. You have no reason to trust me. You have plenty of reasons to doubt me. It *will* happen again. You may not be just any Hunter, Duke, but you *are* a Hunter. You're going to react in the way you were trained. About all things."

"You're wrong," he said, staring at her.

"Am I?" She sighed and closed her eyes. "Duke, let me go."

"No." He gathered her closer, threaded his free hand through her damp hair and brought her head against his chest. He kissed her shoulder, stroked his hands up and down her back, tried to ease the cold knot of pain he could feel inside her. Tried to ease his own pain. Tried to warm them both.

But warmth didn't come easily.

"I'm not letting go, Ana," he whispered. He couldn't.

CHAPTER 9

SHE came awake, shaking and shuddering and with cold, pressed up against the furnace-like heat of Duke's body. She wore a pair of pajamas, a tank top and long lounge pants. He'd slid in nude behind her and when she tried to push him away, he'd simply ignored her, pulling her up against him and stroking her back until she fell asleep.

He was still holding her, holding her tight and by all logical reasoning, she shouldn't be cold. Between her pajamas, the blankets and Duke, there was no way she should be cold. His body temperature was higher than a mortal's—it was like sleeping with a living, breathing electric blanket, so there was *no* reason to be cold.

But she was.

"Ana?" he whispered, his voice sleepy.

Her teeth chattered too much to respond.

Something slick and icy moved through her stomach as he shifted in the bed behind and braced his weight up on his elbow.

Something was watching them. She could feel it. *Feel* it, pushing in on her, pressing against her shields. It was unlike anything she'd ever felt in her life and it terrified her.

"What's wrong, princess?" he asked drowsily, dropping a kiss on her shoulder.

"Shhh . . . " She licked her lips.

"What's wrong?" he asked again, and this time, his voice was more alert. She felt him tense. Without thinking, she reached out, grabbed his arm when he would have slid out of the bed.

"There's somebody watching us."

Duke went still. In the dim light of the room, she saw him frown, then scan the room. It was still early, just a little past six, but already sunlight was streaming in around and under the blinds, enough that she could see the room clearly.

There was nobody in there—but she could feel somebody watching.

"There's nobody in the apartment, sweetheart. I'd know," he said softly. "Nobody could get in here without me hearing something."

Ana shook her head. "Somebody is in . . . oh. Oh, shit."

She'd known fear before. Had known terror that kept her from sleeping well for nights on end.

But terror didn't quite touch what she felt as a pair of eyes shimmered into view just inches from her face. Eyes . . . followed by a face, the mouth open in a silent scream.

"You were supposed to help him!"

The words echoed around them.

Behind them, Duke hissed out a breath and moved, grabbing Ana off the bed and rolling backward into a smooth feline movement. In the span of a heartbeat, he had them on the other side of the room.

"You . . . you see her?" Ana asked hesitantly.

Duke nodded. "I see her."

"You were supposed to help!" This time, the voice was louder. Plaintive. Screeching inside Ana's head and scraping against her nerve endings like nails down a chalkboard.

Something pressed in on her shields, hard, harder than

before and Ana gasped, instinctively recoiling and slamming extra shields into place. The sensation of being pushed intensified and Ana groaned, pressed her hands to her temples.

"Stop it," she whispered. Her brain felt like it was being compressed, squeezed by a giant fist. "Stop it!"

"Why didn't you help him?"

"Help who?" Duke demanded.

"Paul," Ana rasped out, trying to think past the pain in her head. Damn it, she hadn't thought ghosts could actually *hurt* people. But this one was doing just that. "She wants to know why we didn't help Paul."

Abruptly, the pressure on her head eased. A low, keening wail filled the room. It made her hair stand on end, brought tears to her eyes. It was the sound of pain, she realized. The sound of pain, a deep, heart-wrenching anguish that Ana couldn't even begin to fathom. *"Why didn't you help him?"*

Shaking her head, Ana whispered thickly, "I don't know how. I . . . I'm sorry."

"I told him you would help us . . ."

Then there was a sigh.

Then silence.

Ana closed her eyes and took a deep breath, tried to find the words. She would help. She'd find a way. Somehow—

But when she opened her eyes, the room was empty. Save for her and Duke.

They were alone again.

She sucked in a deep breath and sagged. If Duke hadn't been holding on to her, she would have hit the floor. "Shit," he muttered, still staring at the spot where the ghost had been. "You ever had a run-in with a ghost before?"

"No." She rubbed a hand over her chest.

"Me, neither. I don't want to do it again." He rubbed his chin against her shoulder and cuddled her closer.

She really should pull away. She was still mad at him—well, not mad at him. Disappointed, yes. Hurt, yes. But she was mad at her herself and determined not to get suckered into hoping for anything beyond sex with him. Wouldn't happen. Best thing to do would be pull away.

But she couldn't. Just then, she was desperate for his warmth. She was still so damned cold, even though the temperature in the room was slowly rising. So she leaned against him, let his strength and warmth surround her, even as she pretended that he needed the comfort of her body even half as much as she needed his.

"You got any idea who she was?"

Ana nodded. "Her name was Marie."

"What did she want?"

"Something we can't do now," she said, her voice hollow, her chest aching. "She wanted me to help Paul and I didn't."

"Paul." Behind her, his body tensed, but then slowly relaxed. He blew out a breath and asked, "Paul, as in the guy who kil—"

"He didn't kill her," Ana said, her voice flat. She tugged against his hold. Screw being cold.

Duke didn't let go. "How can you be so sure?" he asked, dipping his head to nuzzle her neck.

Ana hunched her shoulder up, trying to edge away. "Stop it—and I just am. He didn't kill that girl. He's not a killer."

"Then what is he?"

Somebody I failed.

Tears burned her eyes as she thought of the sad, sweet smile he'd give her when she pushed some money, or a sandwich into his hands. The grief she'd seen in his eyes so often. *I'm sorry, Paul.* But she didn't say that out loud. "A victim," she said.

Duke shifted behind her, bringing his hands up to cup her hips when she would have pulled away. "Okay."

Glancing at him over her shoulder, she said, "Just like that? Okay?"

"What else do you expect me to say?"

Ana didn't know how to answer that. She didn't expect him to believe her, but she didn't see him pretending to go along with her, either. She frowned and once more, tugged against his hold and this time, he let her go. Wrapping her arms around her midsection, she paced away from him, circling around the bed and cutting a wide berth around the spot where she'd seen Marie's soul hovering. She ended up by her dresser and since she was there, and still freezing her ass off, she opened up one of the drawers and tugged out a fleece hoodie. She pulled it on and then glanced up.

A startled yelp escaped her as she saw Duke standing right behind her. "Damn it, don't do that," she snapped.

"Do what?"

"Sneak up on me like that."

A grin tugged at his lips. "Sorry, darlin'. I can try to walk a little louder."

Ana scowled. "I'll just put a damn bell on you."

He leaned in, bracing his arms on her dresser, caging her in. "I'm not much for bells." He dipped his head and nipped at her lower lip. "But if you want to buy me one on a collar, I might wear it. For you."

For you. A fist wrapped around her heart, squeezing, even as her belly went cold. *For you.* Like she was somebody special to him, like he'd make a change for her. Like he'd do something just to make her happy . . . because she mattered.

She wasn't going to let herself get deluded into thinking or hoping for anything like that, though. She'd let herself indulge in that kind of daydream for a couple of days and having those illusions smashed was painful. She wasn't doing it again.

"I'll try to find one in a neutral color . . . your next woman can use it when we're done."

"Next woman . . . now, Ana, I said I'd wear one for you. Not one for any other female," he teased.

She frowned at his reflection in the mirror. Instead of even trying to figure out how to respond to that, she said, "Weren't we talking about something important?"

"What makes you think this isn't important?" But the levity in his voice was forced and it wasn't long before his smile faded. He shoved away from the dresser and started to pace. "I can't think around you. You do bad things to my head."

Ana wrapped her arms around herself. Defensively, she said, "I already told you, I'm not blocking."

"I know that, baby." He stopped in mid-prowl and turned to face her, a self-deprecating grin on his face. His lids drooped low over his eyes and he added, "Wrong head."

Involuntarily, her eyes dropped. It was still dim in the bedroom, but not that dim. He was hard, and as she stared at him, his cock jerked.

He laughed. "You look surprised, Ana. I've never been able to think all that clearly around you, don't you know that by now?"

Out of self-defense, she turned around, staring at the wall in front of her. Plain, boring, white . . . safe. "No, I hadn't realized that."

"Then you're in the minority."

She heard fabric rustling. She suspected he was getting dressed, but until she heard the rasp of a zipper, she didn't chance turning back around. He shot her a wide grin and then went to the bed, settled down with his back against the headboard. "So what do you think you were supposed to do, Ana? You're not a precog. No way of knowing what was coming. Why did that . . . " His voice trailed off and he rubbed the back of his neck. "I can't believe I'm talking about a ghost. Why did that ghost think you could help?"

Ana shrugged. "Why is it so hard to think about ghosts? Plenty of people would be hard-pressed to believe in big, shapeshifting cats or psychics. Ghosts don't seem that much a stretch."

"So you weren't the slightest bit weirded out?" He slid her a look.

"I didn't say that." She huffed out a breath and leaned back against the dresser.

Duke patted the bed next him. "Why don't you come over here?"

"Because I don't want to."

"You're still mad at me."

"No." She shook her head. "I'm not mad at you."

"You're mad at something," he muttered, crossing his arms over his naked chest and pinning her with an unblinking stare. "Otherwise you wouldn't be standing over there freezing when there's a nice, warm bed right here."

"I'm being practical."

A faint grin curled his lips. "Practical . . . as in you think we'll get more accomplished if you're not lying on the bed with me."

No, practical as in I think it's best I not get any more tangled up in you. She didn't say that, though. Instead, she hedged. "It's logical reasoning."

She was holding something back, Duke decided, studying her face. She wasn't lying. But there was something not quite right, either. He wanted to press, but now wasn't the time. "Perfectly logical," he finally agreed. "Okay. You stay there."

He slid down in the bed farther and rested a hand behind his head, staring at the ceiling. He rested the other hand on his belly, drumming his fingers restlessly. "Help me think this through, Ana. Why would this ghost think you could help Paul?"

"I don't know."

He glanced at her. "There has to be something."

She shrugged and pushed her hair back from her face. Off to her left, golden sunlight was starting to stream through the blinds, falling across her face.

"The first time I talked to him, I felt something. I don't know what, really." She touched her tongue to her lips, remembered that flash she'd seen—a woman. For just a split second, she'd thought she'd seen a woman out of the corner of her eye when she talked to Paul that first time. "I'm not sure, but I think maybe I saw her. And I don't think too many people see her. Maybe that's why."

Lifting her shoulders in a shrug, she said, "If that's not it, then I don't know. I've seen him a few times since then, talked to him. But that first time was the only time I saw her—or maybe saw her."

"What were you talking to him about?"

"Nothing." She slid her hands into the pockets of the hoodie, staring off into nothingness. "He asked for money. I gave him what I had. Got fussed at for doing it, too. A friend from work saw me talking to him, saw me give him the money, and she told me to keep my distance."

"Why? He dangerous?"

"She thought so, I guess. But he wasn't." She caught her lower lip between her teeth, tugging on it absently. "He's kind of a local legend. Homeless, wanders the city. Some people seem to think he's crazy, but I don't think so. He's not entirely connected to the here and now, but he's not crazy."

"So what do you know about him?"

Ana lifted a shoulder. "Back in the seventies, he was in the air force, lived at the base here. Met Marie, dated her . . . then she disappeared. He was under suspicion for a while, but cleared of any charges. He left for a while, made his way back up here."

"None of that tells me why people think he's crazy—or why you disagree."

She scowled at him.

Duke just barely managed to keep from grinning at her. He'd take that scowl over the blank, cool exterior of the ice princess. "People probably think he's crazy because he talks to thin air, wanders around town talking to a woman who's been missing, presumed dead for thirty years. I know he's not crazy . . . and I suspect he was talking to her ghost, not thin air. I think he could see her."

"Why would he see her? Or rather, why would she appear to him? Think she was haunting him?"

"No . . . I think she couldn't let him go any more than he could let go of her," she said softly. "Or maybe she couldn't move on unless he did the same, moved on with his life, let her go."

"You think maybe she expected you to help him move on?"

Ana shrugged. "I have no earthly idea, Duke."

* * *

Ana smothered a yawn behind her hand and watched as Duke prowled the small alley between storefronts where she had often run into Paul. "I don't know how much longer you plan on pacing the alley, but I've got to be at work in less than thirty minutes."

Duke grunted. "You got any vacation time coming?"

"Haven't we already talked about this, Duke?" Tired, she pinched the bridge of her nose. "I've got a job. I've got responsibilities."

"I'm aware of that. But jobs often come with little perks like time off."

"Yes, they do . . . and I just took two days last week. I can't take any more right now." She tucked her hands inside the pockets of her jacket and tried not to shiver. Summer was close to over. Already the early morning air had that chilly bite to it and it wouldn't be too long before she had to bring out the winter coat. The coat, boots, gloves, hat, scarf . . .

"If you're right about the ghost wanting you to help with Paul, then you're going to have to work that into your little list of responsibilities, princess." He stopped pacing and turned to face her, a somber look on his face. "If she singled you out, you have to try and help. You owe her that much."

She glared at him. She really didn't need him pointing that out to her. "I did what I'm capable of—I got a Hunter here. That's all I can do."

"Liar." He closed the distance between them and curled a hand over the back of her neck. "Marie wasn't pissed at me. She didn't come looking for me. She went looking for you. So that must mean there's something else you can do."

Folding her arms over her chest, she held stiff as he dipped his head and pressed a kiss to her lips. "I need to get to work."

Duke sighed against her lips and then stepped back, letting her go. As his hand fell from her neck, she backed up one step, then a second. She breathed a little easier, but not by much. "You head on to work . . . but, Ana, we've got to work through this. If there was something we were supposed to do, we have to figure it out, get it done."

She wrapped her arms around her midsection and stared at him, feeling so useless. So completely pointless. "Duke, I'm not *supposed* to do anything here. I don't know how to handle anything like this. That's why I called you."

"But it wasn't *me* that she expected to help. It was you, Ana."

"I bet she's wishing she'd thought otherwise right now." She swallowed the knot in her throat. "This isn't for me, Duke. I'm sorry, but it's not."

He gazed at her, his dark gray eyes somber. "You're wrong, Ana."

S HE walked away from him at a brisk pace, so quick, like she was desperate to get away from him.

She was still mad. Duke didn't give a damn what she *said*, her actions spoke a lot louder than her words and she was keeping him at a serious distance. "She's just going to have to get over it," he muttered, shaking his head.

He wasn't going to let her push him off indefinitely. No fucking way.

He finally made himself turn away as she joined with the early morning flow of foot traffic. Staring into the alley, he opened himself up, unsure of what he should look for, where he should find it. Or if he even *could* find it.

He sensed nothing there, at least nothing out of the ordinary. Scents, all of them normal, nothing seeming out of place. Noises—the sound of car engines, the low murmur of voices. Life. Just the normal sounds of life.

Nothing at all otherworldly, nothing that hinted at the watchful presence of any kind of ghost, no lingering scent of power that might indicate some other player in the game. Nothing.

"Gotta be something," Duke muttered, pacing in a tight, constrained circle. There was always some kind of clue. He shoved his hair back from his face and finally stormed out of the alley.

Maybe if he headed back to where the bodies had been found—yeah. The girl and Paul—their deaths, he'd felt them. He wasn't feeling a damn thing here, but maybe if he went back there and prowled around, he'd find something. Yeah, that was what he needed to do. No matter what this ghost seemed to expect from Ana, Duke needed to focus on the job, do some investigating.

Good, old-fashioned investigating. He glanced in the direction where he'd last seen Ana before heading the opposite way. He took exactly one step and then stopped, turning back. His heart slammed up into his throat as his eyes locked on an insubstantial form. Silvery and wavery, almost like a heat mirage off in the distance. Except this heat mirage wasn't off in the distance and it was human-shaped. Human-shaped and drifting down the road.

In the same direction Ana had gone.

His lips peeled back from his teeth in a snarl.

A couple of people shot him an odd look and several cut a wide path around him. He didn't notice as he started down the sidewalk, following that insubstantial shape. It walked through people and they never saw it, although each and every one of them shivered, like they were cold.

"A ghost," he muttered. He was tailing a fucking ghost.

It came to a halt just outside the building where Ana worked and Duke halted five feet back. His gut turned to ice as the thing turned to face him—no. Not thing. Woman. It was a woman.

Off to their left was a mirrored store window. Duke could see himself clearly, plain as day. And he could see her—her reflection looked a lot more substantial than she did. A lot more real. A lot more human.

She looked like the girl who'd died—the one he hadn't been able to save. The resemblance was eerie.

"What do you want?" he asked.

A woman who was walking down the sidewalk shot him a sidelong glance, but he ignored her.

In the mirrored surface of the window, the ghost stared at him solemnly.

"*It's too late.*"

"If it was too late, you wouldn't have woken her up this morning and scared her to death. If it was too late, you wouldn't be following her. I'm asking again—what do you want?"

She sighed. Duke felt the change in the air around them. He wasn't prone to feeling cold, but as the temperature seemed to plummet, he found himself suppressing a shiver. Her image wavered in the reflection before settling back to its normal state. "*I want him stopped. He's already hurt so many girls . . . I want him stopped.*"

"You're not talking about Paul, are you?"

"*Paul . . .*" Her eyes closed. When they opened, Duke found himself staring into her bereft eyes. A sound escaped her, soft and bereft, achingly lonely. "*Why didn't she help him? Why didn't you help her?*"

"I don't know. I'm sorry."

"*Sorry—*"

She laughed. It was an ugly sound, bitter and heavy, and it dug into him like an ice pick gouging inside his skull. "*Sorry—they are sorry, Paul.*"

Duke sighed and rubbed a hand over his face. When he dropped it, only years and years of controlling his instincts kept him from reacting—only that practice kept him jerking away, maybe even running away with his tail tucked between his legs. She was there—right in front of him and moments ago, she'd been ten feet away.

Now she was right in his face, and she looked a lot more substantial. He found himself staring into eyes that were deep, dark and pupil-less, like gazing into an endless, starless, moonless night. She laughed and he felt the icy chill of her laughter like a cold wind, blowing his hair back from his face, stinking of death and decay. "*Sorry. It means less than nothing. Help her find him. Then you have to stop him. That will mean something—that would mean everything.*"

Her voice faded away. She faded away. As he stared at the place where she'd stood, a shiver ran down his spine. He

shoved aside the uneasiness. It was just uneasiness—Duke
would be damned if he was actually afraid of a ghost.

A ghost—

"Give me a psychotic vamp any day of the week," he
grumbled. He squared his shoulders and took a deep breath.
Ana wanted to spend the day working—that was just fine.
Let her take another day to delude herself into thinking she
didn't have everything to do with this mess.

Duke was going to do some work of his own, some of
that good, old-fashioned investigating. Figure out everything he could about this Marie, about Paul. Figure out a
way to convince Ana that she couldn't just turn a blind eye
to her part in this.

"Man, what a fucking mess."

Preoccupied, he started down the street and then came
to an abrupt stop as he realized he had an audience. The
woman's graying dark hair was pulled back from her face
in a ponytail and she wore a brightly colored tunic. Her
round face was creased with a grin and it only widened
when their gazes locked. She tapped her finger to her
temple and said, "I talk to myself all the time, too."

Then she laughed and walked off.

Duke scowled. Under his breath, he repeated, "A fucking mess."

*D*UKE, *I'm not* supposed *to do anything here. I don't
know how to handle anything like this. That's why I
called you.*

But it wasn't me *that she expected to help. It was
you, Ana.*

Stop it, Ana, she thought. Tucking her hair back behind
her ear, she clocked in and slipped out of the break room. She
needed to get to her desk, get her mind on work and just not
think about Duke. Not think about the ugly cold shroud that
still gripped her from yesterday, not think about her early
morning encounter with a ghost, not think about Duke and
the way he'd watched her as he told her, *You're wrong, Ana.*

I'm not. This doesn't have anything to do with me. Whatever part I needed to play, I've already done it. I got him here, didn't I? What else was she supposed to do?

"You're supposed to stop thinking about it," she muttered as she dumped her stuff on her desk.

"Ana?"

Distracted, she glanced up and saw her boss lingering in front of her desk. "Hi, Mr. Holcomb."

"I'd like to talk to you for a few minutes. Can you come into my office?"

She didn't need to be psychic to pick up on the gravity in his words. Her stomach sank down somewhere close to her knees as she followed him. This wasn't good.

A NA had been right. It wasn't good.

She felt sick.

In her lap, she linked her hands together and squeezed. She squeezed until her knuckles went white and then she squeezed harder. It was either that or sit there and wring her hands and she wasn't about to do that.

Gary Holcomb, her boss—soon to be *ex*-boss, watched her with sympathetic eyes. "I'm really sorry, Ana. It's just that business has been down . . . you know that. And you're the newest employee . . . "

"I understand." She kept her voice flat. The bitch of it was, she *did* understand.

"I'll be more than happy to give you a reference. And it's possible we'll need some part-time help in the next few months . . . "

His voice trailed off as she stood up. "Of course. If that's all, I'll get my things together."

He stood as well. He picked up something from his desk and held it out. "Your final paycheck. It's got your unused vacation time—you'd accumulated two weeks and only took two days, so there's eight extra days of pay. As well as one month's severance pay."

At least she'd have a little bit of money to tide her over

while she tried to find another job, she thought dismally. Might be able to get unemployment . . . she wasn't sure. Hell, she'd never lost a job before. Of course, this was the only real job she'd ever had.

And damn it, she'd *liked* this job. She left his office without saying anything else, determined to get out of there as quick as possible—and without talking to another soul.

She didn't quite make it. Darlene came out the bathroom and stopped in her tracks. "Hey, Ana . . . what's wrong?"

"I was just laid off," she said.

Darlene's eyes rounded. "You were what?"

"Laid off." She headed toward her desk and found a nice, neat box already sitting beside it. How thoughtful. She ignored the box and grabbed her bag. It wasn't like she'd had that much stuff she kept here. A book she'd been reading off and on during her lunch hour. A picture of her and Brad in a frame. A comb. A couple of tampons. Nowhere near enough stuff to fill a box.

"Oh, shit. Ana, I'm sorry." She shot a dirty look down the hallway just as Gary stepped out of his office. He quickly retreated back inside and Darlene crossed her arms over her chest, tapping one booted foot. "I can't believe this."

Ana shrugged jerkily. "Business is slow. I'm the newest employee. It happens."

"Yeah. It sucks, though." Darlene shifted from one foot to the other, looking uncomfortable.

Ana could sympathize. She was feeling pretty damned uncomfortable herself. "Yes. It definitely sucks."

"So what are you going to do?"

"I don't know." She pushed her hair back from her face, staring down into her bag. Her gaze landed on a book. *Unsolved—Mysteries of the Far North*. The book where she'd read about Marie's murder. Duke's voice whispered through her memory.

Marie wasn't pissed at me. She didn't come looking for me. She went looking for you. So that must mean there's something else you can do.

"Well, you'll have a little bit of time to figure it out, I guess. You can file for unemployment."

Ana glanced at Darlene. "Unemployment—oh, yes. Yes, although I'm not too sure what to do."

"Oh, I am . . . here's what you do . . . "

Ana paid attention—mostly. But in the back of her mind, she was thinking. Remembering. *There's something else you can do.*

D UKE, laden down with a recently purchased backpack, mounted the steps. Ana was home—early, again. He frowned, hoped she wasn't having more issues with her shields. That wouldn't be a good thing, for a number of reasons.

Numero uno being that shaky shields wreaked havoc on a psychic. He wasn't worried about how it would affect her gifts, not anymore, and he was still pissed over how he'd hurt her when he had questioned it. But he was worried over how it would affect her. She didn't need the stress, didn't need the strain. Especially not when he was getting ready to dump more on her.

If she was that dead set on not taking some time off, he couldn't force it on her. She had a life, one that would go on after this mess was dealt with, and he had no right expecting her to set it aside. Frowning, he slowed to a stop as he cleared the steps. Yeah. She had a life, one that didn't include him, one that didn't include the bizarre baggage that accompanied Hunters.

She'd get back to that life . . . without him.

That thought pissed him off. For reasons he really wasn't ready to examine too closely. So instead of thinking about that, he decided to focus on the here and now. Namely, all the information he had crammed into the backpack. Copies he'd made at the library, some books he'd picked up. The books weren't going to come in real handy for anything other than supplying names, but the names would give him a starting point when he started surfing the web for more detailed info.

And Ana was going to hit the books with him. Maybe

if they were lucky, something in those books could help trigger her.

The door was unlocked and he went inside, following the sound of movement coming from her bedroom. He came to a stop in the door and stared. The normally neat space was in a state of organized chaos. He studied the large suitcase open in the middle of the bed and then looked up.

Ana was by the closet. She glanced up at him as she walked to the bed, arms full of clothes.

"Going somewhere, darlin'?"

"Yes."

He waited for her to elaborate, but that was it. Taking a deep, controlled breath, he leaned one shoulder against the doorjamb. "Wanna tell me where? And why?"

"The Mat-Su Valley, for starters. That's where I was the weekend before you got here. Heading back." She dumped her armful of clothes on the bed and started folding them.

"Okay. There's the where. Where's the why?"

She glanced at him, her mouth flat and unsmiling. "You wanted me to do something. I'm doing it."

"And it involves this Mat-Su Valley. Ana, I'm not quite following your thought train here. Where's the Mat-Su Valley? Why are you going there? And why aren't you at work?"

Her lip curled in a sneer. "The Mat-Su Valley is about an hour north of here. I'm going there because that's where I feel like I need to go. And work—" She broke off, laughing but the sound had absolutely no humor in it.

It was heavy and weighted, and her purple eyes were sad.

"What's wrong, Ana?"

"I got laid off. Business is slow, I'm the new employee— nobody they can't manage without. The story of my life, pretty much." She finished folding her clothes and then headed back to the closet.

Shoving off the door, he caught up with her before she managed to get her busy little hands on more clothes. Catching her elbow, he tugged her to a stop, made her turn around and face him.

"I'm sorry, princess."

She cocked a brow. He could scent the anger and frustration inside her, but none of it showed on her face, none of it showed in her voice as she calmly said, "Why are you sorry? You wanted me to do more. This pretty much opens my schedule up." She grimaced and added, "Not indefinitely—I'm going to have to look for a job at some point. I'll get unemployment for a while, and I've already taken care of that. I'd rather not rely on that, but it gives me a little bit of breathing room before I have to worry."

He brushed her hair back from her face. "There's no reason to worry. I can help out—"

"No." She stepped back, evading his touch. "That isn't necessary."

"I know it's not necessary. But I want to."

"Too bad. I *don't* want you to," she said, her voice cool. She turned back to the closet and tugged a couple of hoodies from their hangers.

Duke scowled and stepped out of her way, watching as she went back to packing. She added a couple pairs of shoes and socks and then snapped the suitcase closed. He grabbed it before she could haul it off the couch, depositing in on the floor and then once more facing her.

"How long are you going to stay pissed off at me? I already told you that I'm sorry. I was wrong. I know that."

"I've already told you that I'm not mad at you," she said calmly.

"Bullshit. You *are* mad."

"I'm not mad at you," she repeated.

He narrowed his eyes. Okay—she wasn't mad at *him*. But she sure as hell was mad. "Fine. You're not mad—at me. Who in the hell are you mad at and why in the hell are you still avoiding me if it isn't me?"

Her eyes fell away from his. Her shoulders rose and fell on a sigh and then she met his gaze again. "I'm mad at myself, Duke. But I'm handling it."

"Why are you mad at yourself?"

She just stared at him, her violet gaze unreadable.

"Ana . . . " He took a step toward her.

She went to back away but stopped herself. Unable to help himself, he took another step and watched her body tense as she fought the urge to put some distance between them. Dipping his head, he rubbed his cheek against hers. "Talk to me."

"What do you want me to say?" She turned her face away.

"Tell me why you're mad at yourself . . . tell me why you don't want me touching you anymore. Tell me what I can do to make it better."

You could love me, Ana thought desolately. His voice, dark and warm, wrapped around her, sending heat rushing through her. It warmed all the dark, cold places that had settled back within her soul over the past day. In a matter of days—hours—Duke had somehow managed to fill the emptiness inside her. Then, in a matter of seconds, with a couple of terse words, he'd hollowed her back out.

Now he was trying to do it all over again, warm her, soothe her, comfort her . . . but she couldn't do this roller-coaster ride. It was too exhausting, too confusing, and she just didn't want it.

She didn't.

Then why don't you pull away?

Good question. She tried to make herself do just that, but instead, she found herself turning her face into his neck and breathing his scent in. He was always doing that to her, and it might have made her feel self-conscious if she wasn't getting pretty damned addicted to the way he smelled. Warm, strong, male . . . just a little wild.

She rubbed her lips against his neck and then licked them, tasting him there. Slowly, she brought up her hands and rested them on his waist. He eased her closer and she didn't pay any attention to the voice of reason that told her to pull back. No, she didn't want to do the roller coaster, but she couldn't manage to pull away, either.

He threaded a hand through her hair and tugged, easing her face upward. Through lowered lashes, she stared at him. He was going to kiss her.

But as he dipped his head, she pulled back.

A muscle jerked in his jaw, but he said nothing as he let his arms fall away. With distance between them once more, that miserable knot of cold settled inside her. Now there was another voice whispering in her head, but it wasn't the voice of reason.

He's going to be gone soon enough. Gone, and he won't be back. It's entirely possible you won't see him again.

Possible . . . and very likely. The pain that hit her as she realized that was staggering. She had to lock her knees just to stay upright. Never see him again . . . never see Duke.

In a matter of years, her brother Brad would be done with his training at Excelsior. He'd leave, settle into whatever assignment the Council felt he was best suited for and once Brad was gone, Ana would have no ties to Excelsior, no reason to go back.

Which meant little chance of her seeing Duke anymore. He alternated between running patrol and training the newer Hunter recruits at the school, but he tended to stay in the eastern part of the country. Once he left Alaska . . .

Ana took a deep breath. When he left, it was going to hurt, no matter what. He would leave—was it going to make any difference if she held him at arm's length now?

Hell, no. She was in love with him. She suspected she'd started the fall the very first night they'd met. His soul had called to hers and nothing had changed that.

Whether she pushed him away or not, she'd still love him.

Whether she pushed him away or not, it was still going to tear a hole inside her when he left. The only thing she could control was whether or not she'd have some good memories to ease the ache of loneliness.

Lifting her head, she stared at him and made the decision.

Damn it, I'm going to live it up while I can. Every bit of it. She reached for the waistband of her sweater and drew it off.

Duke's breath escaped him in a rush and his eyes went

dark. "Ana, are you trying to confuse me or does it just come natural?"

She forced a smile and went to him, pressing her body to his. Just like that, the icy knot inside her dissolved, replaced by the heat of desire, the wistful ache of yearning. She pressed her lips to his chest and slipped her hands under his shirt. "I guess it's natural."

"Hmmm." He cupped the back of her head and tugged on her hair.

She lifted her face to his. This time, when he lowered his head to kiss her, she pushed up on her toes and met his kiss. Met heat with heat. Yearning with yearning. They fumbled away the rest of their clothes and as their bodies pressed together, he growled in pleasure. She sighed in satisfaction.

Duke walked her backward until her legs bumped into the mattress and then he stopped, sank to his knees in front of her. His mouth burned a trail across her belly, his tongue circled her navel, and then he went lower, lower. Ana gasped as he pressed his mouth to her sex and licked her, spearing his tongue through her folds and teasing her entrance. Legs watery, she braced her hands against his shoulders and stared down at him.

He growled against her, the guttural noise vibrating against her sensitized flesh in the sweetest way. She whimpered. He trailed his fingers up the outer curve of her leg, up over her hip. "Fuck, I love the way you taste," he gritted out, pulling back just long enough to glance up at her. The heat in his gaze warmed her clear down to the soles of her feet. Then he put his mouth on her again and used his tongue to tease her clit as he pressed two fingers against her entrance.

As he pushed inside, she whimpered, barely able to breathe. Her legs wobbled, threatened to buckle. He eased her down, skimming his lips over her flesh as she settled on her knees in front of him, straddling his lap.

"Pretty Ana," he muttered, straightening up and staring down at her, watching as he fucked her with his fingers. "Watch . . ."

Leaning back, she braced her elbows on the mattress

and watched, wide-eyed. Watched as he stroked her, teased her, pumping his fingers in and out. Blood rushed to her cheeks and she squirmed with embarrassment, but she couldn't look away. It was too damned erotic, watching him play with her, hearing herself moan as he worked her closer and closer to orgasm. But just before she could find it, he stopped touching her.

Moaning in disappointment, she wiggled in his lap and Duke laughed, easing her off his lap and turning her away from him. "You're not coming without me inside you," he said, urging her forward so that the mattress supported her upper body.

Fuck, she was already so close. Duke gritted his teeth as he pressed the head of his cock against her entrance and started to push inside. He had to force his way past muscles that were already clenching tight in anticipation. Sweat was dripping off his body by the time he had his dick completely buried inside her snug pussy. His hands flexed and power rippled through him, his grasp on control slick and shaky. Lightly, he raked his nails over her back and swore. His nails had lengthened, darkened to jet-black with just the faintest hook-like curl. He slammed his fists down onto the mattress and dug his fingers in. Material ripped—he heard the whisper of it even above her whimpering cry and his own ragged breathing.

"Killing me," he muttered, shaking his head and trying to clear the lust-and-need-induced fog. Body trembling, he pressed his brow to her back and reached for control. He wanted to plunge deep, ride hard, until she was screaming, whimpering and as mad with desire as he was.

She moaned and rolled her ass back against him and Duke swore. "Don't. Ana, fuck . . . please don't move. Not yet . . ."

She gave him a teasing smile over her shoulder and did it again. Duke snarled and banded his arm around her hips, locking her against him. "I'm about to crack, princess. You're driving me insane . . . fuck, you're so soft . . . so wet . . . just gimme a minute."

"Uh-uh." She didn't want to give him a minute, he

realized. Not even five seconds. She might not be able to move her hips or wiggle that sexy ass of hers, but she could damn well tease him in other ways. Painfully erotic ways—like clenching down around his cock, her silken, slick pussy tight as a fist around him. Then releasing, then tightening, a maddening rhythm that had him snarling in desperation.

Letting go of the mattress, he put one hand in front of her and flexed it, baring the nails that had yet to shift back to normal. "You're pushing me, Ana. I'm about to break," he rasped against her ear. He dipped his head and raked his teeth down her neck. Then he clenched his hands into fists, clenched his jaw closed and willed the beast inside him to recede, to pull back, give him some measure of sanity back.

But Ana just milked him again, reaching down and trailing her fingertips along his thigh. Swearing, Duke grabbed her hands and shifted, taking her down to the floor. He crushed her flat against the hardwood and used his knees to spread her thighs wider. Capturing her wrists, he jerked them high overhead and then he growled, "Are you trying to push me over the edge?"

"Yes . . . " She pushed back with her ass.

He stilled—even as the beast inside him screamed. "I don't want to hurt you."

"You wouldn't."

She clenched down on him, once, twice, a third time and Duke gritted his teeth, tried to battle down the need. "Fuck . . . you better be sure . . . " Control withered, frayed, snapped and he shoved backward onto his knees, bringing her with him. Gripping her hips, he held her steady and then drove deep, hard, fast. He held nothing back, fucking his dick inside that tight, wet pussy.

Ana cried out his name, arched her back and came. Duke rode her harder. Took her deeper. Canting her hips higher, he changed the angle so that the head of his cock rubbed against her G-spot. He watched, staring down at their bodies, her hips, that perfect, heart-shaped ass lifted for him. Hunger burned, ate at him. He licked his thumb and then pressed it to the tight pucker of her ass.

She tensed. He pushed.

She shuddered and tried to pull away, but Duke held her steady. "You wanted to see how far you could push me," he rasped. "Now it's my turn . . . I'm going to push you. And push . . . push . . . "

Her slender body trembled and bucked, her spine bowing up as he continued to push. Hot and snug, the walls of her ass closed around his thumb. He pushed onward until he could go no deeper and then he started to ride her again. Slower this time, gentle. She was tighter now, but still so fucking wet, so hot.

The scent of her hunger wrapped around him and he sucked in desperate draughts of air, tried to breathe past it, tried to think past it.

With her flaming face pressed against the smooth wooden floor, Ana whimpered and trembled. She was afraid to move, afraid to even breathe too deeply although she desperately needed air. Desperately needed to move. Inside her sex, his cock throbbed and jerked. He settled into a slow, easy rhythm, stroking her deeply, completely. But too damned slow—she wanted more, wanted fast, wanted hard.

But the newer invasion kept her from pushing back. It was new, unexpected—something she'd read about, but nothing she'd ever done. It was almost too much. Too damned tight. Too damned intimate. He moved his thumb and she moaned, tried to pull away.

Duke slid his hand around and under, raked his nails across her clit. "It's my turn now," he muttered, using his body to control hers, keeping her from pulling away, keeping from doing much of anything that might relieve the burning, aching pressure building inside her.

He moved his thumb again, falling into a tandem rhythm. His cock stroked in, his thumb stroked out. Her breath locked inside her chest. Couldn't breathe, couldn't breathe—then he raked his nails over her clit a second time. Third time.

The fourth time had her coming.

The fifth time had her moving, rocking forward to meet

the teasing strokes of his fingers, then back, riding his cock and his thumb, taking both penetrations as deeply as she could. A harsh growl escaped him and he went faster, rode her harder. She met each stroke, reached back and gripped one muscled thigh, crying out his name.

Heat, need, hunger, yearning . . . they swamped her, and as she came one more time, she pressed her mouth against her forearm, muffling her cry . . . muffling the words she couldn't say to him.

CHAPTER 10

"WHY are we here again?"

Ana climbed out of the car and looked across the roof at Duke. Blood rushed to her cheeks. She just barely managed not to nibble on her thumbnail as he leaned forward, bracing his elbows on top of the rental car. He'd paid for it—he'd insisted and she'd let him have his way.

She'd already put the call in to the B and B where she'd stayed the week before and paid for the room with her debit card. She'd briefly considered staying at a hotel, since they might be here for more than a few days. She'd bypassed the idea, though. Hotels might be cheaper but they were too crowded. Too much pressing in on her. B and Bs were just so much easier for her and right now, stressed as she was, easy was good.

"Ana?"

She huffed out a breath and said, "I've already told you . . . I'm not exactly sure why we are here. I came here last weekend and did some tromping around through the woods."

"Why?"

She shrugged. "I don't know. A girl disappeared from here ten years ago—she looked a lot like Marie. She was found off one of the trails by some hikers a few weeks after she'd disappeared—or rather, by their dog. She'd been buried, but not deep enough."

He pushed off the car and studied the area around the house. "Ana, I haven't really taken much time to do the tourist bit, but I get the feeling there are an awful lot of trails in this state."

"You have no idea," she muttered with a grimace. She'd spent plenty of time doing the tourist bit, as he called it. She'd spent a great deal of time exploring in the year she'd been in Alaska and she hadn't even touched the tip of the iceberg. She mustered up a charming grin and said, "I'm kind of hoping that you could maybe act as a bloodhound."

He snorted. "Wrong animal, princess. I don't go bow-wow or bay at the moon."

"But you can track by scent. More . . . well, you might pick up on something."

"Something you didn't pick up on?"

"I don't have that internal homing beacon that you've got, Duke," she said, shaking her head. Against her will, she found herself staring out at the sprawling mountain vista just behind the B and B. It was a beautiful view. But something about it sent shivers running down her spine. There was something out there.

She didn't know what. But she could feel it.

"Hey . . . "

She jumped, unaware that Duke had pushed away from the car and come up behind her. His hands landed on her shoulders and he dipped his head, brushing his lips against her cheek. "Easy, princess."

Grimacing, Ana said, "Sorry."

"What's wrong?"

She nodded toward the mountains. "There's something there. I felt it the first time I was here. That's what called me. That's what's still calling me."

Duke fell silent, gazing off into the mountains, his gray eyes unreadable. "I don't really feel anything . . . but I'm not psychic."

Ana shivered. His arms went around her waist and she covered them with her own. His fingers twined with hers and for some reason, that simple gesture had a knot of emotion settling in her throat.

"I'm kind of wishing I really wasn't psychic, either." She made a face and muttered, "Of course, that's not unusual for me."

He nuzzled her neck. "Don't wish you were different than what you are, Ana."

"If it wasn't for me, Cat probably never would have gotten to you. She never would have found me or Brad. Your life would have been easier if I had just been completely and utterly normal," she said, sighing. "Your life. Mine. Brad's."

"If you were completely and utterly normal, my life would have been lacking something very important. If Cat was the price I had to pay for that, so be it." He rested his chin atop of her head, unaware of the look skittering across her face. "Besides, what in the hell is completely and utterly normal?"

In a lighthearted tone she didn't really feel, Ana said, "Normal—that means no psychic skill, no getting furry, no hiding away while the sun is up."

"Where's the fun in that?"

"The fun would be in being normal," she said, melancholy. "In not hiding." She was so damned tired of hiding. So tired of keeping to herself just because it was easier to not be around others. It ended up leaving her life rather empty and very alone.

She disengaged herself from his arms and grabbed her tote from the floorboard. "Come on. The people who own the house told me they'd probably be gone when we got here but they were leaving my room unlocked."

"Now that sounds safe," Duke drawled, shaking his head.

"Welcome to small-town Alaska." She shot him an amused glance over her shoulder and slung the tote over her arm.

The owners were out, the private entrance to their room was unlocked and there was the scent of something sinfully sweet in the air. On the table was a big platter of chocolate chip cookies, as well as some maps, some tourist books and a handwritten note. Ana recognized the handwriting from her previous stay and just skimmed over the note before grabbing a cookie. Duke was already on his second.

She demolished half of it before she made the mistake of looking out the big picture window. Her appetite promptly vanished. Halfheartedly, she nibbled at the rest of the cookie as she stared out at the mountains. Duke came up to stand behind her, resting his hands on her shoulders. Ana relaxed back against him and smiled when he rubbed his cheek against hers. "Something in those mountains really has you spooked, doesn't it?"

"Yeah." Although she wasn't entirely sure *spooked* was the right word. She wasn't exactly afraid—it was more like resigned dread.

"Any idea what?"

She took a deep breath. "I think he's hiding them out there."

I DON'T like this. Duke hooked his thumbs in his belt loops and stared into the trees. It was early, not even seven, although the sun was already high in the sky. It didn't penetrate very far down into the canopy, though. The air was dark, ripe with the scents of forest, game, life—and death.

He could smell it. It lay on the back of his tongue, foul and bitter.

New death.

Old death.

Blood.

Something ominous weighed down on him. Everything about this place said, *Go away.* The message came through pretty loud and clear. As pretty as the area was, they hadn't seen a single tourist, not even a couple of bikers on the drive out here. Even mortals with absolutely lousy instincts would probably feel the need to get very, very far away from here.

But aside from the death he could scent, he wasn't picking up a whole hell of a lot. The internal voice that had guided him as a Hunter was utterly silent, and if it wasn't for the physical signs that he couldn't ignore—the stink of death—Duke doubted he'd hang around long enough to do any exploring. He wanted to get out of there that bad.

It felt wrong.

It felt false.

It bore a weird similarity to something that had happened to him years earlier, back when he first met Ana. The area where he'd been on patrol with Kendall, the vampire that had trained him, had been a void—a lot like this.

It had been there that he met Ana, and once he laid eyes on her, the desire to get the hell out of dodge was replaced with a different one—*her*. Ana, picking him up in that bar—they'd left together and he'd been too focused on his dick, too focused on getting inside that hot little body and having another taste of that mouth.

Ana had screwed his head to hell and back, to the point that having her damn near obliterated all other impulses. Still, when he'd been with her, he hadn't felt this oppressive weight in the air—just a weird emptiness. Then Cat had shown up and his instincts kicked back up—that insistent whisper that spoke of trouble, evil, ugliness and malice.

The warning had come too late—Ana had served the exact purpose that Cat hoped, blocking out the presence of paranormal activity. It left Duke vulnerable and unprepared and could have left him dead.

The skin along his spine crawled and to his disgust, he realized his hands were wet, clammy from a cold sweat. A series of memories, one fucking horrifying image after another rolled through his brain. Chained with silver, starved, beaten. A knife cutting into his flesh while the woman laughed. She'd watched him as she licked the blood from his body. Watched him with lust in her eyes—lust for his body, lust for his blood.

Cat had been one crazy-assed bitch. But she was dead now. Dead. She couldn't hurt anybody again, and he'd sooner slit his wrists with one of those silver blades than let himself be that helpless again. Forcing thoughts of psycho bitch out of his head, he focused on the forest again and tried to pinpoint where it was coming from.

Tried to figure out what *it* was.

"Duke?"

He swiped his hands down his jeans as Ana came to stand beside him. "You feel it?"

"Feel what?"

He shook his head. "I can't quite describe it. It's like there's some invisible shield around this place, something that doesn't want us in there."

Ana shrugged. "No. I don't feel it. I can feel them, though. Souls, or something. I sensed them the first time I was here, but there's nothing I can follow."

He could. He could follow the blood. But he wasn't ready to do it yet. "What else do you feel?"

"Nothing." Ana shook her head. "Just them. Like they're calling me. It's too chaotic for me, like a bunch of voices all screaming at once. None of it makes sense. But that's all. Why . . . what do you feel?"

"Just the urge to get the hell away from here," he said. He almost didn't say it. Didn't really want to. But he knew he had to. Get it out, get it done, before they went there and got caught up in whatever mess waited for them. "Only time I've ever felt anything even remotely like this was back in Cincinnati. Right before I met you."

She glanced into the trees and then back at him. She swallowed and shook her head. Something flickered in her eyes—hurt.

"Duke, I'm not doing—"

"I know it's not you," he interrupted. "It's not the same, not exactly. Back in Cincinnati, you just cast a pall on everything, hid anything that might have set my instincts off. Whatever this is, it's more than that. There's a pall, I can smell death, but I don't *feel* it. And this isn't just some passive blocking. It's more like something's actively screaming at me, telling me to leave. You didn't ever do that. You were like a vacuum—this is one massive, motherfucking black hole."

She blanched. "Shit. You . . . Duke, you think there's somebody around here, like me?"

"I don't know." He didn't know. He really didn't *want* to know. But he was going to have to find out. He rolled his head back and forth, loosening up muscles that had long since gone tight and tense. "Come on. Let's get this done."

Done. As in quick. Real quick, because he wanted *out* of there. Wanted away.

"Yeah, well, you don't always get what you want," he muttered a few days later, remembering his very definite desires to get away from the small town of Palmer. An hour north of Anchorage, the small town didn't seem to have any answers for them.

A damned waste of time. After four, fruitless, empty days, he'd decided it had been a damned waste of time coming here. Four days—four *fucking* days.

Spent tromping out in the forest, following overgrown trails, basically just chasing his own damn tail, it seemed like. His senses weren't working. He could smell the blood, could smell the death.

It burned inside him, that death. Blood spilled, calling out to him a way that left no doubt about why he might be here. If he could just track the source, he could find something. He hoped.

But searching for the source had proved to be another lesson in futility, as far as he was concerned. He couldn't find it. It was like he'd gone scent-blind and couldn't smell anything more than the blood. The stink of that surrounded him. It felt like it permeated his entire damn body.

As he followed Ana up the stairs that led to the private entrance of their room, he wondered what in the hell was wrong with him. Wrong with his head, wrong with his nose.

"I need a shower," he said curtly, brushing past her and stalking into the bathroom. She was quiet but that was nothing new. Over the past four days, she'd retreated more and more inside herself and that wasn't helping his frame of mind any, but he didn't know what to do about it.

He was on edge just being here and while whatever it was that affected him didn't seem to bother her, she was a mess of tension, too. He didn't want to say anything that would make it worse, so basically, neither of them were saying anything beyond what was necessary. Son of a bitch, he couldn't take much more of this.

Stripping out of his clothes, he climbed into the shower and turned up the water as hot as it would go. He scrubbed every inch of his body, washed his hair twice, and still smelled the blood.

Maybe we should just leave. This is a waste of time—

"No." Appalled, he jerked his thoughts back in line and mentally kicked himself. Not a waste of time. So what if they weren't finding what they needed? This was how things were found, through process of elimination, weeding down to the possible problem by getting rid of the more improbable ones.

Furious with himself for even thinking about getting rid of it, he turned the water off and climbed out, drying himself off. He went to reach for his clothes, but he'd forgotten to get clean ones and there was no way he was putting on the dirty ones. Hell, if he had the clothes to spare, he'd burn them. Might do it anyway. It wasn't like he couldn't afford to buy more.

Blowing out a disgusted breath, he looped the towel around his waist and slipped out of the bathroom. He came up short, though, as he caught sight of Ana standing in front of the gas fireplace and staring at the dancing flames. They flickered across her face and glinted off her pale, gold hair.

She looked so beautiful, he thought. Beautiful and sad.

That sadness he glimpsed in her eyes hit him in the gut, low and hard. "Ana."

She glanced up at him, gave him a faint smile and then resumed her study of the fire. "Are you done in there? I think I'd like to take a bath."

"Have at it." As she passed by him, he reached for something to say, something that might ease the misery inside her. He couldn't think of a damn thing to say. He knew what he wanted to do—pull her up against him, hold her, stroke her—it didn't even have to be anything sexual, though he knew it would probably come to that.

He just wanted to touch her. Needed it. She was too deep inside him, stuck inside him. The kind of stuck that just didn't get *un*-stuck.

The sound of running water started in the bathroom. He had half a mind to go stand in the doorway, watch as she stripped out of her clothes, while she climbed into a steaming tub of water. But he knew how she'd react. It would make her damn uncomfortable and that wasn't going to help any.

T WENTY minutes of soaking in a hot tub of water didn't do a damn thing to help. Her back and neck were still a mess of knots and tension. Thirty minutes on a massage table probably wouldn't do jack to help her stress level right now.

Ana stared up at the ceiling, her head resting on a folded-up towel, and tried to keep her mind blank. Tried not to think about anything, not to let herself feel anything. She might as well try to walk on water. The dread, the apprehension knotted inside her, leaving her with tense muscles and a horrendous headache.

She was frustrated and she felt utterly and completely useless. She wasn't helping Duke at all. He'd seemed so sure she could do something to help, and she'd wanted to believe that. But it wasn't happening.

They hiked through the woods, searching for a needle

in a haystack, and each day that passed had him more and more tense. She could feel it, coming off of him in waves, feel it as his frustration started to turn into anger. Too much of it was self-directed and she hated that he was beating himself up over this.

Hated that she couldn't do more to help.

You can't hide in here forever.

No. She couldn't. The water was getting too cool, she was way too tired and she wasn't about to let him stay out there and keep beating himself up over this. That decision made, she made quick work of washing her hair and her body.

Dripping wet, she stood up in the tub and wrapped her hair in one of the towels. She was reaching for a second towel to dry off when he opened the door.

Their eyes met. Duke didn't say anything. He took the towel from her and held out a hand. She climbed from the tub and stood in front of him, shivering and silent as he dried her off.

Ana hadn't ever realized the simple process of drying off could be made erotic. Although she was fast learning that Duke could make almost anything erotic, even things as simple as eating or walking. She caught her lip between her teeth as he stroked the soft, thick cotton over her nipples, down over her belly. He knelt in front of her to dry her legs off, taking a lot more time doing it than she ever did.

She was all but quaking with need by the time he finished. All but ready to pounce on him. Her breath caught in her throat as he stood up. He pulled her against him and she tipped her head back . . . only to have him curve a hand around the back of her neck and cradle her against him. His free hand glided up and down her back, long, soothing strokes. When he rubbed his lips against her temple, her heart melted inside her chest. A soft, shaky sigh escaped her lips and she turned her face into his neck, breathing in his scent.

She'd gotten too used to him being there, she realized. Too used to having him close, too used to having his warmth and strength within reach, close enough to touch. Her throat went tight as an unwelcome thought danced through her mind. How much longer? How much longer was he going to be right here, close enough for her to touch, close enough that his warmth chased all the darkness and ice from within her heart?

Her hands clenched and opened, unconsciously kneading the firm flesh of his back as she held him close. However long it was, a few days, a few months, even a few years weren't going to be enough. Not with Duke. Not with a man she'd loved almost from the first. His strength, the kindness he kept hidden so deep inside, the passion he brought to everything he did.

Memories—she needed to hoard them, to stockpile them up so she had enough to get by one once he left. Warm memories—they weren't going to do much to dispel the chill of loneliness, but it was better than nothing, she figured.

He rubbed his cheek against hers and said softly, "You're thinking awful heavy thoughts."

Tipping her head back, she smiled at him and said, "How do you know how heavy they are? Did you go and get psychic?"

"Don't need to be psychic to feel that," he said, tracing the line of her mouth with his finger. "What are you thinking about?"

"You," she said honestly. Then she surprised herself, and him. Reaching between them, she molded her fingers to his length, feeling him through the thick weave of the towel. "Let's go to bed. I want you."

Want . . . did that even describe what she felt? Want—it seemed so fleeting. An urge easily satisfied, a temporary desire that came and went. She didn't *want*—she craved. She needed. She longed. And for now, she could have.

As he lifted her up, the towel fell to the floor. She wrapped her legs around his waist, shivering as her position had him nestled in just the right spot. Each step he took toward the bed had him brushing against her. A deep, empty ache throbbed inside her and she arched her back, working herself against him, trying to deepen the contact.

Duke growled under his breath as he took her to the bed, crushing her into the mattress as his mouth swooped down on hers. She met him, heat for heat, hunger for hunger. He tore her towel away and she reached for him. But he didn't come—he sprawled between her thighs and urged them open. He pressed his mouth to her, licking, nuzzling and teasing the sensitive flesh and the empty ache inside her womb grew.

"Duke, please," she whimpered, fisting her hands in his hair and tugging.

His groan rumbled through him and he tore his mouth away from her, staring up at her with eyes that swirled and danced with heat.

"Please . . . " She'd beg if she had to. She needed to feel him inside her, needed to feel his weight and his strength—*him*.

Golden hair fell into his eyes and he tossed it back impatiently, staring up at her over the length of her body. She didn't know what he was looking for, but she didn't really care, not when he crawled up and settled atop her body, wedging his hips between her thighs. She sighed in satisfaction, her lashes fluttering down over her eyes.

"No," he muttered, dipping his head and nipping her lower lip. "Look at me. I want to see you . . . I want to watch you."

It took a monumental effort, but she forced her eyes to open and stared up into his face. A satisfied smile curled his lips and he shifted, reached between them and tucked the head of his cock against her entrance. "Look at me," he muttered. "Fuck, Ana . . . I'm getting lost in you."

Lazy. Sweet. She hadn't realized how quickly desperate desire could turn into something so lazy and sweet. He sank into her, inch by slow inch, his eyes locked on her face. He reached down and caught her hands, twining their fingers and pressing their palms together. Then he kissed her and it was so gentle—full of wonder and delight and pleasure. It left her with tears stinging her eyes.

"My Ana," he muttered against her lips. Then he shifted and rubbed his cheek against hers. "My Ana. Say you're mine."

"Yours, Duke." She sighed. "For as long as you want."

"And if I want forever?"

Her heart stuttered to a halt and if she could have jerked back, she would have done so. Dazed, she stared at him.

"Forever?" He didn't mean forever.

Not with her.

"Forever," he whispered, and then he kissed her again and the doubt inside her mingled with hope and joy.

Too quick. Beauty never lasted long enough, and neither did this. He crushed his mouth to hers, muttered against her mouth, "Forever, Ana."

She desperately wanted to believe that. For now, maybe she could even let herself. Wrapping her arms around his neck, she clutched him tight and shuddered as he moved against her, moved within her. Deep, so deep . . . filling her, warming everything cold and empty. She cried out against his mouth and then moaned as he shifted higher on her body, rubbing against her clit with every deep, driving thrust.

"Mine." His voice was a rough, guttural growl and it sent shivers down her spine.

"Yours . . . " It was what she'd wanted for so long. And somewhere, even as doubt lingered, part of her began to hope. Began to believe.

E ARLY the next morning, Duke lay with one arm around Ana's waist and his face buried in her hair. He'd actually managed to sleep some, and Ana was still dozing. Something had woken him up though, and he wasn't sure what.

He pushed up on his elbow and cracked his neck. Didn't help. Still felt something dancing along his spine—

"Shit." He managed to keep from shouting it—just barely.

It was Marie.

Again.

She was hovering on the floor just a few inches away. If he reached out his arm, his fingers would probably go right through her. Ana tensed in his arms, coming out of sleep slowly. "What . . . Duke, did you . . . "

Her voice trailed off. From the corner of his eye, he saw her, knew the second she'd seen Marie. She tensed in his arms and he absently rubbed his hand up and down her hip.

"Marie."

The ghost glanced at him and then focused her attention on Ana. *"Don't you feel it?"*

Ana sat up, tucking the sheet under her arms and holding it over her naked chest. "Feel what?"

"Them. I hear their screams . . . there are so many. Why don't you help them?"

"We're trying. We're just not finding anything."

"Then look somewhere else . . . before he does it again."

"Marie, where do we look?" Ana asked.

She sounded so calm. She was handling this ghost deal a lot better than he was, he decided.

"If it was that easy for me to tell you, don't you think I would?"

Her voice was plaintive and unless it was a trick of the light, Duke thought he saw tears in her eyes. Did ghosts cry? Sure as hell seemed like this one did.

Her bottomless gaze cut his way and Duke managed not to flinch. The air around him went cold and as he blew out a breath, he could see it leaving his mouth, a foggy puff of vapor.

"Do you know who he was?"

Ana's quiet question drew his attention back to her, that and the fact that she was shivering, her teeth all but chattering from the cold.

It got even colder. Marie's response was a low, plaintive cry. *"No."*

Her head fell forward and the illusion of long dark hair drifted down, hiding her face. She whispered it over and over. *"No, no, no, no . . . "*

The temperature was getting cold enough that it was even bothering him, so he imagined it was damn near intolerable for Ana. Grabbing a blanket, he tucked it around her shivering body. "Marie—enough."

The woman just kept whispering and moaning, the sound raw and tortured. In the bed, Ana was racked with cold and her eyes had a weird glazed look to them that had Duke's protective instincts rising hard and fast. He narrowed his eyes and climbed out of the bed, crossing to stand in front of Marie. "Stop it—or I'm out of here and I'll take her with me. How is she going to help you then?"

No change at first. Then slowly, Marie quieted and lifted her head, staring at him with those bottomless black eyes. They were full of misery, rage and pain—he wasn't any kind of psychic or empath, but he didn't need to be to feel *that*.

Duke could feel all her emotions hovering in the air around them, the anger burning hot as hell, the misery and pain an icy morass that could freeze the blood. He wondered how much of that Ana was picking up through her shields. He could only hope it wasn't much.

"She has to help me."

"No. She doesn't. She *wants* to, but if you keep making her miserable, I'll be damned if I let her keep trying."

"I'll make her," Marie said.

Duke felt—something. He wasn't sure what. But behind him, Ana cried out. He had to fight the urge to turn and go to her; instead he focused on Marie, watched as her form wavered and flickered. She was doing something to Ana, hurting her somehow. He could scent Ana's pain as clearly as he scented the fear. But whatever it was, it didn't come without a cost to Marie.

"Stop," he said, and he stopped trying to control his anger. He felt it punch through the air, mingle with the ice of Marie's desperate anger. The heat of his own power cut through the ice and within seconds, the frigid air began to warm. "Stop it now, or we're both gone."

"I'll just keep coming to her." Marie's ghostly body flickered, all but faded and then whatever power she was putting off ceased, cut off like somebody flipped a switch. He heard Ana's desperate gasp for air, but still, he didn't take his eyes off Marie. This woman, ghost, victim, whatever else she was, was a threat. A threat to Ana and that wasn't anything he was going to tolerate.

He bared his teeth in a mocking smile and drawled, "Not if I take her far enough away, I bet." He'd damn well do it, too. Take her back to Virginia kicking and screaming before he let some illusive, angry spirit cause her any more pain.

Doubt flickered across Marie's face. *"I need her help—I know she can help."*

"Then maybe you should stop with the threats, stop hurting her and let us do what we can to help."

Marie's eyes bored into his. But she said nothing else.

Within a few more seconds, she was gone.

He felt it the moment her presence had completely retreated. That heavy, weighted feel of being watched disappeared and once he knew they were alone, he turned to Ana. She was on the bed, her knees drawn to her chest and her body shaking.

"Ana . . ."

She lifted a tear-strained face to his.

"What did she do?"

She released a pent-up, unsteady breath and shook her head. "I don't know. It was like I could . . . " She stopped and licked her lips. "I don't know. I could feel her, trying to push inside me."

"Inside your shields?" He cupped her face in his hands and used his thumbs to wipe away the tears.

"No." She closed her eyes. "No. Inside of *me*. It was like she was using a knife and just trying to scrape me out and force herself inside."

A cold chill went down his spine. Shaken, he pulled her into his lap and held her tight.

What in the hell had they gotten into?

*L*ook *somewhere else.*

Halfway down the steps, Duke stopped.

It had been four hours since he'd come awake and realized he had a ghost watching him, and once more they were heading back into the mountains.

Look somewhere else.

"Ana."

She glanced over her shoulder at him. "Yeah?"

"Let's not do this again."

She frowned. "What do you mean?"

"Marie said look somewhere else. Let's do just that."

Ana stopped on the steps and leaned back against the railing. Troubled, she stared at him. "Duke, I don't know where else to look. There's something here . . . I feel it."

"Yeah. I do, too. There's death here. But there's something else that's clouding things for me, maybe even for you. So let's look elsewhere. If nothing else, it will give us some time to settle down a little, clear our heads."

"For what purpose? We'll still have to come back here—"

"Just because you feel something pulling you here doesn't mean you'll find the answers you need here, princess," he said quietly. He took two more steps, closing the distance between them. Bracing a hand on the railing beside her, he dipped his head and brushed his lips across her cheek.

"If those answers aren't here, then where are they?" she asked, her brow puckering with a scowl.

"I dunno. But there's always good, old-fashioned detective-type work." He caught a lock of her hair and tugged on it. "Come on. You can play Nancy Drew, I'll be one of the Hardy Boys for a few days. We'll poke around and see what we can find out about the girls that have disappeared and just see where that leads us. If it leads us back here, so be it. If it doesn't . . . " He grimaced and glanced toward the Chugach Mountains. One particular area, on the outskirts of the range, the area that felt so heavy and dark with dread. "If it doesn't lead us here, that's fine by me. I could happily go the rest of my life without stepping foot on those particular paths again."

They'd probably have to at some point, he knew. Death waited there. He knew it as well as he knew his own name. But for now, he'd focus on something a little more concrete.

CHAPTER 11

D UKE was pretty sure he'd seen smaller towns. This one at least had two stoplights, a small cluster of shops—leaning toward the artsy and glitzy type of stuff, a hotel, a café and a bar. But damn. He bet he could walk at a normal pace and get from one end of town to the other in less than twenty minutes.

Bentley was even smaller than Palmer. They'd left Palmer earlier that morning after checking out of the bed-and-breakfast where they'd spent the past four days. Once they'd packed up the car, he turned the keys over to Ana and settled down in the passenger seat to read through Ana's neatly written notes. Those notes were the reason they were there.

One of the missing girls had come from Bentley. Leah Parrish had been twenty-two, a pretty girl who had dropped out of college in 1983 to work at a restaurant in Anchorage. She'd been heading home for Christmas the weekend she disappeared.

Her coworkers had seen her the night before when they all went out for dinner, and that was the last time anybody could remember seeing her.

No body had ever been found, just her car on the side of the road, found empty the day she disappeared. There was no proof linking Parrish to any of the other disappearances in the state, but the hair on the back of Duke's neck had stood on end when he saw her name and that was the only connection *he* needed.

The car came to a stop in the parking lot of the town's lone hotel, the Put Your Feet Up Hotel. It didn't look like much, but they didn't have a whole lot of other choices. Ana leaned back in her seat, eying the hotel. The look on her face was inscrutable, but Duke could feel the tension inside her.

"You okay?"

She shot him a sidelong glance and shrugged. "Yeah. I just don't care for hotels."

"Don't care for them as in . . . you don't like them, or as in they can cause you problems?"

She grimaced. "Problems. Sometimes they just have too much going on—presses in on me a bit."

"Well, I think it's safe to say that this particular hotel doesn't see a lot of action," he said, grinning wryly. There were all of three cars in the parking lot, including theirs.

"There is that."

They climbed out of the car, but didn't bother grabbing anything from the back. The hotel consisted of a series of small, separate units, more like cottages than a real hotel, so they'd just have to move the car anyway. Side by side, they headed up to the office and already, Duke could feel eyes on them. Through the window, he could see three people, two of them sitting around a checkerboard, the other standing behind the counter.

"I get the feeling that tourist traffic doesn't come through here a lot," Ana muttered.

"Yeah, I was thinking that, too. Going to make it real easy to ask around about the girl who disappeared from here, huh?"

Her voice grim, Ana said, "I don't see much point in asking anything. We're not going to find anything here."

Duke didn't know if she was being pessimistic, or if she just knew it somehow. He didn't have time to ask, either, unless they wanted to draw more attention to themselves by loitering in front of the office. The guys playing checkers weren't even pretending to play anymore.

Blowing out a breath, he rested a hand on the base of her spine and said, "We'll talk about all of that after we get a room."

A NA lay on the bed, staring up at the ceiling. The mattress was rock hard, thin and probably a good twenty years old.

The room was clean, though, and well cared for. The small unit they'd paid for was probably only a couple of hundred square feet max, but it had a kitchenette, a TV and the bathroom, thank God, was very, very clean. Plus, all the rooms came equipped with wireless Internet access.

Apparently the small town had more tourism traffic than they'd thought. All the rooms but this one were booked and the owner had proudly told them all about the small town. If they were in the mood to hunt, hike, fish or go for a horseback ride—just be sure to let him know because he could hook them right up.

Still, they were wasting their time here.

She wasn't sure how she knew. She just did. Duke was sitting at the desk, already surfing the web and looking for more information about Leah Parrish. Leah . . . the name meant less than nothing to Ana. She'd jotted the name down in her notes, because Leah, like a number of other teenaged girls and young women, had gone missing within the past three decades.

But she got no buzz from the name, and when she closed her eyes, she didn't see the image of the girl being slaughtered. Unlike what happened every time she thought of Marie. Unlike what happened when she remembered the girl who'd died a few days earlier.

There was nothing here.

"You'd make a lousy detective."

Ana rolled her head on the mattress, looking at Duke. He had shifted in the chair, sprawling with his legs stretched out in front of him and an amused smile on his lips. "Why is that?"

"You have no patience."

"And you get that idea because . . . ?"

"Because you're so ready to hop off that bed and head back to Palmer, I can all but hear the wheels in your head turning," he replied.

"It's not Palmer," she said, shrugging. "It just that I *feel* something there. I don't feel anything here."

"What did you expect?"

"I don't know. I guess I expected to feel . . . something. But there's nothing here."

"There is something here." Duke focused his attention back on the computer, ignoring her as she sat up.

"What do you mean, something here?"

He lifted a shoulder in a restless shrug. "Just something. I can feel it. Waiting to see what comes of it. Going to take a look around once the sun sets." He flicked a glance toward the window and added wryly, "Assuming it does set."

"Between ten and eleven. But you won't have that much time. The nights are still pretty short up here for a while yet."

"Won't need that long," he said.

She rolled onto her side and propped her head up on her hand. "What are you going to look for?"

"I don't know. Just got an itch in my gut."

"Do you think it has anything to do with Marie?"

"Don't know," he said, but his voice was distracted.

Sighing, Ana fell into silence and watched him for a while. Expressions flickered across his face. Disgust, resignation, outrage. From time to time, that sexy mouth of his would draw into a tight line and his gray eyes became flat and cold as ice. A good thirty minutes passed before he made another sound, before he so much as glanced her way again.

She didn't mind too much, though. Just watching him was a pleasure, and it was one she could indulge in now for the first time in several days. The small town of Bentley didn't have that heavy, oppressive weight that had lingered around Palmer. She didn't have that premonition of doom hovering around her and that pain and desperation didn't cloak any and every thought.

It was actually kind of restful . . . Ana never even noticed when she drifted off to sleep.

I T wasn't nightfall yet, but Duke couldn't stay in that small room another minute. He scrawled a note for Ana and left it on her laptop. He left in silence. He was just going to walk around a little, stretch his legs . . . and maybe see if he couldn't pick up on just whatever it was out there that kept whispering to him.

But he wasn't going to let himself get too worked up over those quiet little whispers. It might not be much of anything. For all he knew, it was another shifter, one who'd already established some kind of ownership over this area. Or maybe somebody needed help—his kind of help.

Whatever it was, it wasn't a scream. His gut told him that if there was a connection to Ana and her ghost, it was going to be a scream. Marie would make damn sure of that.

The scent of rage came on so sudden, it caught him off guard. Rage. Anger. Disgust.

In seconds, it went from a whisper of unease to a panicked scream. Instincts kicked up and he shut out everything else. Focused on the scent, and followed it.

A LONE in the small hotel room, Ana shivered. The temperature in the room dropped, growing

colder and colder. Something whispered through the air.
A quiet sigh.

Marie shimmered into view, watching Ana with mixed
emotions. Anger. Hope. Rage. Desperation. Disgust. Fear.

I can't do this, she thought.

But she didn't see how much choice she had. There was
so much that this woman wasn't seeing. How much was it
because she couldn't see? How much because she wouldn't
look?

Marie wasn't alone for long. So many lost souls were
waiting for this girl, waiting for her to help find their killer.
That would cut them loose, free them from their ties to
the land of the living so they could move on. Sisters—they
were all sisters in death, bound together by the acts of a
madman.

As one of her sisters came to stand beside her, the air in
the room became even colder and on the bed, Ana shivered
and trembled.

"Let me."

Marie looked at her sister and wondered if she could. If
she should. Marie was the strongest here. She'd been gone
the longest, and though the others had suffered, she wondered if any of them had suffered as much as she.

Her anger, the betrayal, all of it fueled her and grounded
her so completely to the world, and it made her stronger.
Sometimes she hated it. Hated how they turned to her for
help. Hated how they trusted her.

"What if you harm her?" Even the dead could feel
guilty, Marie realized. Because she'd felt a great deal of
guilt in the past week, every time she'd inflicted pain on
the girl. But the guilt wouldn't stop her. *"What if you hurt
her too badly? She doesn't deserve that."*

The other shook her head. *"I won't."*

Marie eyed the other sadly. She could see the woman
clearly, although none of the living could. Perhaps it was
because Marie's anger grounded her so completely, it
allowed her to see in both worlds. *"You don't know that.
You've never done this. You don't even know if you can."*

"I can do it. I know it. I can feel it—feel her. Let me."

Marie closed her eyes. With a desperate prayer, for both forgiveness and guidance, she looked back at Leah and said, *"Be quick about it. And don't harm her—if you do, that man she's with will take her away. What if we can't follow?"*

Leah was quick. It seemed as though returning home had strengthened her and as she hovered above Ana's still body, Marie could feel that added strength.

For just a moment, Marie could see both of them, Leah's spirit drawing ever closer to Ana's body. And then Leah settled inside her. A war was waged. Ana's eyes flew open. Sanity and understanding glinted in that strange purple gaze. She fought and struggled and Marie could feel Leah losing ground.

But then it was over. Not because Leah won, but because Ana allowed her in. Marie felt it—like a door was thrown open. Not a door, though—it was that wall, a wall that Marie had shoved up against endlessly in the past few days. A wall that kept others out. Ana was somehow shielding against them and keeping herself distant from the others.

Now that wall was down and around her, Marie could feel the avid interest of others, sense them pressing close to the woman's vulnerable mind.

"Don't," Marie warned them. *"Don't. Too many of us and we'll hurt her. If we hurt her . . . "* Again, guilt swamped her. She hadn't meant to hurt the girl that much.

They remembered. They had been there when Marie had lost her temper, just a day or so past. It was just the other day, right? It was so hard for her to tell. But yes . . . it had just happened, she was sure of it.

She'd lost her temper and pushed in on Ana, too hard. But the woman's shields had held and instead of overtaking Ana, all Marie had done was cause her pain. That was when her friend, that strange man, had threatened to take her away if Ana was harmed.

So they waited.

So they watched.

* * *

*R*UNNING *late—damn it, I knew I should have set the alarm. Too late now. I'll just have to make it up on the road—*

It was cold, but that was nothing new. Snow fell in puffy flakes from the sky and Leah smirked as she headed toward her car. Under her breath, she sang, "I'm dreaming of a white Christmas . . . "

The guy who wrote that song obviously hadn't lived in Alaska. Leah would just love to have a green Christmas. Sunny, blue skies, warm sunshine, palm trees and piña coladas. Oh, well . . . maybe next year.

The trip home was a long one and she cheered herself up by singing as many carols from memory as she could, as loud as she could. And as badly. The radio on her car was busted and she didn't have the money to fix it, but she managed to pass the time quick enough.

Right up until she blew out on a tire on the highway. Swearing, she climbed out and crouched down, studying the flat tire and trying not to cry. She could change it to the spare—she thought. It had been ages since her dad had shown her how to do it, but damn it, she wasn't going to let a flat tire keep her from having some of Mom's pumpkin pie—

The sound of a car approaching was the sweetest sound she'd ever heard. She stood up and smiled brightly as a man climbed out of his car. The knit cap he wore covered his hair and the oversized glasses hid a lot of his face.

But he had a nice smile. Friendly. Safe—

*D*UKE stood by the back door, listening as the small-time town sheriff quietly, coldly threatened his wife. Disgust and anger curled inside.

"When I was called back out to deal with a problem, you knew that I'd want a decent meal waiting for me when I got home. A warm, decent meal, not something you reheated and not a damn sandwich."

She took a deep breath. Duke couldn't see her face, but his heart clenched at the unsteady rhythm of her breathing and her heart as she answered, "I know, Will. I'm sorry."

"I've been awake since five a.m. It's midnight. I'm tired and I'm hungry. I expected a decent meal."

"I'm sorry," she repeated. "It's just the baby was so fussy today and I didn't know when you were going to be home. He's got an ear infection and his fever has been running really high. But the—"

"I didn't ask for explanations. You are to have dinner done when I come home. Go lay the baby down."

There was a pause and then a hiccupy, little sigh, tragically sad. "Will, please . . . he's been sick."

"Lay the baby down. You don't want him to see."

Duke edged around just enough to look through the window, and damn, what timing. It was just in time to see the bastard taking his belt off. *Oh, hell, no.* He straightened and glanced down at his clothes, and then around. He stripped down quickly and left the clothes in a neat pile by the back door. He'd prefer someplace a little more hidden to put them, but he wasn't about to leave that woman alone. Besides, the house was isolated, damn isolated, outside the small town and set back from the road a decent ways. Not very likely that anybody would head out this way, and if they did, he'd hear.

He didn't shift completely. Took more control to maintain a halfling form, but it suited his purposes just then. He could rip out the sheriff's throat easy in full cat form, but he was more interested in scaring the bastard to death than actually killing him.

Killing wife beaters didn't faze him, but it usually called for a lot of cleanup and he didn't have the same resources up here that he'd have at home. Dealing with the woman was going to be a different story, but he'd work something out.

Power rolled through him, bones breaking and realigning, fur rippling along his limbs until his bare, golden skin could no longer be seen. He flexed his hands, watched as claws shot through the end of his fingers, hooked and black. But the shape of his hands remained the same, bigger, still very much on the human side—all the easier to open a door, my dear.

The poor woman was already back in the kitchen, trying not to cry. She saw Duke first as he slid inside. Duke wished he could reassure her just then, but it was already a dicey road he was walking, trying not to shift completely, trying not to kill the bastard who stood there eying his wife and holding a belt.

Duke had no doubt the sick fuck had used the belt on her before. He could even smell blood on the leather. Old, faint, but there nonetheless. No amount of cleaning ever completely removed the stink of blood.

As she stared at Duke, her eyes rolled back and he moved past her husband, catching her just before she would have hit the ground unconscious. From the corner of his eye, he saw the sheriff, saw the shock on the man's face. The disbelief.

The belt fell from his hand as he reached for his gun. But he'd already taken the gun off—the holstered weapon neatly hanging off the back of a nearby chair. "What the . . . "

"What are you planning on doing with that belt?"

D EAR God, Leah hurt. She huddled in the trunk, terrified and shaking, the taste of blood making her gag, but she couldn't throw up. If she did, she'd suffocate. The tape over her mouth pretty much guaranteed that.

When the car came to a stop, she whimpered and squeezed her eyes closed. *Oh, God . . . help me*.

The trunk opened and she squinted up at him. He smiled down at her and out, stroking her face. "Hello, Marie."

Leah shook her head desperately, but it was a waste of time. He didn't care that she wasn't Marie. She'd tried to tell him and he'd just hit her. Over and over. He wouldn't listen to her now, either, even if she could manage to tell him.

As he hauled her out of the trunk, she closed her eyes

and prayed. She didn't want to look at him. She didn't want to see.

Later, she closed her eyes and tried to hide from the pain. She didn't want to look at him. She didn't want to see.

Duke didn't have too much time to enjoy the satisfaction of a job well done. He'd put some wheels in motion and now the sheriff's young wife was safe, or rather, she would be safe, if she took advantage of the options that Duke had offered her. Whether she took them or not would depend on how badly she wanted to escape, but he had a feeling she was going to take that chance.

Because of her son, more than anything else.

Sometimes they couldn't do much, not when it came to mortal problems like this. Too often, victims wouldn't, or couldn't, leave. It was frustrating as hell, but this time, Duke felt like he'd accomplished something.

But his satisfied smile faded a few hundred yards from the hotel.

Ana—he could smell her.

He rounded the corner and came to an abrupt stop at the sight before him. Ana was out in the parking lot, standing at the back of the car, staring down into the open trunk. Something about the way she stood there screamed a warning at him, but it wasn't until he got a little closer that he realized that something was very, very wrong.

Her scent was different. He couldn't quite describe it. He scented fear, he scented that warm, singular scent that was Ana, but there was more to it. It was almost . . . almost like it wasn't just *her* he was smelling. But there was nobody else around. Cautiously, he approached her.

"Ana?"

She didn't look at him.

She just stared down into the trunk although he'd be damned if he could figure out what held her attention so completely.

"What's wrong, princess?" He reached out with half a

mind to stroke his fingers up and down her arm, but at the feel of her skin, the vague sense of worry exploded into all-out alarm. She was *freezing*, so damn cold he wouldn't be surprised to see her lips going blue. The cool night air actually seemed warmer than Ana did.

"Ana!" he snapped, his voice taking on a harsh edge.

"She can't hear you right now." The blast of cold air against his face almost came as a welcome respite. He scanned the area, searching for Marie—he knew she was there. Knew it, but even as she wavered into view next to him, it still almost had him jumping out of his skin. And *damn it*, he was having a hard time holding on to his skin anyway, thanks to how fucking pissed he was.

"Why can't she hear me?" he demanded. "Why the hell is her skin so cold?"

"It's one of us."

"One of us?" Duke squinted, trying to puzzle that one out. The answer came easily enough, but he sure as hell didn't like it. "Damn it, are you saying she's been . . . what, possessed?"

"Not possessed. Just . . . kind of borrowed. But it's temporary. We're not strong enough to fight your woman's power for long."

"Who in the hell is it and *why*?"

"One of us," Marie repeated. *"One of us, the girl you came here to find. She was almost home when he found her. Now she's so close to being home again—that's all she wants."*

"Leah . . . shit, if all she wants is to go home, then why is she *borrowing* Ana? Why in the hell don't you just tell us what to do?"

"Because we can't. But don't worry . . . she isn't hurt. She won't be hurt." Marie sighed and faded away.

Duke snarled and spun back around, staring at Ana. She was crying now, silent tears that fell from unblinking eyes as she stared into the trunk. He set his jaw and reached out, slamming the trunk door closed. Then he picked her up, cradling her stiff body against his chest. Her body was rigid in his arms, but he didn't let that stop him. They couldn't stay out here staring into the trunk indefinitely.

But once he had her in the hotel, he didn't know what to do. She wouldn't respond to his voice or his touch. She barely even blinked when he passed a hand in front of her eyes. It was as though she was held in a trance, but this one wasn't of her own making.

He could only pray it wouldn't harm her.

But as the hours passed, sitting and waiting just wasn't enough. Worry drove him to the phone and he found himself waiting on hold indefinitely while they tracked Kelsey down. In the ten minutes he spent waiting, he found himself getting more and more short-tempered, and by the time she came on the line, he was ready to attack at the first smart-ass comment out of her mouth.

But when she spoke, her voice was heavy with worry. "Duke. Something's wrong."

It wasn't a question. She knew. Blowing a breath, he said, "Yeah, something's wrong. Crazy-ass shit like I've never seen." He kept it short and concise, all the details leading up to this, at least the details *he* knew. He hoped there wasn't something vital he was missing here, but even if there was, he couldn't do jack about it right now.

He finished and for the longest time, Kelsey was quiet. When she finally spoke, the tone of her voice didn't exactly send warm fuzzies rushing through him, either. "Duke, I've got to admit, you've got me stumped. I haven't ever had a run-in with a ghost, and I can't think of too many people who have. At least that I know about."

"I don't care about run-ins with ghosts, I just want to know what in the hell you think is wrong," he said, staring across the dark room at Ana's still body.

"Duke, I don't *know*. This is kind of outside my area of expertise. Honestly, I don't think ghosts like us—they work too hard to steer clear of us."

Duke frowned. He sure as hell wouldn't have called Marie's actions as those of somebody who was trying to steer clear of *him*. "This ghost sure isn't showing any sign of avoiding me."

"Maybe it's because if she avoids you, she can't get to Ana."

He squeezed his eyes shut. *Shit, shit, shit.* Although he couldn't quite get his mind around the logistics of it, he had a bad feeling that was exactly the case. The hair on the back of his neck was standing on end. He wished he could believe it was just an overactive imagination or something.

He couldn't. Plastic creaked and he swore as he realized he had the phone squeezed so tight, he was about to crush the phone's plastic casing. "Why would she want to get to Ana? There's not much in the way of shifters or witches up there that I've sensed, but it's one big-ass state. There's got to be others. Why Ana? Why her?"

Kelsey sighed. "Duke, you're asking me questions and I have no clue to the answers. Ana's gift isn't one we're entirely familiar with. Psychic skill can vary so much from one to another—it's one area we really just don't understand as much as we'd like, which really sucks because psychic skills are actually a hell of a lot more common than people realize. But there's only so much study that can be done when the abilities vary so widely and when we can't locate psychics as easily as we can track vamps and the like. Their gifts are too low-level, even the strong ones, and unless they're doing something wrong, we don't know who they are from Adam."

"So you have no idea."

"Ideas—maybe. How plausible they are, I don't know."

"Well, even implausible ones are better than I have," he muttered. He paced back over to the bed and studied Ana's pale face. Although he could hear her heartbeat, he checked her pulse anyway. Something about the strong, steady beat against his fingers did something to ease the ball of fear in his gut. "She's scaring me to death, Kelsey."

"I get that." She paused and then asked, "Is she physically in danger? She need a healer?"

"Physically . . . no. Not right now." Then he scowled. Hell, what if he was wrong . . . "Maybe you should come."

Cold ripped through the room. Duke jerked his gaze away from Ana, searching the room until he saw the shifting form of Marie—she didn't do one of those reverse fades into existence this time. One second, she wasn't there, then she was and those black eyes of hers were shooting daggers at Duke. *"No."*

"No what?"

Kelsey said, "I didn't say anything."

"I'm talking to Marie," he said into the mouthpiece.

He shifted the phone away from his ear and stared at Marie. He could heard the tinny echo of Kelsey's voice through the receiver as he asked Marie again, "No what?"

"I don't want more of you here," she said. The distaste on her face was very clear.

"More of me?" He glanced at the phone. "I'm trying to get somebody else here who could help us—"

Marie laughed. *"Nobody else can. She can. Ana can."*

"How do you do know?"

"I just do . . . " As quickly as she'd come, she was gone.

Duke flipped her off, or rather, he aimed the gesture in the area where Marie had been standing but a few seconds ago. Then he set the phone back to his ear and gritted out, "The ghost doesn't want more company."

"The ghost," Kelsey said slowly. "I'm supposed to listen to the whims of a ghost instead of one of my Hunters."

"Supposed? Hell, beats me. I don't even know what *I'm* supposed to do."

"Well, let's try this . . . what does your gut say? Is this ghost a threat to Ana? I know you said she'd tried to push her way into Ana's shields, and it gave Ana one hell of a headache. But do you get the sense she'd do worse? Is this ghost the threat?"

He wanted to say yes. But in the end, he couldn't. Marie was desperate, scared, mad, lonely and grieving—but his gut said regardless of what had happened before, Marie wasn't going to harm Ana. "No. She's not the threat—a pain in the ass, but not the threat."

"Then you don't really need me or anybody else there. Sounds like she's got her mind set on you and Ana—that means you and Ana are probably the only ones who can give her the help she needs."

She hung up without another word and Duke tossed his cell phone on the bedside table. Stretching out beside Ana, he rested a hand on her belly. "God, don't let me screw this up," he muttered.

T HE pain was obscene. Shame and desperation and fear had her begging until her voice was raw and still she tried. Tried to beg for mercy, tried to beg for help, until her voice gave out on her and then she just sobbed.

But still, she wouldn't look at him. She just didn't want to see him—

It wasn't until hours later that she made herself look at him. Made herself focus on his face, and look. And remember. He'd taken off the glasses, glasses he didn't really need. He'd taken off the knit cap as well, and there was nothing to keep her from seeing him. Really seeing him, and memorizing his face, because somehow, sooner or later, he was going to pay for what he'd done.

Sooner or later. When he killed her, wrapping his hands around her neck and choking the life from her, she'd ignored the beckoning light and focused on her memories of him. Because he had to pay. Sooner or later.

Sooner or later . . . it was a mantra, one she repeated over the endless nights, weeks, months and years. Long after he'd buried her body in an unmarked grave out in the Chugach Mountains, she comforted herself by repeating it.

Sooner or later, he would pay.

Sooner or later, somebody would find him.

Sooner or later.

* * *

WHEN she came awake in his arms, it was morning. Sunlight filtered in through narrow gaps in the curtains, slanting across the floor. She tensed and then whimpered, deep and low in her throat. "Duke?"

He rubbed a hand up and down her back. "Shhh . . . it's okay. I'm here." His hands were shaking, he realized. He gave up trying to comfort her and wrapped both arms around her waist, clutching her tight. "Damn it, Ana, you scared me to death."

"What . . . what's going on?" she asked, her voice muffled against his chest.

He stilled. Then carefully, he eased her body away enough so that he could sit up and reach for the light. After turning it on, he studied her pale, wan face. "I don't know what's going on. I was hoping you could tell me," he said softly.

She licked her lips, staring at him with turbulent eyes. "I don't know . . . "

Then she stopped. Closed her eyes. "Oh, God." She wrapped her arms around her middle and rocked forward. "Oh, God. Oh, God. Oh, God."

He went to touch her but she bolted from the bed, rushing for the bathroom. She barely made it to the toilet before she started to vomit. Long minutes passed as she emptied her gut and even after she had nothing left inside her, she continued to dry heave. When it finally passed, she was red-faced, sweating. Duke wiped her face and mouth, but when he offered her a drink, she just stared at it.

"Ana?"

She looked at him and her eyes were glassy.

Too damned glassy—shock.

"Fuck." He pulled her against him and carried her back into the bedroom. Feet up. He needed to get her feet up— damn it, what else was he supposed to do? He used a pillow to elevate her feet and bundled her up under the blankets, terrified. Should he get her to an emergency room? He was pretty sure the nearest hospital was too damn far away.

"Shit," he muttered desperately. He fumbled his phone out of his pocket, but before he could punch a number in, Ana moaned.

A low pitiful sound. Then she struggled free from the blankets and hurled herself at him. Wrapped her arms around his neck and sobbed. She clung to him as though she was trying to crawl inside his skin and he felt each harsh, wracking sob so that his chest ached in sympathy.

"I saw him, Duke." She took a deep, desperate breath, fought to control the tears and the grief. Her eyes were haunted as she lifted her gaze to his. Her hands fisted in his shirt, her knuckles white. "I saw him, Duke . . . God, I saw his face. I saw what he did to her . . . "

"What?"

"I saw him. I saw what he did to her," she whispered. She licked her lips, staring off over his shoulder. "She had a flat tire—he stopped. She thought he was going to help her . . . but he knocked her out, threw her in his trunk, raped her, beat her, choked her . . . "

With a shaking hand, she reached up and touched her neck. "I can feel it, the way he squeezed and squeezed until her heart gave out. But she couldn't let go. All this time, she's been waiting." Another sob escaped her.

Duke eased her close again and pressed his lips to her temple. "Shhhh. It's going to be all right."

But he wasn't entirely sure he believed it.

And as she cried herself hoarse, the seconds stretching into minutes, then into an hour, he knew he'd lied. It wasn't okay and judging by the heartbreak, fear and grief coming out of Ana, he didn't know if "okay" was something that could happen in the near future.

She finally cried herself to sleep, and if nothing else, Duke was grateful. He wasn't sure if he could have handled those awful, heartbreaking tears for too much longer.

HOURS passed. Noon came and went and still Ana slept. He worried, but his gut told him she needed the sleep. Needed the escape for now. Fuck, *he* needed the escape, but he couldn't sleep, couldn't rest, couldn't shut out the horror she'd shared with him. He lay on the bed with her, zoning out and trying not to think just yet.

He couldn't do anything else right now anyway. Not until Ana was ready.

She'd seen his face. The killer.

She'd seen him. When Leah "borrowed" Ana's body, she must have shared her memories, and Ana had seen the killer's face. Leah had been dead for twenty years, so whoever it was, he had done some aging. At least they had something to go by. Or they would once Ana was ready to think about it.

Although Duke wasn't entirely sure anybody would ever be ready to think about what she'd been forced to experience.

Thankfully, Marie hadn't made any appearances. Duke was biding his time, because that woman would be back. Until she'd satisfied her need for revenge, for justice, she'd just keep coming back, but for now she seemed content to let Ana sleep and try to cope.

Cope . . . Duke pressed his lips to her brow and wondered how she could ever cope with what she'd just had to go through. Through the memories of another, she'd been kidnapped, raped, beaten and murdered. How did one cope with that?

The sharp, shrill ring intruded on his rambling thoughts—a very unwelcome intrusion. With a grunt, he fumbled behind him on the bedside table until he got a hold of Ana's cell. Five rings later, he finally managed to turn it on, although the main reason he was answering was to keep it from ringing any more since voice mail wasn't kicking in.

"H'lo," he said, keeping his voice low.

There wasn't an answer at first, although Duke could hear breathing on the other end of the line. A man's voice finally broke the silence. "I'm trying to reach Ana."

Duke squinted and tried to place the voice. Carter. Her landlord. He scowled and almost broke the connection. But then the man might just keep calling back. "She's sleeping, Carter."

"You got good ears . . . Duke, right? It was Duke? Did you say Ana was asleep? It's the middle of the day. She's not sick, is she?"

For some reason, the concern in the bastard's voice put Duke's teeth on edge. A deep, primal and possessive part of him started to wake and he tamped it down through sheer will. "She's fine. Just couldn't sleep last night so she's taking a nap."

"Ahh. Okay. Yeah, I've noticed she doesn't always sleep well. I see her moving around or the lights on late at night. Of course, if I wasn't having trouble sleeping myself, I'd never notice," the other man said, self-deprecating humor apparent in his voice.

But Duke wasn't in much of a mood to listen to the guy's humor or his concern or anything else.

"Is there something you needed?" He glanced at Ana and then slipped out of the bed. He didn't want to leave her, but he wasn't going to risk waking her up, either. He stepped into the bathroom and closed the door most of the way behind him.

"Well, actually, yeah. Her friend Darlene came by, mentioned that she'd been laid off. I just wanted to check in, let her know that if she needs some time to make her next payment, not to worry."

How friendly of you. Duke kept the snarl behind his teeth. Barely. Keeping his voice neutral, he said, "I'll pass the message on, but it won't be necessary. I'll take care of anything she needs." So what if he put extra emphasis on the *anything.* He was her lover—he was entitled to be a little protective, right?

Carter's laugh sounded pretty damned forced and he hung up after a quick good-bye. Duke scowled at the phone and then memorized the number on the display. He wasn't going to risk talking to that guy again.

Calling to offer her some extra time to pay—how considerate.

He turned off the phone. In case the guy called anytime soon. Ana didn't need anything else to worry about at the present, right?

CHAPTER 12

Ana came awake slowly and she fought it every damn step of the way. If she was still a child living at home, she would have been cowering under the covers for fear of the monsters waiting under the bed, ready to pounce on her if she so much as needed a drink of water.

Eventually, though, she had to wake up. For the longest time, she lay there, staring straight ahead and taking stock of everything around. Duke was in the bed with her. He was awake, he was watching her, but he hadn't said anything. She could feel the warmth and weight of his stare, feel his strength, and she was perfectly fine to just lay there in his arms for a while longer and absorb it.

The room was dim, which meant it was either getting really late or it was clouding up outside. She didn't know, but somehow, she suspected it was getting pretty late. An entire day lost. She didn't remember much of anything beyond going to bed the day before—no.

No. That wasn't right.

Memory crashed into her and unconsciously, she shivered and made a soft, terrified noise deep in her throat as she edged closer to Duke. His arms tightened and she felt him press a hard, desperate kiss to her temple.

"Shhh, baby. It's okay, princess," he whispered.

Okay? No. It wasn't okay—

Tears burned her eyes and threatened to choke her, but she gulped air desperately, blinked her eyes and tried to fight the tears as image after image rolled through her. Her hands clenched spasmodically, her nails lightly raking over Duke's bare chest as she curled her fingers into impotent fists.

In the back of her head, she heard him whisper. A voice that was strangely familiar, but she couldn't place it. Not yet. *My Marie . . . say you're mine, Marie.*

Desperate pitiful pleas—*But that's not my name!*

It hadn't mattered. For him, each and every one of the girls he'd killed had been Marie, Ana suspected. Although she hoped and prayed she never had to experience the memories of another woman he'd killed. She'd never survive it. The horror in her mind already threatened to drive her crazy already.

"You see now why you have to help."

At first, the voice didn't connect. Ana lay huddled against Duke, fighting to control the onslaught of pain and fear wracking her, fighting to control the memories. She'd let them inside, she thought belatedly. It was a vague memory, but somebody had been pushing at her. She'd felt it, fought—and then for some reason that she didn't understand, she'd stopped fighting and just let the presence inside. Inside her head, inside her soul, so that Ana experienced every last, awful minute of her life.

"Marie, give her some time," Duke snapped, cradling Ana closer.

"There's already been too much time wasted. Do you want him to kill again?"

"He just killed a girl. He's not going to do it again this soon," Duke snapped.

"You talk as though he is rational. As though he cares whether he just killed a few days ago. He doesn't care. He

*already needs again. I can feel it. The last one, she wasn't
enough. He didn't get enough."*

"Enough what?" Ana asked, cutting Duke off before he
could say anything else.

*"Enough time with her. Because of Paul. That stupid
idiot . . . why didn't he just leave that girl alone?"*

Marie's form wavered and flickered in and out of view
for a minute. Then it solidified and Ana flinched as those
intense, bottomless eyes locked on her. *"He heard her crying. He didn't know who she was. But he was out there . . .
looking for me. He could always find me, like he felt me or
something and I was there. Because of the girl. I couldn't not
go—I didn't even know where it was, I just felt . . . felt . . . "*

Her voice trailed away, but Ana knew. "You felt the man
who killed you. You felt him and you followed it."

*"Yes. Although I don't know why I can feel him, why I
followed it. There's nothing I could do to help her. I can't
stop him. I've tried, but when he's near, I lose strength and
fade away."*

"What do you mean fade away?" Duke asked.

Marie tore her gaze away from Ana, but there was a
look on her face like she really didn't want to. *"I mean . . .
fade. It takes strength to be here, like this. To see things,
hear things, talk to you . . . and when he's near, I have no
strength. I have nothing. It's like I don't even exist. After
what he did to me, what he's done to the others, you'd think
I could find the strength to face him, but I can't."*

"How many others?" Ana was pretty sure she didn't want
the answer to that. But it didn't keep her from asking.

"I don't know. Too many. Each time, I hope he's done.
But he never is. He never stops. He'll keep seeing me inside
them, and he'll keep killing."

Seeing me inside them. Those simple words made a
shiver run down Ana's spine. He was killing Marie, over
and over. But why?

An image of his eyes, wild and excited and desperate and needy, flashed through her mind. The connection
danced, just out of reach. But Ana couldn't lock on it.

Not yet.

Damn it, who was he? Ana thought, half desperately. There was something familiar about those eyes. She'd seen them before. Maybe—no. Shit, she couldn't ask that. She started to shove the question aside, but then she stopped. She didn't *want* to ask that, but it might help get answers a lot quicker. "Did you know him?"

An icy blast exploded from Marie and her nebulous features took on a demonic cast. Skeletal bones became visible through translucent skin and her mouth opened in that familiar soundless wail.

"Know him?" She laughed, but it was a mocking, angry sound. *"Do I know the man who killed me? If it was that easy, I would have already told you who he was."*

Blood rushed to Ana's cheeks and she had to squash the urge to pull back and hide behind her own walls. "I'm sorry."

"It's a good question," Duke murmured, resting a hand on the back of her neck. "One I was getting ready to ask, too."

"Wouldn't I tell you if I knew who he was?" Marie asked, scathingly.

"Beats the hell out of me," Duke snapped. "You're kind of into being cryptic."

In the span of heartbeats, Marie's anger faded. The temperature in the room returned to normal and her features evened out. *"I can't help you with finding him—I barely remember anything from that night. It's just a blur. And the others . . . it's like I can feel his anger, feel his need . . . God, it's awful to even think about it. I can feel it when he's killing them, but until he's done with them, I can't get close."*

She sighed and it blew through the room like an icy blast. *"All of this, it's because of me. All of this has happened because of me."*

"That's not true," Ana said flatly.

"Isn't it? Killing me wasn't enough—he keeps looking

for me, seeing me even though he's already killed me once, and he keeps trying to kill me again and again. If it wasn't for me, he wouldn't keep doing this."

"It isn't your fault."

"She never said it was her fault," Duke said.

Ana looked at him, frowning. He shrugged and glanced toward Marie, then back at Ana. "She said it happened because of her—that's not really the same thing as saying it's her fault. And if he's killing these women because of some similarity to her, then yes . . . it is happening because of her."

Ana opened her mouth to argue, but she realized that she couldn't do it without either lying or looking like a naive idiot. It was the truth—it was happening because of Marie. Not her fault, no, but because of her. And until they could figure out who, it would just keep happening. She had the worst feeling though, she wasn't going to figure out *who* until she understood *why*.

"Damn it," Ana muttered. She scrubbed her hands over her face and then jammed fisted hands into her pockets, fighting the rising tide of anger. It swamped her and left her feeling helpless and impotent.

Through her shields, she could feel the echo of Marie's pain, echoes of a soul in turmoil, a maelstrom of grief, pain and frustration.

As the women stared at each other, Ana felt the weight of all the years Marie had been trapped pressing down on them. But there was more—there was longing. Pure and sharp, it pierced even through Marie's rage.

Longing . . . ? But even as she wondered at it, Ana knew the answer.

"Where is Paul now, Marie?"

"He's moved on," Marie said. Her "voice" was thick with misery and bitter anger. *"He barely lingered before moving on, even though I think he tried to stay. Tried to stay with me."*

"Why didn't he?"

"I don't think he could. He was just too tired. And now I can't get to him. I can't move on."

"Have you tried?" Duke asked, voicing the question that Ana wouldn't ask.

"Yes. Dear God, yes. But I can't. I can't leave them."

"Them . . ." Ana and Duke said it together, puzzled. As if on cue, a wind blasted through the small room and a chorus of sighs rose in the silence. No words were said, but they felt the presence of others with sharp clarity. Ana shuddered as the weight of their combined wills pushed in on her mind and threatened to decimate her already shaky control.

God, there was so much pain—

A low, pathetic whimper cut through the silence but Ana didn't realize it was her until the sound had already died. She covered her face with her hands and desperately reinforced her shields. They were already too precarious and Ana didn't know what would happen if they slipped and too much filtered into her.

"Do you understand? Do you understand we need help? Do you understand why we need you?" Marie asked, her voice plaintive.

"I don't understand why me. I do understand why you need help . . . but why me?"

A look flickered across Marie's face, too hard to describe. *"You saw me. Talking to Paul, you saw me. And you just felt . . . different. I saw you and I just knew you could help."*

"I will," Ana said as she squeezed her eyes shut. She'd help, even if she couldn't figure out *how* yet.

The weight of their presence faded until only Marie remained. *"I knew you would,"* Marie said quietly. *"I knew you'd understand. I knew you'd help us."*

Ana swallowed. Other than Brad, nobody had ever counted on her. Ever trusted her and depended on her for help—it was a burden she wasn't sure she was equipped to handle, but she'd be damned if she let them down. She'd help or die trying.

Taking a deep breath, she squared her shoulders and looked Marie in the eye. "I'll find him. No matter what it takes. I'll find him."

Marie closed her eyes. A look of peace settled on her face. As she faded away into nothingness, her voice drifted through the air around them. *"Thank you."*

T HE drive home was tense and silent. Duke hadn't said much of anything after she'd told him she wanted to go home. Ana didn't have much to say, either. Her head was too full, her gut a mess of knots, and she was confused as all get out. She didn't know how to handle this.

The only thing she knew for sure was that she had to get away from Bentley. She couldn't go more than five minutes without remembering the hours she'd spent trapped inside the memories of a dead woman. Whether or not distance would help, she didn't know, but she sure as hell hoped it would and it was the only thing she could think of doing once Marie had left.

It had been nearly an hour since they'd left the small town behind, and slowly, the knot of icy fear inside her had eased, but so far, no path of action had made itself clear to her, either. She'd hoped once they left Bentley behind she'd think of *something*, but no such luck.

Damn it, she felt it like she was feeling her way through a cave, sans flashlight or guide. Didn't know what her next step should be, none of it.

Ana's mind kept whirling back to those brief flashes from Leah's memories, the few moments she'd caught a good look at her killer.

Marie couldn't bring herself to remember the man who'd taken her life. The woman who'd taken up residence in Ana's memories remembered him, but Leah's knowledge of him was twenty-plus years old. Seeing a stranger through the eyes of a murdered woman, staring at him as he looked twenty years earlier wasn't anything that was going to help a whole lot.

"You got any idea on what we do from here?" she asked, rolling her head on the back of the seat and looking at Duke.

He snorted. "No."

"Me, neither." She smirked and muttered, "We're really accomplishing a lot here, aren't we?"

"We'll figure it out, Ana," he said softly. He reached out and hooked a hand over the back of her neck.

But Ana had her doubts. Big, whopping doubts that threatened to eclipse her own determination to find justice and peace for Marie. "How can you be so sure?"

"Because if we weren't meant to figure this out, it wouldn't have been dumped on us."

Ana snorted. "It didn't exactly get dumped on *you*. It got dumped on me and then I dumped it on you, if I remember correctly."

Duke shrugged. "If I wasn't supposed to be up here helping you, I wouldn't be. I didn't have any reason to keep hanging around the school, kept thinking it was time I headed back out and hit the road, but something wouldn't let me." He slid her a quick glance before focusing back on the road. "I was waiting for this. So yeah, it did get dumped on me. Got dumped on both of us, and we'll figure it out."

He caught her hand and laced his fingers with hers, brought her hand to his lips. "I know you don't have a whole lot of faith in your gifts, or in yourself. But you can handle this. If you couldn't, it wouldn't have come to you."

"Big believer in fate, aren't you?" she said, trying not to get all mushy inside as he rubbed his thumb back and forth over her hand. He had this way of doing those small things, toying with her hair, or massaging her shoulders. The way he rubbed his cheek against hers or buried his face against her neck, just to breathe her in.

He shrugged. "Seems kind of counterproductive *not* to believe in fate. It's not a predestined type of thinking. It's just that things come to people who are most suited to deal with them."

"Then fate screwed up royally. I'm *not* suited to handle this."

A grim look settled on his face. "You're more capable than you realize, Ana. If you can't trust yourself, then trust me on this. You can handle this. *We* can handle this."

N IGHT had fallen. In the dim room, Duke leaned against the wall and watched as Ana slept on like the dead.

It had been hours since they'd gotten home. The clock was pushing midnight when they finally climbed the stairs to Ana's neat little apartment and she'd collapsed onto the bed without even bothering to undress. The interaction with the ghost was still taking a toll; at least Duke hoped that was all it was.

He didn't scent any kind of sickness on her, and he'd know if there was something of that nature wrong. All he could pick up from her was a deep sense of exhaustion, nothing that sleep wouldn't cure, but that didn't make it any easier to wait as the seconds, minutes and hours dragged on.

By morning, he was itchy, pacing the small apartment liked a caged tiger—or a cougar. Restlessness drove him from the house, but he spent the time walking in endless circles around the yard or just sitting on the steps by the door and staring east toward the mountains. He wanted to run—needed it, actually. The frustration from the past few days was bad enough, but there was a darkness building inside him. It had been inside him since they'd started searching the mountainous trails near the small bed-and-breakfast in Palmer.

Like a harbinger of things to come, the darkness and despair he'd felt there kept trying to settle inside him. And blood—old blood, he could taste it, clinging to his nasal passages, lining the back of his throat and taunting the beast that lived within him.

The sound of a powerful engine turning down the driveway pulled Duke from his thoughts and he looked up, watched as Carter Hoskins rode his bike up the gravel-covered path. The other man looked a little surprised at the car in the driveway, but then he caught sight of Duke.

A myriad of emotions flickered across the mortal's face and Duke watched the struggle. Saw something possessive light the man's eyes, saw his mouth tighten, saw the internal battle and he couldn't help but smirk as Carter threw a leg over the bike and headed in his direction. *Too late, pal. But even if you weren't, I'd fight you for her,* Duke thought, half amused, half sympathetic. He recognized the look in Carter's eyes easily enough.

Ana had the quiet, mild-mannered professor tied up in knots.

Since she'd had Duke tied in knots pretty much from the first time he laid eyes on her, yes, he could sympathize. Still, he didn't bother rising to meet Carter as the man started up the steps. He stayed in a lazy sprawl and waited.

"I didn't realize you two were back." There was a brief pause and then Carter added, "Ana *is* back, right?"

"Yes."

"Is she awake?" Carter glanced toward the door and another struggle appeared briefly within his eyes. Courtesy won out. "I'd like to speak with her for a few minutes."

"She's lying down."

"Lying down?" Carter frowned. "She's not sick, is she?"

There was genuine concern in the man's voice. Duke could appreciate that, too. Except the concern rose from desire, and the man had no business desiring the woman who belonged to Duke.

She *did* belong to him. Damn it, he couldn't believe how long it had taken him to realize that. He stared at Carter, half forgetting the man had asked him something until he opened his mouth—probably to ask again.

Carter Hoskins, Duke decided, talked way too much. "No, Hoskins. She's not sick. Just tired. She's been a little stressed out, and we've been on the move pretty much since we left here."

Carter blew out a breath. "Yeah, I imagine. Look, tell

her she doesn't need to worry about rent for the next few weeks. She can pay me back once she's on her feet."

"Nice landlord," Duke murmured. But he wasn't going to let Ana owe this man anything. Hell, he'd be happy if Ana wasn't near him—or any other human with a dick. *Possessive, much?* Way too possessive, and he knew it, and it would probably piss Ana off, but just then he wasn't overly concerned about it. Holding Carter's gaze, he reached into his pocket and pulled out a roll of bills. "What's her rent?"

Carter blinked. "I said she can take some time to pay . . . "

"She's not paying. I am. What's the rent?" Duke repeated and he didn't bother softening the edge in his voice this time. Carter told him and Duke counted off enough to cover the next six weeks. "If it looks like she'll need more time, I'll get you more money before I go."

Carter stared at the money in his hands for a long, tense moment and then he lifted his eyes to study Duke. "You always carry around this kind of money?"

"No. But I'd planned on taking care of her rent when I saw you." He waited a beat and then added, "I'd rather you not mention it to her. She's got enough on her mind."

"You know, I don't think you ever mentioned exactly what it is you do."

Duke almost laughed. He could hear the insinuation in Carter's voice loud and clear, and the speculation in the man's eyes was anything but subtle. "I do whatever I feel like doing. A little bit of this. A little bit of that."

"And it pays that well?"

Duke shrugged. "The money is legit . . . and it's mine. So what does it matter how I earn it?" he asked.

"Because you're hanging around Ana and I don't want her involved with somebody that could bring her trouble. She's a nice lady."

How in the hell did he respond to that? Carefully. Probably best to do it carefully, he figured, so he took his time weighing his words.

"Ana is a nice lady—and she's more than that." He blew out a breath and straightened up, bracing his elbows on his knees. "I've known her for five years—you don't need to tell me what a nice lady she is. And you don't need to worry that I'm going to bring her trouble." *Liar—you did bring her trouble.*

"You trying to tell me you won't bring her trouble?" Carter's smile looked entirely too derisive. He looked Duke over from head to toe—apparently whatever he saw seemed lacking in his eyes. "You think you can make her happy?"

"Happier than you could," Duke said, rising to his feet. He met Carter's gaze with a flat, level stare. "You don't understand a damn thing about her, and you don't *know* her. How in the hell could you hope to make her happy?"

Carter clenched the money in his hand and lifted it. "I know her well enough to know she'd be madder than hell that you were paying her rent."

"Hell, ain't you a fucking genius?" Duke drawled. "I know she'll be mad. That's why I asked you not to mention it to her. She's got enough to deal with right now and worrying about money isn't going to help."

"She'll worry about it anyway. She's never been late by even a day, so she's already trying to think about how to juggle bills. You want me to believe that's not why she's so stressed out?"

Bills are the last thing she's worried about right now, Duke thought disgustedly. But he couldn't exactly say that, either.

"She's got enough money in the bank to last her for a while, so no, I don't think getting the rent paid is the top of her priorities." Although, under normal circumstances, it probably would be. "And I'm hoping that with all the other priorities, she isn't thinking about money."

"Not her priority? And you think you *know* her?" Carter demanded.

That smirk on his face was really rubbing Duke the wrong way. If he didn't have a decent amount of self-control, he might just be tempted to knock the smirk off Carter's face and knock the bastard flat on his ass while he was at it.

Instead, he climbed down a couple of steps, stopping only when Carter's body barred the way. "Yeah. I know her. I know her well enough to know that you're wasting your time here. She's not into you. Deal with it."

Carter's eyes flickered. Blood rushed to his cheeks. Still, he wasn't one to turn tail and disappear—which kind of sucked, at least the way Duke saw it. "You so sure of that?"

"If she was into you, I wouldn't be here," Duke said. And that was God's honest truth. If he had to stay this close to Ana while she was into some other guy, he'd be hovering on the knife edge of control. Not even he was that into self-torment. Even if she was into Carter, Duke would have fought for her, but not here—not so close that he could smell her desire for another man. "Not something I want to see, and it wouldn't have Ana that comfortable, either."

A muscle jerked in Carter's jaw. Duke almost felt a little sorry for the guy. Almost. Hooking his thumbs in his pockets, he lifted a brow and said, "Was there anything else?"

Carter turned away and took a couple of steps down and then stopped, staring off into the east, at the same mountains that kept grabbing Duke's attention. The other man sighed and shoved a hand through midnight black hair. At his temples, the hair was starting to silver, but just a little. Fine lines fanned out from his eyes, the kind that came from a lot of laughter, a lot of smiles. He wasn't smiling now, though.

He shot Duke a dour look and said, "Here I was thinking she probably figured I was just too old for her, and I was hoping I could work past that. She's been living here nearly a year—I didn't know there was some other guy in the picture for her."

Duke didn't know what to say to that. Frankly, he didn't want to say anything to it. He remained quiet and Carter blew out another harsh sigh and glanced at the money in his hand. "Be a lot easier on me if I could actually believe

there was something up with this money—or with you,"
he muttered. Then he tucked it in his pocket and glanced
at Duke. "I won't say anything about the money. I've got
enough going on with my classes starting back up that I
won't be around too much—she's always given me a check
in person, so maybe if I'm not around to do that, she won't
think about it as much for a while."

He headed back down the stairs and then stopped, looking back up at Duke. "You better take care of her."

That was exactly what Duke planned on doing. Starting
now. He didn't bother waiting until Carter had disappeared
inside his house before going back into Ana's place. She
was still sleeping. He could hear the slow, steady sounds
of her breathing, but she'd been asleep long enough. She
needed to wake up and eat—if she was still tired after that,
fine.

No. Not fine. If she was still tired after that, he was calling Kelsey and telling the woman to get her ass up there
and check Ana over.

But Ana could sleep while he made up a meal.

CHAPTER 13

Those damn eyes.

Ana stared at the TV, but she wasn't seeing the blank screen, the living room, nothing. She couldn't quit seeing those eyes. The man who'd kidnapped and killed Leah—Leah's determination to look upon her killer, memorize his face, those memories burned inside Ana like a fever.

Kind eyes—or rather they seemed kind, but below that mask lay madness.

"Who are you?" she muttered, absently rubbing her hands up and down the legs of her cotton capris.

Abruptly, she climbed off the couch, moving so fast she knocked the remote onto the floor, but she didn't notice as she strode across the living room toward the kitchen table. It was covered with books, notes, maps and pictures—research into the death of women who'd died too young, too violently.

She riffled through them until she found Leah's picture, a copy made from a newspaper article that had run in the weeks after her disappearance. Grainy and small, it showed a young woman with a wide, open smile and dark, friendly eyes. "I need more," Ana muttered, but if somebody had asked, she couldn't have said if she was talking to herself or somebody else.

Of course, there was nobody there to answer.

Other than Duke, she hadn't seen a soul—or a spirit, since returning home two days earlier. He wasn't there now, out to get some food—she thought. The guy ate like a horse.

Dropping Leah's picture, she went through everything, searching for the pictures she found of Marie. "Where are you?" She found the picture and stared at it, all but willing the ghost to appear.

Leah hadn't known her killer, even though she'd died with his image emblazoned on her mind.

Marie didn't remember anything about that night.

And none of the others had ever made their presence known to Ana. She needed answers, but she really didn't know where to look. She needed to find *him*, but she didn't know how to go about doing that. "And sitting here talking to yourself is going to do a lot of good." Taking a deep breath, she pulled the chair out and settled down at the table.

"Start at the beginning. Isn't that what people always say?"

The beginning.

With Marie.

But there wasn't anything within these books and papers that she hadn't already read over ten times. At least.

She needed more.

There were answers, she knew it. She could all but see them in front of her, obscured by the mists of time, hiding in them. Damn it, she'd seen that man before. Frowning, she grabbed a pencil and a blank piece of paper, jotting down the features she remembered clearly. White male. Age—? She left it blank, because she couldn't be sure. Twenties, maybe. Or a little younger. A little older. Brown eyes. Thin lips, but not too thin. Close set eyes, skinny blade of a nose. Hair? She couldn't recall the hair color.

Chewing on the eraser, she studied the sheet of paper. "This is just going to be another waste of time," she muttered. But instead of tossing the pencil aside, she bent forward over the page and got back to work.

Duke juggled the grocery bags when his cell phone started to ring. Eying the number on the display, he debated on whether or not to answer. If he thought, for five seconds, he could avoid messing with Kelsey Hughes, he would have just ignored her. But she'd keep calling. And calling. And when he didn't answer, she'd start calling Ana.

That was one thing he definitely didn't want just yet. That nosy woman would just start asking Ana questions, and Duke knew the witch too well to think they'd all relate to the job at hand. Chances were, once she knew Ana was okay, very *few* would relate to the job.

The phone stopped ringing while he was still trying to decide and he heaved out a sigh of relief.

It was short-lived, though. He'd only managed to stow one of the reusable grocery sacks Ana had given him before the phone started ringing again. "What?"

"Duke, we really need to work on your phone skills," Kelsey said, her voice amused.

"If I was paid to answer to a phone, maybe. Since I'm not? Not worried. What do you want?"

"Just wanted to see how things are going."

Duke rolled his eyes. "Since when did you start checking up on people, Kelsey?"

"I've always checked up on people—when I feel the need."

Yeah, and he could just imagine why she felt the need, too. "I'm alive. Ana's alive. We're working on the problem. Anything else?"

"How is Ana? She handle things okay from the other day?"

"Okay? No. As well as can be expected? Yes." Absently,

he braced his elbows on top of the car and stared across the
street, without really seeing anything. He opened his mouth
to reply—most likely with something biting or insinuating,
but the words shriveled up and died, leaving a bitter taste
in his mouth as he found himself looking at a face that was
very, very familiar.

Carter.

"You still there?"

Distracted, Duke said into the mouthpiece, "I got to go,
Kelsey." He disconnected in the middle of her sentence,
tucking the phone back into his pocket and tossing the second tote of groceries into the car.

He almost started for the crosswalk, but at the last
moment, he decided against it. He could see just as well
from over here, and he was much less likely to be noticed
by Carter or the woman he was with.

Woman—hardly more than a girl, Duke decided.
Twenty. Maybe twenty-one. Pretty. Dark. The golden skin
and near-black eyes of a native. A smile that lit up her entire
face. And she looked far too much like Marie did.

S HE was still trying to jog her memory when the door
opened a little while later. Glancing over her shoulder,
she watched as Duke came in, two black totes hooked over
his shoulder.

He gave her a distracted smile but didn't say anything
as he started unpacking the bags. A whole hell of a lot of
junk food, then some stuff for sandwiches and salads. Ana
pushed back from the table and went to help put things up,
neatly sidestepping in front of him when he would have
just dumped stuff into the refrigerator.

He was acting weird, she decided as he went back to
unpacking the rest of the stuff without saying anything,
without even really looking at her.

"Are you okay?"

His only response was a noncommittal grunt. Rolling
her eyes, Ana turned back to the refrigerator and put up

packages of cold cuts, lettuce and tomatoes. She finished and turned around to find him staring down the book she'd bought weeks earlier.

Unsolved—Mysteries of the Far North. He flipped it open, going directly to the short section that detailed Marie's disappearance. "Did you think of something?" she asked, but she didn't really have any hope in the answer.

"I don't know," he said, and his voice had that same distracted tone to it.

She glanced back to the table, eying the notepad with her neat little lists. She'd spent the past couple of hours trying to think of the men she knew. Most of them were either too young, or too old, and none of them really seemed to *fit*.

"You don't by chance know any police sketch artists, do you?"

That caught his attention. Curious, he looked up at her and lifted a brow. "Sketch artists?"

"Yeah."

He shrugged. "Afraid not. At least none that I can go talk to."

"Why not?" she asked, puzzled.

A grin curled his lips, showing a ghost of his normal humor. "Because I'd scare the shit out of them if I showed up on their doorstep. They think I'm dead, sweets. I knew them back before . . . well, before I ended up at Excelsior. It's a different life. Everybody from before that point thinks I'm dead. They had a funeral and everything."

"How can they have a funeral without a body?"

He flipped the book closed and shrugged. "As far as I know, there was a body. Just not mine."

She gaped at him.

He sauntered over to her and placed his finger under her chin, nudging her mouth closed. "I fell into a group of people that know how to make messes go away when it suits them. I was gunned down in front of at least one human. They had to do something."

"So they just found a body and said it was you? What if somebody said otherwise?"

Duke shrugged. "The only person around that could have said otherwise was in a coma until a few weeks after my so-called funeral. They weren't going to dig up a casket just to let him take a look-see." He draped his arms over her shoulders and dipped his head, nipping her lower lip. "So why do you want a police sketch artist?"

"Because I have somebody I want sketched and I'm no artist."

"Who?"

Cold fear settled in the pit of her belly. She licked her lips. Man, her mouth had just gone seriously dry. "Him."

"Him." He studied her thoughtfully. "Ana, it's been twenty years since Leah saw him. He isn't going to look the same now."

"I know that." Ana dropped her head forward and let it rest against his chest. She slipped her arms around his waist and settled against his body. "Yeah, it's been twenty years. Yeah, he's going to look different—there's something familiar about him, Duke. I don't know what it is, but I swear, I know I've seen him before."

He stiffened. Big hands came up and closed around her arms. "What?"

She swallowed and lifted her head, wincing as she caught sight of the look on his face. "I've seen him. Somewhere. Hell, for all I know, it's one of the local news anchors. But I know I've seen him."

He cupped her face in his hand, eyes locked on her face, staring at her as though he was trying to see through to her soul. "Where have you seen him?"

Ana rolled her eyes and said, "I just told you. I don't *know*. Wherever it was, he doesn't look the same as he did then. I can't . . . I dunno, but something about him is just too familiar. His eyes . . . " She closed hers and pulled the memory of his face to mind. The eyes.

"It's his eyes," she repeated softly. "I've seen those eyes somewhere."

Then she sighed and rubbed a hand over the back of her neck. "I just can't remember where."

Duke bit back a snarl. It wasn't going to help anything if he lost his temper, but damn was his control pretty much shot. Every protective instinct he had was screaming, jerking and struggling to be free. He wanted to hunt. Wanted to lose his skin and find his other self, take to the hunt until he scented his prey.

Carter—

Calm down. You don't know it's him. Hell, she sees him every damn day. If it was him . . .

But then again, Duke had seen the bastard several times and he hadn't once gotten that vibe off of him. Of course, he hadn't been able to fully rely on his instincts the entire time he'd been here. The few days they'd spent up near Palmer, his instincts had just about gone haywire on him.

Then there was the night the girl had died—he hadn't felt a damn thing.

Abruptly, he recalled how he'd automatically assumed it had been because of Ana. He knew better now and he'd just started thinking that maybe he wasn't meant to save that girl. It hadn't ever happened like that before, but it made a lot more sense than anything else he could think of.

Ana hadn't done it, so why else would he have just blanked out? Unless there really was another like Ana. Unlikely as it was, over the past few days, he was starting to realize that it had to be the case.

Unlikely as it was, Ana had stumbled across a serial killer with a gift way too similar to her own. It would explain so much—why he hadn't felt anything, why Ana wasn't affected as much up at Chugach—she'd been more immune to it, since she lived within her shields all the time.

With somebody else blocking him, possibly Carter, he wouldn't have felt anything until it was too late. More, if somebody was blocking him, it could keep him from picking up on the clues he'd normally follow. Leaving him in the dark.

Carter . . .

Was it possible she'd been living next to a killer for a

year without ever realizing it? Possible—well, hell. Yeah, it was possible. Those shields of hers—unless she was in physical contact with somebody, it definitely was possible that she wouldn't be picking up anything from the guy. If he'd been a threat to her, her instincts would have kicked in, but Ana didn't fit the profile of the guy's victims so there was little chance of him being a threat to her on that level.

He felt half sick even thinking it. His stomach knotted and he flexed his hands. His body wanted to shift so bad, it left his bones aching. He took a minute to drag in a couple of breaths, hoping to cool the rage. It didn't do much, but he did manage to get some measure of control back.

"You're sure you've seen him before?"

"Sure?" Ana repeated. She shrugged restlessly. "I don't know, Duke. But there's something about those eyes . . . no, I'm not *sure*, but I really think I've seen him before."

Duke ground his teeth together. It helped keep the growl locked in his throat. Still, his voice came out deeper, rougher, harsher than he'd intended. "But you don't know where?"

"No. No, I don't."

He scrubbed his hands over his face and swore. Now what? Did he tell her? And what if he was wrong?

Ana, I saw your landlord a few hours ago. He was sitting with a girl that looked enough like Marie to be her sister. I really don't know if there's anything to worry about, but . . . Yeah, that would go over real well.

"Fuck, ain't this going to be fun?" he muttered. "Okay, so here's what we need to do. We need to sit down and just make a list, I guess . . . " Actually, what he needed was for Ana to be distracted so he could either run a search on Carter himself or call somebody back at Excelsior to run it. Maybe a picture of the guy from twenty years ago—

Or you could just try telling Ana that you saw him with that girl, lay it out. See what she says.

Screw that idea. He wasn't going to get her pissed off at him unless he had a bona fide reason for it. He glanced up and realized Ana was watching him expectantly. Pinching the bridge of his nose, he said, "Shit, Ana. I'm sorry. I wasn't paying attention."

"I'd noticed. You've been acting a little off ever since you walked in the door." She quirked a brow at him.

Go ahead. Just lay it out.

No. Screw the voice of reason right now. He wanted the voice of facts before he went and did or said something that would make her mad—or hurt her. Scare her. Of course, he wouldn't be able to hide it if Carter was his man, but he'd damn well have a little bit of time to work out how to tell her. And maybe there wasn't even anything to tell. Heaving out a breath, he scrubbed a hand over his face and said, "Sorry. Distracted. All this shit's driving me nuts."

"You and me, both," she murmured. She leaned forward and kissed his chin, then settled back against the counter with her hands tucked inside her pockets. "Anyway, what I'd said was that I wanted to go back and talk to Marie's sister again."

Marie's sister? Duke frowned, thinking back. Vaguely, he had some memory of a discussion involving the murdered woman's sister. "Again . . . when did we talk to her the first time?"

"We didn't." Ana smiled. "I did. It was before you got up here. She couldn't really tell me much. But . . . I dunno. Maybe I wasn't asking the right kind of questions."

"So now you think you know what the right questions are?" The wheels in his mind started to spin. This could work—if he went, he'd know where the sister lived, and then track down a picture of Carter from twenty years ago, go back out and see her without Ana . . . maybe he could get lucky and the woman would know Carter, remember him from all those years ago—if it was him. That would be something linking them, at least, and he could decide what to do from there.

His gut insisted that Marie had known her killer, somehow. Okay. Yeah. This could work.

"I don't know if I know the right questions now, but I've got a better idea of what to ask at least. This might sound crazy, but I get the feeling that Marie somehow knew the guy that . . . well, the guy that killed her," Ana said in an eerie echo of his own thoughts. "I don't know how and I could be wrong. It's just a feeling I've got. But maybe if I describe the guy I remember from Leah's memories, maybe . . . I don't know. Maybe Beverly knew him, too."

Then Ana closed her eyes and sighed, her shoulders slumping. "We're putting an awful lot of hope onto *maybe*."

"You have to go with what you got, Ana." Closing the distance between them, he went to her and hooked an arm around her neck. She had some maybes—and he had a gut instinct. With any luck, one of them would pan out and they could actually get something accomplished.

He pressed a kiss to her brow. She snuggled up against him, rubbing her cheek against his chest. Duke's heart clenched inside his chest and he skimmed a hand up her back. Protectiveness, need, other crazy emotions he wasn't ready to examine just yet swamped him. Staring out the kitchen window toward her landlord's house, he told himself there was time.

They'd get this done—figure it all out. Then he could get to work on what to do about Ana.

CHAPTER 14

IT took them an hour to get out the door. Ana finished putting up the groceries after Duke said he needed a few minutes on the computer. Keeping an ear out to make sure she didn't get close enough to see the screen, he logged into his email and sent a note back to Excelsior. He needed information on Hoskins, and until he had something concrete, he'd rather not have Ana catch him digging around on the Internet looking for dirt on her friend.

The few minutes ended up being forty-five and by the time they climbed into the car, it was edging on three thirty.

"We're going to have to make this quick," she said as he pulled out of the drive. "She watches her granddaughter during the day and she isn't going to want to talk to us when her daughter comes to pick the girl up."

"Should we wait until tomorrow?" Duke shot her a glance. If they waited, maybe he'd get lucky and get something back on Hoskins—like a picture from twenty years ago. He could even figure out a way to show it to Ana, see if it matched the image she'd caught while Leah took her on a grisly trip down memory lane.

She smashed the plans even as they formed.

"No. I don't want to wait." Ana shook her head and fought the urge to nibble on her fingernails, squirm around in her seat or fidget with her hair. She was restless. The memory of those eyes kept nudging at her and she had a headache from figuratively pounding her head against the wall as she tried to figure out where she'd seen him before.

They pulled out of the drive just as a familiar motor- cycle pulled up. Ana absently waved at Carter as he turned into the drive. He slowed the bike but Duke turned out of the drive like he hadn't noticed. She glanced at him and rolled her eyes. The carefully blank look on his face some- how managed to speak very loudly.

"You really don't like that guy, do you?"

He shrugged. "I don't really know the guy, so I couldn't really say one way or the other, could I?"

"Now, Duke . . . that was actually very diplomatic. Especially for you."

"Diplomacy isn't my style."

No. It really wasn't. Still Ana had a feeling there was something that Duke wasn't telling her. She didn't have time to focus on that, though. Before she stepped inside Beverly's house again, she needed to bolster up her shields. She wasn't taking a chance of having any of the woman's grief filter through into her head again.

She needed to keep focused and it wasn't possible to focus with random thoughts dancing through her head or a storm of grief that threatened to blow her over.

Reaching out, she flicked on the radio and tuned it to a classical station. Duke rolled his eyes and started to change the channel. She slapped his hand. "Leave it alone."

"Hey, I'm the one renting the car."

Ana crossed her arms over her chest. "Too bad. I need to focus, want to layer on some extra shields. The last time I saw this lady, all the grief she had inside her hit me hard." Ignoring his scowl, she turned the radio up louder and leaned her head back against the padded headrest. It wasn't dark and quiet, but the classical music helped her block out everything else. It would have to work.

Thanks to road work and the summer traffic, it took close to thirty minutes to get to Beverly's. Ana used the time to reinforce her shields as solidly as she could. By the time she climbed out of the car, she was wrapped in a psychic cocoon so pervasive, so complete, she felt like she'd lost one of her senses.

She hated going around shielded like this—left her feeling too vulnerable. She wouldn't be playing unintentional voyeur, and she definitely wouldn't be giving off any psychic vibes, but it meant she couldn't pick them up, either. She was used to feeling . . . something.

Duke climbed out of the car and waited for her, staring up at the house with an unreadable expression. "You said you've been here before?" he asked, his voice tight.

She nodded. "Yeah. Not for long."

"Anything weird?"

"Weird? No. Just a woman who's still grieving for her sister, but that's not what I'd call weird." She glanced at him, and again, that preoccupied look on his face had her wondering what was going on. "Are you okay?"

He rolled his shoulders, rotated his head from side to side. "No. I dunno. Edgy. I've just felt a little off today, I guess. You feel anything?"

"I don't feel *anything*," she said. "I might as well be walking around wearing Bubble Wrap, I've got so much shielding up."

Duke eyed the house, wondering if this was really worth the waste of time after all. He had other things he wanted to focus on—other people, namely Hoskins. Although it had seemed a good idea back at Ana's, now he wasn't so sure. He didn't want to spend any time on this if it wasn't going to get them anywhere.

Somehow, he doubted it would. His instincts were

screaming, but they'd been doing that ever since Ana had told him she thought she'd seen the killer somewhere.

He didn't like this Nancy Drew and Hardy Boys shit anymore. Well, he hadn't ever liked it, but he was now in a state of serious hate. He wanted Ana out of there. Narrowing his eyes, he slid a look toward Ana and made a decision. She was leaving Alaska for a little while. It would take some doing, and she'd be madder than hell, but if he made some calls, exaggerated a bit while he explained he had his hands full and worrying about her wasn't helping, he could make it work. He thought.

But even as he made that decision, Ana was heading up the walkway. Toward the house.

Safe behind her shields, Ana rang the doorbell and waited. When Beverly opened the door, Ana didn't need to rely on her gift to let her know what the other woman was thinking—it was written all over her face—*Should have looked before I opened the damned door.*

Something kept her from closing the door on them, though. Ana didn't know if it was morbid curiosity or courtesy, but she was betting on courtesy.

"I should have known I wouldn't get lucky enough for it to be done with you, especially after Paul died," Beverly said. She glanced at Duke, curiosity lighting her eyes. "Who is this?"

"He's a friend," Ana said.

"A friend." She made no attempt to hide her skepticism. "I've had a good five people show up on my doorstep since Paul died, trying to get me to talk about what happened the summer that Marie died. Even though I don't *know* anything. Apparently some people think it might be *therapeutic* or give me some kind of *closure* to talk about my sister disappearing and speculating on some asinine newscast for five or ten minutes about how her disappearance has destroyed my family."

Beverly crossed her arms over her chest and glared at them. "If you're here thinking along similar lines, save us all the trouble and just leave. I'm not interested in being interviewed or reliving any of that time. Nor am I interested in speculating on how Paul managed to evade the authorities for so long."

"You and I both know Paul didn't hurt Marie," Ana said quietly.

Averting her gaze, Beverly said nothing.

"I thought you didn't believe Paul was guilty."

Beverly looked back at Ana, grief darkening her eyes. "I don't know what to believe now. I never could believe it was Paul—he wouldn't hurt a fly. But then cops find that girl's body, and his . . . what else should I believe?"

"I'd say trust your instincts. What do they say?"

Beverly took a deep breath and closed her eyes. When she looked back at Ana, there was some measure of peace in her dark gaze. "I say, somehow, they're wrong. But that means he's still out there, whoever he is. He's been out there all this time, killing girls that look like my sister. Destroying more lives."

She looked from Ana to Duke and then finally back at Ana. "I guess you should just come on inside. Although, honestly, I'm not sure what you think this is going to accomplish."

They followed her inside and this time, Beverly led them into the kitchen, gesturing to a long, narrow bar. "Have a seat. I've got water, soft drinks or coffee if you'd like some."

Duke asked for some water, but Ana declined. She suspected if she took so much as a single drink just then, she'd puke it back up. Her stomach was a mess. A tension headache had settled right at the base of her skull.

After giving Duke a bottle of water, Beverly said, "I'm going to pour myself a glass of wine. I think I'm going to need it."

Now a glass of wine, Ana might have gone for that, except she was the cheapest drunk in the world and even though the wine might steady her nerves, it would also loosen her tongue—and probably her control.

The last thing Beverly needed was for Ana to blurt out

something without thinking it through first. And the last thing Ana needed was shaky shielding. So no alcohol.

Ana and Duke waited in silence as Beverly poured herself a glass of wine and then settled on a stool across from them. "My daughter took her little girl on a last-minute vacation. After they found Paul . . . well, you know how some reporters are. They can be such vultures, always looking for a story. They tracked my Jeannette down at her work and started pestering her for an interview, took some pictures of her and little Marie when she came to drop her off. So she decided to take a week or so off.

"As much as I want my family gone until this dies down, I miss them . . . " Beverly swirled the wine in her glass, staring down into the deep red liquid, but somehow, Ana suspected the older woman wasn't interested in the quality of the wine. "Little Marie, she keeps me hopping. I didn't realize how much I'd miss the distraction of picking up toys and answering her ten thousand questions until Monday rolled around and they weren't here."

Ana hated small talk. But if she could put Beverly a little more at ease, it might help. She thought. She hoped. Forcing a smile, she reached out and tapped her finger against one of the framed pictures that adorned the countertop. "Is this your granddaughter?"

The older woman smiled. "Yes. That's my Marie."

"She looks a lot like you," Ana murmured. And like her great-aunt. It was in the shape of her eyes, the set of her mouth. When the little girl grew up, she was going to be a knockout.

"Some. But she actually looks more like her namesake than her grandmother. I've got pictures from when my sister was that age—the similarity is startling."

"Does your daughter look like your sister?" She reached for another picture, eyeing the young woman who held little Marie.

"No." Beverly sipped her wine. "She looks like her father."

Ana frowned, seeing little similarity between the willowy woman in the picture and Beverly's husband. Both were tall and slender, but that was it. "I'd say she looks more like you than Kyle."

"Kyle's her stepfather." Beverly smiled and lifted her wineglass. "Jeannette's father and I didn't marry. He was up here for just a summer. Once it was over, he left—he never knew I was pregnant, and I never bothered trying to track him down to tell him. It was . . . well, I guess a summer fling, and as much as I enjoyed my time with him, I didn't want to spend my life with him. He wasn't exactly what I'd call father or husband material. Of course, back then, I wasn't really parent material, either. Having Jeannette changed a lot of things for me. And I'm glad I never tried to locate her father after he left. I ended up married to a wonderful man who loved Jeannette like he was her own. And he got me through a very hard time in my life."

"Of course, he still has to hold me together. It's not over. I'm starting to wonder if it will ever be *over*. Every time somebody disappears, I think, *Is it the same one? The one that killed Marie?* This last time was the worst—finding out that Paul had died, it was almost as bad as the summer Marie disappeared." She sat her wineglass down and rubbed her eyes. "I can't stop thinking about it. About Paul. About Marie. About that summer."

"I can't imagine how hard this is," Ana said quietly. Her heart went out to the other woman and she wished there was something she could do. But the only way she could help was to help Duke find the man who did this, to keep him from hurting anybody else.

"I can't even describe it." Beverly reached for her wine and took another, longer sip. Followed by two more.

"After twenty years, you'd think I'd be a bit more used to it. Or that it wouldn't sneak up on me so easily, catch me by surprise and leave me this close to tears. Poor Kyle, he's been at his wit's end ever since I heard about Paul. He tries to keep me from thinking about it, and then when I can't help but think about it and I get upset, he's trying to comfort me and I think he blames himself for not doing a better job." She shook her head and murmured, "I never thought anything could be as hard as that summer. Never. But this is close. Very close."

"Is your husband here?" Ana asked. "I know you didn't want him knowing that you and I had talked."

"Kyle's in his office. He works at home, has his own consulting business. Of course, he hasn't been able to get a great deal done over the past few days, since he's had his hands full with me. I'm trying not to let it show, but he can always tell." Her voice went cool and angry. "He's got high blood pressure, had a mild heart attack a few years ago. He doesn't need this stress right now. God, does anybody ever need something like this in their life?"

Guilt sank in Ana's gut like a stone. No matter how this all played out, Ana didn't see much chance of doing anything to ease Beverly's pain. The only thing that would do it would be the knowledge that her sister's killer had been stopped. But that would mean letting her know what they were doing, it would mean finding some kind of proof, and somehow getting that proof into the right hands so mortal justice could deal with him.

Her instincts told her that this was going to end with the bastard dead. Dead people weren't questioned about murders or put on trial. So the answers Beverly needed may never come.

"Why don't you go ahead and explain why you're here," Beverly said. "More questions about Paul?"

"Not exactly." Ana licked her lips and shifted on the seat, glancing at Duke.

He wasn't looking at her. He was staring at the unopened bottle of water, focusing on it like he expected it to take flight or something. Something about that absolute focus had her instincts humming, but right now, she had to figure out how to get the information she needed from Beverly.

Focusing back on the older woman, she braced her elbows on the counter and leaned forward. She'd mentally rehearsed how to do this back at home but now, none of the questions she'd put together made sense. God, how was she supposed to explain she'd seen her sister's killer and that she needed help trying to figure out who he was?

Beverly continued to watch her and seconds stretched out.

"Ana, what's this about?"

"Do you believe in psychic ability, Beverly?"

It wasn't a question she'd planned to ask. It wasn't a question she'd wanted to ask. But it slipped out of her, almost of its own volition and now that it was hanging in the air between them, there wasn't a damn thing Ana could do to jerk it back.

Beverly blinked. "Ah . . . psychic ability?"

"Yes."

"Hmmm." She lifted her glass to her lips but put it down without drinking. "You mean like those *Ask your psychic friend* scams?"

"No. As in real ability. As in . . . "

Duke reached over and laid a hand on her thigh, squeezing. She ignored the warning, just as she ignored his intent stare. With him touching her, some of his thoughts still managed to filter inside her thick shields.

Harsh. Demanding. Intense. *Look at me!* She could all but feel the command. But she didn't dare. She couldn't really back out of this now unless she wanted to alienate Beverly and that wasn't about to happen.

"Psychic ability as in I think I've seen the man who killed your sister. But I don't know who he is. And I don't know if I can find him without some help."

The emotions flickering across Beverly's face ranged from grief and disappointment to outrage and disgust. A muscle twitched in her cheek and fury flashed in her eyes as she glared at them.

"Why do you people have to do this to us? God, this is my fault. I don't know why in the hell I thought you were better than the scum that keep after us."

Ana's belly went tight and blood rushed to her cheeks. "Beverly, please, listen to me. This isn't a sham and I'm not trying to do anything but help—"

Duke's hand came up, closing over her elbow. He squeezed tight. She shot him a pleading look—she didn't know if she wanted him to back her up, back off on whatever he was trying to project her way or just give her a few more minutes.

The look she saw on his face killed any thoughts of backing up or backing off. He stared at Beverly like she'd gone and sprouted a second head—a second head with a mouth full of daggerlike teeth.

Fuck. Something was wrong, she realized, staring at him. No wonder he'd been so damned quiet. No wonder he'd been projecting his thoughts so loud.

From the corner of her eye, she saw Beverly rising from her stool. "I want you to leave now, Ana. Leave, take him with you and don't come back." She pointed an arm toward the door and continued to glare at them.

Ana was having a hard time taking her eyes off of Duke, even when Beverly raised her voice and said, "I said *leave.*"

Duke growled.

Silence fell. Beverly, pale and startled, backed up a step. Ana reached up, covering the hand that still held her right elbow. She squeezed gently, unsure of what to do or how to handle a pissed-off shapeshifter. Of course, knowing what had set him off might help.

"Duke?"

The hand on her elbow tightened and he lowered his gaze to Ana. His eyes no longer resembled anything human. Ana hissed out between her teeth, staring into the swirling pinwheels of gray and black.

"Duke." She tried to put as much warning into her voice as she could, but she wasn't sure if anything could penetrate the fog of rage she sensed rising inside of him.

He spoke, and his voice, thank God, was relatively normal, just a little deeper, a little gruffer than normal. "We're leaving, Ana. Now."

Leaving? She wanted to argue. They couldn't leave. But Duke wasn't in any shape to stay. He looked like he was holding on to control with nothing more than will alone, battling back the beast she could see staring back at her from his eyes.

With little choice, she took her purse from the counter and slung it over her shoulder. She paused long enough to look at Beverly. "Regardless of what you think, all we want to do is help."

Beverly said nothing.

Ana wanted to say more, but Duke was urging her toward the front of the house—hell, screw urging. He was all but pushing her out the door with Beverly trailing along behind them. They were almost to the front door when Beverly's husband emerged from the depths of the house.

Duke went still. Slowly, he turned to face the other man and Ana turned with him. That heavy, choking sense of doom was back, ringing through her mind like a funeral dirge.

Kyle studied Ana through the lenses of his glasses, blinking in curious, owlish way, like he couldn't quite comprehend what he was looking at or where he was.

"Beverly?" Kyle said. "Is everything okay?"

"Everything is fine," Beverly said, her voice wooden. "They were just leaving."

Ana looked back at Beverly, then glanced at Kyle. Duke tugged on her arm, hard enough that she stumbled against him. Automatically, she flung out a hand and grabbed the edge of the wood-and-glass étagère that graced the entrance way. Pictures wobbled. One started to fall and she reached out to steady it.

And she found herself staring into *his* eyes.

Him—

Blood roared in her ears. Jerking her arm away from Duke, she grabbed the picture, stared at it. Dazed, she lifted her gaze and stared across the room. Into *his* eyes. Eyes hidden behind a pair of glasses, but they were the same damn eyes.

Screams rose in the depths of her mind, a cacophony that drowned out anything and everything else.

"Duke . . . "

His only response was a growl. He knew. He'd picked up on it way before she did and that was why he'd been trying to urge her out the door so fast, trying to get her out of harm's way, probably.

He moved in front of her, placing his body between her and the others. But Ana wasn't too into that idea. She moved back around him, staring at Kyle with horrified fascination. "You. It was you."

"Excuse me?" Kyle frowned at her, a puzzled, almost absent sort of frown. "Have we met . . . oh, wait. You're the student who came by last week, right?"

"She's not a student," Beverly said, her voice harsh, shaking. "You two need to leave."

But Ana couldn't have left that house just then if her life depended on it. "You killed her," she whispered. "You're the one who killed Marie."

Beverly stared at Ana, stunned and horrified. "That's an awful thing to say."

But Kyle was smiling. A humorless twist of his lips that did nothing to soften the ugly void she sensed inside him. "I knew you were going to be a problem," he muttered, smoothing a hand back across his thinning hair. "Even under all those shields of yours, I thought I felt something odd about you. Trouble. Nothing but trouble."

The smile he gave her was cold. "Just like that bastard, Paul. Always trying to interfere. Should have taken care of you the first day you came around here."

Duke edged in front of her one more time and this time, she was too dazed to even notice. Staring at the picture in her hands, she waited for her mind to catch up with what her instincts had already figured out.

It was a picture of Beverly and Kyle—at their wedding. Judging by the clothing styles, it was probably taken back in the seventies. Something on the frame caught her eye—a small piece of metal, engraved with the date August 16, 1975.

Eight months before Marie had disappeared.

Dear God. Beverly had spent more than thirty years married to the man who'd killed her sister.

He keeps looking for me, seeing me even though he's already killed me once, and he keeps trying to kill me again and again.

Ana could so clearly remember those words, like Marie was standing right there, whispering them to her. "Marie . . . "

As though simply saying her name had opened a door, Ana felt them. She shuddered as screams echoed through her memories. Shivered as the temperature in the room started to plummet.

It was them. All around her, she could hear the echo of ghostly sighs and wordless whispers. All of them, reaching out, to push against Ana's shields. Demanding entrance— no. No they didn't want inside her shields . . . or even inside her. They wanted her voice, wanted once more to settle within her body, but not for a jaunt down memory lane this time.

They wanted to confront their killer . . . using Ana as the conduit.

Thank God she'd added to her shields, because even the weight of their presence was painful . . . so many. All of them pushing at her. If her shields faltered and they slipped inside her . . . she shied away from that thought. It would be a bad thing . . . a very bad thing. Even if they didn't mean to hurt her, they would.

But her shields held, strong and steady, thanks to the extra work she'd put into them.

She took a deep breath, fought to settle her ragged nerves. She could handle this—Duke seemed to think she could, and it was about time Ana actually tried to be strong, instead of running away.

For Marie—

Marie . . . ?

Ana reached out, but she already knew the answer. Marie wasn't there. Somehow, Ana knew this man's first victim wasn't there. She couldn't be around him, couldn't find the strength to manifest around her killer. God, no wonder. It had been her sister's husband who'd done this to her.

Carefully, Ana placed the picture back on the shelf and looked around Duke's body, staring at Kyle. "You killed Marie," she said quietly.

Beverly shouted, "Don't say that!"

Kyle just smiled.

Save for the way the skin tightened around his eyes, there was no warning. Something slammed into Ana's shields with enough force, the impact sent her to her knees. Duke moved, all silent, feline grace, catching her and steadying her. He wasn't looking at her, though.

This guy felt all wrong. Duke stared at him, struggling with the animal inside. He was a tangle inside—part of him wanted to rip and tear, yet another part of him want to recoil. It wasn't fear, but some strange aversion he couldn't quite understand. He recognized it, though. It was the same way he'd felt a few days earlier as he and Ana prowled the forest paths in the Chugach Mountains.

The desire to leave was strong, but it warred with his own instincts, the part of him that looked at the older man in front of him and saw the threat.

The guy looked so fucking normal—like somebody's grandfather, like a preacher, like a doctor—somebody people looked at and just instinctively trusted. If it wasn't for the part of Duke that made him a Hunter, he just might have looked and trusted.

Hell, Ana had looked at him and trusted. She'd known this man, had met him before and nothing about him had set her instincts screeching. Nothing about him had penetrated her shields—the shields.

Fuck. The damned shields she'd lived behind were probably the reason, kept her from picking up stuff that might have clued her in before now.

Of course, those shields had also kept her from putting

out her own vibes. If this man had any clue about Ana's gift . . . No. He couldn't go there. Not now.

Distantly, he heard a woman's soft, erratic breathing, gasp and catch, like she was trying not to cry.

"Kyle?" Beverly whispered. The desperate plea in that simple word, it was so full of pain and grief.

From the corner of his eye, Duke watched as Beverly gazed at her husband. The blank look on his face had the woman utterly terrified.

The air suddenly was ripe with the stink of fear. Sharp and acrid, burning on the back of Duke's tongue and teasing instincts that were already working overtime.

Cold, too. Damn cold. The hair on his arms and the back of his neck stood straight up, but he didn't dare look around to try and see if Marie was here. Not that it would do any good—the ghost had already told them, she was useless against her killer.

Next to him, Ana shook, trembling in the cool air.

"Kyle, make them leave," Beverly said, once more pleading with him. She didn't want to believe it. Didn't want her head to accept what part of her had already figured out. "Make them stop saying these things."

He ignored her. Like she didn't even exist for him, he sauntered closer, watching Duke and Ana. He didn't seem to notice the chilly air, immune to it as he came to a stop just a few feet away. His smile, that friendly, affable smile, widened as Duke shifted to keep him away from Ana.

"I knew you'd be trouble," Kyle said again.

Curling his lip, Duke said, "You have absolutely no idea."

Kyle wasn't watching him, though. He was staring at Ana—like Ana was the threat. Like she was indeed some kind of problem.

Stupid bastard. Duke was the one who was going to be a problem. He was trouble—as a matter of fact, he planned on being more trouble than this sick bastard had ever dreamed of. The only thing that kept him from shifting and ripping Kyle's murderous heart out with his own claws was the fact that Beverly was still watching them with horrified fascination.

She watched them, and in her eyes was a growing understanding. Already her scent was changing, as disbelief and grief morphed into rage.

Shit, things were going to get bad fast if Duke didn't get it under control. Ana stood behind him, still half in shock if he was guessing right and Beverly was struggling to deal with everything playing out in front of her.

And Kyle—he just stood there, smiling. Duke watched him, felt something spike in the air, felt it flow toward them. Duke tensed, prepared for some sort of impact. Most psychics had gifts that worked more in a defensive manner, or were better suited to information gathering.

But on occasion, some of them had a gift that could be used to cause direct physical harm. Duke had a bad feeling this fuck was one of them. Duke was useless against psychic power, so his only chance would be to eliminate the threat before they got hurt.

He shifted, keeping his body between Kyle and Ana. Even as he tensed for impact, the tension in the air mounted. From behind him, Ana laid a hand on his shoulder and hissed out a breath. Nothing happened—no, not exactly right. There was no impact, but that mounting tension in the cold air remained, swelling to a crest before slowly fading away into nothingness. Kind of like he'd taken a walk outside in a downpour—he felt the impact of the rain glancing off the umbrella, scented it, heard it, but it failed to reach him.

It hadn't failed, though, whatever strike Kyle had flung at them. It had been blocked. Somehow, Ana had blocked it and Duke had a feeling it was because she'd deflected it with her own shields. It wasn't something she'd done without price, though. He could scent her pain. He didn't dare take his eyes off of Kyle, but the beast inside screamed in rage as he scented pain.

What the fuck—

It hit again, something massive, unseen. On his shoulder, Ana's hand tightened and this time, there was a bigger impact. Harder and stronger, enough to send him staggering back a step. Without looking away from Kyle, he reached out, brought Ana closer and steadied her body against his own.

Beverly, unaware of the unseen battle, finally managed to find her tongue and she stormed up to her husband. "What's going on, Kyle?" Her teeth chattered as she spoke and she had her arms crossed over her chest as though to warm herself.

Kyle reached out and stroked a hand down her hair, a gentle, loving gesture, one he'd probably done a thousand times during their marriage.

It happened quick—too quick—another psychic surge of energy came flying their way. Duke and Ana braced for another impact and that was when Kyle grabbed his wife and jerked her against him.

She cried out, startled, and then that startled cry turned to an outright scream, piercing and terrified, as her husband lifted his hand. In it, he held a knife. Poised at Beverly's neck, the silvery blade flashed light back at them.

Cold—a wind whipped through the room, like a blast straight from the arctic.

Duke growled, the muscles in his body tensing, preparing for action. The skin along his spine rippled and he fought against the Change, struggled to remain in his human skin. He couldn't spare the few seconds it would take to shift, not right now. But he didn't need to change to kill this bastard. He could do it just fine with his own two hands—

Ana caught his arm before he moved. "Don't," she whispered. "He wants you away from me. My shields aren't strong enough to cover you if you aren't touching me."

Divide and conquer—

"How strong is he?" Duke asked.

Her lips twisted. "Stronger than me. Better than me . . . I had no idea he had any sort of gift. I'm sorry."

Beverly struggled against Kyle, but the man's wiry body was stronger than it looked and he held her easily. Barely even seemed distracted by her struggles, because he managed to lob another psychic burst at them. It hit harder this time and Duke muffled a startled grunt as it hit him. Full-body, blunt-force impact, that's what it felt like. Ana cried out and swayed. If he hadn't had an arm around her waist, she would have gone down.

"Kyle, what are you doing?" Beverly asked, her voice trembling.

Kyle kissed Beverly's temple and murmured, "They want to ruin it. They want to keep me from finding her."

"Finding who?"

But Kyle didn't answer her question. Instead, he focused on Duke and Ana. "You should have just left me alone. Left us alone—I have to find her. She needs me."

"Don't you think you've found her enough?" Duke asked. When he spoke, his breath came out in heavy bursts of vapor. The room was now so cold, steam was rising off his body. Behind him, Ana was shuddering, shaking with cold. And distantly, like a forgotten song, he heard them.

Whispers. Moans.

From the corner of his eye, he glanced at Ana. Her gaze met his for the briefest second, but he saw it. She heard it, too.

Kyle frowned. "If I'd found her, I wouldn't still be looking for her." He sighed and nuzzled Beverly's hair. "I'm close. I know it. I can almost feel her . . . "

At first, Duke thought he was imagining it. A louder voice, familiar. One that had given him more than a couple of bad moments. *"Feel me, can he?"*

Ana tensed next to him. "Marie . . . "

Unaware of the voices, Kyle sighed and a dreamy look replaced that blank, disturbing look in his eyes. "Marie. She's so beautiful. So fragile and delicate . . . like an angel. I need to find her, protect her."

"Protect me."

Her voice echoed so loud, Duke and Ana flinched.

Beverly went pale. Duke didn't even have to ask—she'd heard the voice, too.

Judging by the wide-eyed look on Kyle's face, he'd heard it, too. But he didn't look as pale as death the way Beverly did. Tears flooded his eyes. A smile curled his lips. He craned his head around, searching the room. "Marie?"

While he was distracted, Duke edged a few inches away. Then the bastard's eyes cut back to his, scowling. "Where is she?"

"Where is who?" Duke blinked, feigning innocence.

"I heard her—I just heard Marie, calling to me, crying out." He looked down at Beverly and frowned. A confused look danced across his face. "I have to protect her."

"Protect me." A laugh, cold and icy as an Alaskan winter, echoed in the room, coming from all around. It bounced off the walls, growing louder and louder until abruptly, it ended. *"Protect me, Kyle. What are you going to protect me from?"*

Still standing frozen in Kyle's grasp, Beverly whispered, "Marie?" Her tear-filled eyes sought out Ana's, and Duke felt his heart break a little as the older woman asked, "Is that Marie? Or is this some kind of trick?"

Marie sighed. A sad, lonely sound. *"It's me, Beverly. Honey, I'm so sorry."*

"What's going on?" Beverly demanded. She jerked against Kyle's hold and his arm went tight.

Marie wailed. High and keening, it was the kind of noise that could keep a person from sleeping easily—or sleeping period.

Duke scented the blood before he saw it, dark crimson flowing against golden skin. His muscles tensed and under the weight of his anger, his control fell in shreds around him. The muscles in his hands shifted, reformed as the bones broke and realigned. The semi-shift was soundless and swift, taking but a few heartbeats. The pain of the shift was barely noticed, he was so fucking enraged.

Ana reached out, laid a hand on his arm when he would have attacked. "Don't."

"Don't?" Duke snarled.

"She's not hurt, not right now," Ana whispered, staring raptly at the woman and the psychopath who held her.

Fighting the rage, Duke focused on Beverly, listened to her heartbeat, eyed her color. The nick on her neck was small, bleeding freely, but it wasn't deep. Behind her, Kyle seemed mostly unaware of what was going on as he hauled Beverly backward with him, skirting the perimeter of the room as he called out for Marie.

She didn't answer, but Duke knew she wasn't gone. Neither were the others. He could hear them, feel them.

"Damn it, where is she?" Kyle demanded, pointing at Duke with his knife. "Did you hurt her?"

The smear of blood Duke glimpsed on the knife didn't do a damn thing to cool him down. In a harsh, barely intelligible growl, he said, "You're the only one who ever hurt her, you stupid, crazy fuck."

Kyle flinched. "That's not true!"

"You hurt her." It was Ana who spoke this time. "Just like you hurt the others."

"I didn't want to." Kyle squeezed his eyes closed, knocking against his temple with the hand he still had fisted around the knife.

Duke tensed and edged a little closer. But like the bastard had radar or the hearing of a shapeshifter, the faint sound Duke made had Kyle's eyes flying open while he edged farther away. "I didn't want to hurt her. But she wouldn't listen. Told me that she didn't love me, and she laughed, told me I didn't really love her. I couldn't let her keep saying that. Marie—Marie, where are you? Help me find you and I'll take care of you."

For the longest time, it was quiet. Duke and Ana waited while the tension built and Kyle continued to drag Beverly around the house. Beverly stumbled along with him, not fighting, not speaking. She stared ahead with a flat, blank expression that warned Duke they didn't have too much time, because the older woman was going into shock, in a big way.

"Where are you?" Kyle demanded, his voice growing angry.

"I'm right here."

She drifted into view and to Duke's surprise, she looked a hell of a lot more solid than she had the few times he'd seen her. Solid—almost real. Except she glowed. Except her body was a paler washout than she would have been if she'd really stood there.

"Hello, Kyle." Even her voice sounded—more real.

Kyle stared at her, his mouth falling open. "Marie . . . "

She glanced at Beverly and then looked back at Kyle. *"Why are you hurting my sister?"*

"Hurting . . . " He looked down, staring at Beverly like he couldn't quite believe what he was seeing. "I'm not— I'm not hurting her. I think . . . wasn't she trying to hurt you?"

"No," Marie said, her voice oddly gentle. Soft. Completely at odds with what Duke glimpsed in her eyes. Completely at odds with the frigid temperature of the room. If it got too much colder, it was going to be dangerous for Beverly and Ana. *"She wouldn't hurt me."*

"Somebody hurt you." Kyle lowered his gaze to Beverly's head, staring at her dark hair. He rubbed the back of his hand against her cheek, then caressed it with the flat of the blade. "I know somebody hurt you. I can still hear you screaming."

Kyle's breath left him in foggy little puffs, but he didn't seem to notice as he gazed at Marie with wide, worshipful eyes.

"I'm screaming because I'm scared. I'm scared of what you're trying to do to Beverly," Marie said.

"I won't hurt her."

"Then let her go."

That confused look crossed his face again and he looked down at Beverly, stroked her hair. Then, carefully—as though he had to concentrate on each movement, he let her go and stepped away.

Beverly stumbled and swayed. As she took a step, her eyes rolled backward.

Duke didn't wait two seconds. Before she could hit the ground, he caught her unconscious body in his arms and carried her across the room. The muscles in his back were tense, prepared and ready for a strike that never came. Laying her on the floor, he paused only long enough to check her pulse before he stood. Turning back, he stared at the scene before them.

Kyle, gazing at Marie, that empty, almost rapturous look on his face.

Marie staring at him.

And glowing . . . her body was rapidly losing its solid look, Duke realized. The gentle, understanding smile on her lips faded away, replaced by something hard and cold. *"You want me to stop screaming,"* Marie said, laughing coldly. *"Perhaps I could stop—once you start."*

Ana gasped next to him, her hand flying to grab his arm. Short, neat nails bit into his skin. He looked at her, watched as she stared at Marie and Kyle. "They want in."

"In . . ." They? Fuck. "They can do this without using you as a taxi this time."

"Not me. *Him.* But his shields are too strong." She shook her head. Mesmerized, she stared at Kyle. "So were mine. I had to lower them to let Leah in."

"Whatever you're thinking . . . don't," he warned.

A smile flirted with her lips and she looked at him. "His shields are stronger than mine . . . but there are more of them. So many of them." She caught her lower lip between her teeth. "If I can blunt your abilities when I'm blocking, maybe I can block his."

"Bad idea, Ana." Duke shook his head. She'd have to lower her shields, and he wasn't taking a chance with a bunch of vengeance-hungry ghosts hovering around them. If they decided to hitchhike a ride in her . . . no fucking way. "Besides, you don't even know if it will work on somebody who's got a gift like yours. And what if he fires it back at you?"

Ana slid a look toward Kyle. "He's a little preoccupied." Then she closed her eyes.

Duke felt something shift around her and he growled. "Ana, don't!"

She wasn't listening, though and he grabbed her, hauled her against him as the moans in the air rose. From the corner of his eye, he could see them. Insubstantial, wavering shadows, pressing close and closer, bearing down on Ana.

"Not her," he snarled.

They stilled. Oddly enough, they stilled. He felt their hesitation and he cut his eyes toward Kyle. "Isn't *he* the one you want?"

They swarmed toward him and Duke could only hope it worked. Ana shuddered in his arms and lifted her head just as the first shadow drew close. Kyle was still staring at Marie, although she became harder and harder to see with every second that passed. But then he flinched.

Duke's breath hissed out between his teeth as he watched.

One after another, the shadows descended on Kyle and his body began to spasm and shake. Four . . . five . . . eight . . . nine . . .

Kyle's head jerked back, the cords in his neck standing out in stark relief. His eyes were wide and his mouth was opened in a silent scream. And Marie stood in front of him, staring at him.

Spittle sprayed out of his mouth as he reached toward the ghost. "Help . . . help me!"

Marie ignored him, turning to look in Ana's direction. She turned her back on the man who'd taken her life and drifted toward them in a graceful, eerie glide. *"All these years, I thought I'd laugh. Thought I'd dance. If I ever had the chance to see this end, I'd want to celebrate."* As she sighed, her form wavered in and out of view.

Behind her, Kyle's body, still upright, jerked about, seizure-like. He stared at them, helpless, confused . . . and aware. "Help . . . " he whispered again.

Duke drew Ana close. When Marie came back into

view, they focused on her, ignoring the man behind her. "It's over," Duke promised. "I'll make sure of it."

Marie smiled. *"No. They are making sure of it."* Even as she spoke the words, Kyle sagged to the ground, swaying on his knees for a few moments before crashing backward.

His color was bad, going gray quick. His breathing began to hitch inside his throat, and Duke could hear the man's heart as it started to falter. *Death by ghost*—that's a new one.

It seemed to last forever. And no time at all.

Duke heard it when the man's heart beat its last. His eyes stared lifelessly up at the ceiling and one by one, the souls that had settled inside him came drifting out. They hovered around his body in a shifting, insubstantial circle.

"It's done now," Marie said, her voice flat.

They echoed her in whispers and sighs—sighs that ended abruptly. As one, they looked up. A ring of light hovered above them.

Ana wrapped her arms around his waist and held him tight. Duke bent his head and pressed his lips to her crown, squeezing his eyes shut. Done . . . it was done. Through their clothes, he could feel her heart slamming away against her ribs—beating every bit as fast as his own, he figured. Yeah, give him a psychotic feral vamp over ghosts any day.

"They're leaving," Ana whispered, awed.

Startled, Duke looked up. "Son of a bitch."

They *were* leaving. One by one, each of them drifted into the circle of light until only Marie remained.

She lingered next to Ana for endless moments and then she sighed and started forward.

Behind them, there was a soft moan. Then Beverly's voice. "Marie?"

Such a familiar voice. Marie didn't know how much time had passed since her death—time lost meaning once the heart stopped beating. But it had been a while, a long while, she decided as she turned and faced her sister. Years upon years, because Beverly looked old.

She summoned up every last bit of her fading strength and focused. Bit by bit, her body became more substantial—or at least, she knew it looked that way.

"*Hi, Sis,*" she said, and she was startled at how *real* her voice sounded.

"My God, how can this be?"

Marie shot a look over her shoulder, staring at Kyle's body. Kyle—she cut her thoughts off before the pain could rip through her. It was over. It was done. He couldn't hurt Marie anymore. But this would continue to hurt Beverly. Poor Beverly . . .

"*I don't know,*" Marie said. She didn't, not really. She knew it had to do with how she'd died, but she didn't understand why she'd lingered for so long. Why she hadn't been able to move on. That was done though. Without understanding how, she knew it. Something was calling her. Pulling her. And faintly, she thought she heard another voice, whispering her name. "*And I don't really think I have the time to explain.*"

Beverly's face crumpled and she looked beyond Marie to stare at Kyle. "Kyle. It was really him?"

"*I'm sorry.*" Another pull, this one harder, stronger. Commanding. She shuddered and felt it as she started to fade away again. With one desperate attempt, she pushed herself back and faced Beverly. "*It's over now, Sis. Over and done . . . don't let this tear you apart now.*"

And then she couldn't fight it any longer. The warmth drew her and after being cold for so long, she didn't even *want* to fight it.

A NA nibbled on her thumbnail as the cop continued to speak with Beverly. Duke sat next to her, silent, and listening to the conversation taking place fifteen feet away.

So far, the older woman hadn't said much of anything that could cause problems, but Duke wasn't going to bank on their luck holding there. Already, he had a plan. If they got arrested, they'd get a call. One call was all it would take and this whole mess would be done.

But if it happened, Ana would have to leave Alaska. If she disappeared from jail, her face would be everywhere. The Council could and would clean the mess up but still, Ana wouldn't be able to come back here for a good long time.

Oddly, he couldn't find a whole lot of joy in that, though. She loved it here. He didn't want her to lose that.

Behind them, the door to Beverly's house was closed. The house was empty and silent. The oppressive weight that weighed down on his shoulders was gone, and so was the edgy, driving need that had been shouting warnings at him. Warnings he hadn't focused on, because he'd been too convinced he knew who the killer was.

He hadn't expected to see a threat here and Kyle had made damn sure that nobody could sense anything. Thank God the bastard hadn't counted on Ana and her ghostly accomplices.

It really was done.

He reached up and rested a hand on Ana's back, stroking it up and down. She leaned into him and he wrapped his arms around her, pulling her close. He needed the contact just then. Needed to touch her.

"What's going to happen?" she asked quietly.

Duke glanced at the back of the ambulance, watching as one of the EMTs hopped out. "The EMTs think it was a heart attack. Makes sense that's what they'll find. His heart just gave out—I could hear it. It's not like he's young. Heart attacks are pretty commonplace. So it all depends on Beverly."

"I don't know if that's good news or not," she muttered. Her shoulders rose and fell on a sigh as she stared at the emergency vehicles parked in front of the house. "Either she lies or she tells the cops that her husband was killed by some angry ghosts because he was a killer."

Duke rubbed his cheek against her head. "It will be okay. Just do me a favor—*if* by chance she mentions anything about ghosts, psychics, that sort of thing and the nice police officers decide we need to go in for questioning—play dumb. Act like you have no idea what they are talking about. And don't worry. If this ends up causing problems, I'll take care of it."

"Go in for questioning—that's something I don't even want to think about." She stirred in his arms and looked up at him. "Exactly how will you take care of it, though?"

"Remember that clandestine, uber-rich assembly of superheroes?" he asked teasingly. "They come in handy from time to time. We get tripped up from time to time. They won't leave us hanging because we got in trouble doing what we're supposed to do."

"I'm not part of that, Duke. They've got no responsibility to me."

He cupped her chin in his hand when she would have looked away. "You really think they'd leave you hanging, Ana?" There were other things he wanted to ask, wanted to say . . . like, *You're part of me, does that count?* But this wasn't the place. Wasn't the time.

"Probably not," she said, her mouth curving in a bitter smile. "Although I doubt any of them will be real happy that I'm causing them even more problems. After all, I'd probably be considered one hellacious liability if I ended up in jail."

"You're not a liability." His hand tightened and then fell away. "And *you* didn't cause this. I won't let you catch trouble over it."

CHAPTER 15

H E was gone when she woke.

Ana lay in the bed, painfully aware of the fact that she was alone in her apartment. She closed her eyes and took a deep breath, tried to breathe through the hideous pain spilling through her. But even the simple act of taking a breath hurt—hurt like fire, hurt like a razor slicing through her. Each beat of her heart was agony. Each movement was hell.

Slowly, she sat up. Drawing her knees to her chest, she tried not to let herself be surprised. She'd known this was coming. The job was done.

It really was over.

It had been three days since Kyle Hartwick's death.

The day before, Ana and Duke had driven back up to Palmer. Ana could still feel something in the forest, but it had been faint, so much weaker than before. And Duke had been able to track it. She'd trailed along behind him and wasn't the least bit surprised when he left the marked trail.

Nor had she been surprised when he came to a halt and said, "There are bodies buried here."

"Bodies?"

"Yeah."

She hadn't asked more than that. He hadn't offered. As they left the trail, he had written notes, documenting directions down on a piece of paper, making note of the trail and how far they'd walked before they left it.

He'd send an email, he had said. Or an anonymous call. The bodies would be found. Maybe they could even find something linking them back to Kyle and get real closure. Something concrete, something other than Ana's insight into what had happened.

"So it's done?" she'd asked late last night.

"Yeah. It's done. We did it, Ana."

Done . . . so there was no reason for him to stay any longer.

Kyle Hartwick was being buried in a few days. The official cause of death, thanks to Duke doing some nosing around, was a heart attack, so they were clear. Of course, Ana still worried that Beverly would suddenly decide to tell people about the ghosts, or about how Ana spilled her guts about psychics . . . or even about Duke and his weirdly glowing eyes.

But it really was over.

That heavy oppression that had weighed down on her for the past few weeks was gone. That feeling of impending doom had disappeared.

If it wasn't for her broken heart, Ana would probably feel okay. Maybe even a little satisfied that she'd helped Marie.

But she couldn't feel anything beyond the ache in her chest. Duke had left . . . and he hadn't said so much as good-bye. She swallowed the knot in her throat and tried not to cry. Took a deep breath, then another—but before she could manage a third deep breath, she started to sob.

He was gone . . .

DISTANTLY, she heard the phone ring, but it barely registered.

Some time later, there was a knock at the door. She had half a mind to ignore it, but as the knocks grew more and more demanding, she figured she needed to get up, if for no other than reason than to make whoever the hell it was go away.

And turn off her cell phone, she thought, as it started to ring.

Dragging herself out of bed took more energy than she thought she had. Dragging on a robe and tying it took more coordination than she could manage. But the diligent thought each action required was a bit of a blessing—she managed to go twenty whole seconds without thinking about Duke.

There was one more knock, harder than the others. "I'm coming, I'm coming," Ana muttered, shoving a hand through her disheveled hair. She used the sleeve of her robe to wipe the tears off her face but she didn't care enough to do much more than that.

She opened the door but there wasn't anybody there. Frowning, she leaned forward and glanced down the staircase. Her eyes landed on Beverly's back. "Beverly?"

The older woman paused near the bottom, her hand resting on the banister.

Edging out onto the small landing in front of the door, Ana crossed her arms over her chest, feeling ridiculously self-conscious. Red-faced, eyes swollen, her hair was a mess and all she had on was a T-shirt and a robe.

"Ana." Beverly turned and faced her, a wry smile appearing on her face. She started back up the stairs. She had a black tote bag in her hand. "I knew I wouldn't be lucky enough for you to not be home."

Ana wanted to recoil just at the sight of the bag, although she had no idea why. Tearing her eyes away from it, she looked at Beverly instead. "Ahhh . . . do you want to come inside?"

"Yes, please."

Ana left her unexpected guest in the small kitchen while she went back to her room and tugged on a pair of jeans.

She almost pulled the shirt off, but she couldn't—it was Duke's. She wasn't quite ready to separate herself from it yet. Later. She did take a few minutes in the bathroom to brush her hair and wash her face.

When she left the bathroom, Beverly was sitting at the table with her hands folded neatly in front of her and the black tote laying several feet away. From the way the other woman carefully avoided looking at it, she suspected she wasn't the only one who didn't want to look at whatever it held.

"How did you know where I lived?" Ana asked.

Beverly smiled. "The police report. I've driven by here a couple of times. I think part of me was hoping that you'd lied about your address—then I wouldn't have to see you. Plus, if you'd lied about your address, I could pretend you'd lied about other things."

Ana swallowed, unsure what to say.

"But you didn't lie, did you?"

She shook her head.

"It really would be easier if I could convince myself that you had." Beverly sighed, her shoulders slumped. She closed her eyes and for a minute, both women were silent. Beverly looked back up, her eyes red-rimmed and puffy. Her warm golden skin had a sallow look to it and there were dark circles under her eyes.

"I wish I was lying—I wish none of this was the truth."

"If wishes were horses . . . " Beverly mused. "Well. They aren't. The truth is what it is."

She gestured toward the tote at the other end of the table. "I spent most of yesterday gathering up every last thing that belonged to Kyle—I was going to have one very nice fire in the backyard. Then I found that."

"What is it?" Ana asked, wary. She suspected she really didn't want to know. And she also suspected it really didn't matter. Beverly wanted her to know.

"Souvenirs." Her voice shook. "Even if I could have convinced myself you were lying, it wouldn't have lasted, not once I found that. Marie's ring is in there—Paul gave her that ring. She wouldn't have parted with it for the world."

Ana stared at the tote, blood roaring in her ears. She really, really didn't want to look inside. Swallowing, she looked at Beverly and asked, "What are you going to do with it?"

"Take it to the police." She lowered her eyes to the table, studying her hands.

"Are you sure you want to do that?" Ana asked gently. "You know what will happen. People will find out . . . your daughter, your granddaughter . . . everybody."

"Oh, I'm well aware." Beverly laughed. The sound bordered on hysteria. "Believe me. I spent most of last night trying to decide what to do. But in the end . . . " A sob escaped.

Helpless, Ana gazed at her and tried to decide what to do. In the end, she did nothing, waiting as Beverly took a deep breath and composed herself. "Would you like some water? Some tea?"

"I'd rather have whiskey, but I need a clear head to get through this." She gave Ana a weak smile. "I know what's going to happen. But I also know I've spent thirty years wondering what happened. Why. Who. I can't condemn other people to that. If I *don't* take this in, those poor families will just keep on waiting. They deserve to know."

"I wish I could be that strong," Ana said sadly.

"You think you'd do it differently?"

Ana smiled bitterly. "Oh, I'm pretty certain I'd do it differently. Strength isn't really my strong suit."

"I think you'd surprise yourself," Beverly replied. "It took strength to do what you did."

"I didn't really do that much. Duke—"

"Your friend wasn't there the first time you came to see me, Ana. Whatever led up to this, I don't know. And honestly, I don't want to know. But you can't convince me that you don't have strength, not after what you did." She glanced around the small apartment and asked, "Where is he?"

"Gone." Ana pushed back from the table, unable to stay still. She would have preferred to run back inside her room and hide, but she settled on going into the kitchen and making some tea. Even if Beverly didn't want any, it gave Ana something to do with her hands.

"Gone—I get the feeling he's not gone to the store, is he?"

Ana looked up over the breakfast bar and met Beverly's sympathetic gaze. "No. He's not gone to the store. He's just gone—he came here to help me take care of this. Now that it's done, there's no reason for him to stay around."

"I guess that explains why you look so miserable."

"I guess it does." Silence stretched out as Ana made two mugs of tea. The sweet scent of cinnamon and cloves filled the air as she put the mugs on a platter, added the bowl of sugar and the small container of half-and-half from the refrigerator.

"Does he know how you feel about him?" Beverly asked as Ana settled back down at the table.

Flushing hotly, she busied herself with adding sugar and half-and-half to her tea, making it even sweeter than she usually drank it. Curling her hands around the cup, she darted a quick look at Beverly and tried to decide how to answer that.

"He doesn't, does he?"

"No." Ana lifted the mug to her lips, even though it was too hot to drink. She breathed in the warmth and wished it could do something to ease the chill inside her.

"If you'd rather I not pry . . . "

Ana snorted. "Beverly, considering what I've done to your world in the past few days, it would be pretty shitty of me to get upset, wouldn't it?"

"But you didn't do it to my world, Ana. I was living a lie, living with—" Her voice broke off and she blew out a harsh breath. "I still can't believe it. I've been married to the man who murdered my sister. *You* had nothing to do with that, Ana. You might have been the one to bring the truth to light, but it was the right thing to do. Besides . . . I got to see Marie once more. There have been times when I would have given anything to have that, to see her just once more, to tell her . . . so many things. I didn't get the chance to tell her all the things I wanted to tell her, but she's at peace now. Isn't she?"

"I think she is."

Beverly nodded. "She is. She has to be. And that means a great deal to me."

She sipped from her tea, although Ana had a feeling she did so more out of a need to be polite than anything else. Beverly's gaze bounced back and forth between Ana and the black tote.

"Do you want to look inside?" she finally asked.

"I'd rather not." Ana barely managed not to shiver. "But if you think I should . . . ?"

"It's entirely up to you." Beverly took one more sip and then stood.

"If you don't want me to look, then why did you bring it by?"

The older woman shrugged. "Perhaps I just wanted a reason to knock on the door. To see if you really did live here—and maybe I needed to see your face again, to make sure I didn't imagine the kindness I thought I saw in you. I'm glad to know I didn't."

Ana blushed.

"I'm going to take this to the police station now." She took a deep breath.

Bracing herself, Ana knew, bracing herself to do something very, very hard. "Would you like some company?"

Beverly laughed. "Actually, yes, I would. But I'm not going to ask you. Nor do I want you to offer." She reached for the bag, holding it gingerly, careful not to let it touch her body. "Please don't take this wrong, but I get the feeling its best if the cops know as little about you and your friend as possible. Am I right?"

"Ahhhh . . . " The spit in Ana's mouth dried up and for the life of her, she couldn't think of a damn thing to say.

Laughing, Beverly murmured, "That's what I thought. Don't worry, Ana. They won't hear anything from me about you or him." She headed to the door but halfway there, she turned back. "I'm leaving Alaska. I haven't decided when, or where I'm going to go, but I don't want to be here anymore. I think my Jeannette and little Marie will come with me, although I can't be certain. Nonetheless, I'm ready to leave here. I won't be seeing you again. And although I don't blame you, I'm very glad of that."

Ana couldn't blame her a bit. She followed her to the door and watched as Beverly headed down the steps.

At the bottom, she stopped once more and looked back up at Ana. "You really should tell him how you feel, Ana."

Then she left, climbing into her car. Ana watched as Beverly drove away and once the car turned out of the driveway, she slid back inside the house and closed the door. Leaning against it, she stared at her small, empty apartment.

Empty.

Shoving off the door, she paced over to the breakfast bar, staring at her phone. A little red *1* flashed at her, but she ignored it. Should she call him? Tell him?

No. She really shouldn't.

There was just no point.

She turned the ringer off, and for extra measure turned off her cell phone. Then she went back to bed.

I T took a hell of a lot longer than Duke had thought it would, and he still didn't get as much done as he'd planned on. Too damn bad, though, because he wasn't going to stay away from Ana for any longer.

And the first thing he was going to ask was where in the hell she'd been all day and why she wasn't answering her damn phone.

As he turned into the drive, the sight of the lights on in her apartment eased the huge knot in his gut. He parked his new Jeep Grand Cherokee in the driveway and climbed out. The first thing he'd done that morning was return the rental. If he was going to be staying in Anchorage, he wanted his own vehicle. Somehow or other, he'd have to get his bike up here, but he'd worry about that later.

All sorts of little details he needed to take care of, things he'd planned on doing today, but time got away from him. Getting the Jeep had been the most important, followed by some calls back to Excelsior to help with other technicalities.

He and Ana were going to need a bigger place—one away from Carter Hoskins, preferably—the guy still set Duke's teeth on edge, even though it wasn't anything other than possessiveness.

Getting a house required all sorts of information, paperwork, a work history, credit history . . . all sorts of shit.

All of it had been previously arranged and in a few days, he would be ready to do the next thing. He'd already found a place—at least he thought so. He had to make sure Ana liked it, too. Realistically, he knew it might not be as easy as all of that, but he'd cross that road when he came to it.

For now, all he could think about was how perfect she'd look in that house.

Aside from the house, the Jeep, getting the wheels in motion to settle down here, there was another important matter that had taken up half of his afternoon—notifying the police about the bodies he sensed buried in Palmer. That had taken a little bit more doing, and in the end, he'd settled on another call back to Excelsior. Let them handle taking care of the anonymous tip. Duke didn't have so much as a laptop up here and he wasn't sending it from Ana's, either. Not considering the stuff the cops could do with technology these days.

Too much of the day gone, though. Nearly four o'clock. It had been an hour since he'd tried calling Ana at home— no answer, just like the other four times he'd called. He'd called her cell three times and each time, it had gone into voice mail.

He loped up the steps and used his spare key to unlock it. It was quiet. Distantly, he could hear Ana, her breathing slow and steady. Sleeping? Frowning, he crossed the floor and paused by the counter. Her cell phone was there, turned off. A red, digital 5 flashed at him from the cordless phone.

Dropping his keys on the counter, he headed down the hall.

She was sleeping, all right, curled up in a ball with her back away from the door. He paused in the doorway, uncertain if he should wake her or not. If she was that tired, maybe he should just be nice and let her sleep. They could always talk later, right?

Screw being nice.

Silently, he slipped out of his shoes, jeans and T-shirt. She could sleep. That was fine. But she'd do it while he was there with her. He circled around the bed and slipped under the blanket, stretching his length out next to her. His heart froze in his chest as he caught sight of her face. Her eyes were red and puffy—had she been crying?

He forgot about his intentions to let her rest. Reaching up, he cupped her cheek and rubbed his thumb over her lip. "Ana?"

Still sleeping, she sighed, a soft, shuddery whisper of sound. She rubbed her cheek against his palm. Her breath caught, hitched in her throat.

For reasons he didn't really understand, his heart started to ache. Leaning in, he pressed his lips to hers. "Ana."

She murmured his name against his mouth.

Duke lifted a hand and rested on her thigh, easing it up over her hip, then to her waist. He rested it there, on that soft curve and kissed her again. "Ana."

S HE was dreaming.

Ana knew she was dreaming.

She also knew she didn't want to wake up. Duke was here, in her dreams, lying next to her and his long, warm body managed to chase the chill from hers. If she woke up, he'd be gone, she'd be alone and cold.

So logic dictated she just not wake up. At least not yet. Not until she had to.

But dream-Duke seemed to want her awake. He kept

whispering her name and kissing her, soft, teasing little kisses. "Wake up, princess."

"Don't wanna," she muttered truculently.

He laughed and whispered, "Why not? Come on, Ana . . . open your eyes."

He wouldn't quit. Her logic made perfect sense to her. If she woke up, he'd disappear. But he didn't seem to get the point and kept nagging her, and nagging her . . .

Then he slid a hand up and cupped her breast. Sighing against his lips, she arched into his touch. That was better. Definitely better. Dream sex was better than waking up, any day of the week.

She reached for him, her fingertips grazing over the hard, naked muscles of his chest, the sculpted lines of his belly. He groaned as she closed her hand around his cock, then he rolled on top of her, kissing her hard and quick.

"You going to wake up?"

"Make love to me," she whispered, refusing to listen to him talking about waking up. She'd have to wake up sooner or later, no reason to do it now.

"Not until you wake up," he muttered, his voice a harsh, rough growl.

His lips covered hers and she opened for him, but he didn't have a soft, seductive kiss in mind. Not even a deep, demanding one. He didn't kiss her at all. He bit her lip, hard enough to sting and the shock of it had her eyes flying open.

The dream fell apart around her and she could have cried—but then her eyes focused and she saw Duke above her, his sandy hair falling into his face as he stared down at her.

"Duke?"

He dipped his head and nuzzled her neck. "You sound surprised . . . were you expecting somebody else?" But he kissed her before she could answer, kissed her—and pushed inside, driving deep until he'd buried every last inch of his throbbing length inside her.

When he would have lifted up to look at her again, she

locked her arms around his neck. Clinging to him, desperate. Kissing him, starving.

Not a dream. That was all Ana could think. *Not a dream—he hadn't left.*

She didn't know what that meant, except maybe he just hadn't gotten tired of her yet. But she wasn't going to think about that—not when she had those big, hard hands gliding over her body, cupping her hip, her bottom, palming her breasts. Not when he kissed her, those deep, hot kisses that made her feel as though he wanted to gorge on her taste. Not when he moved above her, riding her, pushing her higher . . . and higher . . .

Tears burned, slipped out from under her closed eyes. She didn't care. He lifted his head, made a rumbling sound deep in his chest—a wordless question. Then he kissed her tears away, catching them with his lips.

"My Ana," he whispered. "Mine . . . "

"Yours." *For as long as you want me* . . . before she could say those words out loud, she pressed her lips to his. "Kiss me, Duke."

Warm hands, strong and calloused, stroked her body, fisting in her hair and arching her head back as he pressed kiss after ravenous kiss to her mouth. Gliding down her side, palming her ass and canting her hips higher, taking her deep, but so slow. So slow . . .

She raked her nails down his back and arched, grinding her hips against his.

"Such a hurry," he teased.

Ana stared at him from under her lashes, watching him as she clenched down around him, milking his length with her inner muscles. Duke groaned and arched his back, shuddering.

She did it again.

He swore.

Again and again.

He growled.

Again.

He slammed into her. Hard and fast, shafting her,

riding her, possessing her. Ana whimpered his name, then screamed it. He slid a hand between them and pinched her clit, then stroked it, teasing the little bud of flesh. Her breath froze in her chest—she couldn't breathe. Couldn't breathe.

The orgasm ripped through her, starting in her womb and rippling outward, spreading through her, filling her. Then Duke buried his face against her neck. She wailed out his name, just as he whispered—

Her brain didn't process what he'd said right away. Hard to think when the body was all but wracked with pleasure. But as she drifted back down to earth, the words started bouncing off of each other, back and back, rattling around until finally they connected and made sense.

As he rolled off of her body, she went stiff. He settled on his back but when he reached for her, she jerked back and scrambled down to the foot of the bed. Once she had a few feet between them, she settled back on the mattress and drew her knees to her chest. She licked her lips—her mouth, how had her mouth gotten so dry?

"What did you say?"

Duke stared at her, his lids low over his eyes. "Huh?"

Ana scowled at him. "What did you say to me?"

The muscles in his torso shifted as he pushed up onto his elbows. "I didn't quite plan for it to come out like that."

Her heart sank to her knees. Fighting not to cry, she slipped out of the bed and grabbed her T-shirt from the floor.

Duke watched her. She could feel it as he tracked her every last move. When he slid out of the bed, she sensed him approaching even though she couldn't hear him. Only seconds before he went to put his hands on her shoulders, she stiffened because she knew it was coming.

"You don't have anything to say?" he whispered, brushing a kiss over her shoulder.

She gave him what she hoped was a casual smile. "There's nothing to say. People say stupid things all the time and they don't mean any of them. Don't worry—I'm not going to hold you to it."

"Stupid things," he repeated.

"Hmmm." She eased up from under his hands and headed to her dresser. She needed a shower. Needed a drink. Needed to get him out of her house before she broke.

But Duke wasn't too interested in letting her put any distance between them. Even as she tried to slip away, he caged her up against the dresser. "People say stupid things they don't mean," he said, echoing her words.

"Yes. Don't worry about it. Look, I've had a rough day. I'm tired, I've got a headache and I need a shower."

Her words had no effect. He leaned into her, pinning her body between his and the dresser at her back. "What about words they do mean?"

Ana froze in place. He dipped his head and nipped her chin. *Words they do mean*—This was too damn cruel.

He continued to stare at her expectantly, but she didn't know what he wanted to hear from her, what he wanted her to say, what he wanted her to do. He caught a stray lock of hair and brushed it back from her face, tucking it behind her ear. "What's wrong, Ana? Why do you look so scared?"

"I'm not scared," she said. And she didn't lie. She *wasn't* lying. She wasn't scared—he didn't mean it, so what was there to be scared of?

"Then what's wrong?" Duke asked, getting frustrated. He hadn't meant just to blurt it out like that, but he wasn't going to take it back or apologize. He didn't see the point. She felt something, a whole hell of a lot of something, if he trusted what his gut said when she looked at him.

"Nothing's wrong," she said as she untangled herself from his arms. "It's just been a crazy couple of weeks, and the past few days, they've just been insane. I'm tired. I'm ready to relax. I'm ready to get back to my life."

"Is that why you were crying earlier?"

She went stiff and under that deep, insightful gaze, she felt the rush of blood rising to her cheeks. "Why do you think I was crying?"

He reached out, trailed a finger over her eyes. "Maybe

I'm psychic," he teased. He slid his arms around her waist and drew her close. "Why were you crying?"

She swallowed, searching desperately for something that would explain the tears, something that wasn't truth, but wasn't lie, either. If she lied, he'd know. "Maybe things are just catching up to me," she hedged.

But he didn't buy it. "That's why you were lying in here, crying and not answering the phone all day? I kept trying to call."

"You did?" Startled, she looked at him.

He frowned down at her. "Of course I did." His eyes narrowed on her face.

"I . . . I thought you were—" *Shut up. Deal with it when it happens.*

"Thought I was what?" he demanded.

Twisting out of his arms, she said, "Nothing. Don't worry about it, Duke."

"No, I think I will worry about it. You thought I was what?"

Gone. She squirmed in his arms and pressed against his chest. "Damn it, Duke. What does it matter?"

But he wasn't going to let it go, no more than he was going to let *her* go. He kept her locked against his body, and considering how he had his hips wedged against hers, she could tell that her wiggling around wasn't leaving him unaffected. Her belly clenched at the warmth of his cock as it cuddled against her belly and she tried not to shudder in reaction.

"It matters," he murmured. His voice went low and rough as he added, "I think it matters a lot."

Ana swallowed the knot in her throat. Lowering her gaze, she stared at his chest. "I thought you were gone, okay?"

"Gone." He threaded a hand in her hair and tugged, angling her head back so that their gazes met. "You mean—gone. Like leaving-on-a-jet-plane kind of gone, don't you?"

She lifted a shoulder in a shrug.

"Answer me."

"Yeah." She blew out a breath and said, "Gone as in gone. You happy now?"

"You actually think I could leave without so much as saying good-bye? Wait—don't answer that." He let go of her and took a step back. "Get dressed."

Ana blinked, a little thrown by the abrupt change. One second she was pressed up against his warm body, even as he stared at her in disbelief. Then she was cold and alone. "Get dressed?"

"Yeah." He flicked a glance at her that encompassed her from the bottom of her bare feet up to her neck. "Unless of course you feel like going outside naked. Then we'll have problems because if a guy so much as looks at you, I'm gutting him."

"Duke, what—?"

"Get dressed."

S HE really thought he could just leave, Duke thought, alone in the living room.

Shaken, he rubbed his hands over his face and tried to figure out what in the hell was going on inside her head. She'd spent the day crying . . . because she thought he wasn't coming back?

Or was he just assuming too much?

No. His gut insisted that's what it was. She'd been crying, because she thought he was gone. So what did that mean? He thought he knew. He wanted to think he was right. But he wasn't going to do that just yet.

She came out of the bedroom, her shoulders slumped, her hair brushed back from her face and secured in a tail at the nape of her neck. He wanted to tug the band that held her hair confined and tug it free so that pretty, pale hair fell loose around her shoulders. Instead, he slid his feet into his shoes and kept his distance.

He didn't keep quiet, though. Too many questions, he needed answers and he sucked at being patient.

"Would it really bother you so much if I just left?"

She flicked a sidelong glance in his direction. Instead of giving him a straight answer, she shrugged. "You've got a life to live, Duke. Same as me. I can't begrudge you for getting back to it."

"But would it bother you?"

"There's really no reason for it to bother me," she said.

His nostrils flared as he caught a trace scent. She was lying. Lying—or at least not telling the complete truth. Ana knew better than to outright lie to somebody like him. He would know it before the words even left her mouth.

But something about these words, circumspect as they were, didn't ring entirely true.

"You don't want me to leave, do you?"

Duke stared at her bowed head as she slid her feet into a pair of flat, black shoes and grabbed her keys from the bar. All without looking at him. But he didn't need her to look at him.

Body language doesn't lie. Scent doesn't lie.

Dominic had said that to him more than a year ago—it seemed like a whole other lifetime.

No. The body didn't lie. Scent didn't lie. Neither did the heart.

And neither did those eyes that hid everything and nothing at all.

A NA tapped her foot restlessly against the floorboard, squirming on the unfamiliar leather seat. It was a Jeep, a dark, deep shade of red and *nice*—seriously nice. "Was there something wrong with the other rental?" she asked as he turned onto the Glenn Highway, heading north out of town.

"Nothing was wrong with it—and this isn't a rental."

Frowning, Ana sat up straight, studying the Jeep's dashboard. "Not a rental—you meant you *bought* this?"

"Yep."

She slicked her tongue over her lips and settled back against the leather. "Why?"

"Because I wanted it."

"I guess that's one way to get out of flying back to Virginia." She crossed her arms over her chest, staring out the window. Tall fences bordered the highway, interrupted every so often with an open area—for the moose to cross the highway. "You've got one hell of a long drive ahead of you, though."

He made a noncommittal grunt and drove on in silence.

Ana rested her head against the padded headrest and just stared outside. Minutes ticked away as they drove across Eagle River. Outside her window, she could see the mountains and she focused on them. It was a lot easier to look at them now than it had been the last few times she came through here.

"Are we going to Palmer?"

"Nope."

Ana rolled her eyes and glanced at the clock on the dashboard. A few minutes ticked by.

"Where *are* we going?" she demanded after four more miles sped by in silence.

He glanced in the rearview mirror and turned his signal on, cutting across traffic and taking the exit to Chugiak. "Damn it, Duke, where are we going?"

"You're swearing again, princess," he said, his tone affable. He shot her a look from the corner of his eye. "If you could just be patient for another ten minutes, you'd see where we were going."

The smirk on his face had her seething. Clamping her mouth shut, she closed her eyes. Wherever they were going, she just wanted it over, so she could get back to her apartment, back in her bed, pull the covers over her head while she tried to figure out how to handle Duke.

He hadn't left.

She couldn't figure out why.

Was he just not bored with her yet? No matter what she might tell herself while she was wrapped in his arms, lying under that long, lean body . . . her mouth started watering and she had to jerk her mind back to the matter at hand.

When they weren't touching, her brain functioned halfway normally, and when her brain was functioning the way it should, Ana knew this wasn't the best thing for her.

She loved him—she'd *always* loved him, it seemed. When he left, she was still going to love him. No, she didn't regret sleeping with him, didn't regret that he'd been the one to show up in Alaska. In a way, some things were a little easier now. She knew he didn't hate her.

That was good, right?

Except . . . except when he hated her, it was easy to accept facts. There was no happy-ever-after lined up with Duke. At least not one that included her. And when she believed he hated her, she hadn't found herself daydreaming about it. Or at least not *too* much. Now . . . Ana blew out a breath and shifted in her seat, leaning her head against the window and staring outside.

Scenery sped by in a blur, but even if they'd been crawling along at a snail's pace, she wouldn't have seen anything.

Now she found herself thinking about a future, yearning for something with Duke. Something that would last.

Impossible things.

The car came to a stop, but it wasn't until Duke reached over and brushed his fingers across her cheek that she realized it. Frowning, she straightened in the seat and glanced at him.

"What do you think?"

Ana frowned. "About what?"

He glanced out the front window. Automatically, she followed his gaze and found herself staring blankly at a house. A big, beautiful house made up of gleaming, golden planks of wood and lots of glass windows that glittered under the brilliant August sunshine.

"What do I think about the house?" she asked, feeling a little bit stupid. "Why are you asking me what I think about the house?"

Instead of responding, he climbed out of the car and came around to her side, opening the door. When she didn't climb out, he rolled his eyes and reached in, unbuckled her seat belt and caught her hand. "Come on. Let's go look around."

"Duke, this is private property." She dragged her feet as he tugged her along.

"Yeah." He glanced at her over his shoulder and grinned. "But if they want to sell it, they probably expect people to come around and look at it. Or at least one would think."

"Sell it . . . " Dazed, she tugged her hand free and edged in front of him. Her eyes landed on the Realtor sign in the front yard. Although calling that rolling expanse of grass a *yard* was rather like calling a diamond a rock. Technically correct, but the term just didn't do it justice. She stared at the For Sale sign and felt her heart skip a beat or ten.

Her mouth was dry.

Blood roared in her ears.

"Duke, why are we here?"

He didn't answer her, and she turned around to stare at him.

"What's going on?" Her voice was shaking, but there wasn't a damn thing she could do about it. Just being able to *speak* right now seemed like a huge accomplishment. It wasn't terribly easy to speak when something had squeezed all the oxygen out of her lungs. Wasn't terribly easy to speak when her heart was suddenly pounding a mile a minute and giddy laughter warred with pessimistic doubt.

Duke stared at her, his hands shoved deep inside his pockets, his legs spread wide. His golden blond hair fell into his eyes, trying to obscure his pale gray eyes. Eyes that watched her, stared at her as though trying to see clear through to her soul, clear inside her heart. Reflexively, she slammed extra shields up—thick, solid shields that muffled everything.

"Why were you crying?"

"Why are we here?" Ana ignored his question in favor of her own. Glaring at him, she closed her hands into tight fists, her nails biting into her palms.

He sauntered forward, a smile curling his lips. "You

want to know why we are here?" he asked, his voice soft—almost gentle.

With that intense gaze, he watched her. With that intense gaze that sent shivers down her spine and had her belly clenching with need. Her heart hammered away inside her chest even as her head started to scream a warning at her.

She could feel his thoughts, pressing against her shields, almost like he was trying to tell her something. Ana, safe behind her shields, did her damnedest to ignore the thoughts he was sending in her direction.

"If I didn't want to know why I was here, I wouldn't have asked," she snapped, shooting for flippancy, hoping it would hide the nerves. Futile hope, she knew it, but she had to try, right?

"I'll tell you why we're here." He drew even with her, his booted feet nudging the toes of her black ballet flats. A warm, calloused hand cupped her chin and he gently angled her face up. "As soon as you answer my question. Why were you crying, Ana?"

Why am I shaking? She stared up at him, trembling, half terrified and half . . . half she didn't know what. Was it hope? She didn't want to think about that, because if she did, she'd have to wonder what in the hell she was so hopeful about.

"Ana." He dipped his head and rubbed his cheek against hers.

That familiar gesture had a knot swelling in her throat and tears stung her eyes, threatened to fall.

"Tell me why you were crying."

Swallowing a cry, she tore away from him and moved away, quick, quick as she could, even though she knew he could stop her in two seconds. She needed distance, had to have it before she threw herself against him and made an idiot out of herself. The words, the answer to his question, danced on her tongue but she didn't want to answer him.

"Why were you crying?"

She hunched her shoulders when he came up behind her

and touched her. Tried to edge away from his hands even as she tried not to lean against him.

"Ana . . ."

Something snapped inside her. Spinning around, she pushed up on her toes, nose to nose with him. "Damn it, I was crying because I thought you'd left! I thought you'd left, that you were gone and not coming back and . . . and I . . . and . . ."

Turning away, she covered her mouth, tried to muffle the sob before it tore free. Duke wrapped his arms around her waist, drew her back against him. She struggled against him, tried to get him to let go even though it was like trying to put out a house fire with one lone bucket of water—pointless. Still, she fought against him, kicking him in the shins, driving an elbow back into his gut. He grunted and even though pain shot up her arm, she felt a little bit better.

That was until he spun her around and lifted her in his arms, slanting his mouth across hers. "Damn it, you son of a bitch, let me go," she snarled as she tore her mouth away.

"Shit, princess, you must be really pissed." He was laughing.

He went to kiss her again and she jerked her head away, arching back as far as his arms would let her. Which wasn't far. Then he cupped the back of her head in his hand, drawing her close again. "Let. Me. Go." She gritted each word out, the last one muffled against his lips as he kissed her again.

"Awwww, Ana. I can't do that. Took me five years to finally get you, and you think I can walk away as easy as that?"

His tone might have been lighthearted, but there was something . . . something under the words. Something that echoed in his eyes and in the smile that curled his lips as he stared down at her, stroking her hair back from her face. He laid a hand on her cheek and pressed his lips to her brow. "Don't ask me to do that, Ana. God, please, don't ask that."

"Why not?" She squeezed her eyes shut and made herself concentrate on breathing. She kept forgetting to do it, and she felt a little light-headed from the lack of oxygen.

"Because I can't." He lifted his head, gazing down at her.

She could feel the weight of his stare, and once more, she could feel the intensity of his thoughts beating against her shields. If she lowered them, just a little, she'd hear whatever it was he was thinking. She suspected she'd hear it loud and clear, too, with none of the jumbled chaos that too often came when she picked up on the thoughts of others.

Even though she knew he wanted her to look at him, she didn't do it. If she did, it would strengthen that connection between them and she didn't know if she could avoid hearing his thoughts.

"Aren't you going to ask me why?" Duke asked, staring down at her bent head. He reached up and tugged the band out of her hair, combing through the silken, pale strands with his fingers. Then he tangled his fingers in it and tugged until she finally lifted her head.

"Enough, Duke." She closed her eyes and took a deep breath, then looked at him again. "Enough. Just tell me what is going on. Why are we here?"

"Because I want to know what you think of the house," Duke said, tracing the line of her mouth with his index finger. "I think I want to buy it. But I can't do that unless I know you like it."

Her breath hitched in her throat. "Why do you want to buy it?"

"Because your place is too damn small, and I can't stand living in a city."

"Living . . . " She paused and licked her lips. Sharp little teeth caught the lower one, biting down nervously. "Living in a city. You mean Anchorage?"

"Where else would I be talking about?"

"You're talking about living here." She gulped and a

series of emotions flashed through her eyes. Panic. Hope. Doubt. Need.

Need . . . that was the look he focused on. Cradling her face in his hands, he dipped his head and pressed his lips to hers. "Yeah, I'm talking about living here. You're here, Ana. So this is where I want to be."

"Why?" she whispered against his mouth. Then she jerked her head away and glared at him. "And give me a straight answer, damn it."

"I already gave you a straight answer." Duke combed her hair back from her face. "But you told me people said stupid things all the time, stupid things they didn't mean. So I figured maybe I should show you that I did mean it."

I did mean it—Ana wanted to believe that. She blinked furiously, trying to hold back the tears blinding her. "You meant it. You really meant it?"

He linked his arms around her waist, locking them at the small of her back. "Yeah, I meant it. I don't much waste time saying things I don't mean. I don't see the point in it." He skimmed his lips over her cheek, then along her jawline, down her neck. There, he brushed the neckline of her shirt aside and raked her neck with his teeth.

A shudder wracked her body, from head to toe and back up again. Heat flashed through her, but for once, it didn't threaten to overwhelm her, consume her. "You meant it," she repeated dumbly. Maybe she hadn't heard him right. Were they talking about the same thing?

Duke chuckled and reached between them, toying with the buttons of her shirt. "I love you. I was born to love you. And you feel the same way, don't you?"

Cool air kissed her flesh. Startled, she glanced down and realized he had gotten her shirt completely unbuttoned. She hadn't put a bra on—blood rushed to her cheeks as she stared down at her braless breasts and then shot a look back at the house.

"Nobody's there," Duke whispered, tracing her collarbone with his fingertips. "Nobody has been out here in a day or two. And it's the only house down this road . . . lots of land. Plenty of privacy."

"You . . . uh . . . I guess you'd do better having a lot of privacy." She licked her lips and looked at him from under her lashes.

He was still watching her. Patiently. Expectantly. "You do better with privacy, too. Figure it's the best for both of us." He reached up and pushed her shirt back off her shoulders.

It fell and caught at her elbows. She reached up and pressed her hands against his chest, flexed her fingers. "Privacy's good."

"So are answers." He pressed his brow to hers. "I gave you your answer, Ana. Can't you answer mine?"

I love you. She wanted to tell him, wanted to throw her arms around his neck and tell him, over and over. But she held back. This wasn't right. Wasn't good, not for him. Even back when she let herself daydream about having Duke in her life, she'd known it wasn't right. Duke deserved better than her. He deserved so much more.

"This isn't good for you." She blurted the words out before she lost her nerve. Pulling away from him, she jerked her shirt back up but her hands shook too much to button it. Instead, she just held it closed between her breasts. "This is bad for you. *I'm* bad for you. You've got to know that. Even if you . . . even if you think you feel how you're saying, you have to know I'm bad for you. I'm not the kind of woman you need in your life, Duke. I'm not strong enough. You need somebody strong. Somebody more like you—"

Duke reached out and hooked his hand in the front of her jeans, gently. She resisted. He jerked harder and she crashed into his chest with a startled "Ooommph."

"I know what I need," he growled. When she would have argued, he covered her lips with his finger. "I know what I want, what I need. And it's you, Ana. If I wanted somebody like *me*, I would have gone chasing after Kendall or half a dozen other women that I've met. I didn't go after them, because I was too hung up on you and I have been, from the first damn time I laid eyes on you. I *love* you. I *want* you. I *need* you."

"But—"

He cut her words off with a hard, short kiss. "Don't want to hear it," he snarled. "I love you. You don't have the right to tell me what I need, or what I deserve. That's my call, princess. Now give me an answer—do you love me?"

Old doubts—so many of them—swarmed up, swamping her, pulling her down, destroying her. Staring into Duke's stormy gray eyes, she gulped. Her hands were damp, cold with sweat, and her heart raced. Her breathing hitched in her throat. Tearing her gaze away from his, she stared at his chest. Couldn't do this, not while he was looking at her like that. Like he really did love her. Like he really did need her.

Like she mattered.

"How?" she asked. "How can you love me?"

"How?" He kissed her temple and stroked her hair. "Hell, Ana. How can I *not*? You're stronger than you think. You're better than you think. You . . . "

Blinking away the tears, she looked up at him. "I'm what?"

"You're everything." Gray eyes, warm as a summer rain, gazed down at her.

Her heart stuttered inside her chest, then melted as he kissed her. Soft. Slow.

"Everything, Ana." He cupped her cheek in his hand and whispered, "Let me in, princess. Give me a chance . . . give *us* a chance."

Hesitantly, she started to lower her shields. Complete and utter shock had her letting go of them altogether. Love. Desire. Need. She felt it welling inside Duke. Spilling out into her as she dropped her shields. It swarmed in. Swamped her. Pulled her under . . . and remade her.

Swaying against him, she felt something inside her crumble—a wall of self-doubt and anger. Crumbling down into dust under the weight of the need she sensed inside him. Need . . . for her.

He wanted her.

He loved her.

He *needed* her. Abruptly, she started to laugh, a giddy, elated laugh that felt altogether too foreign, and altogether too good. Throwing her arms around him, she covered his mouth with hers, even though she couldn't quite manage to stop the giggles.

Duke lifted her off the ground and spun her around. The world blurred around her, and then faded away, along with her laughter, as he slowed to a stop. They ended up by the Jeep, and he leaned back against it, holding her close as he kissed her.

He kept his eyes open, watching her—as he took the kiss from gentle and light to deep and hard, he watched her. He eased back and reached up, once more taking the edges of her shirt and tugging them apart, pushing it down until it caught at her elbows again. They turned, until she had her back resting against the Jeep, trapped between a warm, hot body, and a warm, hard machine. Through her jeans, she could feel the warmth radiating through from the engine.

"You still haven't answered me," he said, cupping her hips in his hands.

"About what?" She groaned as he leaned forward and caught one nipple in his mouth and suckled deep, teasing the hardened tip with his tongue.

"About whether or not you feel the same way."

From under her lashes, she looked at him. A smile teased her lips and she said, "You kept me waiting while we went on this little field trip."

Duke pulled away and groaned. "Damn it, Ana . . . "

"Shhh." She caught him, grabbing his arm and pulling him back. Through the thick layers of denim, she could feel him, hard, thick, full—her belly clenched demandingly while a sweet, painful ache settled between her thighs. She draped her arms over his shoulders and pressed her brow to his, staring into his eyes. Lost in them. Lost in him. "I love you, Duke. I think I've always loved you."

He shuddered. His lids drooped low, shielding those enigmatic gray eyes. Then he looked at her, relief, delight, lust, love, all of it swirling in his eyes. "What . . . no teasing me? You're not going to draw it out?"

"Maybe we've both waited long enough."

He grinned. Against her lips, he muttered, "Damned straight."

Turn the page for a preview of

VEIL OF SHADOWS

By Shiloh Walker

Coming Fall 2010 from Berkley Sensation!

T HE first time she saw the man, Laisyn Caar knew he was going to be trouble.

Syn really, really didn't have the time for it or the inclination to deal with it. Not that fate obviously gave a damn.

Like a lot of the refugees they'd taken in over the years, he wore threadbare clothes and he carried little in the way of material goods. A lot of the refugees arrived on the base-camp on solar-powered glide-carts or riding a baern. The big pack beasts could carry two people easy, and they were somewhat protective of their owners and proved to be very handy guard animals.

This man was on foot. He had a pack strapped to his back and enough weaponry to have her eyebrows going up.

All those weapons, it was the first thing that set him apart.

Even though he was surrounded by other refugees, he looked to be traveling alone—that was the second thing that set him apart.

It wasn't wise to go anywhere alone. Not here. Not even now that the Gate was out of commission. They no longer

had to worry about raids from Anqar, but it was far from
safe in their devastated pocket of the world. Demons ran
amok in the heavy forests covering the valleys at the base of
the Roinan Mountains. There were still Warlords, as well,
those who had been in Ishtan when the Gate collapsed. Syn
suspected those Warlords weren't too damn happy about
being trapped in a primitive, inferior world, good only for
the slaves it provided for them.

Going anywhere alone was a bad, bad idea.

But there he was—a lone, rather wild looking wolf amid
a bunch of scared and nervous sheep.

His hair was black, as black as her own, but it didn't
have her blue-black hue to it. It was dense and dark, no
hints of blue, red or brown. He wore it pulled back in a
stubby tail that left his rough features unframed. He had
high cheekbones, a broad forehead, and his mouth looked
as though he never smiled. Broad shoulders stretched the
worn cloth of his tunic. If it had ever had sleeves, he'd long
since ripped or cut them off. His arms were long, tanned
and roped with muscles. He had thick wrists and she had
suspected part of the reason for those rather impressive
arms was the blade she saw sticking over his shoulder.

It wasn't a sword. She didn't need to see it to know that—
long swords weren't exactly the weapon of choice. Pulsars
were—handheld weapons that delivered a pulsating blast
that could either disable or kill. But all of her soldiers carried blades and they could use them if they had to.

Somehow, Syn suspected this man would prefer the
blade over the pulsar he had strapped to his thigh.

The most arresting feature about this man wasn't his
weapons, or his face, or the way he seemed to take in
everything with one quick, trained glance.

It was the patch he wore over his left eye.

She would bet the lack of vision on one side didn't slow
him down one bit. He kept to the back of the group and if
she didn't know better, she might have mistaken him for one
of her own. Except for the threadbare clothes and noted lack
of cavinir, the flexible body armor most of the rebels wore,

he blended in perfectly with her troops. Ready and aware, fully prepared for danger even this close to the camp.

It made her wonder how rough the journey from Sacril had been. It also reminded her that she had a job to do, and she forced herself to look away. It may be great fun to briefly ogle one of the more interesting men to enter through their gates. But doing so didn't get the job done.

Right now, she needed to get ready to speak with the commander, she needed to speak with men who'd accompanied the refugees and then, she had to speak with the refugees themselves. And that was going to be such fun.

Sighing, she flicked a hand through her short, dark hair. "At least this is the last time."

She hoped.

The Roinan territory was just too dangerous now. The refugee camps had been decimated over the past few weeks. Most of the refugees entering through the main gate didn't realize it, but within a few days, they were going to be on an eastbound convoy. Kalen was evacuating the territory. Civilians wouldn't be forced to leave, but they couldn't remain in the camp and the only people getting an escort were those on the convoy.

If they didn't join the convoy, they were on their own.

Once these refugees were out of here, the rebel army would focus on the demon infestation and *only* on the demon infestation. Splitting their time and energy between helping the refugees and culling the demons had proven too dangerous. They were losing lives, they were loosing ground, and losing both too fast.

It had to stop. Considering their limited resources, they had to focus on the threat presented by the demons. It was the only logical choice.

But somehow, Syn suspected these men and women weren't going to be pleased with logic.

I T was organized chaos.

There was no other way to describe it. Xan stood on

the sidelines, watching as the soldiers herded every last refugee into a long, low-ceilinged building.

Two men stood at the door, questioning each person that entered.

"Any combat experience? No? Sit on the right. Yes? Sit on the left. That's all you need to do for now."

Any and all questions were ignored. But that didn't keep the refugees from asking. The line moved interminably slow. Xan kept a light hand on one of the straps that held his pack in place, the other on the shorter blade at his waist. He had dealt with enough thieves over the past few months to know that none of them were above robbing people blind right under the noses of the only law this part of the world had.

From all reports, this forsaken territory had been cut adrift, left to falter or thrive on its own as the rest of the world recovered.

Well, perhaps the Roinan territory was not completely on its own. The outside still took in refugees. Xan had heard they even had "programs" designed to help the refugees integrate into life outside a war zone. Motivated by guilt, perhaps. It might be the only way they could allay the guilt they carried for allowing these people to fight a war that should have been fought by all.

At one time, the raids from Anqar had been a worldwide concern, but after the other gates were destroyed, the world outside of the Roinan territory seemed content to pretend that everything was just as fine as could be.

For some time, only Kalen Brenner and his army of rebels stood between the one remaining Gate and the rest of Ishtan. The rest of Ishtan seemed quite to content to let it remain so.

But they took in the refugees who couldn't fight.

Sometimes, they even sent back supplies.

When they remembered.

Xan finally reached the door and met the gaze of the soldier closest to him. The man looked Xan over from head to toe and then a smile of camaraderie lit his face. "I don't think I need to ask if you have combat experience, do I?"

Xan just shrugged.

"You do have combat experience, right?"

He gave a curt nod and was waved inside. He didn't sit. He took up a position with his back against the wall. He wasn't the only one. A handful of others were doing the same, guarding their backs, even now, when they were in the one safehold this territory had. One by one, each of them met his gaze. A quick glance, a nod, and then they all resumed their survey of the crowd.

Xan settled in beside them and started his own survey. It was a sorry lot of people, that was for certain.

As more and more people packed in, he gripped his blade tighter.

What in the hell had he gotten himself into?

I T was standing room only. Close to three hundred, she figured. Fortunately, a good twenty percent of the number consisted of soldiers who'd made the decision to return east. They'd served at Sacril, one of the rebel outposts, and when Kalen made the decision to call them back, most of them had decided they'd just as soon join the convoy.

Syn would be glad when this was over. She'd been glad when she could give her troops a clear, direct focus—the demons. She'd be glad when she no longer had to balance and juggle numbers to figure out how to provide the safety the refugees needed without compromising the safety of the camp and without cutting back on the efforts to secure more of their land.

In short, she'd be glad when this day was over.

It was hard enough maintaining order in the post-war chaos, but dealing with a bunch of lost and scared civilians had her wishing for a dark quiet room, a hot bath and a big, bottomless glass of frostwine.

Later, she could get the dark quiet room, and probably even the hot bath. She needed that hot bath, too. If nothing else, it might ease the raw ache of cold settled inside her. She was always cold these days, always chilled. Nothing helped for long.

The frostwine would do a decent job of warding the cold off for a while, especially if she could have it with the bath. But that particular luxury was one she didn't have. One she probably wouldn't have again for years to come.

She followed along behind Bron and Kenner, letting them clear the way while she took in the last group of refugees. The last . . . it was hard to even consider that idea. For as long as she'd been here, there had been refugees arriving at the camp. Most had come seeking to serve in the army, but over the past year or so, that number had slowed to a trickle. Too often now, those arriving at the camp had requests for "security" while the refugees tried to rebuild. Or food. Shelter for a few nights. Aid in rebuilding their homes.

The rebel army's resources were stretched thin as it was and these people wanted Kalen to give them yet more.

Those with half a brain had abandoned this area years earlier. It seemed as though the only ones who remained were those in the base-camp—the rebel army. Except that was far from the truth. Every week brought in more refugees, many of them so gaunt and thin, it hurt to even look upon them.

She didn't need to ask their stories.

She already knew.

They fled to the mountains, fled to the north, to the south. They couldn't go east—this was their home. Going east, to them, seemed too permanent, some kind of unspoken acknowledgment that they had given up. They had to stay. They wanted to rebuild. They just needed some help . . .

That was the story.

In actuality, they needed their heads examined.

It would be years before these mountains were completely safe again. Maybe longer.

And the typical soul just wasn't equipped to fight the demons that crept out in the night. So they ended up at the different outposts, or right here at the base-camp, begging and pleading for help that the army couldn't keep giving.

Something had to give.

She knew Kalen had made a wise decision, but that knowledge didn't make her job any easier.

With her men at her back, Syn forged her way to the front of the hall. Bron and Kenner took their respective places on either side of the dais as she strode up the steps, the soles of her boots making deliberate thuds on the wooden floor.

With every step, she felt more and more eyes cut her way. Slowly, the dull roar of voices faded down to a muted murmur as one by one, row by row, the refugees took note of her.

She could move without making a sound when she wanted to.

But she didn't want to at the moment. She was here to make an impact. She stood a good head shorter than most of the people in the room and although she was strong, she knew she didn't look it.

But Syn knew that attitude made all the difference.

And attitude she had in spades.

She stopped in the middle of the dais and linked her hands behind her back. It was loud, people whispering to one another, looking all around, staring at Bron and Kenner with wide eyes, and then up at her with confusion.

"My name is Laisyn Caar. Around the camp, I'm known as Captain. My superiors call me Syn." She lifted her voice, knowing it would carry through the door and even out into the common area in front of the west hall. Most of the talkers fell silent.

"Let me make a few things clear right up front." Now just a few were whispering.

One of them was a woman sitting next to the man who'd caught her eye yesterday. She was leaning over him, all but climbing into his arms trying to get his attention. Syn dropped off the dais, talking as she went.

"This is a military base. It may not be recognized as such to those out in the rest of the world. But that is how we see it. That is how we run it." She took her time, making her way up the aisle, occasionally looking at some of those sitting down and watching. As she passed, those still whispering fell silent.

All save one.

She drew her culn from her belt and twisted it. Immediately, the metal baton expanded to three times its size. It was now nearly as long as she was tall, and solid.

She used it to tap the shoulder of the only person still talking.

"And that means, when I am talking, every last one of you will shut up."

The brunette turned around and stared at Syn with irritated eyes. "Excuse me—"

Syn lifted a brow and repeated herself. "When I am talking, every last one of you will shut up."

The woman went red. Then white. "Who in the hell—"

Somebody next to her jabbed an elbow into the woman's side. Syn pretended not to see it. "What's your name?"

"Vena Saurell." She glared at Syn, a disdainful look on her face. "And who are you? The commander's personal assistant?"

Syn smiled. "No. I'm one of his captains. I'm third in command and I have the authority to have you hauled out of this camp, this very second, kicking and screaming, should I chose."

"Like hell."

Syn glanced toward the door. The two soldiers standing at ready stepped inside and flanked Vena. "I'm going to start from the beginning. My name is Laisyn Caar. Around the camp, I'm known as Captain. My superiors call me Syn. Let me make a few things clear right up front. This is a military base. It may not be recognized as such to those out in the rest of the world. But that is how we see it. That is how we run it. And that means, when I am talking, every last one of you will shut up."

Still smiling her nice, pleasant smile, she cocked her head and said, "Now, Vena Saurell. Are you going to shut your mouth or should I have my men escort you out of the camp?"

"You can't make me go out there alone. It's not safe."

"No. It's not safe. And yes, I can." She wouldn't. She'd just have the woman tucked away inside a dormer, with the door locked, until she could be placed on tomorrow's convoy. She'd done it before and she had no problem doing it now. "Now, am I clear?"

Vena glanced at the two soldiers flanking her. They didn't look at her. They stared straight ahead, just like a good soldier should. Then she looked at Syn and nodded, slowly. Something ugly flashed in her eyes but she fell silent.

"Good." Syn twisted her culn and it folded back in on itself. Tucking it back into the loop on her belt, she returned to the dais.

There always had to be one person. Always one person had to challenge her. After all these years, Syn was almost used to it. But it still annoyed the hell out of her. She focused on those sitting on the right side of the room. "Are there any among you that has any sort of real combat experience?"

A few lifted their hands. She nodded and then focused on the other side of the room. "Every one of you told the men at the door you have combat training—is that correct?" Some nods, a few muffled affirmatives. Back in the back, her newest, dearest friend Vena just glared at Syn. Smiling at her, Syn asked, "Vena, I take it that means you have real combat experience?"

"I—" She opened her mouth to say something, then snapped it shut. Either somebody had gouged her with an elbow again, or she was growing something more than just a brainstem. Instead of saying anything else, she just nodded.

Damn. Syn would much rather just get that woman off of her base.

Looking back at the nonfighters, she asked, "Are any of you healers, witches, psychics or medics?" There wasn't a witch among them—Syn had already looked. It didn't surprise her, but it was disappointing. They needed more witches. Unfortunately, though, witches, as a whole, had the common sense to get out of a bad place when it was clear the bad was only getting worse.

There were two medics and one psychic. She made a mental note of their faces and then selected the others who'd claimed some combat experience. She gestured all of them to the front and then looked at the remaining civilians.

"This is a military camp," she said, her voice soft, but firm. "We're still fighting a war here, even though the Gate is gone."

Something about the gravity of her voice had them stirring uncomfortably in their seats. Syn could see it.

Her gut twisted as she went on. "As of today, a new policy is going into effect. The army is making the demon threat its new focus—until that threat is contained, it will be our only focus."

People started to whisper among themselves and some of them were watching her with outright hostility.

"We've called our men in from the outposts. Sacril and the other outposts are being abandoned for the time being. We will no longer maintain them."

"But—"

Syn lifted a hand. "Please, let me continue. When I'm done, if there are questions, I will answer them. In the past month, attacks on the outposts have increased. Attacks on the eastbound convoys have increased. Attacks on our hunting groups, our scouts, have increased. The demons are becoming more aggressive, more violent. The army's focus must be containing that threat."

"But we're safe here." This came from a middle-aged woman, her voice soft, her eyes censuring.

"We don't have the resources here to feed, protect and see to an additional three hundred souls," Syn said quietly. "And if we allow non-fighters now, then in a few weeks, we have more coming seeking refuge. As of today, the only civilians allowed in the camp are those who can provide us with certain useful skills—namely, witches, healers, medics and psychics. Since none of those apply to you, you're being sent east tomorrow on the outbound convoy."

Voices rose.

She lifted a hand and cut them off. "This isn't up for discussion. I'm sorry. But we're not here to play bodyguard, we're not here to provide security for you while you rebuild your homes. For the next few months, probably the next few years, the mountains will be too dangerous for civilians and we don't have the manpower to offer you any kind of protection, not if we want to concentrate on eliminating the current threat."

"What threat?" one of the men demanded. He stood up, glaring at Syn. "The Gate is gone—we don't have to worry about raids anymore. We just need some help . . ."

Syn shook her head. "You need more than *some* help. Every last one of you. Otherwise, you wouldn't have abandoned your homes and gone to Sacril. You come to us seeking shelter, or food, or hoping we can provide you with some sort of bodyguard detail while you rebuild your homes. One of the last confrontations with Anqar decimated nearly half of our forces. We have roughly fifteen hundred able-bodied soldiers and we're already stretched thin—we can't possibly provide the security needed to every last soul that asks. It can't be done."

"But this is our home," he gritted out.

"I know that. And I am sorry. But this isn't up for discussion."

"I want to talk to the commander." He glared at her.

Syn angled her head to the back. Kalen Brenner had quietly slipped in just a few minutes ago. His timing, as always, was impeccable. "Feel free. There he is."

The man turned around. Kalen strode forward and stopped in front of him. "This is your home," he said, his voice flat. His gray eyes were not unkind, but there was nothing soft in that gaze, nothing yielding. "I'm aware of that. It's mine as well. I can fight to protect it. I can fight to protect your land. I can fight to clear it of the demon

infestation. But I can't do that if my men and I are playing bodyguard for all the civilians who want their homes
rebuilt."

"But . . ."

Kalen shook his head. "There are no buts. If you want
your home rebuilt that badly, then do it. I can't force you
onto the convoy tomorrow—I won't force anybody. But I
can force you out of my camp. If you want safety, go east.
Find a life there. This isn't the time to rebuild here."

He scanned the faces of the civilians. Syn did the same,
seeing the disappointment, the grief, the denial in their
eyes. They'd come here with hopes, dreams of rebuilding
their lives, and in under five minutes, Syn had been forced
to smash every one of those hopes and dreams.

Sometimes she hated her job. The cold knot inside
her chest grew, expanded until it seemed to encompass
everything—all of her. She suppressed the need to shiver,
kept her teeth from chattering. But still, she was so cold.

The job. Focus on the job.

Kalen joined her on the dais, off the side. Syn didn't
waste any more time. She gestured to the civilian medics
and the lone psychic. "You three remain here. The rest of
you, you're dismissed. Outside, there are some of my men
who'll get your information and explain about the convoy."

They departed, an air of defeat clinging to them. Syn
was sorry for it. But they'd be alive. Alive . . . and maybe
in a few years, they could return to their home. She had
to take comfort in that. If they allowed them to stay here,
they'd likely be dead within a year.

Her men and women couldn't protect everybody—there
just wasn't enough of them.

After the door closed behind the last one, she focused on
the remaining civilians. "Medics and psychics are always
needed here. You have the choice to stay here or you can
join the convoy tomorrow. It is your call, completely. But if
you stay, be prepared to work. Be prepared to work hard.
And be prepared to die."

Horror flashed through the eyes of the youngest medic.

Syn focused her gaze on the young woman's face and said, "We're still fighting a war. We can't go a week without a demon attack and they are getting more desperate and more aggressive with every passing day. Those are the ugly facts of life here. If you can't handle them, then you need to leave. Any of you three want to leave? Do it now."

Not one of them moved.

"You're going to be trained to fight. You'll be expected to take place in daily training. You'll be placed on job rotation. You'll have one rest day a week. Other than that . . . you work. You eat. You train. You are ready to fight, should the need arise. This is our life—if you don't want that fight, then leave."

Still, none of them moved.

Damn. She wasn't as good at scaring people off as she used to be.

With a curt nod, she gestured to one of her men waiting by the door at the back. "This is Lothen, one of my men. He'll get you a permanent dormer and get you added to the job rotation. If none of you have any questions, you may go now."

Now it was just the fighters she had to deal with.

"Man, she's a serious bitch."

Xan didn't bother looking at her. Vena Saurell wasn't letting that slow her down. She seemed determined to glue herself to his side, staying with him even as he waded through the crush of people gathered in the common area outside the west hall.

"Don't you think? I mean, hell, I came here to fight and all, but she doesn't have any right to tell these people they aren't worthy of protection."

Ignoring her wasn't going to make her disappear, he decided. So he stopped in his tracks and crossed his arms over his chest.

"I don't recall hearing her saying that. What I heard was a woman willing to fight to secure these lands—she can't do that if she's too busy taking care of refugees."

The woman's lip curled. "Seems to me that the purpose of this whole damn army is to protect the refugees."

"The best way to do that is to eliminate those who are preying on the refugees," Xan replied with a shrug. "Once the demons are gone, the refugees will no longer need the protection of the army. It is not an easy choice to make, but it seems a wise one."

"Maybe." Vena shrugged. "I'm not too impressed. But she doesn't need to be such a bitch, does she?"

"If it keeps people alive, she can be the queen bitch," somebody said from behind Vena.

She went red and then white. Xan barely managed to restrain his grin as she turned to face the commander of the Roinan rebel army. Kalen Brenner was a name known pretty much throughout the world. One would have to have lived under a rock to not know this man. Vena obviously hadn't lived under a rock.

Syn stood at his side, her slender arms crossed over her chest. With a faint smile on her lips, she glanced up at the commander and said, "I prefer Captain Bitch, if it's all the same to you, Commander." Then she dismissed Vena and focused on Xan.

Xan had spent much of his life learning to school his emotions, his reactions, everything. In that moment, he was very glad. Because he would hate for his emotions to show in just that moment. He would hate for his reactions to show in just that moment.

He looked at Captain Laisyn Caar and thought only one thing:

WANT.